SOUL SEEKER

SOUL SEEKER

A JOHN EISENMENGER FORENSIC MYSTERY

Keith McCarthy

This first world edition published 2010
in Great Britain and in 2011 in the USA by
SEVERN HOUSE PUBLISHERS LTD of
9–15 High Street, Sutton, Surrey, England, SM1 1DF.
Trade paperback edition first published
in Great Britain and the USA 2011 by
SEVERN HOUSE PUBLISHERS LTD.

British Library Cataloguing in Publication Data

McCarthy, Keith, 1960-
  Soul seeker. – (John Eisenmenger forensic mystery)
  1. Eisenmenger, John (Fictitious character)–Fiction.
  2. Pathologists–England–Fiction. 3. Serial murder
  Investigation–Fiction. 4. Detective and mystery stories.
  I. Title II. Series
  823.9'2-dc22

ISBN-13: 978-0-7278-6987-6 (cased)
ISBN-13: 978-1-84751-318-2 (trade paper)

All Severn House titles are printed on acid-free paper.

Severn House Publishers support The Forest Stewardship Council [FSC],
the leading international forest certification organisation. All our titles that
are printed on Greenpeace-approved FSC-certified paper carry the FSC logo.

Typeset by Palimpsest Book Production Ltd.,
Falkirk, Stirlingshire, Scotland.
Printed and bound in Great Britain by
MPG Books Ltd., Bodmin, Cornwall.

PROLOGUE
a rare kind of cancer

D ominic Trelawney coughed, the noise viscid, low and somehow threatening, as if he had swallowed a swamp monster. He was still not used to the sound and to the sensation of pain and burning deep in his chest; had never become even slightly inured to that strangely salty taste that his copious phlegm had developed. He had lived in Stroud with its wonderful valleys, its entrancing views of pastureland and its strangely irritating and odd inhabitants, for a long time. He had trained sixty years ago as a carpenter and joiner, then moved into the building trade, eventually running his own company employing six permanently, another ten on a pro rata basis; he had not made a fortune, but he had made a reputation for reliability and craftsmanship. The problems with his chest had started fifteen years before and had done nothing but progress ever since; at first the medics had thought it was bronchitis, but then the pain had started to bite, to eat him indeed; the breathlessness had increased and his weight had evaporated.

Cancer, they had said. A rare kind of cancer, one that is associated with asbestos, they had said. They had given it a long, fancy name that meant nothing to him, and he had come to understand that he was going to die of a thing that he could not name, because there is no proper treatment, they had said. He tried to tell himself that he did not care, but it seemed an insult to be killed by something he could not name, that was mysterious and shadowy to him. It made him feel diminished, unmanly.

His chest hurt and he felt more ill every day; every morning he awoke and in that moment of awareness, there was first an instant of normality, followed at once by the realization of his situation, of his destiny, that he had no future, only a past. He had lost Aggie, his wife of thirty-nine years two years before and his dependence on alcohol, until then contained and supported, broke free; it had shown itself to be a ravenous beast, one that had all but slain him; only the support of the few friends that remained and, until a few months ago, a voluntary group for those with a drinking problem had saved him, he was sure.

He did not have long to live, he knew, and his only reason for seeking help had been a plea from Daphne, his only child; now that she had died in a road traffic collision a year before, he saw no reason for continuing to try to abstain. Abstinence seemed to him to be a poor way to see out his life. He wanted the pain to end, although he had never articulated the thought to himself.

When the knock came on the front door of his small cottage at ten thirty-seven in the evening, just before he was going to bed, it was the first intimation that he was going to get his wish; it was also the time that he truly appreciated that one should be careful what one wishes for.

ONE
her scream, bouncing off the walls, outlived her

The world flooded in upon her, but gently and therefore deceitfully, because for a few moments she did not realize that this was not a nice world.

Not nice at all.

She was in darkness. She felt stiff, heavy-limbed, groggy; too groggy to appreciate that she had been drugged.

It was a cool darkness, but only slowly did she appreciate how very cold it was.

And then she suddenly realized that she was naked and, with that, came the terror; this did not creep up on her, but came all at once, a huge, chilling flood in which she all but drowned, a shock wave of sudden wakefulness.

Where am I?

Complete blackness. No vague outlines, no faint shafts of light, no variation in the density of the darkness around her. She could have been in a cupboard, could have been in an aircraft hangar. She was on a hard surface, she realized, and she had been there a long time, because she was numb. It was not cold, though; not metal. Perhaps polished wood? And she could not move her arms or legs; although she could see absolutely nothing, she came to appreciate that her wrists and ankles were held tight by some sort of clamps; they chaffed her skin. In her efforts, she craned her neck but . . .

Around my neck, too? The terror increased. *What is this?*

And her head. It did not feel right. Her scalp felt cold, too.

Just a moment passed before she realized that she must have had her hair shaved and this, more than all else that she had discovered before, terrified her, made her almost lose control of her bladder.

She thought about calling out, but something stopped her. Something more powerful than fear of the dark – fear of the one who had done this to her. He was out there, in the darkness. He was watching her, would be listening . . .

Oh, shit!

She had always enjoyed horror films – the *Saw* series, *Hostel*, the *Cube* films – but now it seemed as if she were being punished for this predilection, because now she was in one. She shivered and, despite the cold, it was because of fear and nothing else. She was naked and her legs were held open; he could be waiting there in the nothingness, looking at her, thinking about her.

She screamed suddenly. She didn't want to, but it was not she who decided. It was a word that she only heard when it echoed from walls that she could not see, but that she could hear were cold and hard and maybe even damp . . . *'Pleeease!'*

And her reward was nothing; no response and no change in the cold black. There was a silent yet piercing tone in her ears as the complete lack of sound got louder and louder by the second, until it seemed to split her skull, curdle her brain, stoke her fear.

Her heart was thumping . . . no, pounding . . . no, *bursting*.

She began to squirm, at first gently but then with increasing violence, and as she did so, she discovered something new. Her head was shaved – she missed the movement of her shoulder-length hair – but it was more than that. Someone had put something on her scalp, a sort of metal stiff net, she guessed. This was bizarre, a further dollop of inexplicability, and one that increased her fear exponentially. Nothing had resulted from her efforts, other than pain as she chafed her skin. Around her neck there was more room but that meant only that she bruised her neck as she moved with increasing violence to free herself; after a few minutes – she didn't know how many (how could she?) – she gave up, breathless, aware that with every gasp she was perhaps pleasing some pervert looking at her through night-vision goggles.

For a moment she lay still, but that sound in her ears continued; no, it took advantage. It was an accomplice of whoever had done this thing to her, one that screamed in her ears, that taunted her and left her more frightened still . . .

A light came on, one that shone excruciatingly down into her eyes, the light that blinds, the light of the gods, that disables, not enables. The click disturbed the scream in her ears, made it vanish yet grow louder in her memories. Instinctively, she turned her head. To the left. Towards a camera lens.

What the . . .?

It was a big camera lens – the type that sports photographers use, that are hideously expensive and that produce a big cheer from the crowd when the ball smacks into them – and the light only produced arcs of reflection against dark, perfectly smooth convexity. It was perfectly inhuman, perfectly cruel.

She twisted her head away, to the right, where she expected relief.

She found another camera lens; it was identical.

Two eyes that watched her without eyelids, without emotion, almost without interest, at least without human interest.

She looked down at herself, saw electrodes on her arms and legs, on her abdomen – even, she saw with nausea, up between her legs.

She had nowhere else to go but back up into the light.

Which was when she saw more than the light, when she saw the wooden struts rising above her on either side of her head. They were a deep, dark red that seemed highly polished, beautiful and running up a groove on each inner surface was a rope; she had been brought up in a Victorian house and they reminded her of a sash window.

But it was a very tall, very narrow sash window, one that rose into the bright light above her . . .

One that disturbed her oddly.

She screwed her eyes to stop the pain that looking into the light brought, to try to see beyond the brilliance. In doing this, she made out . . . something.

It was angular and bright.

It was sharp.

It was a guillotine.

She began to scream, almost without thinking about it, once more thrashing from side to side, even though she knew that she could not break free. Her terror made her do it, was in total charge, stifling rational thought that had had its chance and lost. She was reverting to animal because there was nothing else left for her.

Something flickered to her right, catching her attention, stalling her panic. A large flat-screen television was suddenly alive, showing . . . showing what? For a second she thought that it was her – a naked figure, covered in electrodes, and strapped down on a table – but she saw almost at once that this was an elderly male figure. Like her, this man lay under the threatening blade of a guillotine and, like her, his head was shaven. There was no sound, but she could see him thrashing from side to side, his mouth opening in what was clearly anguished pleading.

What now? What was going on? Who was this?

She watched for long minutes, horrified and therefore fascinated, mesmerized despite her own situation.

The end when it came was shockingly quick. The man had quietened, gasping for air, clearly exhausted . . .

And then the blade fell.

She screamed.

The body convulsed, the head fell backwards, blood spurted once, twice, three times in dying arcs from the neck as the fading sight of the eyes looked directly at her.

'Noooooo!!!'

Surely not . . . Please God, no . . .

She screamed again, screamed so that it hurt and somehow that pain was good, and the words were completely incomprehensible, even to herself. She thrashed and strained at her bonds, unconsciously a perfect imitation of what she had just seen on the screen.

Her eyes looked up at the blade just as it started to fall and the automatic shutters of the cameras caught every part of every second as her head came off.

Her scream, bouncing off the walls, outlived her. Far above, hidden in the darkness, five more high-speed cameras – one directly above, one in each corner of the cavernous room – concentrated on the head, watching long after the eyes had clouded and blood had ceased to pump from the neck and ooze from the head.

TWO
'I'm afraid it got chewed up pretty badly'

Another day, another dollar, another head.

Acting Chief Inspector Beverley Wharton had had trouble raising enthusiasm when she had learned of its discovery – indeed, she had trouble raising horror, disgust, surprise or even boredom at it. It was not the first head that had come into her orbit, crying in mute enquiry to be reunited with the body with which it had been born; usually such unnecessary flamboyance was the work of gangs, related to turf wars over drugs, warnings to the cognoscenti and the innocent alike that there were people about who were not to be trifled with. The only exception to this rule had been a butcher who had been suffering paranoid schizophrenia and had become convinced that his wife had been a gorgon, her hair a head of snakes, her ugliness enough to blind (he took to wearing sunglasses when in her presence). Mr Bone – no, really, Mr Bone – had been sectioned but had absconded one day, swung by the retail establishment to pick up a few tools of the trade, and thus made Mrs Bone safe for family viewing.

She judged it unlikely that this case would be as macabre.

And not for the first time, she could not have been further from the truth.

Still, it was a job, although not an everyday kind of job, not a job that would suit many, not one that was particularly safe, either for peace of mind, or the body. She still felt the pain, the humiliation, the burning anger at what had happened to her just six months before; the *violation*, the feeling of humiliation and total subordination that she had endured as she had been raped. She still felt the pain and, make no mistake about it, it still hurt, but not enough to go in for the counselling that the medical officer had so strongly advised. She *wanted* to feel it; she wanted to keep it there, motivating her, reminding her of just how evil, how depraved mankind – a man – could be, and what she had to do to endure, to survive.

Survive, though, she would.

She had even profited. Promotion – temporary but with the hint of permanence, should she keep her nose and other bodily parts clean – had come unexpectedly with the sudden disappearance of Lambert; apparently a promotion for him, but superintendent in the Cinderford Station was not considered the cream of appointments and she guessed that it was one that Lambert would rather not have taken, had it not been politically expedient.

So she *should* be one happy bunny, she reckoned. Lambert had been her nemesis for so many years, an implacable foe, forever sneering, forever undermining, working tirelessly to ensure that she stayed down, cowed, that she suffered merely for being the kind of person he disliked. And now he was gone and, if he wasn't gone forever nor gone a great distance, at least he was far enough away for her to begin to make some headway once more.

The car she was in pulled off the main Gloucester-Ledbury Road, running westwards into the small village of Bromsberrow Heath. The speed limit was thirty miles per hour, but the driver ignored that and she did not choose to reprimand him; they had an appointment with a disembodied head, which trumped the regular global emails from the chief constable droning on about 'respect for all aspects of the law', and 'ensuring that we cannot be criticized for only obeying those laws which suit us'. It was a pretty village, she decided, as far as such villages went; having been brought up in an urban environment, she still looked on rural Gloucestershire as a strange land and she a stranger in it. Mostly bungalows, she noticed, and mostly well kept; biggish gardens but too much chintziness, too many garden gnomes, stone storks and wicker arches; too many called things like 'Dunroaming' and 'Cherry Blossom Cottage'.

There was a distorted crossroads at the heart of the village with a village store and post office at one corner, a bus shelter at the other, then they were past and heading out into open countryside. Open farmland, a row of poplars to the right, a chapel converted into a home on the left. They swung sharp left just past this and continued along a road that became narrower and rougher, more and more like a track. Eventually one more turn to the left and they were approaching Home Farm. Approaching, too, she decided, the eighteenth century.

Gloucestershire, she had long ago decided, was a patchwork of times, ranging through the centuries from near medieval to near modern; not totally modern, mind, not bang-up-to-the-moment, so new it's too hot to touch, but close. Most of it, though, was time-warped into a past that people thought ought to have existed, that existed in actuality only for American tourists and senior citizens, that was as fake as the wooden beams in most people's ceiling. This farm seemed to have stopped somewhere around the time that Marie Antoinette had shown spectacular underestimation of her situation and opted for a career in dietary advice.

'Who owns this place?'

She asked this not of the driver but the woman next to him – Detective Inspector Rebecca Lancefield. Looking over her right shoulder, Lancefield replied, 'Owen Gardner. Sixty-seven years old, widowed, no children. Been farming here all his life. No convictions, except two for tax evasion on red diesel.'

Which, as far as Beverley was concerned, summed her up. Efficient, but efficient only to help herself; efficient only to gain a purchase on that oh-so-greasy, oh-so-high pole. Worse, she was *nice*. Beverley knew how to react to *shitty* – *shitty* was her currency, after all; she worked in *shittiness* almost every hour that she was awake, whether it be dealing with criminals or her real enemies, her colleagues – so she was well versed in it. She could close her eyes and recite *shittiness* without employing much more than one percent of her mental capacity. *Niceness*, though, required some thought; *niceness* was underhand because it might be genuine, might well be a subterfuge. *Shitty* people were straightforward, they did what it said on their tin; she was fairly sure that *nice* people split fifty-fifty down the middle, half being cunts, half being stupid.

She had yet to decide about the curly-haired, snub-nosed blonde who was looking at her now with wide-open, friendly brown eyes, but she wasn't about to give her the benefit of the doubt. Accordingly, she was getting on extremely well with her new detective inspector.

'Good work,' she said and no one would have known.

They stopped in the middle of a farmyard that was no more than ten metres across; it was immediately obvious that Owen Gardner was of the breed of farmers who had no interest in aesthetics; animals made him money, but they also made faeces and if there was no need to clear it up, he wasn't about to bother. Beverley waited in the car while the driver got out and fetched wellingtons from the boot; they weren't Hunters, but she said nothing. When she stood up in the yard, her feet sunk into nearly ten centimetres of some sort of animal shit and the smell that had been permeating the universe since they arrived intensified. She found herself longing – and not for the first time – for concrete, tarmac and halogen lighting, for odours of Indian takeaways and car exhaust.

There were derelict pig-sheds on their left, open countryside to the right, the view broken only by a barn that was empty except for two ancient tractors, some tyres, a lot of barbed wire and a pile of sacks full of farm-type things. Straight ahead of them was a three-storey farmhouse in red brick; it was like a thousand others in the county, except that it was considerably more neglected than most; nine windows, each divided into twelve, and of the one hundred and eight panes, perhaps a quarter were broken and filled in with cardboard, while the curtains behind them (although poorly seen) seemed little more than dirty blankets. The paint could easily have been the original – although there was little left to judge by – and the small garden in front had become something akin to no-man's-land at the battle of Ypres. There were three police cars and two unmarked cars already there, but no sign of human life, until a uniformed constable trudged his weary way around the right-hand side of the farmhouse. His progress was slow and, Beverley noticed, the suctioning effects of the viscous manure had produced its toll upon the blue serge of his constabulary trouser ware; his salute was

tired and his tone equally so when he announced in a voice that
was half respect, three quarters pissed off, 'It's round the back,
ma'am.'

'It', she noted. Lancefield asked, 'Has anyone touched it?'

Beverley found herself wondering how many times she had heard
that question. The uniform – too callow, too scared-looking, just
too bloody innocent, she thought – shook his head with the kind
of nervous certainty that comes only from terrified uncertainty.
'No.'

They followed him around the building. Beverley noted a kitchen
through the windows, one that she recognized from costumed dramas
on the box, and a small back parlour in which there were a widescreen plasma television and a big hi-fi system, items in a small
pocket of the new millennium. Owen Gardner, then, was apparently not completely immersed in the wrong century.

One side was metal fencing with a gate in, opposite this was a
concrete, prefabricated milking parlour, whilst across from the back
of the farmhouse was a slurry pit. Beverley could think of nothing
she'd rather see first thing of a morning when she looked out of
her back door; it was a large one, too, almost full, a hazy kaleidoscope of various shades of bilious green, browns and greys.

It was also the centre of attention. A quick glance told her that
there were four uniforms and three plain clothes police clustered
around it, to all intents and purposes just aimlessly milling, ants
without the queen to direct them.

As soon as Beverley appeared, one of them turned and came
hurrying towards her; it was Fisher. Beverley was not a fan of
obesity, in neither women nor men, whatever their age, but there
was also a certain kind of thinness that she found disturbing; it was
a sallow, unhealthy kind of emaciation and Fisher – newly promoted
to detective sergeant – personified it. Clothes, no matter how small,
seemed to hang off him, his collar touched his neck only ever at
one point, his eyes peered out at the world from two moulded caves.

His expression was one of great relief. 'Chief Inspector! Good
to see you.'

Of course he would think it was good to see her. Until their
arrival, he had been the senior officer and therefore in charge of
the crime scene; responsibility sat on him rather as his dandruff
did; it was a coating, nothing more, and something of an embarrassment. Fisher's promotion had been a surprise, and not just to
Beverley. He was not venal, nor was he lazy which, she supposed,

put him about a fairly large distance above the competition, but he was thick. Beverley had long ago concluded that brains weren't necessary for much of police work; indeed, in the execution of the overwhelming majority of tasks that the police were required to perform, brains were a positive disadvantage. No army wanted infantry that was intelligent, cannon fodder that could think and thus maybe decide that there was more to life than being in the front line and getting hurt. You'd only want brains in those giving the orders; evolution had decided for a very good reason that it was better to have the brains stored in the head than in the hands. She looked at Fisher, looked into his eyes, and suspected that he was a revolutionary dead end. The *Sun* quick crossword was his intellectual zenith, and that only rarely accomplished.

She said nothing, but then she didn't need to; Rebecca Lancefield was already rushing to show her abilities. 'Where's Owen Gardner?'

'In the farmhouse.'

'And the dog?'

'Muzzled and chained around the back of the cowshed.'

Beverley asked, 'What about the dog?'

Lancefield said, before Fisher could even begin compiling his thoughts into his version of human speech, 'It was the dog that found it, sir. I'm afraid it got chewed up pretty badly before Gardner was able to get it off her.'

Beverley raised her eyebrows. 'And where did the dog find it?'

Fisher said brightly, 'The slurry pit.'

She had somehow guessed that this would prove to be the case. 'Where is it now?'

'We bagged it,' was Fisher's bright response, one that produced a correspondingly depressing feeling inside Beverley. *We bagged it*. It was what the police now did; they no longer looked for clues and then deduced from them, they now *bagged* them. If they had made evidence bags big enough, they would be bagging the fucking bodies so they wouldn't have to do any thinking about them. Fisher continued, 'I ordered it to be put in the boot of one of the cars.'

She could hear by the way that he said 'ordered', that he liked reliving the event. She waited for him to suggest that it would be good idea to go and get it so that she might gain some purpose from her visit, but nothing was forthcoming.

It was Lancefield who suggested, 'Perhaps you could go and get it so that we could examine it, sergeant.'

Fisher nodded, oblivious to the undercurrent, and trotted off. Had

Beverley and Lancefield been better acquainted, they might have exchanged knowing glances – the secret messages of the initiated – but neither wanted to lower their defences just yet. Instead, Beverley said to Lancefield, 'I think it's about time that lot started to earn their wages, don't you?' She meant the crowd around the slurry pit. 'First I want three of them inside searching the farmhouse – make sure there isn't a cellar – and remind them to go into the lofts. The rest can go over the farmyard; not fingertip, but I want every nook and cranny investigated; if I discover that one of them has missed something, they'll be sent to the dog-training school as live bait.'

'What about further afield? This is a three-hundred acre farm.'

'First things first, inspector.'

And Lancefield merely nodded, accepting the mild rebuke. She strode off to the assembled police officers, leaving Beverley looking at her back, her expression neutral, her thoughts anything but.

Fisher came trotting back, a human retriever not with a ball in his mouth but a human head in a clear plastic bag in his hand. He proffered it and she could see from the way that he did so that it was heavy; when she indicated that he should put it down on the bonnet of a nearby, apparently derelict tractor, it landed with a dull thud. The weather, until then gusty and only threatening rain, finally made up its mind and began to let forth a fine drizzle upon the just – and, she had a shrewd idea, upon the unjust, equally.

The head was difficult to see, even though the plastic was perfectly transparent, because it was covered in green and brown cow faeces that had smeared the inside of the bag. She could make little out other than it had been seriously chewed, and she was loathe to unseal it. Let the pathologist have that little treat.

Speaking of which . . .

'Who's the duty pathologist?' she asked Fisher. God, she hoped it wasn't Sydenham. Sydenham, who seemed to go on forever, rather like an inferior Wagnerian opera, or a scabetic itch.

But Fisher, for once not because of his incompetence, managed to surprise her.

'Dr Eisenmenger, I think.'

THREE
a box of small treasures

Antonia watched Andrew trudging up the hill, pale-blue shirt open at the collar, showing sweat stains under the arms and, she knew, between his shoulder blades, a damp towel over his left shoulder. Ahead of him ran Josh and Harriet, their liveliness providing stark contrast with his lassitude; their shouts only emphasizing his breathlessness. Not that Andrew was *old*, she thought automatically, but at the back of her head was the realization that she had been saying that to herself for quite a few decades now. He was definitely showing tiredness, though; how could he not be? Thrust into a second bout of parenthood at the age of sixty, destined to miss out on the comparative ease of grandparenthood, all the while grieving for his son and daughter-in-law, bearing the curse of outliving his own offspring. The children burst into the kitchen giggling. They knew better than to let the door slam, but even so it was opened with a degree of energy that neither she nor Andrew would ever be able to match. Josh was eight years old, two months from being nine; he had dark, slightly curled hair and a rather asymmetrical face that somehow worked, that evoked a smile and a feeling of warmth in those who saw it. Harriet was halfway between seven and eight and, similarly, halfway between fates; Antonia could see that in a few years time her granddaughter would either be startling attractive, or plain. It was at the moment impossible to say which way the genes would fall, onto which path Harriet be lead.

'Have you had a good swim?' she asked them, a smile breaking her mood of unconscious melancholy. Of course they had; how could they not? The weather was good and the Parkers had a wonderful pool. Their hair glistened and there was a faint yet potent scent of chlorine. Whilst the children sat at the kitchen table and drank the orange juice that Antonia poured for them, Andrew came in. He smiled because he always smiled, but those decades came back to remind her that it was not as happy a smile as it once had been. She asked him, 'Nice swim?'

'Oh, yes.' He meant it, but she could hear that his head was full of darker thoughts. He sat down and she went to the fridge and, forsaking the orange juice, she poured him some white wine. There was a large dark sweat patch on his back.

Harriet asked, 'Can we have the television on?' Eighteen months ago, when Antonia and Andrew had just been grandparents, the idea of a television in the kitchen was as peculiar as the idea of one in the bathroom. How things had since changed. She rose and went to the wall-mounted set without argument. It was a cartoon, of course, but she said nothing; she and Andrew had learned to blot things out and children's TV was the least of them. After all, they had all but blotted out the events around the car crash that had killed their only son and his wife.

She picked up her own glass of wine and joined the family at the table; the children had become immediately and deeply entranced in the television. 'How is Jane?' she asked her husband.

'Not there. No one was.' Wallace Parker was often away, his wife, Jane, less so; even if none of the three children, now grown up, was there, it was understood that they were allowed use of the swimming pool.

'Really? Jane didn't say she'd be away.'

There was nothing Andrew could say to that and he didn't try. Antonia liked to think that the Parkers considered them more than just neighbours, that they were friends, and friends, moreover, who were approximate social equals. He was of a different opinion: Wallace Parker had been the CEO of a major high street bank, of one of the better-regarded estate agency chains, and, most recently, of an international gas and electricity supplier. Andrew Barclay had recently retired as a general practitioner; not exactly a failure, but he was aware that he had been run of only a slightly esteemed mill. Antonia Barclay ate lunch; Jane Parker 'lunched', a wholly different thing. 'Lunching' was a verb that implied so much more than ingestion of food, it implied a way of life so socially elevated, so distant from the lives of most people that it might have been the group ritual of a different species.

It was not that they were treated in quite the same way as the inhabitants of the council cottages just down the road – the Redferns, Mrs Williams, the Carters and the Coles – who were regarded, he had observed, much as barbarians at the gates, it was just that they were not treated as members of the inner circle. They were merely 'neighbours' and, as the saying has it, one cannot choose one's neighbours or one's relatives. They were *endured*, he suspected, although that was better than the fate reserved for Tom Sheldon and Ellie Taylor, who just didn't register on the social radar; Sheldon, because he was an ex-traveller who had no interest in observing the social conventions that the Parkers considered so essential; and Ellie Taylor because she had three children by three different fathers and never once a husband.

Josh finished his drink and, the television not to his liking, he began to torment his sister by trying to grab and squeeze her knee. She squealed and spilled her juice, causing Antonia to scold first her then, when Harriet protested, Josh.

'Go up to your rooms and I'll start running your baths in a moment. Give me fifteen minutes to relax with Gramps.'

They complied with her command, doing so in an energetic manner that she still found exhausting and thus demoralizing. Once more, she could not help realizing the difference there was between the two generations in the house, one that was twice as wide as was normal, perhaps twice as wide as was healthy. They waited until the door had closed – slammed, actually – before Antonia turned to Andrew. 'How are you?'

He said at once, 'Fine.'

He might have been convincing had she not known he was lying. 'No pain?'

'Not today.'

She eyed him. Being a doctor he was, she knew, a good liar. Eventually she decided that she could not tell whether this was the truth and so gave him the benefit of the doubt. 'Good,' she said with the best smile she could muster. She knew better than to press the point and the conversation continued in the easy triviality of a long marriage for ten or so minutes.

Upstairs, Josh and Harriet shouted cheerful insults at each other from their rooms, feeling a degree of exultation in life that they did not know was a precious, diminishing part of their lives. As she ascended the stairs and heard them, Antonia was once again struck by both joy and sadness, a mix that produced a kind of melancholic euphoria, as she exulted in their youthfulness whilst being reminded of what she had lost forever. She went to the bathroom and began running the bath, pouring in some bath bubbles; it was Josh's turn to go first tonight.

She checked the temperature, swirled the water, dried her hand and then called for Josh.

She tidied his room as he splashed in the bath, listening with half an ear to make sure that everything was alright. Her back

ached and had done so for a long time, although she wondered
occasionally if it had got significantly worse, or maybe even
changed, and if she should mention it to Andrew. There were so
many things now that she never seemed to get around to discussing
with him.

Josh was not an overly untidy child she now realized, although
it had taken a good few hours of conversation with other parents
at the local school to convince her of this. She was certain that she
had not been so careless of orderliness when she was so young.
She had tried to impress upon him the concept – so simple to her
– of putting dirty clothes in the laundry basket, of folding and
putting away clothes that he was hoping to wear again, yet neither
he nor his sister, as bright as they were, seemed able to cope with
this concept. She found herself constantly sighing as she performed
this nightly ritual of tidying up after them.

And toys . . .

She and Andrew had looked in vain for Meccano, and the Airfix
kits that they had found had left her husband deeply saddened,
muttering that he had not realized that things had become so bad.
Even Action Man – and she had moral qualms about the concept
– did not seem to be quite as she recalled him; Lego, too, appeared
to have changed, mutated, degraded. Still, Josh was showing a
healthy interest in board games such as Junior Scrabble, Monopoly
and Mousetrap, although he still seemed blind to the concept of
clearing up after himself.

After fifteen minutes she had almost managed to clear the floor
of pieces of toy, having succeeded in more or less reuniting the
bits correctly. She got tiredly down on her knees – her left hip
became bad tempered at this time of day – and reached under the
bed. She brought out a box of small treasures. More Scrabble tiles,
more small abstruse and highly coloured plastic parts from Kinder
toys, Lego bricks and a small, tatty teddy bear that had once been
Andrew's. Then her fingers found his camera and, tutting at the
careless way he treated precious things, she pulled it out. It had
been his present not six weeks before; it was a ten mega pixel
digital camera and he had been thrilled beyond words to receive
it. Already, though, the casing was scratched. Telling herself she
was not being unduly inquisitive, she switched it on as she sat on
the bed, then scrolled though the pictures. Most were of her and
Andrew, many were of his sister and an equal number had in them
Darren from over the road.

She stopped and stared at one in particular, then sighed again, this time more angrily. She went into the bathroom where Josh was playing submarines and presented the camera to him. 'This was under your bed.'

It was not obvious to Josh's young mind that he had done anything wrong in leaving it under the bed, but his granny's tone told him that it was. He looked guilty and the silence that was suddenly about them was huge. She waited; Josh was well aware, young as he was, that Granny Antonia was good at waiting. He said eventually, 'Sorry.'

'You've been in the grounds of the Grange again, haven't you.' This was a statement without the inflection of a question mark.

There was a hesitation but it was only minimal. 'No, I haven't.'

'Josh, please don't tell fibs.' She showed him the photograph that was displayed on the back of the camera, the one that showed Darren making a silly face; close behind him was a chain-link fence and beyond that could be seen the upper, ruin storeys of the Grange. He looked surprised, then shocked, then crestfallen. He dropped his head.

'We were only in the outer grounds, not the inner,' he said by way of defence. If entering the outer grounds of the Grange was bad, entering the inner – and thereby potentially getting into the building itself – was akin to heresy.

She said severely, 'It's still trespassing, and that's against the law. You don't want to be labelled a criminal, do you?' Before he could answer, presumably in the negative, she continued, 'You were lucky the last time that it went no further when you were caught.' Some months before, they had been caught trespassing there by Alan Somersby, the estate manager. He had been quite angry and gone on about health and safety, although, thankfully, Wallace Parker, owner of the estate, had taken a lenient view. 'Please don't do it again. Understand?'

'Yes.' His tone was as sincere as he could make it.

She looked long and hard at him, searching for a lie. Uncertain, but wanting to give him the benefit of the doubt, she nodded slowly. 'Very well, Josh.'

FOUR

there was just too much shit

He's lost weight.

Beverley had no problem with slimming but John Eisenmenger, she judged, had gone too far. Her contact with pathologists had taught her the meaning of the word cachectic, and whilst he had not quite achieved this, he was looking worryingly thin. She could not blame him, however. Not for the first time, John Eisenmenger had suffered trauma in his personal life. The first time had nearly destroyed him and she had been afraid that this most recent event would do the job properly, but she was surprised and pleased to see that, whilst it might have marked him, it had not done its worst.

He was walking around the side of the farmhouse, following her path unconsciously, accompanied by a young uniform. He was wearing wellington boots that seemed too big for him and she wondered if this was another sign of his weight loss. When he caught sight of her, she saw that his eyes were more sunken than she remembered but, more than that, they were more distant yet seemed to see the world more acutely; it was as if they were unclouded by optimism and therefore saw more things. His shirt collar, too, had stretched, she noted, and his smile was real but weak.

'Hello, Beverley.'

She felt almost like hugging him, but restrained herself. 'Hello, John. It's been quite a while.' Which, of course, led only to painful remembrance for him so she had to say at once, 'We have a head.'

He was surprised enough to lose the slightly lost expression. 'Just a head?'

She nodded to Fisher who had produced the plastic bag with its curious and curiously heavy content, placing it on the bonnet of the car by which they stood. Eisenmenger's face showed part interest, part surprise and part dismay at the accompanying manure. 'Where was it found?' She gestured to the slurry pit where various lowly constables toiled unhappily.

'Over there. By the farm dog.'

He said, 'Ah. Hence the teeth marks.' Which, even though it was difficult to see exactly what had been done, was clearly something of an understatement.

'We're searching for the body, but no luck so far.'

Eisenmenger looked around at the fields that surrounded the farm. 'Might be tricky.' She didn't bother replying and he asked, 'Can I take a closer look at the pit?'

She shrugged; *do what you like, John.* She didn't accompany him as he trudged to the slurry pit where three policemen in boiler suits were being supervised by DI Lancefield; supervised at something of a distance, he noted, and could not blame her when the miasmic stench hit his olfactory membranes. The slurry pit was clearly ancient and, now that the top layers had been disturbed by the less than enthusiastic shovels of the constabulary, the true viciousness of what decay does to all natural things was there to be fully appreciated by all. Eisenmenger felt a twinge of sympathy for the toiling policemen as he asked Lancefield, 'Do we know how deep the head was found?'

She shook her head. 'It couldn't have been too far in, because the dog wouldn't have smelled it out.' Which, given the almost solid wall of odour through which he was moving, Eisenmenger felt unable to dispute.

The slurry pit was about half emptied, a growing lake of displaced cow faeces to its right which was being raked by two more constables, looking for anything and everything that might be significant. Eisenmenger had the feeling that all six of them were going to be disappointed. He turned and walked back to Beverley or, rather, the head.

He was loathe to open the bag until he got it back to the mortuary and therefore he could little more than peer through the plastic and the brown organic matter that coated both the inside of the bag and the head itself. Doing so did little to add to the sum of his, or indeed human, knowledge; there was just too much shit.

'I'd better take this with me.'

'Can't you give me anything to go on now?'

'Beverley, look at it,' he replied. 'Given the amount of faecal spoiling and predation by man's best friend, and the fact that it's been shaved, I can't even be sure at the moment if it's a man or a woman. Please be reasonable.'

Beverley was used to pathologists refusing to give her concrete and useful information but she did not have it within her to castigate John Eisenmenger as she might once have done. 'I had a feeling you'd say that.'

Lancefield came back over. 'There's nothing in the slurry pit,' she announced gloomily, as if she had been promised presents that had failed to appear. The policemen behind her just looked relieved to have finished their job.

Beverley failed to summon sympathy. 'Then make sure that the search of the fields is going well, while I have a chat with Farmer Giles.' To Eisenmenger she said, 'Can I assume that I'm not going to have to wait days for you to get around to looking at that thing?'

He smiled. It was tired but appreciative. 'No more than five, I promise.'

She nodded slowly and with a perfectly straight face. 'Welcome back.'

FIVE
'smack on the head; got a skull fracture'

Malcolm Willoughby had had his eye on the delightfully chubby Sharon Thomas for some weeks. She had the blonde curls and the slightly rosy cheeks that excited him; she also gave the sense that when she jumped, various parts of her continued to wobble for a very short time after they should have stopped, and he kind of liked that. Her blouses always seemed just a little too small, which no red-blooded male like Malcolm was going to miss, much less dismiss.

She usually came with a girlfriend, a scrawny thing with no figure and greasy skin who smelled of cold, greasy burger, but today he was to be surprised. As he made sure that he was out front, ready to serve them at their usual time, she came in alone. His heart did a double beat whilst his brain crowed a silent, *Hallelujah!*

'Hello,' he said brightly. He was good at brightly, because he had practised it a lot, but he didn't need to act it that time.

'Hello,' she said with a small, polite, insincere smile; one that lasted little longer than a spark from a struck flint.

'Usual?'

'Please.'

He was already moving to get down the glass, then turned his back to fetch the bottle of Cabernet Sauvignon from the shelf at the back of the bar. He thought, *She's really asking for it, drinking alone.*

She had the exact money ready for him, as she always did and, again as she always did, she was taking her first sip before the money was in the card-controlled cash till. She was about to go to her customary seat in the far corner of the pub when he said, 'You're Sharon, aren't you?'

She paused. 'Yes.' The smile this time lasted longer, was less guarded.

Before she could ask, he explained, 'Stan told me. You know him.'

'Oh, yes. Of course.' He had told Malcolm a lot more, too – an awful lot more – which maybe explained why she suddenly seemed bashful. She asked, 'How is he?'

'He's fine. In the Algarve at the moment.'

'Nice.' She sipped her wine. Malcolm helped himself to a pint of Stella. 'Should you do that?'

'Oh, yes. Stan said I could have the odd one.' It was his sixth of the day. 'He's a pretty easy-going employer.'

Her reaction suggested she was a bit surprised at that – as well she might have been, considering that Stan was well known to be a tight bastard – but she said nothing; it was no business of hers if this gawky, spiky-haired twat was rooking Stan; she had seen others who had tried to fool Stan, and generally they eventually learned. 'You in charge, then?'

Malcolm thought about lying, decided not to. 'The brewery got in a temporary landlord,' he admitted.

'Oh,' she replied, her voice so bored it was almost asleep.

'You work at the Nationwide, don't you?'

'I can't get you a cheap mortgage, if that's what you want to know.'

He laughed; he was quite proud of his laugh, thought it sounded really genuine, and sometimes it was. 'Don't worry. I'm renting for the foreseeable future.'

'Spanner' Spanswick came in and Malcolm had to serve him his usual pint of Strongbow, so Sharon was left alone for a while. She didn't leave the bar, though, and he did not fail to notice this. When he returned, she asked, 'You haven't worked here long, have you?'

'Three weeks.'

'Is this all you do?' This was in a voice that might have been sneering, might merely have been curious; Malcolm wasn't bright enough to tell.

'Oh, no,' he hastened to assure her. 'This is temporary, while I find my feet.' Before she could ask what he was talking about, he gave her his usual line. 'I've just been discharged from the navy.'

He was particularly fond of this lie; he was not unathletic in appearance and the various jobs he had had during his twenty-six years – mechanic, undertaker, hospital porter and steward on board a cruise liner – gave his patter a fairly realistic patina. Girls fell for it and, as everyone including Malcolm knew, all the nice girls love a sailor.

'Why? Bugger the admiral, did you?'

It wasn't a particular clever joke, but that didn't matter to Malcolm; he laughed uproariously. 'Nice one,' he enthused. 'No. I was invalided out. Smack on the head; got a skull fracture.' He had perfected the precise tone of nonchalance to make this sound quite heroic. He had, in fact, had a skull fracture once, but it was when he had fallen off a skip whilst drunk, the result of a ten pound bet. It produced the required reaction, though. She was impressed.

A group of businessmen came in – they weren't regulars and were slightly incongruous in the surroundings of The Grey Goose where standard dress was either work boots, shorts and builder's crack, or overalls – and he was occupied for ten minutes serving them, by which time she had finished her drink. He gave her the next one gratis.

Over the course of the next four hours he chatted to her – or, more precisely, he chatted her up – and even managed to do his job. He discovered that the reason she was alone was because Deirdre, her companion, was unwell (actually hung-over following a birthday bash), Sharon had no immediate boyfriend because the last one had just been remanded for falsifying MOT certificates, she no longer watched *Britain's Got Talent* because she thought Simon Cowell was a twat, and she was allergic to strawberries and goat's cheese. Occasionally, the temporary land-lord came through – he demonstrated an enviable ability to delegate and an insatiable appetite for soap opera – but Malcolm always managed to look both sober and busy every time he did so.

Sharon managed neither. She became very drunk but also, he knew, very willing; it was with a practised eye that he judged this, and it was with a practised tongue that he suggested how the evening should proceed. There was perhaps a moment when he worried that he had misjudged the cast, but only a brief one;

her smile this time was altogether different, a thing of crass coquettishness.

Malcolm had to do all the clearing up after hours while Stan's replacement indulged his passion for TV quiz shows; normally he would have been done by half past midnight, but Spanner had thrown up in the gents and not told anyone, and someone else had pulled the condom machine nearly off the wall, so he was half an hour late for his rendezvous with Sharon; he missed her by five minutes.

What he didn't miss was the cosh on the back of the head, the one wielded by the man who had been watching him, when he could, for four days.

SIX

'a very capable psychologist, so I hear'

The next morning and Eisenmenger had taken his unusual baggage to the mortuary, where the senior mortuary technician, Clive, was his old friend. Clive had seen most things and a head that had been badly chewed by a dog, was covered in cow faeces and put in a plastic bag held neither surprise nor shock for him. He was a short, stocky man with a devilish yet attractive grin, and hands and a face that were grizzled, as if he had sailed the seven seas, or perhaps just done a lot of living.

'That's some hand luggage, Doc. Try getting that on an aircraft.'

Eisenmenger had arranged for Scenes of Crime to attend in an hour's time, giving him and Clive time to drink black coffee and chew some fat. As it was a Sunday, there was no one else around to disturb them. Clive, a bluff but kind man, knew all about Eisenmenger's recent history and his conversation was accordingly tactful. 'You coping these days, Doc?'

'It's not too bad, Clive.' They were eating digestive biscuits, a staple of Clive's mortuary for all the years that Eisenmenger had known him. 'Not too bad.'

Clive was plugged into all the gossip going in the department and Eisenmenger knew it. He was well aware that no one did or said anything without Clive becoming fairly quickly aware of it; he was well aware also that approximately seventy percent of what Clive learned was completely untrue. He wondered what Clive had heard about him, but was not about to ask him.

'You sure you're looking after yourself?'

'I think I am.'

Clive was delving in the bottom of the biscuit barrel, looking for the broken ones. He didn't raise his eyes as he pointed out, 'I've been meaning to say, you've lost weight.'

To which Eisenmenger replied smoothly, 'No bad thing, Clive. I was getting podgy.'

Clive didn't respond directly. After dunking half a digestive in his coffee, he said a propos of nothing at all, 'You've got to send that heart off, don't forget.'

'I won't.'

A small, not to say microscopic, pause before: 'Only Dr Sherman's secretary rang yesterday, wondering how things were going.'

He was referring to the death of a man with advance cancer of the maxillary sinus who had been about to undergo radical facial surgery; Charlie Sherman had been the clinical psychologist who had been talking him through the ramifications when he had been found dead in his bathroom. The question was, was it suicide or was it natural causes? Eisenmenger's initial post mortem examination had been inconclusive and the results of toxicology on the autopsy were eagerly awaited. Clive knew well that Eisenmenger and Charlie Sherman were seeing each other socially and knew that they would have discussed the case. 'I expect she is,' Eisenmenger observed drily. He kept a straight face, knowing that Clive was on a fishing expedition and quite happy to swim around the bait and wait.

Clive nodded. The fax machine in the corner began to chirrup and then to disgorge a message. 'Settled in nicely, has Dr Sherman,' he said eventually. 'A very capable psychologist, so I hear.'

Eisenmenger did not bother to reply, thinking to himself that he found it unlikely in the extreme that Clive and others he came into contact with would ever have occasion to discuss the merits of a clinical psychologist.

The buzzer announcing a visitor at the main door interrupted their jousts and feints. When Clive returned it was with the Scenes of Crime officer, replete with obligatory metal briefcase and the weak but unmistakeable odour of fried onions.

Antonia's back was aching. She knew that if she told Andrew he would shake his head and say that the back was the most difficult area of medicine, that they had made more progress in curing cancer than they had in curing backache. Symptomatic relief was all that could be done in most cases; which was all very well, but paracetamol had long since failed to work and even the strongest painkillers she could get off prescription had only a slight and short term effect. So why didn't she go to their family doctor? She could not answer this, but supposed that it was a combination of the lethargy of old age, a suspicion that he would not be able to help much, and . . . something else, something that she could not define, but something that felt very like fear.

She would have to stop gardening for a moment and rest on one of the garden benches that gave a view of the entire lane until it bent sharply to the left some half a mile away. She would have to start thinking about Sunday lunch soon, anyway. From here she could see the council houses, the School House and away up on a hill, Keeper's Cottage where that strange man, Tom Sheldon, lived. She had tried to get to know him, but he had resolutely, and not always politely, resisted all efforts to integrate or be integrated into the village. There was undoubtedly something shifty about him, although she tried not to listen to the sometimes lurid gossip that circulated; she had a fundamentally forgiving and tolerant nature, one that yearned for harmony, and until she saw concrete evidence that he was anything more than unfortunate in his manner and tongue, she would give no credence to tittle-tattle.

She even had time for Ellie Taylor, who was regarded by most of the people in the area as some sort of anti-Christ, or at least a white witch. And, in their eyes, why should they not? She was determinedly an earth mother, who loudly railed against conventional medicine and who picked herbs and plants to brew her own nostrums, who was forever to be heard damning the church, who had been seen wandering through the woods of the estate late at night, some said naked, others naked and painted. Of course, Antonia knew that much of this was exaggeration, that she might not believe in organized religion and the risen Christ, that she preferred to find her own paths through illness, and could see that she was just a very independent young lady who had strong views and liked others to know them. True, she was not particularly well-educated, and she lived entirely off the state, but Antonia had been reared

on caring – she had been a nurse when she had met Andrew and
one, moreover, that felt she had a vocation – and refused to see
superficialities.

The children were, after all, quite nice. Two of them were of
'mixed race' as she had learned she was now supposed to call
them, and the youngest was forever being beset by urinary tract
infections and boils, but she did not dislike them because of this.
The oldest, Darren, was Josh's age and they had struck up a
friendship, which she had encouraged because she was aware
that neither she nor Andrew was a substitute for contact with
close family life, even if that family did not necessarily conform
to social convention.

She had been resting for perhaps fifteen minutes – time seemed
to pass so much more quickly these days – when the door to the
School House opened and out came Ellie, dressed as usual in a tie-
dyed smock and patched cardigan with brightly coloured tights.
The children followed, clearly bickering as usual, but it seemed to
Antonia that it was in a friendlier, less aggravating way than her
own grandchildren did.

'Hello, Antonia.' Ellie had a nice smile, one that charmed her.
She seemed to Antonia to be at base innocent, mistaken in her
beliefs, but fundamentally harmless. Antonia stood up with a small
effort. 'Ellie. How are you?'

Whilst the children played around Ellie, she talked over the garden
fence with Antonia. 'Where's Josh?'

'Andrew took them for a cycle ride. They'll be back in half an
hour.'

'Darren was hoping that Josh would be able to play later on.'

She hesitated. 'After tea,' she said eventually. Then more certainly,
'I'm sure that won't be a problem, as long as they're not out too
late. Back before nine?' She knew that Ellie often allowed Darren
out until well after Josh's ten o'clock bedtime.

'Oh, yes.' Antonia heard something that might have been insincerity
in the reply but she was willing to give her the benefit of the
doubt.

Eisenmenger was not a natural showman. He could gain a
modicum of pleasure from lecturing and from demonstrating, but
it was merely compensation, a small morsel of comfort to help
him through the experience. He did not like the idea of making
an idiot of himself in front of others, felt always that one or more

of them were just waiting for him to suffer a pratfall. Of course, his level of anxiety was inversely proportionate to the knowledge base of his audience and so his not infrequent tête-à-têtes with the police tended to be relatively stress-free. They listened and they accepted, but they rarely argued. This time, though, Beverley, however, was not interested in merely being a passive receiver of his pearls.

'How can you be sure?' she demanded. 'That bloody dog has made such a mess of it, I'm not even sure it's human; it could be Neanderthal.'

They were back in the mortuary, standing around the head that had been placed on one of the three dissection tables; of the four of them – she, Eisenmenger, Lancefield and Clive – he felt that only Clive was on his side. 'I know enough anatomy to be sure of the species, Beverley.'

Eisenmenger had removed the brain and examined it, taking samples but not expecting much to come of this. The only sign that anything had been done was a line of stitching at the back of the scalp.

'But the gender?'

She had a point. Fido had chewed away most of the right cheek and much of the flesh around the right orbit, including the eye itself. On the left side of the face, there were numerous deep teeth marks and areas where the dog had made tentative bites so that small gobbets of flesh were gone. Eisenmenger admitted, 'The damned dog must have been hungry.'

Lancefield said with some disgust, 'Gardner all but starved the poor mutt. Most of the animals on the farm are neglected, some appallingly so; we've informed the RSPCA.'

'I don't see how you can be sure that this is a male head,' insisted Beverley. 'The hair has been shaved off, the nose is quite fine, and there's no sign of stubble.'

'There's no sign of stubble because he had recently shaved, or perhaps been shaved. The hair follicles are definitely of a male type and in a male pattern on the lower face. Add to that there are no ear piercings, the eyebrows aren't plucked and there's no make-up, so I think we can safely assume this belongs to a male of species homo sapiens, even if he wasn't built like the proverbial.'

Lancefield asked, 'You said he had been recently shaved. He died in the morning then?'

Eisenmenger said, 'He died after recently shaving or, conceivably, being shaved. That could have happened at any time of the day or night.'

'Age?'

'Roughly late fifties, perhaps early sixties. Terrible dentition – the maxillofacial guys are coming in tomorrow to take a formal record. I've plucked hair for DNA so you might strike lucky with the offenders' database.'

It wasn't much; not much at all. Beverley asked, 'How long has he been dead? How long was the head buried before the dog discovered it?'

She knew what his answer would be – an exemplar of obfuscation – but she had to ask it anyway. He shrugged. 'Not long.'

'Which means what? Ten minutes, an hour, a day . . . what?'

In a perfectly reasonable tone, he pointed out, 'I don't know. I might not be up on the literature, Beverley, but I don't think anyone's ever done the experiment of burying heads in cow shit for differing lengths of time.'

She played her part, asking tiredly, 'An estimate then?'

He allowed her a smile. 'Not long at all. Less than a day, possibly less than six hours.'

She let the bone go, but picked up another one immediately. 'Anything else?'

'He's been beheaded,' pointed out Eisenmenger.

Lancefield's expression was quite clear. *No shit, Sherlock.* Beverley asked, 'Anything we don't know?'

'Beheading people is not as easy as you might assume; cutting through the cervical vertebra can be tricky. One of the reasons it was abandoned as a form of judicial execution was because even the best of axemen tended to take two or three strokes to separate body and head. Clean, single stroke beheading was rare. Similarly, most modern day beheading – that done by terrorists, for example – is not done with a single stroke but with a see-sawing action.'

'But this wasn't?' guessed Beverley.

At Eisenmenger's request, Clive grasped the head in glove hands and turned it on its side to expose the neck structures. With a biro that Lancefield fervently hoped was going to be soon thrown away, Eisenmenger gestured and explained. 'This is a single, clean cut. There is no indication of trial cuts; just the one that did the business. Also, examining the edges of the cut structures under a dissecting microscope suggests that the blade was travelling anterior to posterior.'

Lancefield was lost. 'Meaning?'

'Front to back. He was looking up as the blade fell.' Lancefield felt sick, whilst Beverley blinked and breathed deeply and slowly. They tried to picture what might have gone on but did not want to. Lancefield asked, 'And he might well have been conscious, or at least alive?'

He shrugged. 'Possibly. There's not much I can get for tox from this, Beverley. Hardly any blood and most of that was contaminated. I've kept some brain, though. They may be able to use that. And we'll hopefully get something from the body when it turns up.'

What he meant was, if it turns up, and everybody knew it.

SEVEN

'Are you sure the head belongs to a man?'

Over quite a short time, Josh and Darren had struck up a close friendship, one that had become important to them in the way that is unique to children of their age, that subsumed their whole existence, that was the first and therefore the strongest bond they thought that they would ever form. They were unaware of the eddies and undercurrents around them, of the turbulence caused by friendships and love affairs that crossed the boundaries of invisible yet ever-forceful social strata. Yet, like all such juvenile friendships, they had their secrets; indeed, their relationship was almost built upon them, cemented it, both enabled and imprisoned them within it; liberated them and yet put them happily in chains to it. Thus, their language was shot through with unvoiced messages to each other, non-verbal communications and in-jokes so obscure they were encrypted beyond human ability to decode. When they came together, they entered a world – and that world varied from day to day – that was solely theirs. Unless it was sport – football, cricket, perhaps just catch – usually it was a world of war, or sometimes one of monsters and aliens, occasionally one of police and robbers; they had never thought to play cowboys and Indians, a sign of their times. And they had a wonderful canvas on which to draw their imaginary world, one that consisted not just of their back gardens, but also of the countryside around them.

Their appreciation of 'the estate' was unformed. They under-stood that it was bounded by fencing, and that it was not common ground, but they did not think of it as 'forbidden', as 'private', despite the notices proclaiming otherwise that were planted around its perimeter. It was part of their environment, and they had still to understand that one's environment is not necessarily one's personal playground. They did not have qualms about climbing over one of the many stiles and then dodging into the under-growth, running between copses, shooting and dodging bullets, rolling and leaping ravines, replica guns firing or Super Soakers streaming water. They did not have qualms, but they realized that it was a secret between them, not to be divulged to adults and all the better for it.

During their months of playing together on the estate, they had discovered many secret places to play, in which to be themselves as opposed to what school, or their loved ones, or everyone else expected them to be, and their choice of any such place on any given day was reached by means unknown to them, driven by chance, by desire, by capriciousness, by joy, by last night's televi-sion, by yesterday's play, by the latest film, by . . . anything.

It was, as so many childhoods are, a wonderful time to be alive, one of total innocence, one of total omnipotence, and one of total vulnerability.

When Malcolm failed to turn up for his shift the next morning, the temporary landlord cursed him but was not surprised. It had not escaped him that the little shit was helping himself to the stocks, and he had every intention of reporting this behaviour to Stan when he called up from the Algarve to check up on things.

Lancefield took the call and went straight to Beverley. 'A headless body has turned up.'

Beverley had been compiling a report for the chief superin-tendent on the reasons for the sixteen percent decrease in the clear-up rate of violent crime over the past twelve months; it was, she knew, another exercise in shit-passing; the chief constable of this fair county would, she knew, be getting flack from the Ministry of Justice and from the press, so he in turn shouted at the chief superintendent, who in turn . . . She had become adept at the jargon, the talk that obfuscated, that deceived as it appeared to inform; the excuses and the meaningless statistics, the hot air that caused the inaccuracies and downright lies to shimmer like a mirage of the truth. She was delighted to be distracted by such news. 'Where?'

'Newent.' Lancefield's tone was not as pleased as Beverley might have expected; indeed, she appeared to be worried.

'What's wrong?'

'I'm not sure this is good news.'

'Why not?'

'We've got some more searching to do. Not all the body parts have turned up yet.'

Beverley didn't know what Lancefield meant. How could she? She was talking garbage. They had one head and one body. End of story. 'Why do you say that?'

Lancefield sighed. 'Because this is a female body.'

Three hours later, Eisenmenger was in his office, dictating his findings when his phone rang; it was his secretary to tell him that Chief Inspector Wharton was on the line. She had left no more than ninety minutes before.

'Beverley?'

'I thought you'd like to know, we've found a body.'

'Where?'

'In a wheelie bin outside a house in Newent. Upside down and naked. Mrs Abricot, whose bin it was, is in Gloucestershire Royal suffering from shock.'

'I can imagine.'

'Unfortunately,' continued Beverley, 'it's the body of a woman. Are you sure the head belongs to a man?' She knew he was, though.

This was met with silence for a moment until Eisenmenger said, 'I'd better come out and take a look, then.'

Malcolm came to with a head that ached in between throbs of agony. He was very groggy but it did not take him long to understand some unrelated observations.

He was cold. He was incredibly thirsty. He was sitting but could not move . . .

He was in a padded cell.

He twisted around slightly when this jumped into his brain, but not only were his hands and feet restrained, but so was his head. *What the hell . . .?*

There were leather straps on his wrists, but he could feel that the one around his head was different; it was metal. And he was covered in wires – wires on his head, on his wrists, on his neck . . .

The lighting, until then low, suddenly became brighter as spotlights flicked on in the corners and he could see that the padding on the floor was covered in debris and dirt through which rats moved. He could see other things, though, that worried him even more.

Like the cameras that looked at him, one in front, one to his left, one to his right, and the large television screen directly in front of him.

Like the electric chair that he was sitting in.

Betty Williams watched Reverend Pilcher as he got out of his battered red car and walked up the uneven path that ran through the untidy garden of the unkempt house in which Tom Sheldon lived. She was in her front garden which gave her an elevated view of the road and, although her eyesight was worse than her glasses could compensate for, she still managed to see much of what went on around her house. She was old enough at seventy-nine to remember Sheldon's house being built although, oddly, she did not now recall how or when it had managed to become so dishevelled. She assumed, as did most of the village, that it had been Sheldon who had brought this decadence with him, although she could not truthfully give much detail as to how he had done it. This did not matter, though, not in a village like Colberrow, where impression was all that mattered, where there was no room for objective consideration. Sheldon did not conform with what most of the inhabitants regarded as 'normal'; he was neither poor and communal, nor rich and aloof; the rules of his game were not obvious and thus he was a thing of suspicion. Rural communities such as Colberrow had strict conventions and strict penalties for those who transgressed them.

Not that Marcus Pilcher had exactly endeared himself to the village, she thought with a short, sharp laugh. She had lived in the village all her life, in the same house, with the same furniture and the same outlook; she had seen perhaps five vicars come and go, and most of them were seriously flawed in one way or another. Not that that had bothered her; indeed she had liked that about them, because it made them equal with the flock they sought to lead, because the whiff of hypocrisy levelled them. She thought of Jonathon Wheeler, who had had an eye for the ladies (an eye for

Betty Williams, if the truth were ever to be told), and Aubrey Sinclair, who had once fallen from the pulpit during Evensong because of his overenthusiastic communion with wine, and (going even further back) of Edward Peterson, who had been the most caring man of the church they had ever had in Colberrow, but who had disappeared one night having embezzled most of the collection plates for the past six years.

Marcus was *modern*, though; he brought new ideas. Not that she thought of herself as entrenched in the past; she accepted that her grandchildren cohabited, that few people saw the need or the desire to go to church of a Sunday; she watched the television and did not mind (too much) the swearing and the sex. She even used the digital radio that her youngest son had bought her for her birthday two years before. No, her problem was that Marcus Pilcher represented ideas that were just not right, not suited to a place such as Colberrow. He wanted to allow same-sex marriage, female clergy and tolerance of divorce; he wanted not change but revolution. Change, Betty considered, happened without notice and was safe, whereas revolution occurred in front of her eyes and was dangerous.

Take Mr Sheldon. He was never going to become part of the village, would only ever be a visitor. He didn't seem to mind, though. He used the village shop but rarely spoke other than to request ham or milk from the cold cabinet, never passed the time of day; he carved odd statues – not at all to Betty's taste – and tried to sell them from the roadside outside his house. He rarely succeeded, but this did not surprise her considering the prices he demanded. She thought him rather grubby, too, with a certain swarthiness that she could never come to like. Occasionally there had been burglaries in the village and she had heard rumours that he had had something to do with them – if not actually breaking in, then perhaps supplying information to some of his former friends about who was in, who was out, what was worth the risk.

Sammy Carter came out of the front door of the cottage next door having just has his lunch; he was dressed in green overalls and heavy, dirty work boots, and he carried with him an orange flask of coffee, his refreshment for when he was working on the tractor that afternoon. She was close to Sammy, as close as a son; he appreciated what she had done for him when his wife, Carol, had died fifteen years before, and now he always had time for

her, making sure that she was OK when the weather was bad or
she was ill. He had even agreed to having an alarm fitted in his
house that she could set off by a bell push if she became unwell.
And all this despite his own problems with that feckless boy of
his, forever in some sort of trouble or other. She supposed that it
was not surprising – she had noticed that he had been a mummy's
boy from right off – and that was always going to mean trouble.
Her cousin. Arthur, had been a right mummy's boy, and no good
had come to *him*.

'Afternoon, Betty.'

'Sammy.'

'Nice day.'

'It is, that.'

'You all right for everything? I was going to the supermarket
after work.'

She shook her head. 'Thanks for asking.'

He went on his way, striding up the lane, swinging the flask
from its handle and whistling. Such a good man, she thought. It
made her proud to think of what she had done for him, or at
least tried to do for him. It just went to show that a man was a
product of nurture more than nature; neither Carol nor Sammy
had a bad or lazy bone in their bodies, yet Shaun had not turned
out right, not right at all. He had always been argumentative,
always ready to find a reason not to do what ought to be done,
forever keen to start something else before a task was done. Not
ugly, not handsome either; he had his parents' features – and
they were both considered a fair catch in their time – yet it had
somehow not worked for him. It was, she had long ago decided,
the look about his eyes; there was something in the depths that
disturbed her.

EIGHT

a huge but obscene practical joke

Mrs Abricot lived in a cul-de-sac of bungalows, a relic of the Sixties, one that ought to have settled Eisenmenger's nerves and made him feel relaxed by nostalgia, but that merely made him feel uncomfortable, as if he had suppressed memories of something awful happening behind net curtains such as these, as if this eerily restful rural road was just *too* nice, *too* quiet. He could imagine awful atrocity lurking underneath the plaster coving, terrible abuse whimpering beneath the cover panes. Her house was not hard to find, partly because there were only seven houses in the road, partly because there were three police cars and seven policemen doing what policemen do at a murder scene. As was usual on these occasions, there was an audience, this time an aged one, easily kept at bay by the burly sergeant who menaced them at the garden gate.

Eisenmenger was allowed access to find a long tidy garden sloping up to the house. He felt as if he had breasted Kilimanjaro by the time he reached the bungalow and was then directed to the back garden. This was slightly shorter and thankfully on a level; most of the activity was centred at the very rear of it. Beverley was sitting on a low wall, although Eisenmenger noted that she was actually in contact only with a copy of the *Daily Telegraph*; Lancefield was supervising a fingertip search of the garden, looking worryingly enthusiastic, in vivid contrast to those in her charge – who were actually doing the hard work – who were on their hands and knees.

Beverley, by contrast, merely looked detached; she was sitting beside a white tent, rather like one in which knights would once have sat in between jousts. When she saw Eisenmenger, her face brightened noticeably and she stood and went to him. Without greeting him she began, 'The refuse is collected from a track that runs around the perimeter of the cul-de-sac so that the bins are at the ends of the gardens, which means there would be no one around to see the murderer dump the body.' Through an open gate in the back fence, Eisenmenger could see the unmade road that was being carefully searched by three uniforms and a woman he knew to be from forensics. Beverley continued, 'The bins are usually emptied first thing Monday morning so Mrs Abricot come up to put it outside the gate. She found her week's rubbish had been emptied out and . . . and, well, something substituted.' She gestured at the tent.

Eisenmenger went over to it, entered. It contained the wheelie bin, the cover of which had been hinged back; when he looked in, he saw a naked corpse, folded into a foetal position, head – or rather neck – down. There were a few smears of dirt and rotting vegetable juice on it, but it was otherwise surprisingly clean. He said, 'I assume that this has been photographed?'

The woman from scenes of crime was already in the tent and she now showed him the digital images on the camera screen that she had taken. Satisfied, he said, 'We'd better take it out, then.' Which, in the end, merely meant tipping it out unceremoniously on to a clean plastic sheet. Beverley, Lancefield, the scenes of crime woman and a chap from forensics joined him in the small tent, making a rather intimate gathering as he looked down the body. No one said anything for a moment while Eisenmenger went about his business, measuring, probing, squinting and considering, until he said in a tone that sounded half bemused, half intrigued, 'Mmm . . .'

At which he turned abruptly away to leave and put on a white all-in-one suit and thick disposable rubber gloves; without being told, the SOCO began taking photographs and the forensic man began taking samples from the inside of the bin. When Eisenmenger returned he had a briefcase that he opened and put down by the corpse. Then he knelt down by it. He had on his left ear a small microphone into which he spoke. 'Female, young – no more than forty, I'd say, and possibly much younger. Severe abrasion around the wrists, ankles and neck, almost exclusively on the anterior surfaces. No other obvious abrasions, lacerations or ecchymoses.'

Fisher had come up unseen and asked suddenly, 'What's an eckymosis?'

Beverley was about to fire up the flame-thrower but Eisenmenger said without looking, 'Medical jargon for a bruise, sergeant. You're quite right, it's unnecessary persiflage.' He carried on at once, 'The elbows, knees and hips have been traumatized after death, presumably because rigor had set in and the murderer had to do some bending to get the deceased into the bin.'

Fisher asked, 'Doesn't that mean you can tell us when she died?'

'With error limits that are so wide and so contingent upon environmental factors that is practically useless.' He went then to the neck, examining it closely, causing shivers to go up Lancefield's spine when he touched the wound, even put his fingers in what she guessed was the gaping windpipe. At one point he got from his case a torch and shone it down into the tunnel. 'Completely clean, completely smooth decapitation. No signs of any more than a single stroke.' At this, he took from the briefcase a metal tape and proceeded to measure the width, breadth and circumference of the neck. After this he stood up and said to the SOCO, 'A few of the neck, please.' When that was done, he asked the forensics man, 'Can you help me turn her over, please?'

This was achieved without difficulty. Eisenmenger gently wiped rotten vegetable material from the skin and uncovered, on the small of the back, a tattoo. Beverley knelt down beside him. '*Maureen.*' She frowned. 'Her name?'

'Presumably,' he said non-committally. More photos were taken, at the end of which Eisenmenger's only positive conclusion was that there were no positives. 'OK,' he said. 'I think I've done all I can do here. She can go back to the mortuary.'

Whilst he was stripping off the oversuit, Beverley came up to him. 'Any idea how she died yet?'

'Unless she was poisoned, I'd say it's odds on that having her head cut off did it for her.'

'Shit.'

He said thoughtfully, 'And a very professional job, too.'

She practically gaped at him. 'You are joking, aren't you, John? There are no professional executioners any more. Certainly not in this country.'

He shrugged. He had put the oversuit into a small bin liner which he then handed over to forensics as he said, 'I would say that people used to hefting an axe or some such ought to be considered. It's no easy job to produce such a clean cut as that.' Even as he was speaking, he trailed off, caught in the current of another possibility. 'Unless . . .'

'Unless what?'

His head bobbed from side to side, then he said almost apologetically, 'Unless they used a guillotine . . .'

*   *   *

Malcolm woke with a start. His mouth was completely dry, his head was splitting with pain, he felt aches in every part of his body. He had had to urinate, but that was now dry, so long had he been there. His throat was sore, both through dehydration and through the long hours of shouting, pleading, questioning and just plain screaming; and it had all been to no avail, with no reaction. Through all this, the camera lenses continued to look at him without blinking, without emotion, almost without interest.

What the hell is going on? He asked this for the thousandth time of himself and for the thousandth time he could not answer it. How had this happened? Why had it happened? Who had done it? He was in an electric chair, for God's sake. Surely they couldn't seriously be considering . . .? That would be madness.

And the fact that nothing had happened for so long, must mean that this was a huge but obscene practical joke. It had to be that. No one would be so insane as to kidnap a man and then . . . and then *electrocute him*. He didn't know what he had done to deserve this, but he was one hundred percent, totally, completely, no-doubt-about-it certain that he had done nothing that merited being fucking electrocuted.

But something told him that this was no joke. This was serious. This was perhaps the most serious thing that had ever happened to him. The panic in his head went from zero to maximum in the space of a few moments at this realization. He began to pull at the straps again, although he had been doing that for what seemed like hours already. He kicked at the restraints around his ankles so hard that he gave himself stomach pains; he jerked his head time and time again against the head strap. He tried to rock the chair, throwing himself from side to side, and crying out nonsense syllables, but the chair was bolted to the floor and wouldn't budge a millimetre.

Eventually he subsided again, exhausted, aching and raw. Trembling so violently he felt almost beyond control, he had to stop, tried to collect his thoughts back into a semblance of rationality.

I mean, who gives someone the right to do this? This is England, for Christ's sake. We haven't had the death penalty for at least a hundred years and we never fried anyone. Hanged them, and beheaded plenty, but no ever got given the juice in this green and pleasant land.

He forced himself slowly to calm down, reason overcoming panic. Whatever was going on, it was not his death by electrocution.

Some weirdo getting his kicks by filming his fear; some sort of psychological experiment, perhaps. He had heard about scientists doing that kind of thing.

Yes. That was what it was.

The television screen came alive and of course he looked at it, his whole life programming him always to look at it. It showed him a naked woman strapped down on a table; it might have been Malcolm's idea of pornographic heaven, except for his own situation. Her head was almost in darkness, but he could see that it was between two rising posts, their tops in darkness.

What now?

He saw her head was shaved, saw it turn to her right, as if she, too, were watching something.

Is this a movie?

He had a feeling it wasn't, but that would mean it was real . . .

The beheading came at the precise moment that the tingling in his body began.

NINE

'I'll ring you when I'm done'

Beverley sat behind her desk and Lancefield sat opposite her while Fisher, feeling very much like a novice, perched on the window sill. Behind him Lansdowne Road was quiet in the Sunday evening sunlight; Fisher had a hot date in the Strand at the top of the High Street and so his excitement at sitting in on his first murder conference was somewhat tempered by sexual frustration.

Beverley said, 'Tell me what Farmer Gardner had to say.'

Lancefield consulted her diary. 'His background you know. Regarding discovery of the body, he says that it was just a normal Sunday right up until about eleven in the morning; he'd milked the cows and fed the pigs, then spent a few hours moving the sheep to another field. He came back to the farmyard to discover the dog, Sally, with a new toy.'

'Did she often go into the slurry pit?'

'He says not.'

'Had he noticed that it was disturbed at all?'

'Ditto.'

'Is he lying?'

Lancefield thought about this. 'I get the impression he's going to give us the minimum help he can, but I don't think he's telling deliberate lies.'

'What did you find in the house?'

'It's a mess, like the rest of the farm. His wife died twelve years ago and I think it all but destroyed him; he's kept the farm going, but it's just a lifeline, nothing more. I don't suppose he's touched most of the rooms in that house since she died; he lives in a room just off the kitchen, barely eats and certainly wouldn't be interested in feeding the dog regularly. He does the minimum for the animals, too.

'He's shot, chief. He won't deceive us intentionally, but he doesn't care enough to tell the truth, the whole truth and nothing but.'

In Beverley's experience, this was true of most witnesses, for whatever reason. 'Eisenmenger estimates that the head hadn't been in there long. Chances are it was dumped during the night. What does Gardner do with the dog at night?'

'Chains it.'

'Would he hear it barking?'

Lancefield shook her head. 'His hearing is none too good and there were a fair few empty bottles in his bedroom. My guess is he has several large nightcaps before turning out the lights.'

'So anyone could have come in and buried it.'

'He must have a strong stomach,' pointed out Lancefield.

'"He" is beheading people; I think we can put "strong stomach" into his psychological profile without much argument,' replied Beverley as dry as an old man's skin.

Fisher, who thought he should contribute something if only for his own self-esteem, said, 'Or she.'

Beverley didn't waste energy moving her neck muscles to look at him. 'Fisher, if you think I have concluded that this killer cannot be a woman, then the rumours about you having brains smaller than your gonads must be correct. I have better things to do than keep talking about "he or she" every time the subject comes up. Got that?'

Fisher mumbled, 'Yes, chief.' He decided that his self-esteem was best served by silence.

Satisfied that Fisher was back in his small, sergeant-sized box, Beverley said, 'Check the missing person's files for anyone with the first name Maureen. Apart from that, I don't see there's anything else we can do at the moment. Do either of you?'

Neither did. As they got up to leave, Lancefield said thought-fully, 'It's odd, though . . .'

'What is?'

'The only thing we know for certain so far is that one male and one female have been killed. Pretty odd for a serial killer to switch genders like that.'

Beverley pursed her lips. 'That was worrying me, too. Makes me wonder . . .'

But she didn't continue the thought and Lancefield knew her boss well enough by now not to press her.

The headless torso had come into the mortuary two hours before. Eisenmenger had half-heartedly suggested that, as it was now five o'clock in the afternoon, he might delay the post-mortem until the next morning, but Beverley had insisted and he could not blame her, not with two deaths to investigate, both clearly the work of a single individual. He had therefore to change his plans for the evening

'Charlie? It's John.'

'Are you done?' She sounded sleepy and that excited him.

'I'm afraid not. Another corpse has turned up. I'm going to be at least three or four hours.'

'Oh . . .'

'Sorry.'

'No problem.'

'I'll ring you when I'm done. Maybe we can at least get out for a drink, if not a meal.'

'If it's not too late.' He was fairly sure that she wasn't happy. It brought back bad memories of previous relationships; relationships that had failed because of his profession.

In the event, it took a little under three hours to complete the autopsy. Before an audience comprising two SOCOs, Beverley, Lancefield, Fisher and a coroner's officer, he performed a full examination, including a subcutaneous dissection. He took samples of heart, lung and liver, as well as aliquots of blood, stomach contents and urine, and swabs from the abrasions, from under the fingernails and the inside of the windpipe. He also scraped the wrists, ankles and neck after examining these areas with a large magni-fying glass. His initial macroscopic examination had shown no evidence of a natural disease process of significance, nor evidence to suggest significant trauma other than the rather trite observation that she had no head.

He said, 'There are no signs of refrigeration or undue heating, so she died within a time span of between ten and thirty-six hours before being found.' Lancefield opened her mouth to say something but Beverley cast her a look: *No point*. Eisenmenger had never been particularly taken by estimates of the time of death from autopsy examination. He continued obliviously, 'The lungs aren't particularly congested or oedematous and there are no signs of asphyxia. These signs aren't foolproof – and we'll have to wait for toxicology, of course – but I would lay a small sum of money that she was fully compos mentis when the blade fell.'

He made most of the audience shiver with these words, but he had entered into intellectual mode and didn't notice.

'Age?' asked Beverley.

'In her thirties. She was nulliparous and had had no surgical interventions.'

Fisher had no idea what 'nulliparous' meant but kept quiet.

'And that's it?' asked Beverley.

'One other thing. It's a bit odd, actually.'

Beverley was at once interested. 'Tell us.'

He held up the corpse's hand. 'There's something odd smeared on the skin around the wrists, ankles and neck.'

'What?'

'I don't know. It's slimy; some sort of gel.'

'Is it significant?'

He smiled but said only, 'I'll let you know what the tox guys say.'

Outside, Fisher took Lancefield to one side. 'What does nulliparous mean?'

She looked at him pityingly. 'Look it up, sergeant. That's if you can spell it.'

She walked on, leaving a thoroughly chastened newly-promoted detective sergeant, whilst fiercely reminding herself to take her own advice as soon as she got back to the office.

'PLEEEASSE!'

His throat felt like fire but he no longer cared; even had it been real fire, it would have been preferable to that tingling, the one that had been filling his body for what seemed like hours now, that was slowly but inexorably intensifying, that he knew would carry on intensifying until . . .

Nothing else had changed. The light was just the same, the temperature had not changed, the silence remained; the lenses merely continued to stare impassively and at the same time menacingly. The tingling, though, increased; it became stronger and at the same time spread throughout his body, extending tendrils into every organ, every limb, eventually every cell.

TEN
when her head fell off

C live had been a senior mortuary technician for over twenty years and those years had seen his routines ossify into things of resolute inflexibility; things in Clive's mortuary were done as Clive wanted them done, and in no other way. Since he was good at his job and intelligent, this was not necessarily a bad thing; the paperwork was always exemplary, the cleaning was well handled and the pathologists could never complain that he was not a useful man to have around; he eviscerated quickly and quietly, he reconstructed immaculately, and he occasionally spotted things that they had missed. The downside was that he did not welcome change, or those who sought to introduce it; woe betide any manager who thought to suggest that Clive's way was not the best, and any junior mortuary technician was liable to experience something not unlike being scalded if he questioned the rituals he was expected to perform. Most of the time, a quick tongue-lashing was all that was required to restore the status quo, occasionally, two or three were required; thereafter, because for most of the time Clive was a charming and amusing man, they acquiesced. Only once, and quite recently, had these tactics failed to work, and the experience still rankled with Clive.

This particular morning he did as he always did, rising at six, taking his dachshund for a walk (he had only bought the infernal thing to impress a rather attractive married woman some four years before; it had worked – in that he had made a conquest – but this was the unfortunate and rather irritating residue), then cooking himself a fried breakfast. After three rashers of bacon, two sausages, two fried eggs and a round of fried bread, he felt somewhat better

disposed to the world. He thought about writing the birthday card
for his grandson, six on Wednesday, then decided that he would do
it that evening; if he put a first class stamp on, it should arrive in
time. He got on his bicycle, and made the short journey from his
home in Whaddon to the mortuary in good order, arriving at his
customary seven thirty.

He opened the big red double doors, wheeled his bike into the
vestibule and thought about the day to come; it would be a busy
one, especially as he was for the time being on his own until they
could appoint a replacement for Shaun, but he was not particularly
bothered by this. He had supreme confidence that he could handle
things, just as he had had to on many occasions in the past. He
was better off without that wanker, Shaun, anyway. Just remembering his name made Clive's blood become slightly hotter, his
heart beat slightly faster. How dare that little shite tell him what to
do? What did he think he was up to, telling Clive that he knew a
better way of dissecting the middle ear bones, and that Clive's
reconstruction techniques 'belonged in the ark'? It wouldn't be the
first time that Clive had had to run the mortuary single-handedly
for weeks on end, including all the on-call, and the prospect had
long ago become little more than an irritant.

This day was definitely going to be hard, though. He had four
coroner's post-mortems being performed by Ben Gosling in the
morning, then he had the dentists coming in to identify a body
pulled from a local lake. In between, he had to shift some bodies
out to undertakers or else he would run out of space, and he would
undoubtedly have junior doctors coming in to view bodies for the
purposes of the statutory cremation documentation (and also
undoubtedly badgering him to pay them their cremation fees). Still,
he had a good hour before Ben Gosling came down to identify the
bodies for his two autopsies, so he would first of all have a cup of
coffee and a quick cigarette out the back of the mortuary, using the
viewing chapel entrance. Accordingly, heavily sweetened white
coffee in one hand, bunch of keys in the other and rolled-up cigarette behind his ear, he opened the door and stepped outside into
the cool but sunny morning air.

He almost tripped over a huddled figure leaning against the brick
wall. It was dressed in thick clothing that was muddied and frayed,
what looked like an old duffel coat; the head was slouched forward,
chin on chest; this, together with the black fedora meant that he
could not see the face. It was not unusual to find down-and-outs

here; it was reasonably sheltered and they were unlikely to be disturbed during the night. 'Time you were on your way, mate,' he said cheerfully, then passed on down the short flight of steps to the pavement, there to sit on the low wall as he always did. He put his coffee cup down, transferred his cigarette to his mouth and fished for the lighter in his pocket. It was by far from his first cigarette of the day, but it was one of the best; now, in a sort of interlude between the strain of getting up and the hardships of the day to come, he could really appreciate the pharmaceutical effects of nicotine and caffeine.

He stretched the experience out for as long as he dared, then sighed; time to get back to the shithole. The down-and-out was still there. Clive had a viewing booked for two o'clock and he did not want Cheltenham's finest putting on a display for the grieving relatives. 'You'll have to go soon, I'm afraid.' He sighed. 'Sorry, but there it is.'

The next four hours were busy indeed. Ben Gosling was thorough but slow and, much to Clive's discomfort, he had a liking for silence; no radio was allowed when Dr Gosling was working. He rarely spoke and, when he did, it was on purely technical matters; Dr Gosling did not gossip and did not obviously have an interest in popular culture. Whilst assisting him, Clive also had to see to a steady stream of undertakers, as well as field calls from the coroner and the police regarding arrangements for John Eisenmenger's forthcoming forensic autopsy. He managed no breaks and was therefore fairly dry and unnicotinned by the time that noon came and things, temporarily at least, became calmer.

In order, therefore, to bring inner calmness to this outer calmness, he made himself an even sweeter coffee than usual, rolled an especially fat cigarette, and repeated his morning ritual. His state being one of tiredness and agitation, his reaction when he saw the tramp still in exactly the same position was not one of carefully considered entreaty.

'Oh, for fuck's sake!'

He walked forward and prodded the form with his clog.

Nothing

'Come on, my man. On your way.' He repeated the action, this time with a little more force.

What happened then was forever jumbled in his memory, a series of disconnected sights and impressions; his surprise in realizing that it was not a man but a woman; his astonishment that she should be so deeply asleep that she should fall to the side without complaint . . .

His stomach-churning shock when her head fell off.

Josh and Darren had become firm friends over the course of only a few months and, since then, had rarely had disagreements but, when they did, they were usually serious, about such things as what game to play, whose was the best team (Man U for Darren, Chelsea for Josh) and whether *Doctor Who* was better than *Star Trek*. Josh was only taller than Darren by three centimetres, but that is a lot at their age; Darren's feeling of inferiority was compounded by his birthday trailing seven months behind Josh's. Josh, too, was aware of these advantages and – perhaps subconsciously, perhaps with a glimmering of artifice – played upon them, always implying that he was the natural leader. In consequence, Darren was vehement in holding his side of the debate, something that was enhanced by a slight advantage in musculature. They had never come to blows, but that did not mean that their arguments were not passionate and therefore bruising.

The most important argument that they ever had did not seem as such at the time and, inevitably, it was related to play; more specifically, about where to play. It was Darren who had discovered it – many months before Josh arrived – but it was Josh who had seen the potential, who had wanted to claim this place as their own – their own battlefield, their own alien planet, their own kingdom . . . their own universe.

There were problems, though.

'We mustn't. Granny would go berserk if she found out.'

Darren, too, was in awe of Josh's grandmother, but to him she was at one remove and her ire was accordingly less of a deterrent to him. 'She won't find out,' he assured Josh, unknowingly paraphrasing the empty words of every felon in history.

'There's lot of other places we could play.'

'But not like the Grange.'

Which was true. Here was a huge abandoned building, decaying in a sort of romantic yet mysterious verdancy; with four storeys of dark windows, many broken, that they somehow just knew had high ceilings, with dust on the floor, cobwebs in the doorways . . . and ghosts. They knew – as in complete, total, pure, concentrated certainty – that there were ghosts in there. Their eyes might not actually see apparitions, or their ears hear eerie moans, or feel their flesh crawl as icy fingers clutched their hearts, but in their minds, these things would happen, and such an imagining would be better than reality, would be enhanced, more intense and somehow multidimensional, a hyper-reality.

The problem was that everyone knew that it was strictly out of bounds. True, they did not understand why it was so – they were too young to appreciate fully that decayed, abandoned buildings were not wise places in which to act out the realities of childhood fantasy – but they were old enough to comprehend that there was a scale of wrongdoing, that some things were mere misdemeanours, whereas others were felonies

And playing in and around the Grange was definitely felonious.

Yet it was dangerously close to irresistible, and so Josh had to yield the debating point to his colleague. 'No . . .'

Darren sensed an advantage and, with cunning that he had not learned but had been given as an inheritance, said, 'Think of what we could do in there, Josh.'

He had to say no more, for Josh was already thinking of such things. He imagined space battles with laser beams in the long corridors, sword fights in the decaying, dusty, darkness of the empty bedrooms, perhaps cricket in the long sun-stroked corridors, perhaps just simple hide-and-seek in and around the grounds. As fortune – or perhaps misfortune – would have it, a few spots of summer rain began then to fall, warm but still wet. Darren looked up at the sky and murmured perhaps to himself, perhaps to no one, perhaps to his friend, 'It wouldn't even matter if it was to rain . . .'

ELEVEN

'the more bodies you have, the more evidence you get'

Beverley was used to being one of the star performers, had the experienced actor's unconcerned awareness of being constantly observed, a confidence that she would only look good and would not slip up, fluff her lines, trip over the scenery. Even though the body had been enclosed in a temporary marquee within an hour of Clive's call, word had soon spread of the finding and, even though Orrisdale Terrace (the road in which it lay) had been cordoned off, the barriers held back nearly fifty people, some holding mobile phone cameras aloft in an attempt to gain some saleable footage of the event. Not only were there stalls, though; this particular theatrical event had a circle in the form of the upstairs front bedrooms of the houses opposite the mortuary. Every window presented a picture of peering faces, a differing study of human salacious curiosity.

Inside the mortuary, Clive sat in his office, for once not in charge, for once very much in a subordinate position as Beverley and Rebecca Lancefield questioned him and Eisenmenger looked on. He did not enjoy being in this situation and became somewhat short as the interview proceeded; despite this, they were able to establish the main facts and chronology of the finding. To his not inconsiderable irritation, Clive was then dismissed from his own office in order that the two police officers and Eisenmenger might confer. He sat on his customary wall and smoked a thicker than usual roll-up with considerably less sangfroid than his morning smoke; he knew now that the day was a long way from over.

Inside the mortuary, Beverley asked of John tiredly, 'Please don't tell me that this is an entirely new head and body.'

He shrugged and smiled; he had gone beyond worrying about what the police wanted of him. 'Until the body is stripped, who knows? In any case, I can tell you what you want to hear, or I can tell you what I find; your choice.'

She said nothing, although her face was expressive enough. Lancefield put in, 'It *has* to be the missing head and body.'

Beverley was scathing. 'It doesn't have to be at all, inspector. If we're lucky it is; if we aren't, we have another two deaths.'

Lancefield, chastened, hoped that the flush she felt could not be seen. Eisenmenger, perhaps aware that there was embarrassment in the air and, in an ill-judged tone of jocularity designed to lighten the atmosphere, said, 'I was always taught that the more bodies you have, the more evidence you get.' He didn't wait long, though, before he continued, 'I'll get on with it, then.'

Charlie had not answered when Eisenmenger rang her and he had known at once that it would mean trouble to come. He left a message telling her that their planned meal for the evening would have to be postponed and that he wouldn't be finished until late, probably very late. He apologized – grovelled, if anything – and promised to make it up to her, but he knew that this would not make up for standing her up. He was well aware that this was the second time in a row that he had put work before this new and still developing relationship; well aware, too, that he was effectively on probation and not doing too well at it either. He had to put that to the side, though; now, he had a job – a long and possibly very difficult job – to do; two forensic post-mortems that were possibly, and bizarrely, on three different people.

TWELVE
'the male had mesothelioma'

'Well?' Beverley's tone was not abrupt or unfriendly, but it was urgent.

Eisenmenger had to pull himself out of something that might have been sleep. 'Intriguing, Beverley. Definitely intriguing.'

'What the fuck does that mean?'

'The good news is that the head fits the body from the garbage bin, and the body fits the head from the slurry pit. It'll have to be confirmed by DNA, but I wouldn't be too concerned about that.'

Beverley murmured, 'Thank God for small mercies.' She looked less than delighted, although Lancefield at least found a smile. 'Anything else?'

She asked this more in hope than expectation, but Eisenmenger surprised her. 'Yes.'

'Really? What?'

'The male had a mesothelioma.'

If he expected generalized swooning and adulation, he was soon a wiser man; there was nothing but consternation. It fell to Beverley to seek enlightenment. 'Which is what?'

'An exceedingly rare tumour, only occurring in people who have been exposed to asbestos.'

'How rare?'

'Very. And he's had a biopsy. He's been in hospital and will have medical records. He may even have missed outpatient appointments.'

Lancefield said at once, 'I'll start checking straight away,' but Beverley stopped her.

'Don't bother. You won't get anywhere, not if I know medics. They'll clam up, claim patient confidentiality, all that crap.' Of Eisenmenger, she asked, 'Won't they?'

'I expect so,' he admitted.

'But you could find it,' mused Beverley after a moment. 'You work at the hospital. You have access to biopsy results.'

'Oh, no,' he said at once. 'Data Protection Act and all that. I've signed confidentiality agreements.'

'I'm not asking you to tittle-tattle on every patient with this type of tumour. You said it was rare, so there can't be many to find; all I want to know is if you can identify who this might be. If you can, he's dead, so no confidentiality problems.'

It wasn't as simple as that, though. He knew that he would be pushing dangerous, mined boundaries. 'I'm not authorized to access medical records except for legitimate professional purposes.'

'These *are* professional purposes, John. My profession is finding the sick bastard who's doing this, and I need to know the identity of that body and I need to know as soon as possible.'

Still he hesitated.

'John . . .'

He shook his head. He was not a born subversive. 'Let me think about it, Beverley.'

He knew that she was about to coerce him, so he said immediately, 'Apart from that, nothing much. He had cirrhosis, although without complications so far. He had as much coronary atheroma as you might expect—'

'So nothing useful?' she interrupted.

'Sorry.'

THIRTEEN
could he yet call it love?

Eisenmenger did not dream of Helena – for so long his lover so recently dead – as he had once dreamed of Tamsin, a child he had barely known in her life but had known so well as she burned to death. He did not need to. She remained with him in a far more constant, continuous way than merely odd visitations in the night-time, vague ghosts in the darkness, flitting reminders. Even after Helena had fallen out of love with him, he had not stopped feeling for her in exactly the same way he always had done, this emotion tempered only by consternation that it was no longer mutual, disbelief and grief. This amalgam of emotions remained with him, would do so forever, only fading, never vanishing.

And, recognizing this, he had made a conscious effort to move away from this episode in his life, this interlude that could never be relived; move *away*, mind, not move *on*; it was a compartmentalization of the memory, not a journey beyond it. It was still within him, only now it was in a room to which he had shut the door; shut it but not locked it. He did not want to lose the joys of having known Helena, and would therefore endure the sorrows that were their conjoined twins. It had been difficult to persuade himself that this was not the wrong thing to do, that he could love his memories just as strongly while finding new joy in new relationships, but he had known that it was a stupidity he had to defeat; failure would mean only entrapment in his own history.

Of course, his attachment – could he yet call it love? – had come from a direction in which he was not looking. He had originally been attracted to a gynaecology cancer nurse specialist, finding her vivacious irreverence for the lunacies of the NHS refreshing, her genuine feelings for the women in her care, touching. Yet it had not developed beyond mutual liking and, whilst he was discovering this, Charlie had come into his ken when a relatively young woman had come into the hospital with torrential vaginal bleeding. It had been Eisenmenger who, examining the tissue biopsies under the microscope, had diagnosed non-Hodgkin's lymphoma of the endometrium, a very rare condition. She had developed severe psychological problems, including obsessive-compulsive symptomatology and some self-harming; Charlie had treated her, attending the multidisciplinary team meeting, at which Eisenmenger was the pathologist, to outline the progress she had made.

She was eight years younger than him, but cheerful and optimistic, open-hearted and ebullient, something that he seemed to have been missing for a long, long time. She was single, having separated from a long-term partner eighteen months before, but the mother of a twenty-one-year-old son, Paul, who was reading computer sciences at Durham; she was not keen to enter into another long-term relationship, but he was not sure that he was either; they found the middle ground mutually reassuring and had just been taking it from there, at least until the last few weeks. Now, though, he suspected that things were changing; now, his life as a jobbing forensic pathologist was beginning to bite. The death in a fire of an elderly couple in Upton St Leonards followed in less than a week by the death of a seventeen-year-old girl from some heroin she had been given by her father; the headless corpse and unassociated head, and now another head and body, portending as they did the long haul that serial killings usually entailed, were an unwelcome addition to this litany. He could see in Charlie's eyes that she was beginning to wonder.

His muscles were twitching uncontrollably, beginning now to go into long painful cramps. He was intolerably hot, sweat soaking his clothes. He had almost lost his voice and could only now croak odd, tremulous words – '*Pleeassse . . . For fuck's sssaake . . . Oh, G-g-god-d-d . . .*' The tingling had long since changed from a tickling sensation through an uncomfortable pattern of pinpricks to sharp, incessant stabs of razor-thin agony, all over his body, within every cell. He had long ago lost control of his bowels, and his heart he could feel was bouncing around inside his chest, careering off his ribs and, he was certain, beginning to miss beats.

The camera lenses continued to stare, blind to his pain.

FOURTEEN

'this is your case, no one else's'

The summons to Braxton's office was both expected and unwelcome, and was so in equal measures. They had tried to keep the finding of headless bodies and unrelated bodyless heads quiet, but inevitably, given the sensational nature of these discoveries, things had leaked and the press were sniffing; thus the police needed to coordinate a public relations strategy. Beverley hated this side of her newly refound promotion, because it meant telling lies by telling part of the truth, misinforming by informing, being as mendacious as the scum she had to swim through every day. She found the mutually parasitic relationship of the media and the police to be somehow less honest than that between the police and the lawbreakers, in which at least there were some truths exchanged from time to time, and in which neither side was pretending to have respect for each other.

The worst of it, though, was that she actually liked Braxton, a unique feeling for her when it came to her relationship with her superiors. He had never given her the impression that he was sexually interested in her, indeed she suspected that he looked on her from a purely pastoral, purely paternal standpoint. He did not see her as a rival (he was due to retire in less than five years anyway) and consequently did not feel the need to denigrate her, insult her, patronize her or actively plot against her. She judged that he was able to look above the office politics and career ladder to concentrate more upon what, after all, they were all supposedly there for – the solving of crimes. Not that she underestimated him; his manner was mild, his voice was relatively cultured and his smile warm, but the corollary was that he gave these expecting respect and diligence in return, and woe betide those who failed to appreciate this.

His door was open when she climbed the stairs to the top floor and before she could knock he bade her come in and be seated. 'I've read the reports,' he said without preamble.

His tone, she assessed, was that of a man who was not impressed and, accordingly, she said, 'They don't make good reading.'

'No.'

His monosyllabic reply gave her nowhere to hide and she had

to continue. 'We're going through the routine – missing persons, DNA, dental records . . .'

'I know that, chief inspector. I can read, you see . . .' A trace of sarcasm but, like all the best cooks, he had added the perfect amount, especially when combined with a small smile and an almost imperceptible emphasis on the word *chief*. Stung, she was momentarily lost, unsure of what to say, and it allowed him to add with a sad but affectionate sigh, 'Beverley, you haven't got the faintest idea what is going on, have you?'

What could she say? 'No.'

Lambert would have exploded, or been excoriating, or just incredibly angry, but Braxton no longer had any interests beyond the furtherance of the investigation. 'I can't say I'm surprised. Neither do I.' His smile, momentarily gone, returned and was broader but sadder. 'Relax, please,' he suggested and the atmosphere became at once easier. He got up and went to a filter coffee machine on top of a filing cabinet, came back with two mugs, handing one to her; it was black and unsugared, as he knew she liked it. Then, as he sat down: 'I don't envy you this one, Beverley.'

Which conveyed sympathy at exactly the same time as it smacked her in the face with the realization that he was hanging her out to dry; *solve it or else*. Perhaps, she thought, she had underestimated his capacity for viciousness; she had been perhaps naive to assume that anyone could rise to his level without being a hard-hearted bastard. She sipped her coffee, deciding that it was too weak and possibly, the greater crime, decaffeinated. 'Can you offer any assistance?'

'Of course,' he said quickly; too quickly. 'We have to catch this one, especially now it's public.'

She knew better than to take this at face value. 'How can you help me?'

'Manpower and other resources . . .' Of course there had to be a caveat, though. 'Within reason.'

She supposed with the bitter cynicism of experience that it was about as much as she could expect, but it was hardly a blank cheque; it could mean anything from an extra car to a promise of half the Gloucestershire Constabulary under her command; it was likely, she suspected, to be closer to the former than the latter. 'And I could appreciate the benefit of your experience. Have you ever come across anything like this before?'

He looked momentarily astonished, the coffee cup arrested on its journey to his lips. 'Like this? Good God, no.' He didn't quite laugh in disbelief at the stupidity of the question, but it was a damned close-run thing. 'Mix-and-match body parts?'

A stupid question, she saw, but could not find embarrassment within her, so persisted. 'Serial killings, though . . .?'

He did not seem to understand. 'You've been involved with serial killers before now, Beverley. I don't see what I can contribute.'

'But surely . . .?' She saw afterwards that she was being dense in not understanding right away, but dense she was, at least until she saw him shaking his head.

'Beverley . . .' He paused, then almost winced, as though a sudden spasm ran through his gut. 'You must understand. It has been suggested to me that this is your case, no one else's . . .'

She had not finished her coffee, but she put the cup down very carefully, realizations sparking around her like fireflies. 'Oh, I see.'

Do or die. This is your very last chance, and you will not get another one. Nor will we help you.

He grimaced. 'I am sorry, Beverley. Not my decision, but one that I cannot influence.'

She left his office, sadder and, if not wiser, then at least better informed.

'PLEEEASSE!'

His throat felt like fire but he no longer cared; even had it been real fire, it would have been preferable to that tingling, the one that had been filling his body for what seemed like hours now, that was slowly but inexorably intensifying, that he knew would carry on intensifying until . . .

Nothing else had changed. The light was just the same, the temperature had not changed, the silence remained; the lenses merely continued to stare impassively and at the same time menacingly. The tingling, though, increased; it became stronger and at the same time spread throughout his body, extending tendrils into every organ, every limb, eventually every cell.

Back in Beverley's office, everyone was in identical positions, it could almost have been a deliberate re-enactment of their last meeting, only this time in morning sunshine, and this time DCI Wharton was feeling even meaner.

'Have you made any progress at all with missing persons?' she asked of Lancefield.

'We've gone back a month. In that time frame, there are thirteen possible females, eight possible males.'

'Anything from fingerprinting the body?'

'She's not known to us.'

'And I take it the DNA samples have returned no hits on the database?' Of course they hadn't; she would have known about it. 'Have you shown photos of the head to the next of kin of the missing males?'

Even Fisher, who had the sensitivities of a male baboon on steroids, thought that was worthy of surprise. Lancefield asked, 'Are you joking?' which was probably not particularly tactful.

Beverley didn't react. 'No.'

'What are we going to say if we get a positive ID?'

'If you like, you can tell them the truth. Tell them he was beheaded.'

'Don't you think that's a bit brutal?'

Her DCI frowned, shook her head as if slightly unbelieving. 'Not at all. They're going to find out eventually.'

The pain now so huge, so corrosive that he had lost almost all conscious thought. He was nothing but that excruciating agony, and because of that he could no longer smell his flesh burning, feel his body thrashing, hear his last few whimpers. His eyes were jerking around in their sockets but it didn't matter because the proteins in his lenses and corneas were cooking and coagulating like egg whites.

From somewhere his dying screams came, but he did not hear them.

And still the current increased . . .

And increased . . .

And increased until his heart gave mercy, gave him relief from the excruciation, and began to fibrillate.

He was dead and at rest at last.

FIFTEEN
bad dreams in the night

The first time he had met the Reverend Pilcher, Joshua had been so scared he had run crying from the room and had had bad dreams in the night. Marcus Pilcher had understood, though; he told Antonia with a tired but tolerant smile that he was used to the reaction. Antonia, embarrassment almost consuming her, had been rushing to apologize so that she barely heard his words of reassurance; she had been determined to express her shame and anger that Joshua should be so rude. Only after a few moments of patient explanation from Marcus Pilcher, BA, had she come to appreciate that he did not mind, indeed had half expected it.

'I *am* rather a shock to the sensitive soul, Antonia.' She had hastened to deny this, politeness overcoming her strict Christian upbringing as she lied through her dentures, but he had said nothing, a most effective way to silence her. Eventually he had pointed out, 'I am six foot seven inches tall, I am almost hairless, I am not the most handsome of men, and I limp slightly, the result of a rugby injury. Of course Josh is slightly taken aback; shows he's got brains.' His smile was huge and warm as he said this, and Antonia fell slightly in love with this gawky giant with a harelip, who wore a dog collar and who, inevitably because he was Church of England, smelled slightly of damp.

And, as the months had gone by, Joshua had come to realize that looks weren't everything. Marcus Pilcher had soon shown himself to be an exemplary vicar, one with a keen interest in the pastoral care of his parishioners, one who, moreover, had a sense of humour. He had even managed to increase the congregation slightly, although the base was so low as to be subterranean; Antonia and seven others, and she was the youngest by a good five years. He had introduced a children's service every month, one to which Joshua and Harriet were taken regularly despite their mute (and sometimes not so mute) protestations. It had attracted quite a few regular attendees; those who, Antonia judged, were normally put off by the slightly austere and more ceremonial services of the Church. She felt in two minds about this, fearing that the Church was 'dumbing down' to attract the lower common denominators, rejoicing to see some life returning to the thirteenth-century, eternally cold, eternally dark St Barnabas Church.

And Marcus had become a family friend. He was divorced, had previously had a parish in Gloucester, and only been ordained for four years. Prior to this he had been an ambulance paramedic. 'I saw such violence,' he told Antonia and Andrew one evening. 'Such terrible evil and hatred, that I felt that merely caring for the physical side of the injured and dying wasn't enough.'

They had finished dinner on a cold and blustery night in November. The room was brightly lit and all three of them now felt comfortable with each other. Marcus replied, 'And before that I was a prison warder.' He smiled at their surprise. 'I had quite a chequered career before I came to appreciate what I should be doing. What I've told you tonight is only a small sampler.' He paused, then leaned forward in a conspiratorial way. 'For a long time I was an alcoholic.'

Antonia, being an experienced hostess, did not let her shock show, although she did not wish to hear more; Andrew, though, was his usual equable self. 'Were you really?' he asked, as if the priest had just told them he used to be world heavyweight boxing champion which, in truth, his frame suggested was quite possible.

Marcus nodded, apparently oblivious to Antonia's distress. 'I had a huge nervous breakdown and used alcohol as a prop to get me through it.'

'Gosh,' said Andrew. He indicated the half-full wine glass in front of his guest. 'You're OK now, though?' he asked with a smile.

Marcus nodded and returned the smile, 'All things in moderation.'

'*All* things?' asked Andrew mischievously.

They all laughed politely and then Marcus said, 'Which is why I have a particular interest in helping other alcoholics. I used to run a group in my previous ministry, I still undertake visits, and I run a chat room.'

They were impressed and they all drank to his charitable work.

Anthony asked, 'What part of the country do you come from, Marcus?'

'I was born in Suffolk. Quite remote – Walsham – but it was a wonderful place to grow up in. When I went to university, it was as if I was discovering a completely new world.'

'Is anyone else in your family in the Church?'

He laughed. 'Oh, no. I am unique.'

Whilst Antonia was clearing the plates, she asked, 'What did you read?'

'Theology, although I dabbled in the life sciences.'

'Really? Aren't they slightly antagonistic?'

Pilcher laughed heartily. 'Good grief, no. They have much to learn from each other. You have a fool for a priest if he dismisses science out of hand.'

'And vice versa?'

Pilcher nodded enthusiastically, his hands clasped as his elbows rested on the table; it was a characteristic pose. 'Bravo! Science doesn't know everything, and never will, but faith, by its very nature, knows hardly anything.'

'And a little knowledge is a dangerous thing?'

More delight from Pilcher. He said at once, 'Well said, Anthony. Well said.' They toasted this aphorism with the remains of the wine after which Anthony got up and fetched some port.

SIXTEEN
a night of happy, lager-fuelled debauchery

Mr Len Barker had had a stroke six months before that had taken from him his ability to speak, much of his ability to move, his independence and his taste for life. He now lived in sheltered accommodation, some woman or other coming in three times a day to get him up, or to prepare his meal, or clean, or, most humiliating of all, to 'clean him up'. He had served as a police sergeant for twenty-four years, then as a prison officer until his retirement two years before. He had always been active – boxing as a lad, then some rugby and cricket in the force, more recently golf and bowls – and had always had good reports from his medicals; no diabetes, no hypertensions, no obvious problems with his heart. And then this. Out of the blue. He had hardly been exerting himself, had only been enjoying a couple of pints in The Russell Arms, his then local, situated at the very top end of Cheltenham High Street; it served a decent pint and looked like a complete toilet, which acted as a fairly efficient way of deterring all but the initiated. One moment that had been nothing unusual – the lighted gloom, the general chatter pulsed with bursts of laughter, smells of stale alcohol, smells of even staler, but somehow now delectable tobacco smoke

– the next, everything had *changed*. Or rather, his perception of it all changed; everything lost colour, lost tone, lost meaning; everything became disconnected. Then it all faded.

Then he faded.

And now here he was, Bromsberrow Heath, a village to the north of Gloucestershire; he had always been a town boy, had hated the countryside. It was three months later, unable to speak properly, unable to write, attending rehabilitation three times a week at the stroke unit, barely able to get himself to the toilet and clean himself up afterwards, spending most of his time in a wheelchair, watching the television and, when that paled, the view from the window of his living room, the only one worth attention. The view was of a small garden, one laid purely to lawn and the end one of four. Because beyond the far fence there was some dense woodland, the small bird table – the only feature of the garden – was well frequented, although he had no idea what he was looking at, a deficiency that summed his life up quite neatly; in short, everything was now shit. Beyond the farther chain-link fencing – so like a prison wall to him – was some scrubby woodland and beyond that, his carers had told him, was another fence, the perimeter to a quarry, although he could not see this directly. It would not have mattered to him, anyway. There was no life here, no bustle, no atmosphere. And in that there was no life in this place, he saw his own death in it.

He could no longer raise any enthusiasm for the exercises that the physiotherapists put him through, for the interminable and pointless games that the ugly speech therapy girl forced him to play, for the visits from the overweening and slightly pungent district nurse, and for the occasional condescensions of whichever doctor he saw in the hospital outpatients. Part of him knew that it was all hopeless, some of him suspected that he was making some – and slow – progress. After all, he was learning painfully to write left-handed, and was learning to speak again – if lipless groans and tongueless grunts could be described as speech. And there was also his most personally satisfying success, that he had achieved a degree of independence; he could now transfer from his bed to the wheelchair, and back again, without aid. It cost him dear in exhaustion, but he exulted in the small degree of self-confidence and pride he earned. No longer did the carers have to put him to bed like a baby or a retard, although they still insisted on helping.

And recently, in a gesture he knew of defiance, he had taken to rising in the middle of the night when he now habitually awoke, and making the arduous transfer to the wheelchair and then to the small, stuffy sitting room where, when the early-morning television became completely intolerable, he just would sit and stare out into the darkness of the garden, the light off so that he could see better, although he didn't particularly know what he was seeing. Just to be there was in some way significant, even magnificent, to him.

Thus it was he saw the white van backing up into the woodland towards the quarry. He wondered what it was doing, his policeman's instincts aroused.

She was seriously drunk, but she was perfectly confident that she was in control. She had not planned to be travelling home alone that Friday night but, as her father had always told her, shit happens. Sometimes she struck lucky, sometimes she didn't. Mandy – lucky bitch – had left her twenty-five minutes before, arm in arm with a tall and chirpy Afro-Caribbean, clearly hoping for a night of happy, lager-fuelled debauchery. Her only slight sniff had been a spotty juvenile, short but stocky, who clearly fancied himself with no obvious evidence to support that conclusion. He had even insisted on buying her a drink, even though a blind man could have seen her body language which was displaying in neon letters a metre high: *I would rather fuck your dead grandfather.*

So here she was, getting off the night bus with still half a mile to walk to her parents' flat on Hester's Way and, as she did so, she stumbled, fell to the ground. *Bloody hell, I must have really gone overboard tonight.* But, even as she was thinking this, she knew that she hadn't. Three, maybe four lagers, then a few vodka shots – surely no more than half a dozen; nothing out of the ordinary. She had been becoming groggier and groggier as the journey had gone on, but suddenly her legs weren't working and she felt slightly sick.

'You alright?'

A figure was leaning over her, wearing a hoodie, the face in shadow. Hands reached down to help her up; they were gentle hands and her head was woolly, so that she was just relieved not to be on her own. When she was upright, however, her head stopped being woolly, started revolving. She staggered. 'Oh! Oh, shit!'

The hands tightened around her upper arms, took her weight. 'I don't think you are, are you?' The words were cheerful.

She breathed, 'No. I don't seem to be.'

'No probs. I'll take care of you.'

And the sedative took full effect, and she awoke twelve hours later to find herself strapped into an electric chair, watching Malcolm Willoughby being slowly cooked to death by an imperceptibly increasing current.

SEVENTEEN

'It looks as though this one's been cooked'

D r Charlotte Sherman had been a clinical psychologist for four years. During that time she had acquired a reputation as a competent and hard working professional and she had turned a few heads, although she was not a stunning beauty, being somewhat short, with longish, auburn hair, a rounded face and severe short-sightedness; when she had her glasses off, there was something about the narrowed eyes and distorted face that John Eisenmenger had found utterly enchanting. When he had discovered that she had recently separated from her long-term partner, he had found himself in the unaccustomed position of having to take many deep breaths and expose himself to possible rejection. It had not happened and six months later, they were settling into a relationship. Neither of them was keen to advertise this, although they were well aware that the rumours were beginning to circle, like buzzards; he tried to avoid the unfortunate corollary of this, that the liaison was a corpse.

Eisenmenger's primary job was as a consultant cellular pathologist – coronial and hospital autopsies, together with surgical pathology – which meant that he worked as close to regular hours as it was possible for a doctor to do; Charlie, likewise, had fairly regular hours. She had problems, though, with his second profession – that of forensic pathologist – and in that Eisenmenger saw trouble ahead, for he had been there before; his marriage had ended because of it. When he was on call – and he was quite frequently – he could be called out at any time and was likely to be away for several hours; because forensic pathology was not paid for by the NHS but by the Home Office, he had to pay back the time to the hospital when he *was* called out, meaning that he was not infrequently at the hospital at the weekend and late into the night.

And now that they had a murderer with a penchant for behead-
ings, he knew that the hours owed to the NHS were only likely to
increase, which meant that today's lunch with Charlie was especially important to him. He could tell that she was still disgruntled
that he had not been able to make their date earlier in the week
because of the autopsy on the body, and hoped that this would make
up for it. He had booked a table at Brasserie Blanc, next to the
Queens Hotel in Montpelier for one thirty, had picked her up in a
taxi at twelve thirty, then been as cheesy as possible by ordering
champagne; Charlie, who was a connoisseur of fine cheese, had
loved it. They sat in the bar at the front of the restaurant, looking
out on regency buildings, enjoying some relaxation, enjoying each
other, enjoying doing nothing but drinking champagne, talking about
nothing and seeing the world around them with eyes that were
relaxed and happy.

Charlie had a deep, husky voice and it had been this, together
with eyes that were of the palest blue, that had first attracted him
to her. The colour was not deep, yet he could not penetrate beyond
the surface although she herself seemed to see deeply, almost too
deeply. She had been greatly hurt, he knew, by the break-up of her
marriage, but he, too, had been seriously affected by the end of his
relationship with Helena, made worse by events beyond his control.
He felt it slightly unfair that she should not feel the need for comfort
from him as much as he yearned for it from her.

'How's Paul?' Eisenmenger had found immediate rapport with
Charlie's son. He was gangly and thin, with a sense of humour that
chimed with Eisenmenger's.

She nodded. 'He's good.'

'Steady girlfriend yet?'

She smiled. 'He hasn't told me if he has.'

'Would he? If he had, I mean.'

'No.'

'But it's going well for him? Up there?' He was aware that he
was making Durham sound like a geostationary orbit.

'He's really enjoying it. He's working on his final year dissertation.'

'Yes?' It was only politeness that made him ask, 'What's it on?'

She frowned, hesitated. 'Deep surfing?' she answered hesitantly.

Which meant as little to him as it clearly did to her.

And then the waiter came over – Australian, in starched, white
shirt and black trousers so creased and straight he had trouble

bending his knees – so they followed him over to their table at once, ready to eat, and had just settled down to peruse the menu when Eisenmenger's mobile phone went off.

It was with a feeling of huge depression that he answered it. It was Lancefield. 'We've found a body.'

Shit. A third killing. 'Where?'

'A quarry. In a small village in the north of the county – Bromsberrow Heath.'

He'd never heard of it. 'Can you give me a postcode for the satnav?'

She did so, then added, 'There's something about this one . . .'

Eisenmenger had seen most things that could be done to a human being and was not about to be frightened. 'Go on . . .'

'It looks as though this one has been cooked.'

Wallace Parker owned twelve hundred acres, an estate he had inherited from a widowed spinster aunt over twenty years before. It was given over to sheep, cattle, arable and vineyard; he had a well-paid and extremely efficient estate manager who took care of most of the day-to-day running, whilst Wallace continued his time conducting an extremely remunerative career in the City. He met with the estate manager once a week and they planned strategy together (or at least Wallace approved the manager's plans), so that he could say with a degree of truth that he ran the operation; he saw himself as chairman, the manager as CEO and this analogy pleased him.

Inevitably, his wealth and power in the community led to hidden but nonetheless occasionally palpable resentment. Much of the village depended on the estate, which meant that they did not like it, and they did not like Wallace, although no one would ever have said so to his face. Wallace, though, believed that he was the beloved leader of this rural community and that they cherished him. He was Chair of the Parish Council, sat on the Parochial Church Council, was training to become a Justice of the Peace, and was Chair elect of the Conservatives; in his eyes, who could not be endeared by him?

Those who were not beholden to him – and therefore were not resentful of him – acknowledged that he (or at least his estate manager) had done good things. The Colberrow Estate had been looking distinctly rundown when Wallace had inherited it, but over the years the fencing had been largely repaired, new signs had been erected, hedgerows had been regrown and the styles renovated. Wallace might have been acquisitive and selfish and a tad monomaniac, but he had a vision of what a country estate should be, and he had the money to achieve it. He wanted rolling acres of tidy grazing for sheep, lakes, ordered fields of waving wheat and beet, and ancient woodland, and he felt in his bones that he was slowly achieving this.

In fact, it was the woodland that gave him most pleasure. He loved tramping through the outer reaches of his land, through trees that had been there for hundreds of years, listening to sounds that were completely human intervention, smelling sweet odours of decay and growth, catching glimpses of hidden wildlife. Of the many such copses and woods on the estate, his favourite – the one, in fact, that he let no one else enter – was Topper's Drift, in which was situated the Grange. At over one hundred and seventeen acres, it was one of the largest, most unspoilt, and oldest areas of woodland that he owned, and he had plans for it. He made sure that it was fenced off and that only he and his estate manager had a key to the single gate.

EIGHTEEN
Sorry about lunch. XXX

The quarry's gates were closed although not locked; a police car parked across them and two policemen stood in front of it. They did not have to keep back the rampaging hordes, who consisted merely of a dozen people of all ages and sexes, for they contented themselves with peering hopefully past the official presence whilst murmuring a lot but not actually looking at each other. It was a very British crime scene. Eisenmenger showed his identity and was allowed through in his car, driving over the uneven ground.

The quarry was about two hundred yards in diameter, and reddish brown in predominant colour. Its walls rose ahead about forty feet and, on either side, perhaps thirty; to his left parked in a row were four JCBs next to a Portakabin; to his right at the far end of the quarry and tucked under the cliff was the centre of everyone's attention – the inevitable small marquee, around which were two marked and two unmarked police cars together with at least ten people. Beverley was there, together with Lancefield and Fisher, the three of them forming a small huddle around the bonnet of one of the cars. As he approached, all eyes turned to him and he thought he felt something in their looks that he had never seen before on such an occasion; he thought he saw distress. He stopped the car and was getting out just as a forensic scientist was coming out of the marquee; the look on his face was enough to make Eisenmenger pause; he was pale and sweaty, almost trembling, almost ready to cry, it seemed.

Beverley came up to him. 'This is bad, John. Really bad.'

He had started to suspect. 'Any identification?'

She shook her head. 'Like the headless corpse, he's naked, and getting an ID is going to require dental records or DNA.' Which was no great shakes to Eisenmenger; a lot of bodies had gone beyond the state in which it was possible for anyone to recognize them.

He went to the boot of his car to get out his briefcase and his all-in-one suit. Beverley said, 'It really is bad, John. I've never seen anything like it before.'

He paused in the act of putting the suit on. 'Is it a child?' She shook her head and he said, 'Shouldn't be a problem, then.'

She said nothing, although he was somewhat disconcerted by her expression as she nodded slowly.

Jesus wept.

He wasn't sure whether he said this aloud or merely thought it, so taken up was he by the sight that met him in that small tent. The deceased lay on his side, his hips, knees and elbows flexed at almost perfect right angles, a curious posture and one that was enshrined by rigor mortis. There were post-mortem abrasions – some of them quite deep – all over the body, and most of them were covered in dust and grit that had clearly come from the quarry. It was the body of a young white male, although the age was difficult to determine; Lancefield had not lied when she had said that it looked as though he had been cooked. The smell was one of overcooked meat; not the sickly one he knew well from the incinerated remains of car and air crashes, but an altogether more pleasant, and paradoxically more nauseating, one; a perversion of the emotions evoked by a Sunday roast.

The body was desiccated and browned, the skin turned to a hardened, leather-like consistency, like badly made crackling. The eyes were open, but they were no longer eyes by any normal measure;

merely cream-brown orbs with a round dark-blue smudge where
the corneas had once been. His mouth was open, his expression
even in death, one clearly of agony. There were darker areas –
burns, Eisenmenger quickly discovered – on the wrists and about
the forehead. His hair had become brittle, blackened, while his
fingers and toes were mummified. When he looked into the mouth,
the jaw nearly broke, and the tongue was a charred lump.

He did not remain long, merely checking for external injuries
without attempting to turn the body. Emerging from the marquee,
he saw that the inevitable close-order search of the quarry floor
had commenced. He joined Beverley and Fisher at the car bonnet,
Fisher having been told to supervise the search of the quarry. Their
eyes were nothing but curious orbs as he approached, although they
said nothing and it was left to him to speak. 'I haven't found any
evidence of traumatic injury, so he was either poisoned and then
heated, or just heated whilst alive.'

Lancefield looked slightly shocked at his refusal to show emotion;
Beverley, who knew more of the man, could see that he had been
affected just as much as the rest of them. She asked, 'You think
he's been in some sort of oven, then?'

He shrugged. 'Maybe.' She had never yet met a pathologist who
didn't use that word at least ten times a paragraph. Then he surprised
her. 'I think the body was thrown down the cliff face. I'd concentrate on looking up there.' He indicated the chain-link fence and
undergrowth behind it that was about ten metres above them. Before
they could ask, he explained about the post-mortem abrasions
covered in quarry dust. Beverley said to Lancefield, 'You and Fisher
concentrate up there first of all. If we don't find anything, then
we'll go back to the rest of the quarry.'

Lancefield left and Beverley said then to Eisenmenger, 'You
OK?'

He nodded. 'No problems.'

She almost believed him, but she could tell something was bothering him and she wondered what it was.

Sorry about lunch. Xxx. Charlie looked at it and did not know what
to think, whether or not to be angry or frustrated, or angry *and*
frustrated. John Eisenmenger had done it again.

As a qualified psychologist she recognized the type; she met
them every day, counselled them, helped them through their self-
imposed labyrinths. John Eisenmenger was full of positives: he

was clearly of an affectionate nature, and undoubtedly believed that he was in love with her, yet – her own feelings notwithstanding – she was unconvinced that he truly was. Her training told her that fact and faith were often unconnected, that a human being was capable of the greatest self-deception, that John Eisenmenger might think that he was in love with her; was more likely to be in love with the idea of being in love. One of her lecturers had once told her that human beings liked the idea of love, but couldn't cope with its effects. Love, she had said, was as corrosive as hate, as destructive of the self as jealousy, as deadly and as addictive as heroin. In John she saw such a man; she saw someone who needed to love but did not know how to be loved, who forever sought – and was forever afraid of – the grail of the perfect symmetry of devotion, the idealized, romanticized and ultimately fictionalized love affair as told in *Tristan and Isolde*, *Romeo and Juliet*, Tom and Jerry . . .

And then there was the barbed question of whether *she* loved *him*. If it was hard enough to be objective about John Eisenmenger's psychology, it was infinitely more adamantine to be objective about her own.

NINETEEN
'three hundred lambs going to slaughter'

Everyone who was privileged to be invited agreed that the Parkers gave such wonderful parties. They were wonderful hosts, having done the job at least once a week for perhaps thirty years, and having done so for the good and the great, new money and old, the shakers and movers, the shaken and moved. Wallace moved amongst his guests and talked with them in a small talk, a language that was as difficult to learn as Hungarian and in which fluency was as difficult to come by as it was in Ancient Greek. His gracious wife, Jane, was equally gifted in this strange tongue, always smiling, always laughing quite convincingly at the right moment, forever remembering guests' names, their children's names, their illnesses and their recent successes, no matter how small. They had three sons – Will, Greg and Harry – all of whom had attended public school in Cheltenham, albeit with greater or lesser success, three Labradors and a live-in housekeeper. Wallace

had been a successful London financier even before he had inherited the estate; prior to that he had been a captain in the First
Parachute Regiment, seeing action in the Falklands and even
being slightly injured (by a British jeep running over his left
foot). He had filled out slightly since those heady days, although
he still considered himself to be relatively svelte, an opinion not
damaged in its righteousness in any way by his sons' sometimes
ribald comments.

He loved his sons, could see little wrong with them. Harry, the
youngest, was just down from Cambridge, due to go on to Imperial
College to complete his medical degree in a couple of months. Out
of their three sons, it was Harry who had always worried Wallace
and Jane. Cold, almost worryingly so, and prone to rages, there had
been times when they had seriously considered seeking professional, psychological help although, thank God, that had not come
to pass; he had mellowed and Wallace could see that medicine was
a good career choice, not only because he had the brains but because
he also had the temperament for it.

Greg was nearly twenty-five, completely different in temperament;
he had read art at college and was now working as a freelance web
designer, although not, as far as Wallace could tell, with much success.
Yet he had a lively sense of humour and, despite the worrying
choice of career, was blessed with charm and charisma; it gave
Wallace a sense of vicarious pride when he saw how the girls reacted
to Greg.

Will, at twenty-nine the eldest, was the star, though. Tall, although
without the charm of his younger brother, he was eager to take over
the management of the estate in the not too distant future, serious
and committed; he had just left the army having seen service in
Iraq and Afghanistan. Wallace felt an extreme peace in the knowledge that the future – the long-term future, he felt – was assured.

Although he worried somewhat about the short and medium
term . . .

Still tonight there was another party to give and to enjoy, acting
like an amnesiac balm on his irritating money worries. There were
this time ten guests. Two local farmers and their wives – Wallace
did not particularly like them, but he knew very well that it was in
his best interests to court them, even if he was by far and away the
biggest land owner in the area; the Reverend Pilcher – an interesting man, Wallace thought, and undoubtedly the most humane
priest he had ever met; his mother-in-law, who endured and whom

he endured; Allen Somersby, his farm manager, and his wife; and Andrew and Antonia Barclay, a couple that Wallace had no problems with, although Jane thought that they were just social climbers. Still, the perfect host, Wallace did not let these feelings hinder the proceedings. His sons, all home for the summer, moved amongst the guests and made sure that their glasses were never empty, their free hands never without a vol-au-vent or olive, and they never looked bored; boredom was almost as much a sin as public eructation in Wallace's view.

He approached Somersby, bottle in hand, ready to ply, but his farm manager covered his glass with his hand. 'Got to be up early tomorrow, Wallace.'

'Really, why?'

Allen Somersby knew better than to betray his feelings and said mildly, 'Three hundred lambs going to slaughter.'

'Oh, yes. Of course.' He vaguely remembered Somersby had mentioned this at their last meeting and he had OK'ed it. To cover his embarrassment, he said, 'You know everyone here, don't you?'

Somersby gestured with his glass towards the Barclays. 'Everyone except them. I've seen them around, but can't place them.'

'Andrew and Antonia Barclay. He's a retired GP. They're bringing up their grandchildren. Quite a tragedy.' With this telegraphic resume, Somersby was brought up to speed; the tone in which it was transmitted gave him added context; Wallace did not consider them 'one of us'. Whilst he was digesting this, Wallace said, 'We need to discuss the Grange.'

'What about it?'

'The surveyor's report was quite damning.'

Somersby said neutrally, 'I seem to remember it said that it would require considerable capital investment, and that we could only expect reasonable revenue income after some years.' He paused and then added for emphasis, 'Twelve million of capital investment, I recall.'

'And projected revenues of a quarter of a million in the second year, half a million in the second and third, but a million and climbing by year four and thereafter.'

'But a long time to wait for a decent return.' Somersby knew that he was pushing his luck by pursuing this, but it wasn't the first time he had lived a little dangerously. 'Even assuming no hold-ups with the redevelopment. And that doesn't include the interest charges on the loan.'

Wallace had a round, slightly greasy and pale face with the perpetual impression that he needed a closer shave. These slightly doughy features now assumed an expression that was partly sorrow, partly angry; Somersby knew from experience that it was the sorrow he had to be frightened of. 'Allen, you are a good and competent estate manager; make no mistake that I appreciate that. That does not make you an investment manager. We are a good team because we each do what we are good at; please do not fight me on this.'

The sorrow was as disquieting as it was heartfelt and Somersby, a man who had managed to get fairly well on in his career without pushing things too far, said nothing, despite his concerns that this was a vanity project that did not make financial sense. He was saved from further comment by the arrival of Will with more canapés. Whilst the plates were being refilled, Wallace said to his son, 'What's your opinion, Will? Should we risk a little now in order to reap a fine harvest later on? What this area needs is a decent, top-notch hotel and I think that the Grange could be that hotel.'

'Oh, sure.' Will had a broad grin and, Somersby could appreciate, the air of the confident; he could persuade men to follow him into battle. As far as Somersby was concerned, that only meant that he had the ability to make people forget the consequences of their actions, no matter how foolish.

Wallace pressed him, knowing the answer he would get, with Somersby knowing that he knew. 'And? Do you think it's a winner?'

'Absolutely.'

It was said with total conviction. Allen Somersby found himself wondering what an inexperienced junior officer just discharged from the army – under dubious and unexplained circumstances – would know about anything.

Wallace turned back to him. 'You've been against redeveloping the Grange from the start, Allen. Why would that be?'

He shrugged and said as disingenuously as he could, 'It's my job to advise you as to how to best manage the estate. I just don't think that it's the best use of funds at present.'

'What, and leave a hundred acres of the estate all but unusable and therefore non-profit making? You think that's in my best interests? I can't knock the place down because of the listed status. What else can I do?'

Somersby had no reply to that and knew better than to continue the argument. Parker let it go, but he was curious as to why his estate manager seemed so attached to the Grange.

TWENTY

'I don't suppose you saw anything anyway'

L ancefield took a party of four to look around at the top of the quarry's cliff where the body seemed to have been thrown, and then to conduct house-to-house enquiries. She had with her Fisher and two uniforms, neither of whom she knew particularly well, but who Beverley assured her were sound. They examined first the fencing around the quarry; concrete posts with chain-link fencing; they were angled at the top with a barbed wire tiara for more than decoration. They found immediately where a right-angled cut had been made in the fence, a rough door made and then bent inwards. The undergrowth had been trampled down on either side at this point. There was also evidence of tyre tracks leading away from this out onto a nearby lane. Lancefield said to Fisher, 'Get forensics up here.'

Having pulled them back to stop them trampling on whatever evidence there might be, Lancefield looked around a little further afield. The trees and shrubs around the fence were only about twenty feet deep; a low wooden fence then formed the boundary to some small gardens at the back of a terrace of modern maisonettes, all pale yellow bricks, angles and small windows. Someone looking out of their back windows might have seen something . . .

They split into two teams, she with Fisher, the two uniforms together; she took advantage of her senior rank to take the properties closest to the quarry's edge, sending the other team to knock on a scattering of houses further back along the road that led past the quarry's edge to open countryside; it was possible that people in these might have seen something, but unlikely and so it would be a tedious and fruitless exercise. There was a distinct chance that she and Fisher would strike lucky, however.

She started off with high hopes but these were almost immediately destroyed when it quickly became clear that these were warden-controlled flats, and most of the residents were not going to be perfect witnesses. The tone was set by the first one, the maisonette nearest the quarry's edge. The door bell sounded – a cheap, trilling thing – after which there was a brief pause before the door opened (with difficulty because damp had warped the frame) to reveal a large woman of Far East Asian appearance dressed in a pale green housecoat; it was noticeably stained.

'Yes?'

She looked bad-tempered, but Lancefield had the impression that this was nature not nurture. She looked no happier when Lancefield and Fisher showed their warrant cards. 'Do you live here?'

She looked incredulous as if she had been asked an indecent question. 'No.' Her accent was nearly thick enough to asphyxiate the meaning. She added, 'I am one of the carers.' There were indignation and pride in her tone, as if she were shocked that she should be mistaken for what she considered a lower form of life.

'Who does live here?'

'Mr Barker.'

'Could we have your name, please?'

She had probably looked happier in her life, although neither of them was going to lay a large amount of money on it. 'Mary Lavoisier.'

'And you care for Mr Barker?'

'I said so.'

'Full time?'

Her expression didn't change, perhaps because it had already plumbed the depths of contempt. 'No. We come in on a rota.'

'And how long have you been here?'

'About twenty minutes.'

'How many carers does he have?'

'We come in four times a day.'

It was an answer, although not to the question that Lancefield had asked. She asked, 'Can we talk to him, please?'

Mary Lavoisier snorted. 'You can talk to *him*,' she said sourly, 'but *he* won't talk to you.' The undercurrent was one of flippancy, but it was laced liberally with hostility. When she saw their looks of uncertainty she said brusquely, 'Come on,' and turned away. They stepped in after her, immediately aware that the atmosphere was hot and dry, that there was a fusty smell around them. She led them to a sitting room where, among thirty-year-old furniture that was no longer of any use to him, sat Len Barker in his wheelchair.

He looked at them with an expression that was unreadable. Lancefield approached him and knelt down. 'Mr Barker?' His eyes had followed the two police officers as soon as they had entered the room, the only sign of animation until that moment; now he nodded slowly and a soft grunt came from the back of his throat. Lancefield made a face of sympathy that Len Barker was beginning to know and detest, then turned away from him back to Ms Lavoisier. 'We'll need the names of the carers who have visited in the past two days.'

'What's going on?

'Suspicious activity in the quarry. We're looking for witnesses.'

Before the delightful Ms Lavoisier could answer, Lancefield's attention was drawn by an urgent sound from Len Barker. He was agitated, with spittle coming from the corner of his downturned mouth, and he was waving his right hand about feebly. Curious, Lancefield glanced across at Fisher and then at the carer, who said carelessly, 'Oh, don't worry about him. He hasn't come to terms with his condition yet. It's very common for them to become seriously depressed.' She might have been speaking about an old pet dog.

'No one else lives here?'

She shook her head. 'He's a widower.'

Lancefield looked again at Len Barker; he was looking directly into her eyes, shaking almost. Was he trying to tell her something? She asked, 'Can he still write?'

''Fraid not. He was right handed and that's the side that has been paralysed.'

Lancefield sighed. 'Never mind.' To Len Barker she said, 'I don't suppose you saw anything anyway, did you?'

TWENTY-ONE

he had never done a post-mortem like that one

She had lost it completely to hysteria long ago. She had screamed, she had cried, she had begged and she had sobbed. She had wrenched at the restraints, badly abrading her wrists, and now she was exhausted, and whimpering, terrified but unable to do anything more active. She was just wondering when she would begin to die . .

She had watched as someone had been slowly electrocuted in a chair identical to the one she was sitting in; she *knew* that it had not been a movie, that it had been real, that she had really been a witness to a horrible, prolonged death. She *knew* too that it was going to happen to her.

And no one had responded throughout all her entreaties; the cameras in front of her and to her sides continued to stare without comment, the dark corners of the padded cell slept, the television screen remained blank after showing the horrible, hideous death of the unknown man, after she had seen him twitching, and smoking, and distorting.

When would it come . . .?

She found herself almost wishing for something to happen.

She wondered what it would be like.

When it started, though, she had no time to think about it as the current surged through her body and agony ripped her apart, as every muscle in her body went into spasm, as her eyes twitched upwards almost turning around in their sockets, and as she bit her tongue off with barely perceived pain; twice more it came, the current each time incremental, until she was dead despite the twitching that persisted for a few seconds afterwards.

He had never done a post-mortem like that one and it was many years since doing his job had affected him as that one had done. Yet this was not surprising, because this corpse had been cooked. The skin was crisp, darkened but in a way the sun could never do; the eyes were milky and yellowed, those of an ancient blind man; the hair was fragile, almost carbonized, the tongue was like a desiccated gobbet of ham. The changes seemed uniform, except for the

wrists and around the head; there the skin was blackened, blistered,
and the flesh charred.

When Eisenmenger had first cut through the abdominal wall –
a virgin cut – there had been no blood and the feel had been more
solid than he was used to; it had been a curious sensation and not
one he enjoyed. It had a grey, greasy texture, one that he could not
stop himself from comparing to *belly pork*. When he had the breast
plate off and the whole of the torso's contents exposed, there was
not the usual palette of colours to gaze upon – the grey speckled
pink of the lungs, the brown of the liver, the green of the guts,
the ruddiness of the heart – for everything had a greasy, brown
sheen; the smell, too, was wrong. Eisenmenger knew well the
scent of a freshly open corpse, the dank, acrid smell that was
not pleasant, but that wasn't disgusting either; this, in contrast,
forced him to take deep breaths to stop himself vomiting, because
this corpse smelled of cooked offal. 'Oh, shite,' he whispered
to himself.

Normally, dissection of the organs is a fluid thing, lubricated by
blood and tissue fluid, yet this time, it was *dry*, greased only by
fat. Normally, though, the victims of fire were completely different;
they were charred to nothing in places, barely touched in others;
often the organs, although clearly subjected to great heat, had been
protected to an incredible degree from the musculoskeletal system.
Not in this case. Other than at the head and wrists, everything had
been heated through uniformly. He had eaten steaks and roasts and
steamed sponge puddings that were less evenly cooked.

And there were those burns quite specifically at two places, burns
that, now he examined them more carefully, were suspiciously
sharply edged . . .

'Well?' demanded Beverley after he finished, after he had stripped
off the uniform, become something approaching – in shape if not
spirit – a human being, but before he could begin to consider himself
once more a dues-paid, bona fide and self-assured member of the
so-called civilized humanity.

'It depends on the tox—' he began, but Beverley nearly exploded.

'Fuck that crap, John. I know that you can't say for certain, but
I need a pointer. I need something now, not in a week's time.'

He had known she would say that, but he had thought to try
anyway. 'Two possibilities in my head; he was cooked, but he
wasn't roasted, not as he would have been had he been bound and

then the room set on fire. The way he was heated through leads me to conclude . . .' He paused, unable to believe that he was about to say what he was about to say.

'What?' Beverley voiced it but both Lancefield and Clive clearly could have done.

He sighed. 'That either he was put in a microwave oven, or he was electrocuted very, very slowly.' There was a stunned silence.

Beverley whispered in something that was almost fright, 'You can't be serious, John.'

'Oh, yes, I am. He's heated through too evenly for it to be an external source of heat. There are burn marks on his wrists and around his head which makes me think it more likely that it was slow electrocution, but if he had metal manacles and some sort of metal head band, a microwave oven – a large microwave oven – would produce a similar appearance, I think.' He smiled. 'Of course, I'm not an expert in this area.'

'Do they make microwaves big enough?' asked Lancefield.

'Good question.' His tone suggested that he didn't particularly care.

Beverley did not want to look at the corpse, but found she could not stop. It was almost as if in a dream that she asked, 'Is there anything to identify him?'

She didn't expect anything, but he said tentatively, 'Possibly . . .'

He took them back to the head of the corpse and beckoned to Clive to grasp the shoulders and lift them so that they could see the back; Beverley remembered that Eisenmenger had asked for it to be photographed. When they crouched down, they saw a large area of blackening, only just visible because of the effects of heating. Beverley peered at it closely but couldn't make anything of it. 'What is it?'

Before Eisenmenger could respond, Lancefield said, 'It's a tattoo.'

Eisenmenger said, 'I'll biopsy the skin to check, but I think so.'

'What is it?' demanded Beverley. It spanned the back from shoulder to shoulder, ran up the nape of the neck. There was a faint hint of dark greens and blues.

Lancefield twisted her head from side to side as she tried to make out some detail. 'A bird? An eagle, perhaps?'

Eisenmenger shrugged. 'I can't be sure. I've had it photographed, so you can decide at your leisure. In any case, it might prove useful.'

Beverley turned to Fisher. 'Go through the missing persons' file first thing. We might strike lucky.' Of Eisenmenger she demanded, 'Is that all?'

'Liver's slightly fatty, and there's a lot of anthracosis in the lungs; he may even be developing emphysema.'

'But nothing that can help me?'

'Doesn't look like it.'

Josh and Darren spent that evening playing in the grounds of the Grange, which had rapidly become their favourite place, their secret place, where no one bothered them. Although they did not fully appreciate it, they had something that all children seek, for it was a place that they thought only they ever entered, that was walled, that was strange and mysterious, and that was not encumbered with adults and therefore with reality. Anything and everything was potential for imagination, for play, for excitement and for wonder; nothing was beyond the possible; it was as it should be for children.

Nor did they fully know where they were, had no geographical or topographical references, knew only that it was reached by climbing over a five-bar gate not far from their houses, then a walk of fifteen minutes to the stone wall; that the stone wall was five feet high and topped with broken glass was not a problem for them, not when badgers had made a run under it; it was artfully hidden and only a child playing on his hands and knees near it would have discovered it. What they had on the other side was ancient woodland, untended for thirty years, but they saw only wilderness, a tabula rasa, a hidden garden. To them it was huge, a circular universe, as uncharted as the one through which the planet itself travelled.

But it was not as they had once hoped.

It was in one plane infinite, but in others limited. At the outer boundary there was the stone wall, at the other, inner boundary, there was a high fence of black iron railings. A gravel road ran through this, their desmegne, from the stone wall to this fence, bounded at the outer perimeter by a high and solid, heavily padlocked wooden gate, at its inner by one of wrought iron. Beyond this latter the road led on, curving away and overhung by sycamores, until it disappeared into woodland. And above the trees could be seen their true, spiritual home, the Grange, the place where they really wanted to be. It appeared as tall chimneys and decaying roofs clad in black slate and pockmarked with jagged holes. They fantasized that it might be some sort of castle, perhaps an ancient manor house, perhaps even a citadel on an alien planet. That they could not reach it only made it all the more irresistible, and their desire for it had increased with every glimpse over the weeks, until it became in their minds something completely mythical and therefore something wondrous.

They had learned to live with their disappointment; indeed they had incorporated this faraway citadel into their adventures, much as stage decorators used well-painted scenery. After all, they had enough space to play in, it was still summer, and they were not adults. This particular evening, they were using homemade bows and arrows that they had made the day before and, after uncountable attempts, had succeeded in hitting a tree so that the arrow – a small wooden garden cane, a supply of which Josh had misappropriated from his grandparents' greenhouse and then whittled to a point – actually stuck in rather than bouncing off. They were both elated but, as luck would have it, the tree was on the other side of the railings. Exhausted, they stood and looked through the fence; it seemed to them almost a sign of the magical nature of the world on the far side of it.

But it was still a world that was beyond their reach.

Josh said, 'Let's get back to base.'

It was getting dark and, in their enthusiasm for their new game, they had stayed out later than they should have, but the fine balance between their thrill of excitement and their fear of retribution was settling in favour of the former; they would be told off anyway, so why not make it last a few minutes longer? They had brought with them some coke and some oriole cookies and it seemed fitting to finish these now, in celebration of their achievement.

And perhaps there was a little bit of magic – possibly, though, black magic – that made Darren then look to his left and spot for the first time a tree (it was a walnut tree, but neither of them recognized it as such) that was easily climbable and that overhung the fence; the limb that did this was stout, easily able to take their weight.

Darren turned to Josh, pulled at his T-shirt and pointed excitedly. 'We can get in!' With this he rushed to the tree and began to climb the low slung limbs easily. He knelt on all fours on the thick branch that led out over the railings. 'See? We climb along here and then drop down.'

Josh was built of more thoughtful, perhaps more timid, substances. 'How do we get back?'

Darren frowned; he was not of a far-seeing nature. The question was a tricky one, even he could see that. 'Well . . .'

He had in his head ideas of piling up stones to form a mountain to climb up, but when he articulated this, the look on Josh's face told him he had failed to carry his friend with him. He thought again. 'There's bound to be something we could use in the Grange,' he said eventually.

'Like what?'

This was harder. Eventually he said, 'They'll be some steps or something. Bound to be.'

He was not hopeful that this would be enough and Josh's expression at first gave him little encouragement. He pressed his case. 'Come on, Josh. It's not that high. All we need is a chair or something, and there's got to be something like that left behind.'

More hesitation, to which Darren responded with, 'We can't wimp out. It'll be so much fun!'

And slowly, Josh began to nod. 'Yes,' he admitted. 'It will, won't it?'

He did not appreciate it, but Darren would have had a great career ahead as a salesman.

TWENTY-TWO
the smell of vinegar

'Usually, when you are dealing with serial killers, half the work is done by the profilers; a serial killer has an idea in his head and his crimes tell them what that idea is and what kind of head it's in. They establish a pattern that allows you a way into catching them.'

Beverley and Eisenmenger were sitting outside Taylors, a pleasant, ivied town centre pub in Cheltenham. It was not a bad way to spend an hour of an evening and perfect for people-watching. 'But not this guy?' he guessed.

'The profiler is completely lost. Apart from the fact that this guy clearly enjoys killing, he hasn't got a clue about who or what he might be.' Eisenmenger's opinion of profilers stayed silent in deference to politeness. She went on: 'A serial killer operates within his gender and socio-economic class.' She said this as if she were reciting by rote. 'They use the same method of killing, indulge in the same fantasies. They have a pattern, and move solely within the confines of that pattern. Usually, their motivation is sexual.'

'Just because I can find no evidence of genital interference doesn't mean these aren't sexual killings.'

She was momentarily interested, then a soft snort indicated her considered opinion. 'You think he was jerking himself off whilst watching some unfortunate fucker die by slow electrocution? I don't think so.'

'Just an idea . . .'

The look Beverley gave him started as contemptuous, but rapidly dissipated into one of resigned concurrence. 'I know,' she sighed. 'And I'm precious short of those right now.'

The silence of contemplation and sociability landed on them for just a moment as they each took a drink. As the glass came down upon the beer-ringed green shamrock of the cardboard mat, Beverley asked of him plaintively, 'Where's the fucking pattern, John? It's not fair. Serial killers have a predictable MO, yet this one doesn't; different sexes, different ages, different ways of killing . . .'

Inside the pub, the large TV screen was showing BBC News 24, a warehouse fire in Hertfordshire seen from a helicopter. It was a warm evening and Eisenmenger's lager was rapidly becoming tepid, and he hated lager that wasn't ice cold. He drew a pattern in the condensation on the glass, a cross in a circle and found himself wondering what that meant. He murmured almost to himself, 'Execution.'

'What's that?'

He came to, almost had to draw himself together as if deep contemplation had allowed his bones to separate slightly. More brightly, more aware of his surroundings and what he was saying, he repeated, 'It strikes me that beheading and electrocution are means of execution, that's all.'

For a moment, he saw that her expression was one of wonderment, but then that mutated into a frown. 'Our most recent victim was *cooked*, not electrocuted.'

He made a face and rubbed out the symbol in the condensation on his glass; through the window he had made he examined the bubbles rising through the lager. 'I suppose so,' he said thoughtfully.

Despite her objections, she found herself intrigued by the notion. 'Although there have been occasions when they botched the execution,' she said slowly. 'The condemned was to all intents and purposes cooked on a few occasions.'

'It was just a thought,' he explained.

Beverley was enthused and he saw in her the fervour of the convert. 'But you could be on to something, John.'

But he found himself less than wholly convinced now that he had voiced the conjecture. 'Maybe. But if that's the motivation, then presumably these poor sods have done something to deserve it, at least in the eyes of the executioner.'

'So we're back to identification; unless we find out more about these people, we're stuffed.'

He took a drink. 'Wasn't it always so?'

'Nothing ever really changes, does it?' She sounded wistful.

He laughed. 'Human beings are afraid of change and hate it, but they would die without it, Beverley.'

Eisenmenger had the intellectual freedom to deal in such philosophizing and, had she not been perhaps in love with him, she might have lashed him with her tongue. Instead she just drained her glass and he went to the bar to get fresh drinks. As he did so, he looked at his watch; he reckoned he had time.

They were on the point of leaving when Eisenmenger admitted plaintively, 'On this one, I really need to know the tox result, Beverley. Not out of academic interest. I just need to know that he was unconscious when he died, so I can sleep well at night.'

The boys crunched the biscuits busily for ten minutes, the darkness bringing with it a chill that they did not notice, talking through this, enjoying the delight that they had actually made a bow and actually made it fly, and that (unspoken) they might actually be able to kill something; they did not know how atavistic this feeling was, and knew only that it was good.

'We'd better go,' said Josh at last, who was well aware that his grandmother was considerably less easy going than Darren's mother.

'I guess.'

They stood up and with the minimum of preparation began to make their way through the undergrowth; there was just enough light left in the sky ahead of them to light their way. They had not gone far when they heard sounds coming from behind them and they stopped, suddenly afraid of discovery. They had been well aware that this world was not solely their property, but until now they had not come into proximity of those they shared it with. They did not know the identity of these others, but knew that they were adults and therefore inimical. Without saying anything, they crouched side by side, staring into the darkness behind them. The sounds – metallic and harsh – were slightly wet in the damp air, and Josh noticed a slight scent in the air that, for a moment, he could not place. They waited and the faint sounds of an engine came to them, then more metallic sounds. Within a couple more minutes, the engine was revving, becoming louder until it passed them; they could not see what was making the noise for thirty seconds more and even then only in the distance through the trees. They saw something white pass perhaps two hundred yards away, then come to a halt a little ahead of them at the padlocked gate in the stone wall.

They waited, heard a door in the van open, then only the wind in the trees and the sound of an engine idling until there was a faint clanking. The wind died, leaving only the engine to whisper into the dusk for a moment before the peace was destroyed by a door being shut quietly. The engine revved gently and the white shape moved forward for a perhaps five seconds; they heard it quieten, before there was more clanking and, eventually, the same sound of a door closing followed by the engine noise moving off into the descending night.

It was another minute before they dared to move forward to their escape from this hidden world, happy that they had not been seen, wondering what they had been listening to. Suddenly, Josh placed the scent, the realization bringing with it memories of fish and chips; it was the smell of vinegar.

Back in her flat, Beverley found herself to be oddly happy, yet strangely dissatisfied; it was the complete inverse of her normal state, and therefore uncomfortable to her. She felt as if she had an ache in her bone, as if she were sickening for something, on the verge of perhaps flu or some other virus. She had achieved in her professional life a small but significant victory – Lambert was gone, and she had finally been given a chance, without his malign influence, to redeem herself, to show that she was not just a whore, not one of the many makeweights in the CID, but an intelligent, hardworking and reliable copper, one who had what it took to make it big. So why, then, this unease?

She sat in one of the cream leather armchairs that she had recently bought and that seemed to consider themselves far too good to be sat in, a glass of Chardonnay on the small table to her left, stereo system singing something softly in the background. Her social life had been uncharacteristically quiet of late – or at

least that was the phrase she used when she phoned her mother
– but she knew that it was not this that was the source of her
discomfort. She was not, as Lambert and some other of her superiors believed, a nymphomaniac; she enjoyed sex, but she did not
crave it, although she admitted freely both to herself and others
that she used it – it was, after all, an exceedingly powerful tool
– to achieve what she could not achieve by other means. It was
perhaps this, she suspected, that had given her a reputation,
although she was cynical enough to believe that there was also a
considerable amount of envy and jealousy that had gone into the
making of it.

No. It was this present case, she suspected. This was her first big
investigation, one that could be the making or the breaking of her,
and she had enough experience to appreciate that it was going to be
a bitch. She did not believe in God, did not even have time to be an
atheist, really; God – indeed, any god – was irrelevant to her because
she took what came at her and handled it. Thus she told herself that
this, therefore, was not a test set for her; it was merely the way things
had fallen.

Not that this viewpoint helped. Whether this case had been
presented to her by a cosmic deity who kept constant tabs on her,
or by a blind, uncaring, inconstant universe based on constantly
roiling probabilities, it did not matter. She had to succeed, to prove
that the quantum of faith that had been shown in her was not
misplaced, to show Lambert and the others that she was more than
just a vagina with legs, that she was worth a little more than a
quickie in the back of the Jaguar with beery breathe and sweaty
brow, and as much technique as a special needs gorilla.

But what a case!

She could already sense that here was no ordinary serial killer.
Most such people were sad, grey little things, forgotten by life,
forgotten by the world, forgotten even by themselves. They killed
and only then did they consider what to do about the consequences
of the act; their sole aim was killing, for in doing so they satisfied
whatever urges preyed on them, This one, though, thought beyond
the act, thought through the thrill of killing, and that made him
special (and she knew it was *he*, despite what she said to others),
that made him a wilier, more dangerous opponent.

This one had a motive she could not yet even guess at and,
without knowing the motive, she feared she would have little chance
of catching him.

TWENTY-THREE

'There's no need. She won't recognize you'

Rebecca Lancefield had embraced the news of her transfer to Cheltenham, and of the opportunity to work with acting DCI Beverley Wharton with something that was considerably less than enthusiasm – dread, despair, desperation, dissatisfaction, disgruntlement, disaffection and disbelief, perhaps – but nothing beyond those. It wasn't so much the rumours of her easy virtue that seemed forever to circulate around her, nor the stories about a less than rigorous adherence to the strictures of PACE and subsequent legislation formalizing policing procedures; no, it was the whispers that Beverley Wharton did not do well by her colleagues, especially if said colleagues were female. She had gathered that those who crossed Beverley Wharton, or even those that looked as though they might, were sometimes mysteriously treated by the Fates; she had also been led to believe by those same whispers that attractive female colleagues were also prone to this destiny.

Not that Rebecca Lancefield made the hubristic mistake of believing that she was strikingly beautiful; she was, she knew, too short and from that came the impression that she was chubby; also she had a slightly lopsided smile and teeth that came within a whisper of an overbite, and sometimes the freckles became not curiously alluring but curiously off-putting. Yet she was far from ugly and had not gone for want of boyfriends, some quite serious, some whom she had even loved and, she was certain, had loved her. Would that be enough, though? Would DCI Wharton take one look at her and decide that, though she might not be the very essence of pulchritude, she was still enough of a threat to warrant some form of action? She had the impression that her new boss was almost pathologically jealous of all potential sexual rivals, in which case she would only have been safe if she were a practising lesbian or a direct descendant of the gorgon.

And that was not all. The whispers spoke also of DCI Wharton's ambition, a thing that ran her sexuality a close second; Beverley Wharton had sharp elbows and no compunction about using them when it came to displacing people from the greasy pole. She was aware that if she appeared too good at her job, too liable to eclipse

her DCI on intellectual grounds (even if she were in her shade
on those of attractiveness), then her position was liable to be no
less hazardous. To make it worse, she was fairly sure that she
was superior to Beverley Wharton when it came to the job; she
had already noticed that she seemed able to anticipate her
commands, already to have thought of matters before the DCI
had her brain into gear. The only area of their profession in which
she felt herself deficient was that of experience, and only time
could give her that; indeed, she was confident that time *would*
give her that.

But only if Beverley Wharton allowed her to gain it.

TWENTY-FOUR
all relationships end

L en Barker was becoming increasingly angry. He had been
angry from the first moment of coming round following his
stroke, but that had gradually died to dull, despairing discontent, a cold, corrosive resentment that he should have been felled
so unjustly, that a punishment had been meted out upon him for
no crime, no misdemeanour, no wrongdoing worse than any other
human being's; why should he be like this when he looked out of
his window for hours on endless end upon his neighbours and saw
people no less craven, sinning and unworthy than he?

Now, though, events had transpired to surmount this low-level
inquietude; Lancefield's patronizing words still lived, cruelly, within
his head, still resounded with mocking disdain. *I don't suppose you
saw anything anyway, did you*. Bitch! She had looked on him and
seen only a cripple, a wreck, a disease with connotations of uselessness and helplessness, a thing and thing, moreover, with a past but
no future. He had not slept that night, the hot shame admixed with
an even brighter anger; he would show her.

Worse, one of the carers, that withered old bitch-hag Lavoisier,
had started storing his wheelchair in the sitting room at night, so
that he was effectively confined to his bed during the night. She
had hoped to crush him that little bit more, he knew, but he would
have the last say. He would overcome this fucking affliction, this
cunt of a stroke, and he would let them know what he had seen.
His old instincts told him that it was important, that this was a

piece of information that might be small but that was as essential as the keystone in the arch, and only he could provide it. From this he sucked some drops of dry and bitter sustenance for his bleeding, limping, dribbling pride.

Charlie Sherman had pale skin to match her pale blue eyes; she believed that she had too many freckles and too many curls in her auburn hair, believed, too, that she was just slightly too chubby. She was intimidatingly bright and far too insecure for her own good; the combination of insecurity about her own looks and a brain that would not stop analysing, would never accept that some things are best left unexplored, was a dangerous one. She had for a long time accepted that all relationships end, that the best she could hope for was as little pain as possible, and this was a self-fulfilling prophesy; she knew this, yet she could not, as bright as she was, change it. She was amused that she recognized that trap that she was in and that all the brains in the world were of no use in it. In a strange way, she found it reassuring to be forever confronted by her own shortcomings, to be properly reminded that there are many different types of intelligence and that in most of them she was below average.

The signals she was getting from John Eisenmenger played into this complex matrix of emotions and doubts and false certainties. He had caught her on the rebound from a relationship with a fellow psychologist at her previous hospital but she was not, she had hoped, feeling especially vulnerable, nor desperate for male company at whatever cost. And Eisenmenger had seemed to tick most of the right boxes for her; true, he was a little cold, a little reticent, but she had never been particularly interested in macho types, nor in men who mistook monologues for conversation. Nor had he appeared frightened by conversing with an intellectual equal, perhaps an intellectual superior, something that was a refreshing change; he did not seem to mind that she could sometimes complete the cross-word or Sudoku that he could not, and she suspected that this was genuine, not mere politeness.

If, though, there was criticism to be levelled – and she was worldly wise enough to know that it was inevitable that there should be – then it was that he apologized too much, that he seemed forever to see himself in the wrong, was always ready to accept without question that he was the one who should be sorry. Whilst she would have abhorred a man who never admitted his faults, this constant and continuous apologia she found at times irritating. It was made all the worse because of recent times, he had had more than usual to be contrite for. She had known that pathologists who did forensic work – autopsies on suspicious deaths, employed by the police – had necessarily disrupted social lives; her own job did not require her to be on-call at all. But just recently, every single plan that they had made to spend time together seemed to have been destroyed by yet another death; and when Eisenmenger was called out, she knew that he would be gone for many hours, unlike her own on-call commitments which not infrequently required only advice over the phone. She was beginning to wonder if this was to be a perpetual cost of knowing him, and if it was worth paying.

That afternoon, when she had learned that yet again he would not be able to make their date, she had had to fight the anger, dissipate the frustration.

Damn it, John.

She had not yet started to cook, but she was not about to go to the trouble of preparing anything special just for herself; tuna salad and a glass of white wine would suit her just fine. Also, it would give her a chance to chill out in front of some mindless television, and then get an early night. Yet, despite trying to suck compensation from these prospects, she remained unhappy and changed her mind.

No, she decided. Damn you, John.

Beverley called a meeting in her office with Lancefield and Fisher for seven the next morning. Braxton, too, attended, and listened in silence as Beverley told him of Eisenmenger's findings. When she had finished, he merely asked, 'What do you think?'

Beverley wasn't certain whether she was being tested or he genuinely didn't know either. 'We have three deaths, but no identities yet. Two of them were killed in the same way, one by a completely different method. One was a woman, two were men; all were white and, as far as we can tell, they fit no particular age group. The bodies have been left in different locations throughout the county. On all three there is evidence of restraint at the ankles, wrists and neck, and all three were naked when found.'

She had run out of facts, aware that she hadn't been speaking long, although Braxton didn't seem perturbed. He said, 'I assume you're looking through missing persons reports?'

'We have been, but up until now we haven't had a whole body to go on, so I'm hopeful we'll strike lucky now.'

'We have to have hope,' agreed Braxton drily, and it came across as something of a rebuke.

Before Beverley could repair the damage she thought the remark had done to her, Lancefield put in, 'It's all wrong.'

Braxton turned to her and perhaps missed Beverley's expression. 'What is?'

'The disparity of the victims.'

He nodded slowly. 'Go on.' He gave the impression that he was already aware of what she was thinking, but maybe he was just good at appearing so.

'We've had two males and one female for a start. That's odd, since most serial killers confine themselves to one sex.'

He appeared to consider this learnedly which gave Beverley the chance to say smoothly and completely convincingly, 'And, of course, there are the methods of killing. Apparently two different kinds, completely different.' She did not look at Lancefield, but was fairly certain that her inspector was not a happy inspector at that moment.

Braxton nodded. 'Yes . . .' he said thoughtfully. Beverley had not missed the glance that Lancefield had given her, had enjoyed it rather, although her eyes were on Braxton and her expression was neutral. *Fuck you, Lancefield.*

Braxton asked thoughtfully of the room, 'Are you suggesting there might be more than one killer?'

Beverley looked across at her junior and asked interestedly, 'Is that what you think?'

Lancefield found herself under a bright and very hot spotlight. Her demeanour, normally very confident, very self-contained, had become somewhat more frayed than was usual. 'Well . . .' Then: 'It's a possibility . . .'

Beverley said at once, 'Two serial killers working together would be unique.'

Braxton nodded. 'That's what I was thinking.'

Lancefield wasted no time in undertaking a total withdrawal from the field of battle. 'It was just an idea.'

Beverley was magnanimous as she nodded sagaciously and said, 'And worth considering, too.' That she immediately turned from Lancefield only underlined the disdain. She continued, 'We should get the first of the toxicology reports tomorrow from the samples taken at PM. That might give us something.'

'Have forensics given us anything?'

She shook her head. 'Not so far.' He went back into his slightly distracted state; they waited, unsure of whether or not to speak, then he suddenly awoke, seemed almost to shake himself. 'Until we find out who these poor sods are, you don't stand a hope in Hades.'

The subtle shift in pronoun again. She suspected he did it unconsciously, much as a chameleon changed colour. His next words did little to give her confidence that she was part of a team and could count on support.

'This is one of those cases, Beverley. It'll either make you or break you.'

He smiled as he said this, perhaps hoping to make her see the positive side.

Strangely, he failed.

TWENTY-FIVE

the pudding was a butterscotch tart

The beef was tender, although for Eisenmenger's tastes it was a tad overdone; he was not enough of an epicure to note this down as a mark against Charlie and, anyway, she was clearly enjoying it, as was Paul. The potatoes were definitely out of the top drawer, though; Helena's potatoes had sometimes been a little too firm for his liking, although he had never dared say as such. The horseradish was excellent too, sourced – so Charlie had explained when he had commented – from a delicatessen in Leckhampton.

Paul was down for the week and Eisenmenger was not such a blind idiot that he could not see she was happier than she had been for some time; this observation, unlike most of those that he made, caused him pain. Despite such a promising beginning, he could see this relationship going the same way that all his others had done, that it was becoming scarred and flawed by circumstance, experience and misunderstanding. There was a feeling of consequent depression in his head as he laughed at the small talk, appreciated the company and the vivacity of Charlie's small house, drank the wine that Paul had brought with him. He was very afraid that unless he did something, and did it soon, the canker would grow and it would sour all things that he touched, as it had done so many times before.

Why?

He found himself continually repeating this enquiry until it became almost a beat within his head, a pounding yet peculiarly wimpish sound in the background as he watched mother and son engaging in easy conversation, aware of his relative ignorance, and effortlessly including him when they had to.

Why? Why did it always seem to go wrong for him in such matters? What the hell was wrong with him?

He knew that he was not particularly gifted as a social being, that he by nature needed solitude on occasion, that he made few friends and those with difficulty, and that his demeanour was frequently mistaken for arrogance, but he was forever hoping that these were barriers that were surmountable and, once surmounted, were of little consequence. Yet it never came about as he wished; forever he was climbing the barricade only to find potholes, gin-traps, unforeseen catastrophes, it seemed.

Try as he might, his fate did not seem to be his own to command.

Why won't you listen, you fucking old bitch?

Len Barker's face did not mutate from its frozen attitude of idiocy and the thin line of spittle did not pause or deviate as it ran down the rivulet formed by its antecedents from the right-hand corner of his drooping mouth. The scream was silent but was to him deafening; Mary Lavoisier carried on her desultory dusting, no longer bothering to attempt to converse with him, treating him increasingly as a piece of furniture, and one she didn't particularly like. He watched her from eyes underlined by drooping lids, his hatred for her smouldering, a living, writhing thing that he found almost invigorating. She was the carer that came most often and she was the carer who angered him most; she was sloppy, insolent and dirty. They were supposed to give him whisky every evening and sometimes she did and sometimes she didn't, depending on her whim; he suspected she helped herself liberally to his whisky, and who was there to tell on her? He found himself so deeply enraged at being powerless to stop her entering his flat, his tired eyes watered constantly and his left hand, the hand that he could raise, shook. Mary Lavoisier took this merely as another sign of his weakness. Her eyes held only contempt as she watched him lift the hand and grunt in yet another effort to communicate to her. She had long ago given up saying anything in response, even something hideously patronizing, and now contented herself with a smirk that suggested she thought him of a different, lesser species.

And he had to communicate in some way because by now it was an article of faith to him that his information about the white van was pivotal in the investigation; it was he and he alone that would break the investigation. He had seen on the television news about the dead body in the quarry and its likely links to previous murders, although the details had been scanty; from his experience, he knew that this dearth of data was deliberate, that there were things the public were not supposed to know. This was an important case, and he was determined not to fail in what he still saw as his duty. He could not speak and, since he was right-handed, he could not write easily either. He was convinced that he could have scrawled something reasonably legible, but there was never anything around that he could use, neither to write with nor to write on; the fools had tidied it all away and he could not tell them to do otherwise. Hour by hour, day by day his frustration had grown, eating into him, tensing his nerves, acidifying his stomach, bringing him to the point of an agonizing spike of frustration.

The pudding was a butterscotch tart, happily redolent for all of them of primary school meals and therefore of false memories of happiness, innocence and a mythic time when there were no concerns. As Paul poured cream over a second slice, Eisenmenger asked him, 'You're writing a dissertation, then?'

Paul nodded. He was tall and thin with curly, slightly reddish hair and thick-framed glasses that gave him an automatic look of academe and, although Eisenmenger had yet to meet him, he had seen photographs of Paul's father and could see the resemblance. He asked, 'How's it going?'

More enthusiastic nodding. 'Really well, thanks.' They did not know each other well enough for Paul to use Eisenmenger's first name naturally.

Not out of an expectation or desire to learn, but out of politeness, Eisenmenger asked, 'What is it on?' He had declined seconds of the tart, perhaps subconsciously (he wondered) worrying that his paunch was proving a bar to a perfect relationship with Charlie.

'The Deep Web.'

Eisenmenger's curiosity was not peaked beyond more than polite interest. 'Right . . .' He nodded, was suddenly aware that he might look as though he knew more than he did, and asked, 'Which is . . .?'

Paul was an archetypal academic and a young one, to boot. He was enthusiastic about his subject to a point that left the audience bobbing helplessly, not to say drowning, in his wake. 'It's something so few people know about . . .' he began.

Eisenmenger was enjoying the wine; it was the second bottle and the one he had bought; he thought it rather good.

'Most people don't realize that when they "surf" the web, they are literally doing just that. At least ninety-five percent of inter-computer traffic is hidden, certainly not reached by standard Internet search engines.'

'Defence stuff? Commercially sensitive information?' suggested Charlie. Eisenmenger knew her well enough to suspect that, like him, she was pleasantly relaxed and it was good to see. Compared with recent experience, she seemed almost deliriously happy.

Paul shook his head and even this was animated, even passionate. 'Nothing like that, Ma.' This salutation was an affectation to which Eisenmenger had yet to become accustomed. 'It's the "Darkweb"; it's not official in any way; far from it. This is where you find criminals conversing, serious pornography, political subversion —'

Charlie said at once, 'It sounds very unsavoury, Paul.'

He hastened to provide filial reassurance. 'Don't worry, Ma. I'm not becoming polluted.'

Eisenmenger was intrigued. 'So how do you access this?'

'You need specific software to access it, but there's no problem getting hold of it – it's called Freenet. It's been available for years.'

Had Eisenmenger not been the man he was, he might have appreciated that Charlie was becoming unsettled; as it was, he was intrigued, and that had taken hold of him. 'But surely the police know about this? I mean, if there's criminal activity going on in there?'

Paul finished his extra of treacle tart. 'This is the cyber equivalent of the wild frontier. In the first place none of the conventional search engines are configured to do anything other than skim the surface and, secondly, we are talking about people who don't *want* to be found and take very special care not to be; the Internet and search engines that we all know work on the principle that a website wants to be seen. The authorities know about it, but they can't actually police it.'

Charlie asked, 'Have you finished, Paul?'

He had. Eisenmenger stood up to help her clear. 'I never realized, Paul.'

Paul showed some pleasure. 'There's some seriously deep shit going on in there . . .' He ignored, or did not see, his mother's look. 'Snuff sites, that kind of thing.'

Charlie had piled the dessert plates and cutlery, was balancing them on one hand whilst she took the remains of the tart out, but she stopped in shock as he said this. Eisenmenger, cruet and cream in hand asked disbelievingly, 'Really? Are you sure they're not just good simulations?'

Paul also was standing. He was clearing the cloth napkins and mats. 'A lot of them, but a lot of them clearly aren't. Really sick, perverted stuff. People being killed in all sorts of weird ways.'

'They're foreign, though, aren't they?' asked Charlie anxiously, as if that kind of thing couldn't possibly happen in this green and pleasant isle.

But her son could not give her that reassurance. 'They're from all over, Ma. Even this country.'

And something clicked in Eisenmenger's head.

Thus fate intervened in Eisenmenger's life.

TWENTY-SIX
provided one asked no questions

'‎**I**gnore all that for now.' Eisenmenger had struck Beverley as uncharacteristically tense since he had first come into her office and this was undoubtedly a command, issued in an abrupt tone. She looked up at him, then caught Lancefield's eye just before her junior said something. 'Scroll to the end.' he told her. 'You'll find some hyperlinks at the end. They're what you've got to see.'

And so Beverley did what she was told.

Allen Somersby knew that he had landed a good job. He had worked for Wallace Parker for six years now, coming from an estate in Scotland, one that had been five times bigger and that had been owned by a man who had been brought up to own land, who had been constantly on his back, asking why this had not been done, why that had been done that way, why his profit margins on the arable were so small, why they were getting through so much diesel . . . Finding Wallace Parker's estate – Wallace Parker, who was rich and knew a lot about city trading and therefore *thought* he knew a lot about managing an estate – had been like finding paradise. Life was so much easier now. There were so many ways in which to make a bit of money on the side, and Somersby could see no wrong in that; Parker was not the most generous of employers and, accordingly, Somersby was of the opinion that such tightwads were right for the picking. It was a game that had been played from the beginning of time: the employer paid the minimum; all that did was to maximize the ingenuity of the employees, and if that ingenuity was employed in private enterprise, then that was surely only the order of the world.

Thus over the years Somersby had entered into several lucrative but quite unofficial business dealings, although it was only the building itself – a vast, decrepit but impressive early Victorian monstrosity of four floors and many rooms – that interested him; the hundred or so acres that it sat in were just more woodland that he had to manage and that were therefore part of his official duties. A large, derelict and completely isolated building had so much more potential, so much more of interest, provided one asked no questions.

'Jesus-fucking-Christ.'

The blasphemy was barely a whisper, and more of a plea for mercy than an attempt or desire to disrespect any God. In any case, no one reacted to Lancefield's uncharacteristic lapse into profanity; not now, not when they were looking, transfixed, at what was unfolding on the computer screen before them.

They were clustered around Beverley's desk – Beverley in the centre, Lancefield to her right, Fisher to her left; Eisenmenger was behind her, his head leaning against the wall, his eyes looking up at the ceiling. He had been up all night, helped by Paul, searching this terrible place that Paul called the 'Deepweb'. It had taken until nearly dawn and he had almost given up before he had come across this website and, when he had done so, he had been almost paralysed by the turmoil of his sense of triumph and his sense of shock at what he saw. Having seen this show on one occasion, he was certain that it would suffice for at least one lifetime, perhaps even a dozen or more. He had to listen, though; he still had to hear the sounds, which was perhaps worse.

It was bad. Bad enough to make him feel sick, make him sweat, make him wish that tears were not such a private thing, that he could let them flow down his cheeks as they should, instead of remaining welled in his eyes, dammed by his lids. He could not stop thinking about Helena, about how she had gone; he thought, too, about Tamsin and he had not thought of her for a long time. Tamsin, who had died in his arms of the burns that her mother caused her, who had given him dreams, who had been within him for so long after her death, who had taught him – a pathologist who knew all about death – something about dying. It was his first real experience of the process as opposed to the consequences, and it had been a salutary one; yet here was his second lesson and, beside it, the first paled into a mere sickly pallor.

At last it finished, yet it left stains, foetors, tastes.

TWENTY-SEVEN

'a glimpse of hell'

After thirty years of growing vegetables, and not infrequently winning prizes at the Bishop's Cleeve Flower and Vegetable Show, Arnold Dearlove had now passed beyond the competitive phase of his gardening career, and looked on his allotment as more of a social thing, a place to come to garden, yes, but more importantly to pass the time with his comrades who, like him were veterans in the never-ending battle against ragwort, couch grass and bindweed. There was something that stirred his soul when he looked up from digging or pruning or sowing to see the wide sky above him, the buildings and houses far away, the suggestion that the works of man were somehow being kept at bay and, in his small area of twenty acres, nature was allowed at least some play. Having retired fifteen years before from a long career as a small shop-keeper (hardware – he had always had the best gardening tools at trade prices because of this), he had had no fears of languishing, knowing that his beloved allotment would be his saviour. And when Grace had died seven years ago, it had come to his rescue again; the routine of daily labour, of nurturing the seedlings, tending to the fruit trees, caring for soil, combined with the support of his friends had been vital – literally vital – to him. How could he not consider himself to be a happy man?

Every day, as he arrived at eight thirty, there was something to see. The weather varied both on a diurnal basis and on a seasonal basis; autumnal light was so different from that of spring; the smell of rain in the air brought him as much joy as the heat of the sun on the back of his neck; even snow and fog had their beauty, adding something mysterious and alien, yet reassuring to the landscape. Only torrential rain, when the allotments tended to turn to quagmire because of the clay base, and a frost so severe that he could not dig, ever kept him away from his love, and turned him into a man without a cause.

On this particular day, when the air was heavy and hot, and humidity dragged at his feet and at his chest, it was his first day for ten days, as he had only just recovered from a bout of influenza complicated by an irregular heartbeat. The allotments were unusually empty because of the same influenza, and there were only three others working as he arrived, although others would undoubtedly drift in as the morning progressed. He waved as they looked up from their labours and saw him, but none were near enough to talk to; there would be time for that later, when he stopped to have tea from his Thermos and to eat his customary digestive biscuits. He therefore walked at once onto his allotment, past the bonfire, the potatoes, asparagus bed (now tall ferns with developing berries) and the parsnips, to his shed. He felt in his pocket for his key to the padlock, hoping he hadn't forgotten it again, but he hadn't. He grabbed hold of the lock and found to his shock that the hasp came away from the door; that, in fact, it had been forced, with clean, untreated wood splinters falling to the soil. He had been robbed again!

He found himself experiencing a mix of anger and sorrow; robberies from the allotment were becoming such a serious problem, and the police never seemed to take them seriously. They asked routine questions in a desultory tone, poked around as if they were bored, then gave him an incident number to use for insurance; he knew, and they knew he knew, that they weren't going to do any actual police work. And every year his insurance went up; some of those who worked on the allotment were now being refused any insurance at all. He felt it was as much a crime as the burglary itself.

With a sigh and leaden heart he pulled open the shed door to make an inventory of what had been taken, finding to his surprise that nothing had gone. In fact, something had been added, for sitting on his camp stool – and looking for all the world as if it lived there – was the naked body of a dead woman.

'What the fuck was that?' asked Beverley, her voice sounded small and distant, even in her own ears.

Eisenmenger was still making eyes at the ceiling; outside the window, Lansdowne Road continued, the weekday morning rush hour dissipating imperceptibly, the sunshine already becoming yellow and hot. There was a long pause before his voice needled into the shocked silence and answered her question. 'That was, I believe, a scientific snuff video.' He found it difficult to control his voice as he would want, as he always did; found it difficult to be the detached professional, ever ready to give a considered opinion, to be cold and clinical, to be the oracle.

Lancefield's frown caused black lines on her face that were frighteningly sharp against the waxen bloodlessness of her flesh. She said slowly, wonderingly, 'But that was nothing other than a glimpse of hell . . .'

To Lancefield's observation, Eisenmenger said only, without changing his body position, '"Hell is other people".'

Beverley demanded, 'What the fuck does that mean?'

Eisenmenger said nothing to that, for in truth he did not really believe the aphorism. They were entering shock, but he was deep in it, for he had had a few hours to consider what they had only just seen. When he had loaded the software and gone to the precise address that Paul had given him, he had found himself drawn into what had been on show. His emotions had flowed from curiosity tinged with disbelief, through disbelief tinged with curiosity, all the way to shocked unbelief mixed perfectly with despair.

The site was presented as a scientific paper, perhaps something out of the *New England Journal of Medicine*. It was dry, austere, objective, without illustrations, or gimmicks, or advertisements, or even anything other than black text on white. *A First Report on Visual, Physiological and Neurophysiological Observations Made During the Moment of Dying*.

Just as in all legitimate scientific papers, the text was divided into an Abstract, an Introduction, a Methods section, Results, the Discussion and then Conclusions; there were even references cited throughout and then listed at the very end. As a parody, it failed because it was too good.

The Abstract explained that: 'Despite the advances in medical knowledge regarding the physiological parameters that are prognostically significant in determining survival from serious disease or trauma, and similar advances made in understanding the biochemical changes that occur shortly after death, there has been little study into the phenomena that occur *precisely* at the moment of death.' It was that italicized word that chilled, that hinted softly that here was no mere money-for-hire scientist hack; here was a zealot.

It went on: 'It is the intention of this series of experiments to fill this lacuna. The hypothesis that is being tested is that there is a soul, that death is not merely an absence of electrophysiological functioning and a breakdown in internal homeostasis, that there is a separation between body and soul, and that life is not merely a consequence of biochemical functioning.'

The introduction went into further detail on this hypothesis, quoting work that Eisenmenger did not recognize. It was the section headed 'Methods' that led the reader into the regions of madness, however, where reason slipped from the page and left a blankness that only insanity could fill. It informed those interested that the EEG readings, the blood pressure, the temperature, the oxygen saturation levels, the ECG findings, the jugular venous pressure, and even the electrical resistance of the skin, had been measured before, during and immediately after death.

And it was at this point that Eisenmenger had found he could read no longer and was forced by a compunction borne of fear, horror and even an irresistible salaciousness to turn to the hyperlinks at the end of the paper. Which was where the real awfulness had begun. It was these hyperlinks that had just finished on Beverley's office computer, that had presented the 'visual' results of the experiments . . .

TWENTY-EIGHT
'worrying news'

Neither Tom Sheldon nor Allan Somersby had said anything for several minutes, but neither minded this silence between them; a tractor had driven past the cottage, and there was the dry sound of a crow in summer, but apart from that the room had been quiet. There were no clocks ticking out the time of the universe, no radio broadcasting one-sided merriment, no sound of a neighbour's baby crying. It was dark, too, the evening dying beyond the dense foliage that shaded the house even in the brightest of noonday suns. And there were scents . . .

A rambling, run-wild, decadent honeysuckle lurked just beyond the flecking paint of the cottage windows, excreting a turgid, almost oleaginous perfume that mingled with lesser tones of damp, dust, mouse and fertilizer. The chair in which he was sitting was old and uncomfortable, although Sheldon knew that it was more welcoming than his visitor's seat; Sheldon somehow fitted into it, presumably by a process of long years of slow integration and mutual accommodation. Somersby's seat was a thing that looked well over a hundred years old and beyond all available medical intervention; it looked *mean*, with lumps and springs in all the wrong places that were ready to bite; it was worn and dirty too.

Eventually Somersby said, 'This is worrying news.'

Tom Sheldon looked at him, but only after a long pause did he say somewhat grudgingly and with little tone of remorse, 'I'm sorry.'

Somersby sighed angrily. 'It's not your fault.' It was clear from his tone that this was not necessarily his opinion of the truth of the situation.

'It was fucking bad luck.'

Somersby grunted. He was looking at his thin, white hand. 'You're sure they were outside the inner fence?' he asked slowly, his voice conveying tiredness, but the tiredness of a man who has done much and fears he might have to do much more yet.

'Yes.' Sheldon said this sourly, affronted that Somersby treated him like an idiot all the time.

'There's no way they can get into the Grange?' persisted Somersby.

The response to this was nothing more than a grunt and a slight movement of his thickset shoulders in an attempt at a shrug. Sheldon didn't know and didn't think he should be expected to know. Somersby eyed him contemptuously. Sheldon was not his idea of an ideal business colleague, being woefully short of functioning stuff between the ears, but necessity was a harsh mistress; anyway, Sheldon was big and strong, and had the distinct advantage of being pleasantly free from inhibition when it came to violence, and Somersby could always use a man like that. 'Make a check of the perimeter next time you are there. Make sure that there is no possibility anyone can get into the inner grounds.'

'Why me?' This was posed resentfully.

'Because I'm busy, and you're not.' In these words there was the tone of a man who had come to expect obedience.

In Sheldon's silence, there was the tone of a man who did not give it easily.

Beverley was clearly intensely angry, but Eisenmenger did not mind her anger, could not find it within himself to be affronted, for he knew that it was just a way of coping. After a final perusal of the ceiling – a rather boring landscape and therefore of some relief to him, given his barely subdued sense of hysteria – he at last looked down at the three police officers. 'You have just seen a man beheaded on a guillotine, a woman die similarly; you have seen a man cooked slowly in an electric chair, and then a woman die quickly in the same one. It was done, if we are to accept the murderer's manifesto, in the name of science. When you read the paper

that accompanies these recordings, you will be led to believe that
what we have here is nothing less than an attempt to determine
whether or not there is a soul, and what happens to the individual
at the point of death.'

'Scientific?' said Beverley scathingly. 'You mean this madman
is trying to convince us that he's working in the name of science?'

'Absolutely,' replied Eisenmenger after careful consideration and
with slow nodding. Then: 'Yes. That's about right. He thinks of
himself as a scientist.'

Fisher, whose experience of science had ended well before he
had failed a GCSE in the subject, and who read the *Star* every
morning in a state of gullible grace concerning the latest research
on such matters, asked incredulously, 'You mean a boffin? Some
guy in a lab coat is doing this?'

'Fisher, don't open your mouth and then I might forget you're
a cretin.' Beverley didn't even bother looking at her sergeant as
she sprayed him with this acidic advice. She had returned to the
introductory web page. Of Eisenmenger she asked, 'It looks fairly
convincing. Is it?'

'At first glance, yes. It could have been reproduced from any
reputable scientific or medical journal, save that the author is not
named. It is in the correct format, and it presents the arguments for
the research in a very structured, reasoned way.'

Lancefield's voice was of a slightly higher register than usual
as she asked quietly, 'Reasoned?'

Eisenmenger was without compunction as he rounded on her
and replied at once, 'Yes, reasoned. Ask the psychologists. This
man – woman, perhaps – is not chaotic or disordered in his
thinking at all; in fact, he is almost certainly far more structured
than you are, than I am, than everyone else is. He is a *slave* to
his thinking, cannot escape it; he has lost free will, in effect, and
with it a conscience. It's because he is almost robotic in his
thinking that he is capable of atrocity, just as a computer would
see no difference between the killing of an ant or the killing of
a baby.'

Beverley said, 'So we can assume that he is a scientist?'

Fisher may or may not have been trying to make a joke when
he murmured, 'A mad scientist.' No one took any notice because
there was a knock on the door and a female uniformed constable
came in at once. She presented Beverley with a note, waited for
the response – a curt nod without word or change of expression –

then left. She looked across at Eisenmenger, the paper still in her hand, waiting for his answer.

'That's one of the things that bothers me.'

'Meaning?'

'This murderer clearly has academic training and has read scientific literature – the primary research stuff, not the popular journalistic stuff – but I can't believe that he's a working scientist, nor ever has been.'

'Why do you think that?'

'He is testing a hypothesis, not a null hypothesis.' General confusion met this. He went on: 'He isn't thinking like a scientist, more like one versed in the humanities. Someone who is intelligent and used to academia, but who does not understand the philosophy of science.'

It was left to Fisher to ask, 'What's a null hypothesis?' There was a refreshing confidence in the innocence of his tone, one that said that he was not ashamed of his lack of knowledge

Eisenmenger stood up, embarrassed because he was aware that he was going to sound didactic and tedious and probably unintelligible. 'Science works by examining data – whether generated from previous experiment or from observation of natural phenomena – devising a hypothesis to explain the data, then devising an experiment to test that hypothesis.'

Lancefield asked, 'Isn't that what this bastard's doing?'.

'But the hypothesis that is generated by the data must be a *null* hypothesis.'

Fisher was used to hitting people who tried to be clever with him, but contented himself with a frown in deference to his newly acquired rank. It was left to Lancefield to ask, 'What's that when it's at home?'

'The scientist conceives his hypothesis – this is what he believes to be an explanation for what he has observed – but he must avoid bias at all costs when he performs his experiments; he must be objective and detached.'

'You can't get more detached than this joker,' pointed out Lancefield.

Eisenmenger had suspected he wouldn't explain things very well and the facial expression of his audience told him he had been prescient; Fisher looked as if a magician had just plucked an egg from his anus, Lancefield was perplexed and irritated, and Beverley wasn't even obviously in the room. 'The experimenter must try to reduce any room for subjective interpretation to a minimum; in order to achieve this, it is not the hypothesis that is tested, but its antithesis. If I think that drinking while driving causes an increase in accidents, then my experiment must be so designed as to try to prove that it doesn't. I then look at the results and, if they suggest that drink-driving *does* result in an increased risk of accident, I abandon that hypothesis.'

Fisher bore the same expression now as when he tried to do the cryptic crossword in the newspaper. Lancefield demanded, 'Isn't the same thing? You disproved one idea, proved another.'

'No!' Eisenmenger himself was surprised at the vehemence of his voice. He recognized stress in himself. 'No, inspector. I have neither proved nor disproved anything. I have merely made one, infinitesimally small, step in the direction of Truth; but I have done so in a manner that is as disengaged as I can make it. I must now carry on to elicit further information. It appears that there may a relationship between drinking whilst driving, and accidents, but that does not prove *causation*, merely linkage. Further, interventional research must be done.'

Lancefield's mouth was opening, Fisher's merely open, when Beverley said suddenly, 'A single piece of observational research proves nothing. Is that it?'

Eisenmenger took the line much as a drowning solo yachtsman in the middle of the South Atlantic might do. 'That's it. It doesn't matter how big the sample, how long it took; a single experiment proves nothing.' He then saw the look in her eye, was immediately cast into a shadow thrown by a combination of puzzlement, dread and precognition. Without taking his eyes from her, he carried on: 'It promises at the end that this is merely the first of a series of investigations. And we already have one dead body not included here.'

There was a depth and density of silence that met this, until the phone rang, making them all jump, screaming into the silence that had fallen onto them. Beverley picked it up, said nothing as she listened; her face might have been overdosed on Botox. There was a dreadful inevitability – a feeling of a great rock about to crash, of a doom approaching, about to grab them, rip them to shreds – as they waited. Then she put the phone down and sat staring at it, her expression still paralysed, and no one dared asked.

Eventually she said tiredly, almost as if asleep, 'They've just found another body.'

'Where is it?' asked Lancefield.

'On some allotments in Churchdown.'

'With or without its head?' asked Eisenmenger. She opened her mouth to reply, then closed it again; she hadn't thought to ask. He murmured, 'Or has it been cooked, I wonder.'

She snapped, 'You'll find out soon enough.'

She thought for a moment, but just a moment; she had been transformed from the figure of pathos that she had presented just before. 'First, we go to the mortuary. Then we go to Churchdown.'

TWENTY-NINE

Melanie often partook of the 'jazz woodbines'

Melanie Whittaker had waited a long time for her daughter, Evangeline, and she was not in the best of moods. 'Where have you been?' she demanded without preliminary greeting, without even waiting for Evangeline to get completely through the glass doors of the school's science block. Evangeline was very like her mother, except for the sixteen years difference in their ages; this difference could not, however, be disguised by modern cosmetics, despite Melanie's strenuous efforts. They were both, though, obese with small, porcine eyes, a slightly snubbed nose and full lips that could not quite cover their incisors (which in Melanie's case were nicotine stained). They had similar taste in clothes, which was unfortunate for Evangeline's mother because younger fashions did not suit her. They also had similar, incendiary temperaments.

Evangeline had been forced to stay behind after school because of a detention that should have finished fifteen minutes before; she was late from this because she had taken the opportunity to purchase something enjoyable but illegal from one of the school cleaners – a not irregular occurrence – but she was not about to tell her mother that. Melanie often partook of the 'jazz woodbines' but drew the line at that; some illicit drugs, in her opinion, were less illegal than others. Evangeline said impassively, 'I was looking for a book.'

Anyone who knew Evangeline might have detected a lie here, and her mother certainly knew her daughter. 'And the rest.'

Evangeline shrugged; her mother's unbelief was of little consequence to her. 'Where's the fucking car?' she demanded petulantly.

'Round the fucking corner,' was the witty rejoinder.

Thus they expressed their love for each other, just as they had always done, walking away from the tatty, decayed beacon of educational excellence that was Evangeline's school. They both smoked, each of them plucking a cigarette from their own packet without any thought that they should share; they did not talk, as if smoking were enough, as if smoking were a means of communication and speech had become redundant.

The car did not have remote or even central locking; Evangeline's mother made a point of climbing in first before reaching across to let her daughter in, and doing it in a leisurely fashion. Evangeline's first act was to turn the radio to Radio One and up the volume; she did not catch what her mother said, but then did not try to. The twenty-minute journey home did not produce a single word of conversation between mother and offspring. There was, as usual, no space outside their Whaddon house and Melanie was forced to park a hundred yards away and, as usual, she spent several minutes doing so badly; the car ended up a yard away from the kerb at the back, a foot away at the front. Evangeline didn't bother to comment and exited the car as soon as it was stationary; the slam of the door could be heard three streets away.

When Melanie finally made it to the front door, Evangeline was standing in front of it, arms folded, lips pouted, jaws chewing enthusiastically on her gum. 'Where's your key?' mother demanded of daughter.

'Dunno.'

'Have you lost it?'

Evangeline said casually, 'It's in my other jacket.'

That this contradicted her previous statement and that it was, in any case, said in a tone that betrayed what was patently a falsehood, did not escape her perspicacious mother. 'Fucking liar.'

As she pushed past her daughter, she groped in her bright yellow handbag for her own key, her form reflected blurrily in fourteen of the sixteen small squares of frosted glass in the door; cardboard clumsily taped into place completed the array. She opened the door and went straight into the minute hallway; Evangeline followed almost at once, but collided with her mother almost at once

'Get out the way, can't—' she began, but she did not finish the sentence, for she had seen what had caused her mother to stop in such an inconvenient place.

It was a hooded man and he held a sawn-off double-barrelled shotgun on them as he stood at the bottom of the stairs.

Two large spiders watched Eisenmenger with sixteen eyes from their webs, one in each corner of the rickety, cramped shed. He did not like spiders and he found them distracting, almost as if they were judging his competence. The mouse droppings under the camp stool on which the body sat were much less disturbing to him; he felt more at home with mammals, preferring their standard blueprint of symmetry about a single plane with all the external organs and appendages coming in pairs. He kept knocking over things, too. A stainless steel garden spade, fork and hoe; a rusting watering can hanging precariously from an equally rusting rail, an aged Thermos flask; all went over as he tried to examine the body. There were odours though, and not just from the body which had started to decompose, perhaps in protest at having to sit in a shed on an allotment for several days. Potash, manure, creosote and perhaps many other things smote his olfactory membranes. The day being humid, it all added up to being not a pleasant place to be. He went about his job with his accustomed dedication, though.

When he emerged into the bright sunlight, he was perspiring freely. It was with something approaching Schadenfreude that he nodded to the forensic team that they might now perform their tasks in the shed. Beverley was occupied talking to Mr Dearlove in the back of a police car, so he went to his own car, took off his oversuit, put it and his bag in the boot, then sat in the front seat to make notes, the car door open. After fifteen minutes, Beverley appeared, looming over him. 'Well?' she demanded. She was curt, clearly under pressure and he knew better than to be anything other than professional and brief in his reply.

'You'll have spotted that she hasn't been beheaded.' If she were going to react to that, he pre-empted her. 'Nor has she been cooked alive.'

She was in no mood for frivolity. 'Can you tell me anything useful?'

He considered; it was so characteristic of him, she thought, to be so careful, unlike some of his colleagues; it was not, she knew, because of cussedness but because of a desire never to be wrong. 'She was bound in the same way as the others – there are abrasions around the wrists, ankles and neck, but there are also burns to the wrists and forehead, in a manner similar to Willoughby.'

'But you're sure she wasn't cooked?'

'No, not cooked, but I think she might have been electrocuted. A sudden high current, this time.'

She shook her head. She couldn't see how this particular maniac was thinking, and it bothered her. 'Anything else?'

'Been in that shed a while. Some days, I'd guess.' This was about as precise as Eisenmenger ever got when judging the time of a death.

She nodded. 'Mr Dearlove has been unwell. Hasn't tended his vegetables since a week ago Tuesday.'

'Apart from that, very little more at the moment. I'd estimate her to be late middle-aged, perhaps in her early forties, and no other obvious injuries of significance. Other than that . . .'

'Wait for the autopsy?'

'Exactly.'

THIRTY
and he was still wiping his own bottom

Rebecca Lancefield let herself into her house at about a quarter to eight, tired and feeling slightly sick because she could not get the thought of the body out of her head, seemed to hear the sounds of his death, the stench of it, even; she now found herself suddenly understanding how ghosts could perhaps come into existence, how they might be resonances of such awful, horrid death. The house was darkening and seemed emptier than she had ever known it before. It was a north-facing terrace house in Longlevens; she did not like it, but she hardly ever seemed to be in it, at least not when she was awake.

She ought, she knew, have called in on her parents on the way home, but she couldn't face it; not tonight. Accordingly, having taken off her coat, slipped off her shoes and made herself a cup of strong instant coffee, she phoned instead. Her father, of course, answered.

'Dad?'

'Hello, Becky.' He sounded just as he always did, and just as tired.

'Sorry I didn't look in. I've only just got in. We're in—'

He cut her short. 'Don't worry.' If she had ever hoped that her relationship with her father was a thing that could be repaired, she had long ago given up, but all the same she found now that he still had the power to wound her. Her mother's condition had only worsened the schism; indeed she could chart a direct correlation between the severity of her mother's dementia and the degree of sullen hostility that enveloped all her dealings with her father.

She took a deep breath both physically and mentally. 'How's Mum been?'

'Oh, not too bad.' She knew that he was lying; there were never any good days with her mother; not now. He was telling her that he could cope, that she was surplus to requirements.

'Has she been eating?'

'A little.'

'Has she been happy today?'

He hesitated. 'She was until she saw something on the television that upset her. Something about horses.'

'Oh, Dad . . .'

'It wasn't my fault.' He sounded at once defensive. 'It was one of those midday magazine programs and I was in the kitchen clearing the lunch things when they started this piece about point-to-point racing.'

'What did she do?'

'She began to scream and threw her coffee cup at the television. Luckily it missed, but there was a bit of a mess on the wall and on the carpet. Nothing serious.'

Becky's brother, Tim, had been killed when he had been thrown from a horse thirteen years before; now in the corrosive grip of severe Alzheimer's disease, her mother relived the pain at the smallest reminder. Ironically, she could date the degradation of the father-daughter relationship to that event; not that it did her much good to know why and when, not when she could do as little about it as she could about her mother's illness.

She asked, 'Is she calmer now?'

'Yes, thank God. She had an accident, though.'

An accident. Becky almost laughed; her mother was now so far beyond continence, these were no longer accidents, they were normality. 'Have you done anything about respite care?'

'Not yet.'

'Dad . . .'

'I don't see the need.'

He always said that, although she could see quite clearly that he was completely exhausted caring for his wife, he was locked into the behaviour, as much a prisoner of the situation as his wife was. She was locked in by disease, he by pride, though; both were strong, too strong to be fought successfully.

'You must do, Dad. You badly need a break. Just for a few days.'

'No.'

'Why don't you let me do more? I'm a bit busy at the moment, but in a couple of weeks, I could take some leave. I'm due some.'

He said immediately, 'I saw on the news that you've got a couple of murders on the patch.' Beverley had given a news conference that afternoon; to Rebecca's disappointment, she had done a good job. The grislier details of the deaths had been skirted round. 'Your career comes first.' He didn't mean it, she knew. It was a way of changing the subject because he was trying to shut her out. She wasn't going to be put off so soon.

'Even so, I promise I'll try to get over tomorrow evening, to give you at least a brief rest.'

'There's no need. She won't recognize you.'

Lancefield suddenly found tears; she knew of course that her mother would not recognize her, but that wasn't the point, and he also knew it. She would be visiting as much for herself as her mother, and his insistence that she was not required was just dull spite. 'Whatever, Dad. I'll be over as soon as I can.'

'If you want.' His voice had become cold.

She resolved to make the time at all costs, no matter what.

In the end, events dictated that it was a promise made in vain; Rebecca Lancefield would be too busy to visit her unloving parents.

Fisher made the first breakthrough. He had been given the task of searching the files for likely candidates amongst the missing persons, a tedious job but not nearly as tedious as it had once been, before computerization. Then it would have meant pulling physical files, relying on a complex system of cross-referencing that required a degree to understand and a genius to administer, yet that had had only a police sergeant looking after it. Even now, after a two-year procurement process and a six-month bedding-in period in which the system had crashed seven times and they had somehow missed three victims amongst the many thousands in the database, Fisher suspected that he had been given this task because no one would be surprised if he cocked it up, that he was once again being used as a patsy, but he had come to accept his fate. He had made it to sergeant, after all, which was one rank higher than he'd ever expected, than most of his colleagues had ever expected him to make, and all he'd ever seemed to do was take the shit squarely in the face whenever it came; it might not have been the kind of strategy employed by a high-flyer, but he reckoned it was worth persevering with, at least for the time being.

And so he spent some hours contentedly, if not happily, at his task. He had to input the details of each of the victims, as far as they were known, then the program would produce possible matches. It was useful to a certain extent, but he was rapidly coming to appreciate the truth underlying the IT aphorism, GIGO – 'garbage in, garbage out'. They knew so little about the victims that the 'matches' were loose, still requiring a huge amourt of trawling through tedious details, something that was far from Fisher's forte. He was therefore pleasantly surprised when he came across the description of Malcolm Willoughby, who had been working as a barman in Swindon Village until a few days before. It was his widowed mother who had reported him missing when he had failed to answer his mobile on numerous occasions; when she had rung the pub, she had been alarmed to be told that he had disappeared without notice and left no forwarding address. Her description of him included the fact that he had a tattoo on his back of a dragon.

Fisher had the feeling that this might just be the first step on the ladder of promotion.

But then, every week he had the feeling that he was going to win the lottery and have people to do everything for him and he was still wiping his own bottom.

They stood side by side over the corpse that was now turned on its front, as Beverley held a photograph out at arm's length that they were now both peering at. Lancefield stood to Beverley's left and slightly behind, Fisher in a symmetrical position to Eisenmenger's right; there was an air of triumph about him, one that was difficult to define but that was undoubtedly present, like a faint whiff of body odour. Lancefield had the distinct impression he was anticipating some fairly hefty thanks. When Beverley said, 'It's the same tattoo,' Lancefield thought that the atmosphere became noticeably more oppressive.

'I would say so,' agreed Eisenmenger.

She turned to Fisher immediately. 'Right, I want to know everything about Malcolm Willoughby by this time tomorrow, by which

I mean *everything*. I don't give a shit if you think it's irrelevant, because I don't give a shit what you think. Got that?'

Which was all that Fisher got by way of congratulation.

Sammy Carter was cooking tea when his son, Shaun, came in. Sammy was short and burly; although he had endured thirty-five years of working outdoors, and his face and hands were consequently weathered to leather, his eyes were still as bright and blue as the day he had married, and he had still retained a kindly smile. His cooking repertoire was not broad; neither was it wide; indeed, it could not be said to be anything other than shallow. Eggs, rice, oven chips and things in tins tended to form the outermost parameters of his culinary horizon; when he was planning to spend the evening in the local, this horizon contracted to a frozen, ready-cooked meal for two out of Lidl.

Shaun was taller than his father, but just as burly. He was also less easy-going and, his father admitted to himself sometimes as he worked, more arrogant; just like his mother, he thought. During the course of the year, Sammy spent a lot of time alone in his job – in the tractor or perhaps fencing – and he thereby had a lot of time to consider matters; over the years he had done a great deal of consideration of a good many matters. This was not deep, philosophical rumination – he did not, for instance, wonder about the significance of the God particle, or why increasing economic prosperity did not result in increasing personal contentment – but he did wonder about his lot in life, about how his life had changed so dramatically fifteen years before when Carol had died, leaving him to bring up Shaun on his own, about how difficult things had been, about how Betty had helped him through the early days, become something of a grandmother to the boy. He had always been a difficult youngster. Sammy knew well that, in his absence whilst he worked on the estate, Betty had had trouble bringing Shaun round to something even vaguely resembling proper behaviour at the start, and he knew that she had not succeeded entirely; there still remained in Shaun's eyes a glimmer of defiance, spark of contrariness. He contented herself with the knowledge that it was only a glimmer, only a spark, that without Betty's guidance, Shaun might have gone seriously wrong.

He did worry, though, that his son had yet to find his place in life. A job on the estate had been his for the asking, but aside from an interest in shooting, Shaun had never really been interested in

agricultural pursuits. He had gone through a series of false starts
– car mechanic, work on a building site, mortician and, most recently
and disastrously, charity worker – and was now employed as general
labour in Silverstone's, a local junk yard.

Shaun, as usual, was less than garrulous. He barely grunted as
he came in; Sammy had long ago given up asking him to take his
shoes off when he came in the house, was constantly aware that
his wife would not have taken defiance as a reason to stay silent;
he was aware, too, at how big his son was, how there was an ever
present sense of *roiling* about him. 'Good day?'

Shaun shrugged and Sammy, used to having his questions become
rhetorical by means of indifference, said, 'Supper'll be ready in
about ten minutes. There's tea in the pot.'

'OK.' His son had picked up the newspaper and was reading the
back page.

'How was work?'

Shaun shrugged by way of an answer; it was a perfect example
of non-verbal communication and it said, *Fuck off.*

But Sammy was worried. 'I was talking today to Barry Drew.'
Barry Drew was a man about town, a man of many talents, a
man you called when you wanted things found like beaters for
the shoot, or things done like gypsies moved on, or things
removed that were in the way. He dealt quite frequently with
Silverstone's.

'Yeah?' This was a thing of total disinterest; the *Sun*'s football
reporters had apparently produced copy of exceptional quality.

Sammy's four eggs seemed to require more than usual attention
as he stared at them and gently slopped hot vegetable oil over them.
He went on: 'The recession's hitting hard.'

No reaction.

'He said that a lot of the firms he did business with were having
difficulties . . .'

Shaun turned the page without looking up.

Sammy might have been overcooking the eggs, but his mind had
wandered. He said after something of a deep breath, 'Silverstone's
are having trouble, aren't they, Shaun?' His tone was almost
pleading, an attempt to enter his son's world that, despite their close
proximity for so many years, was an alien place.

Shaun at last looked up at his father, his face a mix of controlled
anger and clearly fabricated disingenuousness. 'A bit.'

'Barry said that there was a lot of short-time working.'

His son's face clouded briefly then he shrugged. 'For some. Not for me.'

Sammy stared at the eggs that were now distinctly brown and crispy around the edges for a moment, then he nodded. 'Good.'

Thereafter, their meal went as it usually did; that is to say, wordlessly, except for the chatter of *Drivetime* on Radio Two. After it was finished and Shaun had cleared the table in line with their unwritten contract, Sammy was left alone as Shaun went to his room before going out to the pub. He washed up slowly and methodically as he had always done, his hands encased in yellow rubber gloves, but his face was even more thoughtful than usual.

Barry Drew had been quite certain that Shaun Carter was on short-time working.

He wondered where his son was spending his extra spare time.

THIRTY-ONE
he could die with some dignity restored

Consciousness came to Len Barker slowly, like a warm blanket, a thing that stifled him as it gave him life. With it there was intense pain that he could not localize, together with nausea and giddiness. He was on his side, on the hard, cold floor and it was dark. What had happened? For some moments he found no recall, no light of any kind either around him or within him. Had he been attacked? He felt as if he had been kicked, certainly. Gradually, though, his eyes took in the darkness, made dim sense of it. He was in his small kitchen, close to the fridge-freezer, his head a thing of pain and, he now appreciated, blood; it covered half his face, had pooled around on the floor; he could not move to touch his scalp but he was fairly sure there was a deep gash in it.

He began to remember. He had been unable to sleep, so consumed with the idea that he had to make someone listen to him about the white van; he had finally decided that he would have to do something about it. His sudden recollection of the shopping list in the kitchen had seemed like a brilliant idea; it was a small whiteboard on the wall by the cooker, used by the carers when he was running low on stuff. Once a week on Friday, whoever was the carer on duty would travel into Ledbury and get whatever was on it. If he could get from his bedroom and down the short corridor, the white-board would be within easy reach. He would have to walk, though, because he could not control the wheelchair and anyway it was out of reach in another room.

At first he had thought he wouldn't even be able to get out of bed, let alone stagger from room to room. There were handles suspended from the ceiling to allow him to pull himself up the bed, but actually sitting upright and then swinging his legs over was a wholly different proposition. He did not know how long it took, but he knew very well indeed how much strain and effort it required; he felt as if he had wrestled a python by the time he sat on the side of the mattress, the covering sheet rucked into a ball, his useless right arm hanging down, curled, beside him. Thankfully it was a small room and he could reach out with his left hand to touch the wardrobe handle; by pulling on it he reckoned to be able to lever himself up onto his feet, then use it as a crutch. He could then pull himself towards it, and begin his nocturnal journey by leaning on first the wardrobe, then the chest of drawers, then the door frame and so out into the hall.

Everything almost went pear-shaped from the first. As he pulled on the wardrobe handle to lift himself off the bed, the whole thing began to pivot forward, threatening to pin him between its bulk and the bed, crushing the breath out of him; he had hoped that there would be more than enough in it, especially in the two deep drawers at its base, to take his weight, but it was a close run thing, a moment of uncertainty, when it could have gone either way. Eventually, though, he was up, the wardrobe was back at the horizontal, and suddenly he felt elated. Months of frustration at being impotent and patronized made this small victory a significant one for him; he still possessed some independence.

And the journey from there to the door and beyond, although slow and exhausting and jerky, proved similarly exhilarating. With every shuffle forward, he gained confidence and regained pride, stood a little straighter, became a little happier, despite the thin, cold stream of spittle that would not stop oozing down from the corner of his drooping mouth. He clung to the scuffed, cool emul-sion of the hallway, feeling more and more a man again. He reached the open doorway of the small kitchen, stood there for a moment, aware of how cold the flat was, breathing heavily, feeling tired despite his triumph, then moved forward again, intending to stagger the short distance to the nearby work surface where he whiteboard had been fitted to the wall. It would require only a controlled fall.

He misjudged the distance, perhaps through overconfidence, perhaps through exhaustion, perhaps through increasing hypothermia. He had fallen forward, struck his head upon the sharp edge of the cooker and lost consciousness at once.

Once again, he came to almost imperceptibly, the deep darkness and cavernous silence leaving little evidence of what was unconsciousness, what was awareness. He felt so stiff, so numb, so groggy, yet not at all cold.

He had once attended a post-mortem on a man who had died of exposure and the pathologist had told him that in the later stages the victim loses all sense of cold, feels only tired. Was that happening to him? How could he die of exposure in his own home?

All the feelings of resentment and frustration and anger returned to him, his previous nascent impression of progress, of dawning belief that he was not written off, not forever a cripple, gone into a vapour as insubstantial as his dreams. He had to let them know what he saw. He had to. He would not let this fucking awful stroke beat him, not at this, not when it came to police work.

For a long time – he knew not how long – he lay there, trying to overcome the helplessness, to use his brain in a way that had become foreign to him since the stroke. He could not hope to reach the whiteboard now, nor any piece of paper, let alone writing tool. He would have to use whatever he could to leave a message. If he lived until morning, then all well and good; if he didn't, and he could let them know what he knew, then he could die with some dignity restored.

Beverley descended on Fisher as soon as she got into the police station; his knowledge of the works of Byron was such that he had never heard of the Assyrian and his descent upon the fold but, had it been otherwise, he might well have spotted similarities. 'What have you got for me?' There was a glint in her eye that told even Fisher – his knowledge of body language as meagre as his knowledge of poetry – that she wanted results. She loomed over him as he sat at his desk in the office he shared with Lancefield, the window behind her so that she acquired a spectral, deathly appearance, a thing of wrathful shadow.

Fisher was slow and he was woefully short of imagination, but he was methodical. He had written down in untidy, sprawling, misspelled handwriting the products of his labours. He found this, put it flat on the desk, cleared his throat and began to read while Beverley settled herself in a chair facing him. 'I've interviewed his mother—' he began.

'For fuck's sake, I hope you trod carefully, Fisher. You didn't go in there telling her she had lost her only child without first checking we've got the right body, did you?'

Fisher was hurt. 'I got her to show me a recent photograph first. It is him.'

If he thought to receive some praise, he was to be disappointed, and not for the first time. 'Go on,' she commanded.

'Malcolm Willoughby was twenty-six years old. Cheltenham born and bred, until two years ago, he was living at home with his mother; his father died seven years ago. He left school at sixteen with two GCSEs, then drifted through a series of dead-end jobs, mainly bar-keeping; his mother says that the death of his father affected him very badly. She says that he had no enemies and everyone liked him.'

As far as Beverley was concerned, any character reference from a mother about a son might just as well be written on toilet paper and used immediately. 'When did she last see him?'

'Six days ago. He was working as a barman at The Grey Goose.'

'That shithole on the Tewkesbury Road?'

'That's the one.'

'Have you spoken to them?'

'Willoughby disappeared four days ago. It wasn't that he was dismissed, or anything. He just didn't turn up for the morning shift.'

'Nothing untoward happened? No fight, or anything?'

Fisher shook his head.

'Have you checked the databases?'

Thankfully, Fisher had and was able to say that he had. 'Nothing.'

'Nothing?' she didn't believe it. People like Malcolm Willoughby – people who failed at all the hurdles that you had leap to function in modern western society – inevitably drifted into crime, no matter how petty, no matter how pathetic.

Fisher was confident. 'No.'

She was impressed by his certainty. 'OK,' she said, deciding to give him the benefit of the doubt, happy that she would be able to flay him and then incinerate the remains if he had missed something. She ran through what she had been told, sifted it for gold and found nothing. She was understandably disappointed, though; surely there was something in this little man's past to indicate why someone had taken the trouble to broil him?

She turned abruptly and left Fisher with his thoughts, such as they were; she went straight up to her office where Lancefield was just putting the phone down. 'Who was that?' she demanded.

'Press. They've heard something about the body on the allotments.'

'You didn't tell them anything?' Beverley's tone was threatening.

'I said that I didn't know a thing about it. They asked where you were and I said I didn't know.'

Mollified, Beverley nodded. 'Good.' She sat down, beckoned Lancefield to do likewise; then she explained what Fisher had learned.

'What do you want me to do?'

'Go through those clips on the web posting. Go through them again and again and again. See if you can spot anything that might identify the location.'

'It's got to be isolated.'

'And I'd wager large.'

Lancefield frowned. 'A rich psychopath?'

Beverley snorted. 'Maybe. Or a poor one who's squatting in a large house. Or one who's a servant of a rich man. Or maybe it's a hangar, or an abandoned farm, or any one of a million possibilities.'

Lancefield took the hint. She left to follow orders.

THIRTY-TWO
a shiny bright, smooth and almost beautiful needle

There is nothing touching in the fact that Melanie and Evangeline Whittaker died together in a parody of the companionship that they had failed to find in life. They had come to – Evangeline first, her mother some twenty minutes later after her daughter's loud, incessant and hoarse shouting – finding themselves facing each other at two ends of a long, dark corridor. They were both strapped into wooden chairs that were bolted to the floor. Melanie was groggy, confused and her daughter had to shout again. 'Mum!'

'Angel?' She had not used this term of endearment for five years. There was fear in her voice and it made her sound pathetic; it was her curse that Melanie Whittaker somehow always sounded *wrong*; when she became too excited, she sounded raucous; when she was angry, she became shrill; now she was scared witless, she sounded merely witless.

'What's happening, Mum?' Evangeline's voice was cloyed with tears; she was so terrified that even years of disdain for her mother counted for nothing.

Her mother, of course, did not know, could not even find the words to admit this. Confused, she merely pulled ineffectually at the metal bonds, only dimly aware that they were naked, not at all aware that they were covered in sensors and electrodes, that they had been shaved. She did not even appreciate that her left forearm hurt terribly, at least not until Evangeline asked again, and in a voice that was barely less than a screech, 'Mum? Mum? What the fuck's going on?' Melanie had never been a particularly sharp knife and the present circumstances proved far too tough for her to cut through; she could barely articulate, barely even concentrate. Evangeline asked (and perhaps it was more out of hope than expectation of a useful, coherent answer), 'What's with the tubes?'

'Uh?' Melanie Whittaker frowned, unable to understand such a complex question.

'The tubes . . . in our arms.'

Melanie looked down – still frowning, still confused – and saw through clouds of bewilderment that crudely inserted into her left forearm was a shiny bright, smooth and almost beautiful needle, as wide as a knitting needle; it was strapped into place with parcel tape and led to a clear plastic tube that snaked away to large glass jar on the floor.

And it hurt, she came slowly to realize.

God, how it hurt . . .

There was a click that Evangeline heard, her mother didn't. The girl looked around, unable to see its source, then noticing the tube leading from her mother's arm; it was now red and this redness was splashing remorselessly into the jar by her feet. She looked down to see that her own tube, her own jar, was similarly filling with blood.

At which she point she screamed.

THIRTY-THREE
'at least she died quickly'

Eisenmenger was not insensitive enough to be unaware that Beverley was stressed; as he gave her the results of the body on the allotment's autopsy, he could hear her staccato, almost reflexive replies, and hear in them someone who was waiting to receive an Epiphany; and hear in them someone who was realizing that he was not its bearer. When she asked him how the search of people with mesothelioma was going – and, perhaps more to the point, he admitted that he had not yet started it – she exploded down the phone line at him.

'Why the fuck not?'

'I told you, Beverley. There are ethical considerations.'

'This is murder, John. This isn't a debate at the Royal Society of fucking Medicine. This isn't an intellectual game, a parlour conversation, a late-night television chat show.'

'I do know that.'

'The fuck you do. You're letting me down, John. Big time.'

She had slammed the phone down on him with that, leaving him alone with a feeling of failure. Perhaps she was right. Perhaps he should stop being so limp-wristed. He had, after all, gone into dangerously unethical territory before in his career and come out alive. Perhaps he should once again consider the greater good.

Without conscious consideration, he found himself setting up the search of the pathology database almost without real zing it. It was a laborious process, since the Trust computer system was in IT terms primitive, pre-Stone Age, the era of slick user interfaces far, far in its future; he would have to run the search overnight because there wasn't enough computing power to allow it to be run when it was needed for clinics and ward-based enquiries. The Trust had been discussing a new system for several years now – had almost got one before being ordered to stop by the Department of Health because of the coming of the integrated NHS IT system, a fiasco that had wasted billions and set health-care back years.

As he entered the search parameters, the question why?' kept occurring, kept resounding almost in his skull. Was it purely for justice that he did this? Was he really so wedded to law enforcement and the pursuit of felons – even a felon committing crimes as heinous as these – that he was willing to break the law? Was that really his motive? Or was it some other reason? And, if so, what was it?

Did he feel in some way beholden to Beverley, so that he had to risk, potentially at least, his career? Of course, it wasn't the first time that he had broken one law in order to ensure that the breaker of another, more serious law, was apprehended; he was prone, he now saw, to a sort of intellectual vigilantism, going after criminals by any means, foul or fair, that he considered appropriate; not that he thought himself likely to turn into a true blue caped crusader, operating forever on the far edge of the law, perhaps resorting when the occasion demanded to bloodshed. Yet he was increasingly finding himself frustrated by the restrictions of modern British society where, in an effort to prevent the iniquities that arise when there are only black and white, everything had been turned into a soup of grey, without even any shades. The law of data protection was enforced more energetically than the law of theft (even aggravated theft), because it was easier to do so. Eisenmenger had a problem with that; he did not see all laws as equal, no matter what the high priests of jurisprudence might have to say, not when those charged with enforcing those laws claimed the right to choose between them.

So that was his motive.

Except he feared that it wasn't just that, because once again he was finding himself wondering just what Beverley Wharton meant to him.

Beverley slammed the phone down and everyone around her was aware that she was not a happy bunny rabbit. It was left to Lancefield to approach her and, through the open doorway of her office, ask, 'Bad news?'

'Eisenmenger says that the latest body died of electrocution, just like the last, only this time it was quick, as might occur in execution or accidental electrocution.'

Fisher ventured, 'Well, at least she died quickly.' This earned him a malevolent stare and he shut up.

Beverley continued, 'The tox results have come back on the first two deaths. Apparently there were significant levels of Flunitrazepam in the urine of both, but not in their blood.'

A question hung in the air – *And so?* – but Fisher was too scared to ask it. Lancefield, to his relief, wasn't. 'Is that significant?'

'It means that they were drugged to get them wherever they died, but they were fully awake and aware when they died. Flunitrazepam is Rohypnol, the date rape drug.'

This they understood. Lancefield said with consideration, 'It's not a lead, though. Rohypnol is freely available on the Internet.' It was a piece of wisdom that earned her no praise.

'Then find me one, inspector.'

THIRTY-FOUR
the address struck a chime

Mr Leonard William Barker, aged 57 years.
Address: Flat 5, Hedgelands, Sandy Lane, Bromsberrow Heath, HR8 1XX
Occupation: retired policeman.
Information Received: *Mr Barker was a widower, living in sheltered accommodation with carers looking after all his daily needs following a stroke in 2009 which left him wheelchair bound and unable to speak. He was found on the kitchen floor in a pool of blood from a gash to his head. He is believed to have fallen having hit his head on the corner of the cooker where there are bloodstains. The house is secure. There are three empty whisky bottles in the kitchen cupboard.*
Information from GP: *Until his stroke, Mr Barker had been an infrequent visitor to the surgery. He had suffered from hypertension, haemorrhoids and problems with alcohol abuse.*

As E60s – the request for a post-mortem examinaticn received from the coroner's office – went, it wasn't bad. It was a step up from those that merely said, effectively, *Found Dead*, or those that tried to tell the pathologist what the autopsy result should be: *'Is believed to have had a heart attack'*, or *'Probably struck by lightning'*. Those that worked for the coroner were not necessarily in any way medically qualified and they did their best to interpret the jargon that was fed to them; in this case, Eisenmenger felt that he had at least been given a fighting chance of a reasonable context in which to begin the autopsy.

Somewhere at the back of his head, the address struck a chime; it was where Malcolm Willoughby had been found.

Lancefield had been tasked with checking the website regularly and she found herself becoming more and more tense as, each time she did, it was unchanged. She ought, she thought to be relieved, but she found that she couldn't be; the new posting was coming, she was certain, and all she could feel was a clock ticking down, all she could see in her head was a stream of sand running through a timer.

She had had no inkling, of course, when at last it came; she felt first shock, then elation, then relief, then dread when she saw it, all experienced in a moment, all flushing through her system one after the other, surging, singing, screaming. She looked up, saw Beverley in her office through the half-opened door, called out in a voice that was unintentionally hoarse, 'Sir? There's a new posting.'

'Was the flat heated?'

Mark Sheraton was a good coroner's officer; he was brilliant with the bereaved families, he understood that the pathologists wanted relevant facts that might bear on the cause of death, not meaningless gossip or random facts thrown in as if they were telling a story to a child; in the coroner's court, he read out the written reports with some fluency and authority. 'To be honest, I don't know,' he admitted. Eisenmenger was talking to him on the phone from the mortuary office while Clive was cleaning up.

'Find out, will you, Mark?'

'You think it might be hypothermia?'

'All the signs are there.' By which he meant that there was no other obvious reason why Len Barker had died that evening, and there were a few vague changes at autopsy that could have been caused by hypothermia.

'OK, I'll make some enquiries.'

'Until then, it's "unascertained", I'm afraid.'

Mark Sheraton took this well, although it would mean the inquest process would be set in motion, which meant work for him. 'I half thought it would go "forensic" to be honest. What with him writing in the blood from his head wound. Very melodramatic. The constable who was called out by the carer even got CID in, but they're happy there was nothing untoward; the flat was secure and nothing was taken. Must have been confused, I suppose.'

Eisenmenger had barely heard the last few sentences. 'He did what?'

'Oh, yes. I didn't tell you because it didn't seem relevant.'

For once, a coroner's officer had not put in acres of meaningless anecdote and Eisenmenger wished he had. 'What did he write?'

'It was fairly difficult to decipher, but it looked like a car registration number.'

Occupation: retired policeman. Eisenmenger found himself assaulted by a feeling he knew too well, an itch deep within him, where disparate facts were coinciding.

'And?'

'And what?' Mark Sheraton did not understand.

'Whose registration was it?'

'I'm not sure.'

'Mark, do me a favour and find out, will you?'

'If you say so, Doc, but why? It's not going to alter things is it?'

Eisenmenger did not at first know what to say. 'Probably not, Mark. Not in this case, anyway.'

Betty Williams had not been feeling very well for most of the day. She had no appetite and had vomited twice already. Her chest hurt, too; there was a burning in the middle of her chest but she had had that before and it was just heartburn. For lunch the day before she had finished some chicken that had been in the fridge for some time – she wasn't sure how long – and she had at first put everything down to this ('just a drop of gippy tummy' as she remembered her mother used to say), especially when she had almost had an accident as her bowels suddenly became loose. But she had lived long enough to know that this was different, that she should not be breathless, or so clammy, or so, so tired.

THIRTY-FIVE

'warn him what he is about to see'

This one was ten, a hundred, a million times, worse. This one was not just two people dying, not just a snuff movie portrayed as the graphical (and graphic) illustrations for a pseudo-scientific paper on what dying is; no, this was one was a love affair with the subject, a forever-lingering caress of it, a thesis as opposed to a hypothesis.

The title – 'Further Observations on the Physiological, Morphological and Metaphysical Changes that Occur at the Point of Death; Death By Electrocution' – was suitably turgid and the following introduction could have been describing experiments on locusts, so dry and clinical was the tone, so willing to put 'scientific' enquiry about emotion. Indeed, so formal and cold was it, that they did not read it at any depth, for it quickly bored them. The appendices, though . . . As before there were two main ones, each detailing a death; one was rapid, one was protracted; from each of these was a large number of hyperlinks in which various physiological parameters were displayed in real time as the subjects sat in the electric chair. For one, the woman, the moment of death, as the current surged, peaked, and died within a hundred milliseconds, was brief in real time, and perhaps too brief for the author, because a further hyperlink slowed this, with all the attendant physiological reactions, down a thousandfold. For the second subject, the man, there was no need of such artifice, for his agony was so prolonged as to be a marathon of death, slow crawl of excruciation; and for this the viewer could watch all five hours, or dip in and out at will, picking the choicest morsels of a man's agonizing death.

They could not watch it all, not even Beverley. Fisher gave in first, perhaps because of his youth and innocence, perhaps because of a less eroded humanity; then Lancefield left, when the atmosphere in the room had grown dark and dense with dread, and disbelief and shock. They both mumbled apologies, but they need not have done and, indeed, were barely heard. In the end, Beverley had to skip through the last two hours, a dreadful parody of sporting highlights, and even she felt sick at the end, drained to the point of exsanguination, saddened to the point of despair. She had in her career come into contact with men and woman who were scarcely human in their depravity, who would think nothing of rape, of murder, of torture or mutilation, but she could not see any of them behind this; this was off the scale of inhumanity, the knob turned beyond eleven, into the realms of *un*humanity, the kind of thing an interested extraterrestrial might do, one who had lifted a rock, and found a man, and wanted to find out a little bit about him.

She took ten minutes to compose herself before going to the door and calling for Lancefield. She hoped that she didn't look too pale, and that she wasn't trembling, as she said, 'Tell Eisenmenger about this. Tell him we need him to read the paper, but warn him, Lancefield. Warn him what he is going to see.'

Lancefield said nothing, merely nodded. She hoped that there was no sign of sick on her clothing

Having been to the doctor's once in the past six years (and that against her will when she had felt slightly faint in church and the then vicar – who had been almost as old as she was and, she was sure, gay – had insisted she be seen), Betty Williams considered herself to have little need of medical services. Indeed, she had only been in hospital once – when she had fallen and broken her ankle twelve years before – and hated the idea of dependence. From what she read in the papers, hospitals were dangerous places, anyway. Now, though, she knew that she needed help.

She reached for the phone.

Braxton had insisted on seeing the website, and Beverley had left him to it; she noted with wry and decidedly sour amusement that he summoned her back to his office after only forty-five minutes; far too little time to have done anything other than skim the delights on offer. Even so, she saw that he looked distinctly grey as she sat down before his desk.

'We've got to get this bastard, Beverley.' Which was a truism and so she did not feel obliged to respond. 'I mean, Jesus Christ . . .' The blasphemy was uncharacteristic and therefore significant. He sighed. 'What do you need?'

She didn't understand at first, because she was so constrained by experience; investigations were these days resourced at minimum level, the ever-present mantra one of 'efficiency'. He explained irritably, 'Personnel, back-room staff, overtime, IT . . . Anything, Beverley. I'll clear it. Just make sure that you get him before he does any more of this . . .' He lost the words for a moment, a man shaken from his vocabulary by horrific things, visions from hell's own abattoir. ' . . atrocity.'

As welcome as this offer was, she could suck little comfort from the unexpected almost unprecedented words, found it ironic that for once she had no need of it. 'At the moment, we don't need them. We've only identified a single victim and had no leads from his disappearance.'

Braxton looked pained, approaching angry. 'For goodness' sake, Beverley. Why?'

And she had to explain, although she suspected he knew as well as she did. With only one victim identified, by definition there could be no pattern to recognize, and in cases like this, pattern was everything. With but a single point, there could be no connections.

'Are there no clues from the previous video clips?'

'Lancefield has been going through them repeatedly. Nothing. They're just dark rooms.'

'Someone will have to do the same with these new ones.' He looked at her as he said this, aware of what he was suggesting. It was not news to Beverley, though; she nodded impassively. Braxton then said slowly, 'I'm coming under pressure, Beverley. From above.'

Of course he was; pressure from 'above' was a constant for all middle- to high-ranking detectives; it was as constant and inevitable as gravity, and equally unforgiving; it was also as likely to flatten the unwary if it became too strong. She said nothing so he continued, 'The press are sniffing and there are all sorts of rumours circulating apparently; they seem to have got hold of the idea that these murders are worthy of sensation.' She could not tell if he was being sarcastic or not; if the truth of these particular killings got out, if the context of pseudoscientific investigation and the colossal callousness of the way that people were being slaughtered became known, 'sensational' would be revealed as a completely inadequate epithet, a fig leaf to cover a blue whale's erection. It would come out eventually, of course, but not, she fervently hoped, until after an arrest. He continued, 'Is everyone on the team sound?'

By which she presumed he meant 'trustworthy', rather than pure of tone. She nodded. 'That's the beauty of keeping the team small, at least until we've got more leads to follow.'

He grunted softly. 'Well, just make sure you ask as soon as you need the support. I don't want this bugger getting away just because you're too stubborn to ask for help.'

She bit down on her immediate reply; she did not think that she had ever before been accused of being backward in requesting extra resources; if anything, she had thought she had a reputation of agitating too often for more money and men. 'I won't,' she promised with a tight smile.

THIRTY-SIX
'such a sweet old thing'

B etty Williams had been sick three times now and her breathlessness was increasing. She knew that she was dying and was very afraid. She sat in her favourite armchair, the gas fire on low, the clock ticking softly but menacingly. There was no pain but her chest was constricted, as if she were confined by an overtight corset; distressed as she was, the thought brought her fleeting remembrance of her life sixty years before. She was sweating, but was not hot, and she was feeling light-headed, much as she had done two Christmases before when she had drunk too much port at Sammy's house.

Where was the ambulance?

The door bell rang.

Her heart lifted.

The call from her father came through to Lancefield just as she was making her way to the canteen; she had just rung Eisenmenger and told him about his homework. 'Dad?' She knew that something was wrong because her father was scrupulous about not disturbing her work for trivialities. 'What is it?'

She knew what it was, though. Only one thing would make him phone her at work. 'It's your mother, Becky. She's taken a turn for the worse. Doctor says it's pneumonia.'

'Is she in hospital?'

The hesitation told her much, was as informative as an hourlong speech would have been, and far more illuminating than a flash of lightning. He said only, 'She wouldn't want it.' The tone was defensive, as she had come to expect.

She felt riven by a host of thoughts and emotions, all conflicting, all badgering her at once. *Wouldn't she? How do you know? She's my mother! I love her! She's changed. She would welcome death. She's*

*a fighter. She's the one who should decide. You've fallen out of love
with her. You only loved Tim. I know that you had an affair...*

He said, 'I told the doctor she should just be kept comfortable.'

Because she suddenly felt corrosive rage towards him, and
because she knew that she was being unfair, and because she was
about to fall over the edge into tears that would sound in her voice
and would be seen by those around in the main corridor of the
police station, and because she was running out of words, she said
only, 'I'm coming over.'

Josh and Harriet had had their tea and Antonia had supervised their
baths; as a treat they were staying up to watch DVDs in the small
but cosy sitting room. Antonia was sipping a cup of Earl Grey tea
while she read the *Telegraph* when Andrew came in from a trip to
the local supermarket. As he plonked the linen bag down on the
pitted surface of the pine table, he said at once, 'Have you heard
the news?'

'What news is that, dear?' she asked after they had exchanged
embraces.

'Poor Betty Williams,' he said, taking off his ancient green jacket
that still smelled faintly of tobacco even after fifteen years of abstinence. 'She's passed away.' He sounded slightly incredulous as if
he had had it on the best authority that she had been immortal,
perhaps even had a small wager on her continued refusal to join
the bleeding choir invisible.

'Oh, no.' Antonia was genuinely shocked. She had liked Betty
Williams, although she had sometimes found her a little *uncouth*.
'How?'

'I'm not sure. As I was coming past, I saw the ambulance outside
and Marcus Pilcher and Sammy Carter were just coming out from
the house. I managed to snatch a few words with them, but they
could only tell me that the paramedics had just pronounced life
extinct.'

'Oh, dear.' And she meant this. 'Oh dear, oh dear, oh dear . . .'
This last was a sighing lament, an ululation for the entire concept
of death and dying as much as for the demise of a single little old
lady. 'She was such a sweet old thing.'

Andrew knew better than to take her to task for this bending of
the truth; in his opinion, Betty Williams had been an over-curious,
slightly unwashed and certainly wickedly-tongued harridan, and he
could remember his wife uttering similar sentiments on more than

one occasion. He said blandly, 'Absolutely.' He found it best to be bland on occasion.

Her passing was thus remarked.

THIRTY-SEVEN

'I'm not being patronizing, Charlie'

C harlie had had enough and, perhaps due to her Irish ancestry, perhaps because she was slightly drunk, she did not stint in a demonstration of her exasperated disbelief.

'You are joking, aren't you, John?'

Eisenmenger had a sense of humour, he was certain, although it was perhaps slightly stiff through underuse, perhaps even atrophied; an appendix of amusement. He, too, was less than sober. 'About this? No.'

The remains of the meal lay between them, the second bottle of wine only half full (but only half empty, he caught himself thinking as they looked at each other over this battleground full of the dead). They were in his flat – a temporary abode, not to his taste, between Montpellier and Sussex Parade – and he had cooked a half-decent coq au vin (even if he did say so himself, because Charlie hadn't), followed by rum baba. She was wearing a low-cut pale green dress in Grecian style and he had had trouble not noticing how low-cut it was.

'Can't it wait?'

'I'm afraid not.'

'This is becoming a habit.'

'That's not fair.'

'Yes, it is, John. It's bloody fair. I've hardly seen anything of you over the past couple of weeks, and every time I have, you've cut it short.'

'I don't enjoy this life either, Charlie. Sometimes, it's intolerable.'

'You can say that again.'

This invitation, as per custom, was not accepted. Instead, he said weakly (and was well aware how pusillanimous the words were), 'It shouldn't take long.' He was thinking as he said this that this might be wishful thinking, might perhaps be an exaggeration, might even – were he in a state to be objective – be a lie.

'What have you got to do?'

'Look at a posting on the web from the killer.'

'Is that all?'

He smiled; he tried to make it a friendly, reassuring smile, but perhaps he failed for when he said, 'It's not that simple . . .' she flared.

'What the hell is going on here, John? Why are you constantly blocking me out?'

'I'm not . . .'

The flare became an incandescence, an explosion. 'YES, YOU ARE!' She actually rose from her seat, a slight lift-off, one that did not achieve escape velocity and so she touched down again. Her vehemence tore a hole between them, a vacuum that she felt forced to fill while the shock of her shouting left him momentarily silent. 'Yes, you are, John,' she continued in a low, urgent voice. 'You do your thing, and I'm told you do it very well. I *know* you do it very well, because I can see what kind of person you are. You are intellectual, you are kind, you are dedicated, you are, somehow, *spooky*.' He hoisted eyebrows at that, but she nodded enthusiastically. 'I've spoken to the mortuary man, Clive, and that's what he told me; he said that everyone says so.' This encomium was allowed to stand for less than a second as she added apologetically, 'But you're a loss as a human being.' She stood, an almost reflexive action, way below the level of rational thought. It was completely unapologetically that she said, 'No wonder Helena left you.'

Then, clearly to him aware that she had gone beyond the pale, she murmured, 'I'm sorry.'

He didn't answer, was transfixed by this conclusion, speared, pinned, wriggling to the wall and feeling only the pain of its penetration, and a certain degree of windedness, as if he were unable to breathe. He didn't even move, just sat on his chair, staring, his thoughts active and turbulent, but a long way from his mind, a cinema show in the background that he was distracted from. She came around the table to him. 'John, I am so sorry. I didn't mean to say that . . .'

But you did, and just because you didn't mean to say it, does that not imply that it was in your head, unsaid, but very much alive, a worm of a thought, a mealy-mouthed little thing burrowing away into their relationship.

She sat next to him, reached for him and, as they embraced, she whispered, 'I am so sorry, John. It was an unforgiveable thing to say.'

He was bathed in her perfume and that brought with it memories of other times that he had been bathed in it – memories that were still fresh, still exciting – and these fought with his hurt, so that he felt confused, but still overwhelmingly desirous of her. They kissed, at first an almost formal thing – a tentative gesture that was effectively a mutual offer of reconciliation – but then rapidly it became passionate, and for him healing.

Very much against his better judgement, Eisenmenger let Charlie view the latest web posting with him. 'It's not comfortable, Charlie. This one is seriously, seriously disturbed.'

'I know that, John. Remember, I saw his first posting.'

'This one is worse, apparently.' It wasn't so much Lancefield's words as her voice that came back to Eisenmenger. *Chief Inspector Wharton asked me to say to you that this one is bad. Be warned that the video attachments are difficult to watch.* 'I'm not being patronizing, Charlie, but you're not a criminal psychologist, are you? These postings contain a lot of tough material.'

'I've had some exposure of criminal psychology, John.' Her tone had been edged with hurt honed by pride. 'I'm not completely unused to this sort of thing.'

But she had insisted and he did not want to push her away, not after what she had said over dinner, and so they sat side by side in front of the computer screen. That they were slightly drunk and each had a glass of red wine, only added to a sense of unreality; it might have been a scene from Buñuel, the bourgeoisie at play. They read through the 'paper', he making notes, she adding comments.

The synopsis of the conclusions held a surprise, though. Eisenmenger pointed at the text. 'What does that mean?'

> *The physiological readings – in particular careful analysis of the EEG and ECG – have revealed an anomaly which corresponds with an unexplained observational phenomenon at the point of death in both subjects. Such a correlation was not possible in the previous study because of the nature of the execution . . .*

Charlie shook her head, a frown appearing slightly asymmetrically on her face. They read on. The introduction was mostly a rehash of the previous introduction, referring back to it, and full of pseudo-scientific ponderings about the nature of life, even once referring to it as 'vitalism'. The methods section described in uncomfortable detail what had been done to Malcolm Willoughby and the as yet unidentified female; the voltage and current used in her killing, the rate of increase of both in his. It told of their height and weight (and thus the all-important body mass index), although it did not mention their ages, or any other datum that might have helped identify them. All the physiological parameters that were monitored were listed.

And then to the results section, as any good scientific paper would do but, unlike a conventional paper, constant reference was made to the appendices, to the video recordings of the subjects and the parametric readings. It soon became clear that they were going to have to keep accessing these, although Eisenmenger said nothing until Charlie said, 'Shouldn't we be looking at these hyperlinks? The text keeps referring to them and I think we'd have a better chance of understanding what's going on if we saw them.'

'I'm not sure . . .'

'If we're going to understand this psychopath, the more material we study, the more chance we have.'

He sighed. 'OK, but not the visual recordings.'

'Why not? The text refers to specific events, especially during the course of the male subject's death, which are correlated with the physiological readings.'

'These are snuff movies, Charlie. They depict people being killed for real.'

'I've got a strong stomach, John. I enjoy gore in the cinema as much as most other people. There's no need to namby-pamby me.'

'There's a difference between watching a Hollywood horror film and witnessing someone being executed, someone suffering real pain.'

'Please, John, I am not a child.'

He did not want her seeing the videos but her voice was becoming strained again. He had found the first posting hard going and Lancefield's warning coming on top of this had given him the heebie-jeebies; was he willing to let Charlie experience something so awful, so unique? Yet, she was right; he had no right to act as her guardian, to mollycoddle her; she was an adult, and an intelligent one who was trained in understanding the mind. Perhaps, he decided, he should not be so protective.

And so, he agreed.

THIRTY-EIGHT
photos that were old because they were of the young

R ebecca had always thought her parents' bedroom was gloomy but now that her mother lay dying in it, she realized how wrong she had been; it was funereal now and it had always been so. It was as if it had been waiting for a death, as if they had decorated and furnished this slightly drab, slightly dingy room, a tableau from the seventies, with this scene specifically in mind. Her father had always been a man who was careful with money – always second-class stamps, Christmas wrapping paper reused year after year, socks darned and redarned – and he had never knowingly used a sixty-watt bulb, but the ceiling light seemed to be giving out little more than a candle's glimmer, so that the shadows were barely distinguishable, as if they were hiding in plain sight.

There had been no eye contact between them, not when she had entered the house, nor since; his head had been kept low, as had his voice; the curiously atonal quality of this near-whisper gave an air almost of worship and respect, as if they were in the presence of something supernatural, but she had known in reality it was all a charade; they were in the presence of something dying, was all; they were scared; too scared to bicker for once.

And in this all-too-apt gloom, her mother laying breathing stertorously, thin and pale, eyes half closed and filmed, mouth open. Lancefield had watched her mother imperceptibly lose humanity over the past five years, but never before had she seemed to be so empty, so inanimate; was this the dementia or the onset of death, she wondered. Was this woman – try as she might, she could not come to convince herself that here was her mother – alive or dead? That she was breathing was beyond doubt, but was it a purely mechanical thing that this body did, as decerebrate as a headless chicken?

On the other side of the bed, her father held his wife's hand and she could see that his grip was tight enough to show his knuckles white, as if he hoped that pain would bring her back to sentience, the long sought-for remedy for Alzheimer's. She had given up holding her mother's hand, gaining nothing from it other than the inescapable thought that it was too dry and too inert to be of any comfort to either of them, as if she were trying to commune with a mannequin. She spent most of her time either looking down at the bedcover – it was a sea of memories for her – and when that palled she stared at the photographs on the bedside table to the left of her father; photos that were old because they were of the young, that were nothing more to her then than reminders; reminders of how their lives had gone in both senses of the word.

They had sat there for four hours now.

They would sit there for many more.

Eisenmenger felt that, at last, he was beginning to understand what was going through this killer's head; a feeling of displacement came over him, one that was familiar. He would not go so far as to say that he came to identify with a murderer, he could not get inside the mind, but he could start to see why the murderer did certain things, what the murderer was perhaps seeking, either to find or to demonstrate. And never before had he had such a text to work on as this, so much information to sift. There was the overarching theme of *why* the murderer was doing these awful things – and that was potentially illuminating enough – but there was also the extent to which the text betrayed the beliefs, the experiences, the hopes and the fears of this particular madman. It was, in effect, a manifesto, although he was sure that it had not been intended as such. His fascination grew and, accordingly, his awareness receded, and so he did not appreciate Charlie's increasing discomfort.

It started off well enough. Where the text referred them to particular time points in the various readings – EEG wave patterns, ECG complexes, oxygen saturation, respiratory rate, systolic and diastolic blood pressure, skin resistance – they followed the link; when it referred them to various points in the video presentations – and there were twelve camera views in each – Eisenmenger was at first very aware of Charlie's reactions. The execution of the as yet unknown woman had been slowed a thousand fold, so that reference in the text could be made to points in the course of her death separated by less than a hundredth of a second, and because of this, she hardly seemed to move as the current surged through her and overwhelming agony had overcome her. As far as Eisenmenger could see, Charlie seemed to cope with this, maintaining an objective demeanour, her remarks pertinent and made in a controlled voice. He had begun to relax, to think that he had been unnecessarily protective of her; and, in so doing, had begun to lose himself in the task.

What was this particular mad man after? To capture the point of death was the obvious, trite response to that, but why? Why the desire to chase down something that, to Eisenmenger at least, seemed as elusive as the end of the rainbow, as real as the boundary between two consecutive seconds? Death might in the popular imagination be a single thing, or even a single entity (replete with scythe and skeleton eyes), but to a biologist, it was a fading, a gradual disequilibrium, an entropic dismemberment of homeostasis; consciousness was not a binary state – either on or off – but a property that arose from a breathtakingly large number of biochemical processes occurring at a molecular level; he knew that it was a property of chaotic systems that order would arise spontaneously, and he saw self-awareness as merely a higher level of such order. Just as it did not suddenly come into being, so it did not suddenly cease to exist.

Yet this man believed that it did, was convinced that he could demonstrate it happening.

It was with a shock of incredulity that he was jerked from semi-reverie by the last paragraph:

> *One finding that remains as yet unexplained but we believe to be of potential significance occurs at time point T+0.456 seconds in the first subject, and at time point T+4hours, 57minutes, 6.36 seconds in the second.*
>
> *The following hyperlinks correlate all readings and relevant visual recordings of the two subjects at these points.*

He sat up, and murmured to Charlie, 'This might be interesting.'

He moved the cursor to the first hyperlink, the one that referred to the woman's death, and the screen loaded with sixteen images, some close-up video stills, many frozen readings; he examined each carefully. It took a moment but he eventually saw with some fascination that at this moment, there had apparently been a simultaneous blip in the diastolic blood pressure, a coordinated abrupt, but brief increase in activity in both theta and delta wave activity in the brain, and a rise in skin resistance; yet the photos were the most enthralling. They were of the woman's eyes – horribly bloodshot, pupils dilated to black holes without the power of sight – and in them was a tiny, violet spark. It was tiny but sharp, even at the magnification of the still; it seemed almost to curl around lazily, as if trying to bite its tail.

Was that real? Perhaps it was just a glitch in the software; yet it was symmetrically present in the depths of both gaping pupils. A reflection, then – the head was arched back, the current surge having caused extreme spasm of the neck muscles – and so conceivably he was seeing something that was on the ceiling. But what could it be?

'Weird,' he said, half to himself, half to Charlie. She said nothing, but he didn't notice.

He turned next to the second hyperlink. The layout was similar and again the physiological readings all showed a small distinct change that, if the data were to be believed, was totally synchronous. The video images, though were harder to interpret, because they came at the end of an ordeal of nearly five hours for poor Malcolm Willoughby; his skin was browned, cracked with fissures of dried blood; his tongue swollen and black, his eyes filmed over with coagulation; he could even make out a haze between the camera and the subject, perhaps of steam. All this made detail difficult to discern but he thought that maybe he could just make out a faint violet spark deep in the pupils, underlying the frosting of the corneas, identical to that which had just been seen in the first hyperlink.

He breathed gently. *Surely not?*

'What do you think?' he asked Charlie softly without looking at her. There was no answer, but he did not appreciate this for a moment. Then he looked at her. Her face was buried in her hands, and she was weeping whilst she shook uncontrollably.

THIRTY-NINE
a susurrating background theme

Eisenmenger was tired and he had a huge gastrointestinal cut-up to look forward; the last thing he needed was a phone call from Beverley Wharton at eight thirty, before he had even managed to switch on the microscope. He sat down, sighing and looking out of the window at the car park; there were not enough parking spaces, but then there never had been, and a member of the parking Gestapo was prowling. He knew what she wanted, but couldn't be bothered to think.

'Two more bodies.'

Shit! Shit, shit, shit! 'Where?'

'Cotswold Water Park. I need you there now.'

He was building up a huge time debt to the Trust, he knew. It was likely he would be out most of the morning, and he could not ask his colleagues, themselves stretched by NHS duties, to cover for him. He would have to do the cut-up this afternoon; presumably the post-mortem would have to be done that evening, and the rest of his work would have to wait, perhaps until the weekend. He thought guiltily of Charlie, even as he said reluctantly, 'OK.'

'I'll get a car to pick you up in ten minutes.'

And that was that; no thanks, no acknowledgement, and certainly no realization that he had troubles aplenty. He sought his phone and thought about ringing Charlie, decided to text instead. She had eventually calmed down, full of apologies and, as they went to bed at two o'clock, full of whisky. He had risen again at five, successfully not waking her and aware that he had to finish looking through the web posting. He had taken her a cup of tea at seven thirty, and she had been hung-over but seemingly not too upset. How she would react to the news that he was going to have to work late, he could not say.

Just as he was about to leave the office, his phone rang again; this time it was the coroner's office. 'You asked me to check that registration number. I'm sorry it's taken so long, but it slipped my mind.' He had forgotten as well, so could hardly criticize.

'And?'

'It belongs to the Colberrow Estate, in the north of the county.'

'Where the fuck is Lancefield?'

Fisher was always cheerful – perhaps because he was constitutionally optimistic, perhaps because he was stupid (and opinion in the station was fairly clear on the subject that it was the latter), but even he could see that his chief inspector was angry, and that whatever was said to her was not going to make her laugh and smile and pat him on the head. He therefore kept his answer short. 'Don't know.'

Alas, even this did not save him. 'What the fuck do you mean? She should have been in two hours ago.'

There was no answer to either the question or its pursuant statement. As so often before he felt at sea, and it was a distinctly choppy sea. He opened his mouth but his brain took too long pulling the levers to get his tongue, pharynx and vocal cords into operation, and so only a near-inaudible squeak was born, soon to die. Beverley continued, 'Did she tell you she was going to be late?'

He shook his head, feeling that he was projecting a sense of guilt, although she did not seem to notice. 'Ring her mobile. Tell her to get her arse over to the Cotswold Water Park now.'

The A417 gave a susurrating background theme to the scene, the sound of passing traffic coming over the wetlands, between the sparse trees and low bushes, above the ponds and lakes; the cars providing a sibilant treble, the HGVs punctuating this with intermittent bass roars. The road itself was nearly half a mile away, and only just visible on the horizon, which suited Beverley just fine; for once there was little chance of having a distant audience exuding prurience like pus.

The two bodies had been intertwined both with each other and with the weeds and reeds. They were bloated and pale, taking on an almost translucent appearance, slimy and dank as if made out of squid flesh. They were naked. They were difficult to consider anything more than fish food.

'Well?' Beverley had given up politeness. She felt out of control and it wasn't a nice feeling, not a nice feeling at all; she had worked hard all her life – bent the rules and ruthlesslessly used what assets she had whenever necessary – to avoid being in situations such as this. She and Fisher had just entered the canvas tent on the bank of the pond just by where the bodies had been found. Eisenmenger was just standing there, staring at them.

'Well, what?' enquired Eisenmenger mildly as he looked up at her.

'What can you give me?'

He sensed her impatience, and knew well what her temper could be like, but he had troubles of his own. 'Two females, in the water between twenty-four and forty-eight hours. One is young, the other is considerably older – perhaps fifteen to twenty years.'

'Mother and daughter?'

'How the fuck should I know?' His tone might have been light but there was more than a hint of irritation, and Beverley did not miss it, although she contented herself with a long, cold stare at him.

'Very well. What else?'

'I think it's a fair working assumption that they are victims of our Internet scientist.'

'How do you know that?' This from Fisher. The smell in the confined space was rapidly making it even more difficult than usual for him to think clearly.

'I don't *know* it, sergeant. I said that it was a reasonable assumption. The victims come in pairs and we have here two bodies; all the victims have been naked, as are these. All have had their heads shaved, as these have.'

Beverley had knelt down by the two blubber-white bodies. 'They clearly weren't beheaded. Were they electrocuted?'

'No external burn marks,' he said. 'Although that doesn't exclude it, of course.'

Fisher had the feeling he was going to have to leave the tent pretty soon. As much as to stop himself being sick as for information, he asked, 'Why not?'

Eisenmenger explained, 'The electrodes could have been inserted into the mouth, or the anus, or even the vagina.' He was quite capable, Beverley knew, of delivering news of such atrocities without thinking and in a cerebral sense, as if delivering an academic treatise to fellow pathologists; yet this time she had heard more than academic detachment, this time she heard almost viciousness in his reply.

The feeling of nausea that had been sidling up on Fisher swept over him – indeed, it swept him away – and he left with a mumbled, 'Excuse me.'

Beverley stared at the pathologist. 'What's wrong?'

He returned the stare, his face showing passivity to the point of inhumanity. 'Nothing.'

'You seem out of sorts,' she offered, but he was in no mood for gifts and just changed the subject. 'This guy changes his method of killing every two victims. I doubt whether he's used the national grid this time.'

'So how has he done it?'

He looked for a long time at the two bodies lying side by side, companions in a cold death before saying, 'They're pale, aren't they?'

'Isn't that due to immersion?'

He continued to stare at the bodies; it was a characteristic Eisenmenger pose, she thought; he might almost have been communing with the corpses. 'Maybe. And, of course, pallor is a very difficult thing to gauge – some people are naturally pale – but there are the puncture wounds in the antecubital fossae—'

'The what?'

'The crooks of the elbows.' He knelt down and raised the older corpse's arm. 'See?'

'They've had blood taken?'

He laid the arm back down, as gently as if she were asleep and he were afraid to wake her. 'I think,' he said standing up again, 'they've had *all* their blood taken.'

FORTY

'A white-collar killer?'

Outside, in the cool fresh air that was tinged with the faint but reassuring odour of exhaust fumes from the distant A417, Fisher was leaning against the side of a police car, trying not to look ill. As Beverley emerged followed by Eisenmenger, he came across to them. A family of mallards was paddling in a nearby pool, making occasional, questioning quacks, and a pair of buzzards circled lazily in the high air above a large copse a kilometre or two away.

'I'm sorry about that, sir.'

Beverley shrugged to indicate that it was of no consequence; she was struck that Fisher looked almost as pale as the corpses and that, what with Eisenmenger's bloodlessly uncaring treatment of her inspector, she was surrounded by an army of the exsanguinated. 'Check the missing person's reports for a mother and daughter.' He trotted off, happy to have instruction and she turned to Eisenmenger. 'Did you look at the web posting?'

She noticed that there was something behind his eyes as he nodded and said non-committally, 'Yes.'

'And?'

'And what? It's more of the same. It's someone who has an obsession, but someone who has some intellectual training. Not your usual serial killer. This one is more than an undereducated, ill-informed bigot; this one let his obsession take hold after his education.'

'Let?'

He shrugged. 'Anyone can allow themselves to fall prey to their obsessions; they're within all of us, just lurking, waiting.'

Eisenmenger had always struck her as somewhat dour, but today he was bleak; as bleak as she had ever known him. 'A white-collar killer?'

'I think so.' He then said suddenly, 'But not a scientist, I think. Someone who admires science, and maybe has some training in it, but not who practises it as profession. A good mimic of a scientist, but not the real thing.'

She accepted this, allowing it to meld with her other data. Then she thought to break the formalities. 'Perhaps we should have a drink some time, John. It's been a while.'

He looked surprised at the suggestion. 'Yes . . .' A pause. 'That would be nice.' Another pause. 'I'm a bit busy at the moment, though.'

'Of course. Just give me a ring when you're free.'

And so he forgot to tell her about the last testament of Len Barker.

'Any word from Lancefield?' asked Beverley of Fisher as Eisenmenger walked back to the tent.

'Nothing.'

Beverley said nothing, but Fisher could recognize bloodlust in her eyes when he saw it.

The results of Eisenmenger's search were ready by the time he had completed describing, dissecting and sampling the previous day's gastrointestinal surgical specimens; it was thankfully brief. In the past three months, there had been only six pleural biopsies – the definitive test for malignant mesothelioma – performed in the county. All of them were men, all between fifty-five and seventy, all of them could have been the headless man from the information that he had, but at least he had six names. His next move was to enter each name into the general hospital database, looking each one up for missed clinic appointments; this produced nothing definitive and he swore quietly to himself. What now?

He asked himself the question, although he knew the answer anyway, just didn't want to have to do it. The database held all the personal details of each patient, including their home phone numbers and he made a note of all of them. He looked at the clock. He was due to begin the post-mortem on the latest victims in three hours; then, using his mobile, he began to phone each one in turn

FORTY-ONE
'I don't even care if your mother lay dying'

Lancefield was sitting at her desk when Beverley and Fisher returned. She stood up at once, opened her mouth to speak but was doomed never to achieve her objective. Beverley had seen her from across the room and homed in on her much as a kestrel falls upon a dormouse. 'You. In my office. Now.'

She swept away without a further word and without noticing how haggard her subordinate looked. When Lancefield followed, she was greeted by Chief Inspector Wharton sitting behind her desk arms diagonally stretched away to its corners, fingers and thumbs braced, while she stared unblinkingly and malevolently at her.

'Shut the door.' Lancefield did so, then came to stand in front of Beverley's desk; she felt light-headed, almost as if her mind were about to take wing. 'You should have been at work five hours ago.'

'I know . . .'

'You haven't been answering your phone.'

'I turned it off . . .'

'We found two more bodies this morning.'

'Yes, so I understand.'

'SO YOU UNDERSTAND!!?' The explosion was perfect. She was neither overloud nor strident, nor hectoring; she was merely venomous, incredulous, instantaneous; it came at Lancefield from perfect calm and was all the more effective for it. She was immediately removed from her previous, almost languorous, exhausted numbness. 'So you understand?' repeated Beverley. Without further pause, she continued, 'We are in the middle of tracking down the most deranged killer I've ever come across, one who has killed at least six people, possibly more, and in the most degenerate, depraved way it is possible to imagine, and you decide to swan off for hours on end, with no prior warning and remaining completely out of touch. Do you know how unprofessional that is, Lancefield?'

Lancefield found that she didn't care how 'unprofessional' Chief Inspector Wharton thought it was. She might have gone so far as to say that she didn't give a flying fuck what Beverley Wharton's views on the subject were, but she wasn't to be given the chance, for Beverley had yet to reach the end of excoriating her inspector. 'I don't know what you were doing, or what you thought you were doing; there is no excuse for this type of behaviour; none whatsoever. There is nothing that can excuse unexplained and ungranted absence during the course of such an important investigation. I don't even care if your mother lay dying, you don't just disappear when you work for me, do you understand?'

Lancefield looked at her superior from eyes that were sore and with a mind that was in shock; she saw someone she despised, someone who could never achieve respect from her, much less become a close colleague. She was there not because she wanted to be, but because she was required by others to be; she owed Beverley nothing.

She had just lost her mother – or rather lost the final husk-like thing that her mother had become over many pain-filled months – and she did not yet understand it; it was a fact but not an emotion; she knew it would not be long before that changed, but at the moment, the knowledge lodged in her brain and was stifled by the tiredness of the long hours she had just spent with her father and the departing, decaying spirit of the woman she had once called 'mother'.

She ought, she knew, to feel anger at this preposterous woman's preposterous slanders. But she couldn't be bothered. She would soon need to grieve, to negotiate her mourning as best she could, but not yet. Now, she needed to clamber gingerly back on the rocky boat that was normality. But she couldn't think clearly, could hear the words and think the thoughts, but couldn't connect with either of them.

She nodded impassively. 'I'm sorry, sir.' Then she added before she appreciated the irony, 'It won't happen again.'

Beverley searched for the sound of contrition in what Lancefield said; she heard almost disconnection, as if she were somehow having trouble concentrating. Was she, Beverley wondered briefly, hungover? Yes, that was it. The stupid bitch had been on a bender and overslept. If so, there were grounds for formal disciplinary action.

But no. She certainly looked pretty down in the dumps. She would allow her one more chance, she thought. 'Alright, we'll say no more about it. Talk to Fisher about the latest two bodies. There's a chance they could be mother and daughter, so hopefully easily identified. Go through the missing persons reports in the county, see if there are any candidates. Also, Eisenmenger will probably be doing the autopsy this evening, so I want you there, OK?'

Lancefield took a moment to respond, doing so with a slow nod. She knew that she ought to have told Beverley about the real reason for her absence, but she found it impossible to speak about it, struck dumb with the awful shock; it was as if to share her grief with one such as Chief Inspector Beverley Wharton would be to dilute and pollute it; as if to share it would cheapen it.

'Very well, sir.'

FORTY-TWO
merely fascinated, merely intellectually aroused

That Lancefield was subdued did not strike Eisenmenger; he was not particularly observant of those around him in general, but when he was working, he was dangerously prone to wreck his ship upon rocks that were quite obvious to everyone else. In this instance, though, he was safe, for Lancefield had thoughts of her own to contend with. Clive, too, was quiet, although this was characteristic of him during forensic post-mortems, and in complete contrast to his normal attitude, which was one of calculated cheerfulness. Forensics, Clive considered, were too important for unnecessary flippancy. He was a man who took his job seriously, even if his superficial manner was seen by some as flippant; he cared deeply about the service he provided, whether it be to pathologists, the bereaved, the coroner, the police or to undertakers, and was quick to let others know when he thought that they were not up to standard. It was one of the reasons he liked Eisenmenger, because the pathologist had a similar attitude; some of the pathologists he worked with did not, in his unstated but nonetheless cogent opinion, always behave as they should.

After five hours of near total silence, Eisenmenger had finished. He had worked first on the younger female then, as Clive reconstructed this one, on the older. He now said to Clive, 'OK. You can put this one back together.'

'Not much of a mess, at any rate.'

The autopsy on Malcolm Willoughby had been bloodless because his slow electrocution had cooked his blood into something approaching black pudding; in these two post-mortems, there had just not been much blood at all. Eisenmenger felt slightly put out by this, and was put out because he felt put out; a normal person would have welcomed this absence of gore.

Lancefield had been standing in the corner; it was cold in the mortuary but she looked as though she was only half aware of it to Clive; she looked, he decided, as if she was only half aware of everything. Eisenmenger, until now, only vaguely aware in his concentration on the task in hand that she was there, was slightly surprised when he had to address her twice to gain any attention.

Looking slightly startled, she said, 'I'm sorry?'

'The chief inspector will be wanting my provisional conclusions.'

'Of course,' she said, but he was aware that she was playing catch up and he wondered where she had been.

'Tell her that it looks as though my first impression was right. These two have been bled to death.'

She frowned, appearing to be trying to concentrate. 'Is that a good way to go?'

It struck him as an odd question but he said only, 'Better than Malcolm Willoughby's fate.'

She nodded absently.

Since Charlie Sherman had become a psychologist, she had been used to a commentary in her head, one that was above her emotions and thoughts, and that placed everything in context, that explained and therefore comforted her. It was as though she had been voyaging through life with a constant, reassuring companion – a nanny, perhaps – and she had not had to face the terrors of life alone. Yet now that voice, that explaining, soft and always-believable monotone in the background of her thoughts, was gone. She was alone, and she was suddenly facing the biggest challenge of her personal life without any benefit from her training and experience; it made her feel juvenile, almost adolescent, adrift and at the mercy of her emotions, those daemons that she had thought to have conquered.

She had been in control, she knew, until they had watched the web posting and then the voice had gone, neither fading nor saying goodbye, merely refusing to speak, deafening her with its obstinacy. At once, her life had changed and, worse, her perception of her life had changed; certainty became its converse, confidence froze and became immune to her, impenetrable; an alien thing that was now unknowable, and she did not know how it had happened, but happened it had during the hours in which they had viewed the web posting. In some way, her perceptions and thoughts during that period had altered – perhaps even damaged – the props that sustained her. The images themselves were appalling, sickening, unbearable, but she had guessed that they would be; they were worse than she had expected, but not beyond her endurance. She was well acquainted with the terrible things that human beings did to animals and to each other, but they seemed almost to reserve a special cruelty for the pain they inflicted on other members of their own species, as if the sentience of the victim gave a special piquancy to the pleasure.

But then there was the mind of the killer to think about. She was used to human emotions in their extremities, and until now had met them with professional equanimity. Her species, she was well aware, was governed by emotion, much as the higher socioeconomic classes liked to think otherwise; in the world of psychological academe, the more refined might be aware of and be able to *use* their emotions – have 'emotional intelligence' in the common jargon – but they could not escape them. If they should ever manage that particular feat, then this is what happened; someone who killed, not only without compunction but without interest or understanding, who could not conceive any difference between homicide and any other human activity, like defaecating or eating. There was a monstrous irony that this one was interested, obsessed even, in *life*, in the soul; the killing was done in order to find out about what makes humans live. How could any one mind, no matter how twisted, hold that extreme contradiction and still function? She was well aware that the human mind was quite capable of holding diametrically opposed opinions and believe either, depending on circumstance, but one that was so extreme, so incompatible, found her lost, both professionally and intellectually.

Yet she could have coped with even that, had she not just watched the man she thought she loved seem somehow to lose *his* humanity, as he had taken in all this other-worldly, surreal, hideous existence and been merely fascinated, merely intellectually aroused, much as he might have been by a crossword puzzle or a curious pathological finding, or even a well-played game of rugby union. This was what had truly frightened her; he was still the same human being she had met some months before, still the strangely elusive, slightly shy and extremely irritating middle-aged, greying (but not balding, thank God) man she had at first thought nothing of; now, though, she saw what he was capable of being, and it had frightened her. Or rather, he had shown what he was capable of not being, for he had not seemed to react as she thought he ought to have done. He had shown no emotion, no sign that he was affected in any way; he had almost, she dared hardly think, reacted like the killer.

And this scared her.

Eisenmenger had a name for the anonymous man with mesothelioma, although he still could not be sure that it was the right one. He had managed to talk to two of the three non-attendees and their carers (one was in a hospice and expected to die shortly), but Dominic Trelawney stubbornly refused to answer his phone. He had done all he could, done more than he should have, to help the investigation, and more mundane activities were calling. Ben Gosling had called in unwell with flu and he had to cover routine autopsies for him; time to make Beverley earn her crust. He picked up the phone to tell her his news.

FORTY-THREE
'Eisenmenger tells me he's wondering'

There was only one autopsy the next morning and Eisenmenger thanked goodness for that.

Mrs Elizabeth Williams, aged 79 years.
Address: Ivydene Cottage, Albright Lane, Colberrow, HR8 9QX
Occupation: retired cleaner
Information Received: *Mrs Williams was a widow who lived independently. The death was reported by her vicar who had called upon her to discuss church matters. She was clearly unwell. He states that she had already called an ambulance but, unfortunately, she became unresponsive before the paramedics arrived. The vicar attempted resuscitation but she was pronounced dead at the scene.*
Information from GP: *Mrs Williams was registered with a general practitioner but had not attended the surgery in over ten years, despite being called for routine screening procedures.*

'What do you think, Clive?'

And so, Clive considered.

Eisenmenger had known a great many mortuary technicians – or 'medical technical officers', or 'anatomical pathology technicians' or (a term he abhorred) 'morticians' – in his career, and they proved a constant source of interest to him; humanity in general provided him with a steady parade of entertainment, a sort of never-ending rain of distraction and diversion from the dullness of existence, but this fine breed, these special men, were the epitome of human enterprise, the crown princes and crown princesses of endeavour, the A-list of the common herd. During his long and sometimes apparently tedious career, Eisenmenger had known, amongst many others, one who sang hymns while he cracked the ribcage open both with gusto and with stainless steel shears (and who had earned a subsidiary income by procuring abortions in his back sitting room), another who had had an unhealthy obsession with au pair girls (spending most of his spare time on websites and chortling in what could only be described as an unsettling manner), and one who had professed distinctly 'un-PC' attitudes to both women and people of other races, and who had been heard to refer affectionately to 'Uncle Adolf'.

There were some, though, who were to him priceless. They not only did what they were supposed to do – evisceration of the bodies followed by their reconstruction, scrupulous cleaning, preparation of the bodies for viewing by relatives, sensitive handling of the bereaved, keeping up to date with the intricate paperwork engendered by the Human Tissue Act (that the job was complex was, he knew, little appreciated) – but also pointed out to the pathologists things that they might have missed, took an interest in the autopsy and what the findings were. Clive was one such. Sometimes, of course, Clive got it wrong; pointing out irrelevancies or, through failing to spot things, making the pathologists' job harder. In the main, though, he was a useful man to have around.

Many mortuary technicians would have missed the small pieces of red lint that were under the lips. Unfortunately, he only spotted them after Eisenmenger had completed the organ dissection and when he was dictating his findings; thus he gave Eisenmenger a problem, for Eisenmenger had already found a perfectly acceptable cause of death. Betty Williams had had severe coronary atheroma – the arteries supplying the heart muscles were almost completely furred up – and this was a perfectly acceptable, and natural, way to die; indeed, a third of the population did so.

There is nothing a pathologist hates more than too many causes of death. The autopsy that does not immediately find a cause of death – that is 'unascertained' in the parlance – is a nuisance, but not a disaster; in perhaps ten to twenty percent of post-mortem examinations more investigations are needed: examination of tissue samples under the microscope, expert opinion, toxicological analysis of blood and urine, asbestos fibre counts. Even after these, no definitive cause of death may be found, but the pathologist will be able to state with some assurance that there were no traumatic, toxicological or other unnatural factors. It is an outcome that is less than satisfactory, but has to be accepted. More than one cause of death makes life very difficult, however; doubly so when one of them might be unnatural. Lint in the mouth suggested that someone had smothered her.

Eisenmenger saw another evening disappearing in the dubious company of the local constabulary, and more trouble up ahead with Charlie. He sighed.

'Shit.'

'It happens,' was Clive's only comment, one that was of no help to Eisenmenger.

Eisenmenger peeled off his gloves and went to the alcove where the sheet with the details he had been given by the coroner's office was laid out. As he went to the phone, he glanced again at it and saw this time the significance of the place where she lived, that it was a place name he had seen before.

He began to wonder.

'You alright?'

Lancefield had been staring at the computer screen but clearly not seeing it; even Fisher had noticed a degree of distraction. She looked up, but not in a particularly animated fashion. 'Yes. Why?'

'You've got a face like a slapped arse,' he replied cheerfully and with a characteristic lack of tact. 'Been dumped?'

She was too far beyond anger to respond. Even Beverley's dressing down, mistaken in almost every way, had not been able to rile her beyond melancholia; Fisher's clodhopping banter was certainly not going to do the job. She merely returned to the computer screen while Fisher decided that he had been spot on; yes, he now knew, she had been dumped.

Beverley came out of her office. Fisher looked up to discover that she had not found the secret of undying happiness since the last time he had seen his boss. 'Fisher? How far have you got with the missing mother and daughter?'

'Nothing as yet, boss.'

'Find them, fuckwit. It shouldn't be too hard, even for you. And whilst you're about it, find out all you can on this man.' She handed him a slip of paper with Dominic Trelawney's name on it. With that, she turned to Lancefield. 'You're with me, inspector.'

She frowned. 'Where to?'

'The hospital. Eisenmenger reckons we've got another victim.'

Lancefield frowned, tried to concentrate. 'Another one? So soon?'

Beverley was already turning away. 'An old woman's been smothered. I'm not sure it's related, but Eisenmenger tells me he's wondering, and when Eisenmenger wonders, it pays to start working on the assumption that he's right.'

FORTY-FOUR
Magellan, Columbus and, perhaps, Scott

T he first time that Josh and Darren dared to climb the tree
and drop from the thick, overhanging limb, and thus enter
the inner grounds of the Grange, they were aware that it
was a momentous thing, a defining act; they knew that they were
doing something terrible, something heinous (although they did not
know the word, they knew its meaning); yet, although they were
immature in so many ways, they had already learned that this type
of wrongdoing was delightfully, deliciously, deliriously attractive.
They had planned the trip assiduously, getting up early one morning,
collecting their store cupboard of food from the shed at the bottom
of Darren's small, untidy garden (some chocolate digestives, two
apples, two bags of salt and vinegar crisps, and two small cartons
of juice; all carefully sequestered from their packed lunches over
the previous week and in total representing a considerable sacrifice), and then cycling away up the curving lane to the estate, feeling
like true adventurers, unaware that their emotions probably mirrored
exactly those of Magellan, Columbus and, perhaps, Scott. They
cycled for half a mile, then abandoned their bikes, hiding them
behind the fence, before trekking across the open fields of the estate,
following paths that they and they alone knew well, talking excitedly through the shortness of breath that their exertions brought. It
was sunny but not yet warm, the dawn wind having died but the
earth still cool from it.

They approached the stone wall with more care, staying low,
looking around all the time for spies and snipers, the adrenaline
pumping even more, the sense of adventure ringing and screaming
in their ears; they saw no one. Skirting around the wall, body positions low, heads forever turning to left and right, they eventually
found their secret way in, then made base camp. Whilst consuming
the first of their rations – and doing so frugally lest they have to
stretch them to days, possibly weeks – they rested and took their
bearings, constantly watchful. After ten minutes, they set off again,
deeper into the dark heart of the forest.

They arrived at the inner fence in fifteen further minutes, still
scanning all around them, seeing in the depths of the woodland a

thousand silent enemies, hearing in the soft wind high above them the stealthy steps of pursuers, certain that the birdsong held hidden, coded conversations between the foes. They lay upon the ground, heads down, arms tucked beneath them so that they crawled upon their elbows in the manner that they had seen in war films, skirting the fencing until they came upon the tree that would gain them entrance. Another pause to ensure that they were still unobserved, then they climbed its trunk, edged out upon the limb, and dropped quietly to the grass, the dried leaves and the twigs of the inner grounds of the Grange.

'Did she, or didn't she die of smothering?'

Eisenmenger spent a good deal of his time as a forensic pathologist combating barristers who sought to destroy his conclusions; he spent an equal amount of time combating members of the constabulary who sought to drag from him conclusions that he was not just unwilling to give, he was intellectually incapable of giving. As he had said so often before, he now said simply, 'I don't know.' He knew that this would provoke fury – and he did not like provoking fury – but he could give no other reply.

'Well, can't you even give me a hint?'

'Beverley, Beverley, Beverley . . .'

'Please, John. I need something.'

They were in Clive's office, sipping coffee. Eisenmenger had noticed that Lancefield was looking oddly detached, and had wondered distractedly what was wrong with her. He said, 'I know she didn't die of major trauma, but until the tox comes back, I can't exclude a pharmacological cause, and she has enough coronary atheroma to kill an elephant.'

'So?'

He grunted, lowered his head, stared at the pencil sharpener on Clive's desk that was shaped like a small coffin. Then: 'If you want an opinion now, I'd say she was smothered.'

Beverley let out a long sigh, as if she had been holding her breath for a hundred years. 'Thank you.'

He looked up. 'I might be wrong.'

She shook her head. 'You don't believe that, and neither do I.'

He allowed, 'I think it's likelier than not that she was smothered,' which was as definite as she knew she was likely to get.

'But this can't be the same killer. The MO's completely different.'

'It is, isn't it,' he agreed. 'Yet . . .'

'Yet, you think it is?' she guessed.

He hesitated. It was time to confess what he had discovered about Len Barker's final message to the living. He had a feeling he was about to get bollocked, and he wasn't disappointed.

'Jesus mother-fucking Christ, John. How the hell could you forget?'

He thought that perhaps he had one or two reasons, but said nothing about them. 'It might be nothing.'

'The head was found not far from Colberrow, the registration that Len Barker wrote down is from a Colberrow Estate van, and now this. How can it be unconnected?'

He shrugged. 'We don't know that Len Barker saw anything.'

'He lived at the top of the quarry. Maybe he saw a white van; maybe he saw someone get out of a white van and dump a body.'

'Was he interviewed at the time?'

Beverley's eyes narrowed; she knew full well who had been entrusted with that task. 'He was, but apparently he didn't make this information known.'

Eisenmenger, ignorant of the context, was running through possibilities. 'He was still severely disabled; it was a left-sided stroke that affected his speech; if he was right-handed, it would have destroyed his ability to write. He was confined to a wheelchair, too. Maybe he just never got the chance to tell anyone.' Beverley was thinking, Lancefield should have made sure. She should have given him the opportunity to communicate. I bet she didn't. Eisenmenger continued, 'He was found in the kitchen and had been there several hours. His carer put him to bed, so at some time in the night he got up, and made his way to the kitchen where he fell. If there was nothing in the bedroom, maybe he was looking for something to write with.' He paused. 'It would have taken a great effort, given his condition, though. Would it really have been that important to him?'

'He was an ex-policeman, and a good one by all accounts; I should think he would have been desperate to make the information known.'

'So we can be fairly certain that the murderer has something to do with Colberrow, probably the Colberrow Estate itself.'

She gestured with her head towards the dissection room where Clive was finishing up. 'But how is that connected?'

'Now that is beyond me, but connected it is, Beverley.'

Her mobile went off; it played 'Carmina Burana', Eisenmenger noticed. She said, 'Yes?' then listened intently for a little over a minute during which Eisenmenger sent a text to Charlie, asking how she was. Beverley said to her caller, 'What do you know about him?' The answer did not please, Eisenmenger deduced, because her reply was couched in somewhat brusque terms. 'Well, fucking well find it out, constable. Find out everything there is to know.' She paused, listening to what Fisher had to say. Then: 'Just do it, Fisher. And whilst you're about it, I want someone to go over the Colberrow Estate. They own a white van, registration number . . .' She read out the number that Eisenmenger had given her. 'I want to know who has access to it and where it was the night before the body in the quarry was discovered.'

She stabbed her finger with its long, crimson nail – almost subconsciously Eisenmenger wondered if they were false – down on the phone and almost through it into her handbag. 'That name you gave us – Trelawney – has been positively identified as the beheaded male.'

'That's good, isn't it?' His tone was mild, almost ironic.

For a second she might have been about to rip some of the proverbial out of him, but then she seemed to find a little pocket of patience – perhaps in her capacious handbag – that she had previously overlooked, for she took a deep breath and almost smiled. 'It's another lead,' she admitted.

'There you are, then.'

She suddenly laughed, the tension within her relieved. 'Maybe, John.'

FORTY-FIVE

They'll show me a bit of fucking respect

Somersby looked up. 'Did you hear anything?'

Sheldon's eyes were watering because of the strong smell of vinegar that permeated the shed in which they were working; in any case, he was thinking and thinking was something he had to concentrate on, lest he lose track of things completely. He did not reply. Somersby went to the door, unbolted and unlocked it, then looked out warily. Sheldon continued with his task – stirring as he added water to the now cooling mix – either completely oblivious or completely uncaring of what Somersby was doing and saying. This was the part of the process he hated the most, and he had always to keep thinking about the money he was making, the money that made it all worthwhile . . .

Except that he was starting to wonder if it was worth it. When Somersby had come to him and suggested that he had a sure way to make a decent wage without too much effort, he had been wholly enthusiastic, had been completely believing that this was a sure-fire money-spinner, the honest-to-goodness, guaranteed, gold-plated gravy train that he had always thought was sooner or later going to come his way. Maximum money, minimum effort; wasn't that what everyone was looking for?

The effort, though, no longer seemed to him to be minimum; he always got the shitty jobs like this one while Somersby made out that his workload was just as hard and just as important, although it never seemed quite as unpleasant. When there was unloading or loading to do, it was Tom who did it, Somersby who directed him; washing the vats and utensils was always done by him, too, usually when Somersby had taken the latest batch away in the van, the van that was full because Tom had loaded it.

And he had a grievance about the money, because he wasn't allowed to spend it. 'We'll be making tens of thousands, Thomas,' Somersby had said. 'Maybe hundreds.' What he hadn't said was that he wasn't going to let Thomas see any of it, not for a long time. 'We've got to be careful, Thomas. What are people going to think if you suddenly turn up one day in a Ferrari?'

They'll show me a bit of fucking respect, was what Tom Sheldon had thought, although he hadn't said it. Anyway, he wasn't stupid; he wasn't going to go mad and start buying diamonds and shit like that, but there wouldn't be any harm in getting the odd, small luxury – a new Playstation, and maybe a car that was a *little* newer than the crappy old banger he'd had ever since he learned to drive. Fucking hell, he was entitled to *something* . . .

'I thought I heard something.' Somersby, having closed the door and secured it again, was now looking out of the window. 'You sure there was no way those kids could have got in?'

Tom stopped stirring, his resentment bubbling close to the surface. 'I told you, didn't I? There was nothing.'

'It sounded like a kid.'

'I didn't hear it.'

'You wouldn't have done, what with the noise of the stirring, Thomas.'

'Why don't you do some stirring while I do some listening?'

And why don't you stop calling me Thomas? My name's fucking Tom, you cocky cunt.

Somersby knew well that Tom Sheldon was becoming increasingly aggrieved, but he wasn't too bothered and he had had a pretty good idea that a time such as this would come. He hadn't chosen Tom for his brains but for his brawn, which was not without its dangers; there were stages in the process where things could go horribly wrong – 'horribly wrong' as in 'explode' – and the first few times that they had worked together, Somersby had worked with his arsehole too tight to let a pin in.

He smiled at Tom; a friendly smile, one that to a man of greater intellect would have been seen as inappropriate. 'Why don't I? And why don't you do what I'm doing, Thomas?'

He came across the shed, held out his hand for the paddle. It was handed to him, although with sudden reluctance, for Tom hadn't thought it would be this easy and his intellect wasn't *that* limited. Somersby indicated the desk at which he had been working. 'Go on.'

His voice was so full of uncertainty, he had trouble getting any words past it. 'What are you doing?' His face and demeanour mirrored the indecision.

Somersby replied neutrally, 'I'm searching for suppliers of hydrochloric and sulphuric acid, acetic anhydride and chloroform. You can do that, can't you, Thomas?' But he couldn't, and he knew it and Somersby knew it. Somersby continued, 'I've set up a dummy company, but you've got to order only small amounts, and not all from the same company.' Tom nodded; he did so slowly and could not hide his anxiety. Somersby was relentless. 'And order in the right ratios. I don't want stuff we can't use left behind.'

'Why not?'

'Evidence, Thomas. Evidence.'

Tom nodded but didn't rush to the desk and the computer thereon.

'Well?' There was a trace of viciousness in Somersby's tone now and on his face was a tight, unpleasant grin. 'You can do that, can't you?'

Tom hesitated. From outside but at some distance, there came the faint sound of a child's laugh. Somersby said at once, 'Go and check what's happening outside. Now.'

The imperative tone was enough to make Tom obey at once. Sheldon waited in the shed, looking through the window. About three minutes of quiet passed before there arose, clear and high, a child's scream.

FORTY-SIX

'at least you haven't had the children to contend with'

Lancefield looked around the room, trying to focus. Why the hell was she there? Not just why was she in that room at that time, but why was she not elsewhere, mourning as she should, perhaps comforting her father. Except that there was no comfort to be given or had. She appreciated fully for the first time that she had been so wrong all these years; she had been so aware of gradually losing her mother that she had missed the fact that it was only the illness that had allowed her to keep – albeit in a distorted, loveless way – her father. Now that tenuous, desiccated link was gone, and with it the bonds to her father were gone completely. All future contact would be loveless; worse, in fact, because it would be lovelessness tinged with mutual and self-loathing, each of them aware that they were equally responsible for the impasse, yet each ready to blame the other completely.

She felt ashamed, more than bereaved, and wanted to run from this, yet couldn't. It hampered every thought she had; she knew that she was not functioning properly, yet could not help it; the last thing she would do is take compassionate leave. The next before last thing she would do would be to tell Chief Inspector Beverley Wharton of her personal problems and ask for forgiveness.

Fisher had been looking through the rest of the house. 'No sign of forced entry.'

The cottage was cramped and overfilled. It smelled fusty and old, unchanged for perhaps decades. There was an inordinate amount of furniture, not surprising, she supposed, considering Dominic Trelawney had been a joiner; the small dining table was exceptionally beautiful. It wasn't a neat house, though, and he had clearly been sleeping downstairs on the sagging, worn settee for some weeks or months, with consequent disruption and untidiness; the bed had been made, but badly. She looked out of the front-room windows, through old, warped glass and through smeared grime.

The cottage was on the side of the steep Stroud escarpment, looking across to larger, more luxurious abodes. They were too far away to have seen anything.

'Call on the neighbours. Find out when they last saw him and if they saw anyone suspicious come to call.'

Fisher disappeared and Lancefield managed to energise herself enough to begin looking for something that might help in the investigation. After forty minutes, she had found very little. Most of the expected paperwork she found in the sideboard – cheque book, pensions statement, bank statements, hospital appointment card, television licence, old-style driving licence – and none of it told her anything. In the kitchen was the beginning of a shopping list and a calendar. There was nothing on it that she could see was relevant – no mysterious meetings with 'Q' or unexplained sums of money written in the margins – but she decided to take it back to the station anyway, if only to cover her backside when Beverley Wharton demanded to see it. Behind it was last year's calendar and this dropped to the floor. She bent to pick it up. It had fluttered open and she was looking at the February before last. The initials 'AA' were written in for Tuesday of every week. Beside each was written 'St Mark's'.

For a moment she became excited – who was AA? – but this quickly subsided. Alcoholics Anonymous, of course. They would meet in a church hall. She checked and found the entries stopped after October and there were none in the present year's calendar. So he had stopped going probably when he found out he had cancer; she couldn't blame him. She began to riffle through cupboards, discovering four empty whisky bottles. She grunted softly, then went to the old-fashioned pantry at the back of the kitchen, moved some tins of soup and fruit and found three full bottles of whisky, all of which made her smile.

Antonia had had a migraine for most of the day, one that made it hard for her to think. She was delighted that Josh and Harriet had been out of the house for the day – Josh out playing with Darren, Harriet spending a few days on holiday with a school friend in Scotland – thus allowing her some respite. Andrew had been in London at the Royal Society of Medicine ('my club' as he liked to call it), attending a symposium on new advances in gerontology. Had she not felt so unwell, she would have really enjoyed the day, treasuring the chance to garden, to rest, to read and to listen to her

beloved Radio Four; as it was, all she could do was lie there in a
darkened room and feel blessed relief that she was not being pestered
every ten minutes.

Andrew arrived home at twenty past seven to find his wife of
thirty-seven years asleep. Unaware of her travails, he made his
usual bustle as he came in, calling out for her and slamming doors,
just as he had been doing for all of their married life, just as he
was always being told off for doing. He was pouring himself a
glass of red wine when she came into the kitchen. He looked up,
his face changing from an expression of smiling welcome to one
of surprise. 'Antonia? You look awful.'

She took the compliment with fortitude. 'Good. Because that's
how I feel.' She sat down at the table heavily, waving away his
offer of wine. 'Have you had a good day?'

'Very interesting. Quite astonishing the progress they're making
in ageing. Did you know, they now believe that it isn't at all genetic.
There are no genes directly involved in ageing, it's really all just
wear and tear . . .' He paused. 'But that doesn't matter; what's up
with you?'

'Migraine. It came on not long after you left this morning.'

'You poor old thing. At least you haven't had the children to
contend with.'

She sighed. 'No, no. It's been nice and peaceful.'

He looked around. 'Where is Josh?'

'He spent the day with Darren.'

He looked at his watch. 'Still? Isn't it a bit late for him to be
out?'

'Don't worry, Anthony. He's spending the night at Darren's. He's
perfectly alright.'

FORTY-SEVEN

and she was careful not to let him hear

MISSING PERSON REPORT, REF NO. 10/434/A
Name: *Melanie Whittaker (Photograph attached)*
Age: *34*
Address: *29b Wilson Crescent, Whaddon, Cheltenham*
Date and Time Last Seen: *Wednesday 29ᵗʰ July, at approximately 4.30pm*
Last Seen By: *Mrs Alice Dolittle (Statement attached)*
Reported By: *Mr Isaac Lawes*
Relationship to Missing Person: *Ex-boyfriend and father of the daughter (Statement attached).*
Comments: *Please see Missing Person Report ref no 10/434/B*

'I heard you were after missing wives and daughters. Thought you might be interested.' DCI Smillie lived up to his name, but then he was always living up to it; he smiled perpetually, his facial muscles seemingly paralysed; even when the rest of his face desperately wanted to frown, his mouth refused to come out and play, staying petulantly in its chosen position, deaf to all entreaty. His voice was stuck in one mode too but, unfortunately, it was one of whining condescension, of mockery and Schadenfreude. He was not the most popular of men, which had driven him further into his caricature of satisfaction, one guaranteed to irritate all within quite a wide radius. He had only been working in the station for five months, but already he had engendered a vigorous hatred in Beverley's heart. She looked at the report he had handed her as he said, '434/B refers to her daughter, Evangeline.'

Beverley found herself fighting all sorts of emotions: extreme dislike of the pompous uniformed Smillie, elation that here was another potential lead, exasperation and extreme annoyance that Lancefield had apparently missed this. 'What enquiries have been made?'

'We've taken statements, as you can see. We've also talked to the daughter's school. She's well known for truanting, so they weren't too bothered that she was missing.'

She scanned the statements. They were brief and, as so often, almost indecipherable. The concatenation of police constables who were functionally illiterate, witnesses who were functionally stupid and a photocopier that was functionally decrepit made reading such documents an arduous exercise in deduction and guesswork. She asked, 'Is there any hint that the ex did something?'

'Not a chance. He's an HGV driver, just got back from Estonia. Called in to see his daughter as soon as he got back.'

'And nobody saw anything suspicious?'

'Nope. But then, it's Whaddon, isn't it?' Which was code for nobody ever saw anything of use to the police in Whaddon.

She looked at the photographs. They were definitely of the two people found at the Cotswold Water Park, although the partner would have to identify them. 'Thanks,' she said, unfortunately finding as she did so that she had just run out of sincerity.

Smillie smiled. 'Surprised your guys didn't spot it.'

'So am I.'

'Perhaps a team talk . . .?'

'Perhaps.'

He turned and walked away, and she was careful not to let him hear as she murmured, 'Cunt.'

She waited until he was safely out of earshot before calling Fisher and Lancefield. She commanded them to close the door, then chucked the report on to the desk for them to see. Lancefield picked it up and Beverley let her scan through it. When she looked up, Beverley saw a strange mix of surprise and ennui in her inspector's eyes. She said calmly, 'DCI Smillie has just brought me that. Why didn't either of you?'

Fisher looked across at Lancefield, his mouth open, his eyes betraying fear, as if he could see the train lights coming at the far end of the tunnel and he had his foot trapped. He was well aware that standard operating procedure in the police force was to pass the bomb down the ranks until it exploded in the hands of the most junior officer; as it happened, he need not have worried. Lancefield said only, 'I'm sorry, Chief . . .' She sounded tired, almost absent, certainly unable to appreciate the shit she was wandering into. In his incredulity at such an unexpected reprieve, he looked at Beverley. She was staring at Lancefield, her face unreadable. Without taking her eyes from her, she said to him in what the romantic might have considered a biblical way, 'Go, Fisher.'

He left, mightily relieved.

Beverley leaned back in her chair. Her incandescence had

dimmed, replaced by perplexity. 'Your mind isn't on the case, inspector.' Lancefield didn't react. 'Care to explain why?'

Lancefield took her time focusing on her superior. When she spoke, it was hesitantly, yet without fear; there was something of relief, indeed. 'I watched my mother die two nights ago.' But before Beverley could register her shock at this news, she continued, 'I sat there all through the night, holding her hand, listening to her ramblings, getting more and more tired, more and more depressed, and more and more uncertain. She lapsed into a coma, yet was still alive, still occasionally moaning and muttering. Would you believe it, she laughed once!' With unconscious irony, Lancefield laughed, and it was a thing of bitterness. 'I hadn't heard her laugh in years . . .'

Beverley tried to intervene, to show some of the contrition she was experiencing, but Lancefield wasn't even aware that she was in the room. 'And I began to understand what this killer wants. I started to comprehend him . . .' She frowned in puzzlement. 'He wants to see some sign of the soul, and as I sat with my mother, I found I wanted to as well; after so many years of mental disintegration, I had come to consider her little more than an animal, a not-human thing, and I supposed I came to consider that she didn't have a soul anymore. Then, over the course of that night, I recalled the web postings and I wondered if I would be lucky enough to catch sight of something wondrous, something that would prove that my mother *was* still endowed with a soul, that she was still my mother and not a demented animal . . .'

Beverley didn't know what to say. This was not going at all as she had imagined it would; Lancefield had gone far off script and she found herself unsure of which lines to say. Eventually she asked gently and hesitantly, 'And were you lucky?'

Lancefield considered the question for a long moment, then shook her head. 'No. There was nothing.' She sounded devastated as much by this as by the death. She sat down abruptly and trailed off, but it was only to take a breath before looking up at Beverley and saying simply, 'I'm afraid. Very afraid.'

Beverley asked softly, 'What of?'

Lancefield looked up at once. 'Of ghosts,' she said with scarcely any sound at all.

FORTY-EIGHT
a sorrow for a number of things

Eisenmenger sat in the small study of his flat, the sun dying behind him so that darkness was rising to meet him, to enfold him and to welcome him; he did not mind, indeed his subconscious found pleasure in the thought of dissolution, in becoming indistinguishable from his environment, in ceasing to have a separate identity. His mind was full of thoughts, though all were chaotic, disconnected and sociopathic, seeming to shun contact both with him and with each other; nothing was coherent in his head; there was no smooth flow of thought, just a turbulent mental activity that was completely without direction. In his hand his mobile phone was clenched loosely, might almost have been about to drop to the orange-red of the rug beneath his feet. It was the phone on which he had just spoken to Charlie, the one that had given him the news that she thought that she could no longer continue their relationship.

She had sounded distraught, but that was only the scantiest of comfort and it sounded in his ears very like the words of one who has made a decision but earned a guilty conscience as reward. *I'm sorry, John . . .*

Which was a sorrow for a number of things – for reneging on what she had promised him, for shitting on his parade, for feeling uncomfortable, for feeling like a shit – but he did not gain pleasure from this. How could he? He did not feel vindictive towards her merely because she had done what so many had done before her; his logical mind told him that the one constant – John Eisenmenger – must be the one at fault.

Yet what could he do? He was what he was, and he did what he did. He did not feel that he was evil, nor even unpleasant, although he admitted that he was not ordinarily bothered by unpleasant things; did that make him so difficult to love? Apparently it did, at least as far as Charlie was concerned. He was well aware that pathologists had a reputation for coldness, for disconnection, even for strangeness, but he had always hoped that this could be divorced from the rest of his life, that it could be inserted firmly into a compartment and the lid closed, so that for at least some of his life he could consider himself normal, and have others consider him likewise. Yet it had never yet proved so. There was ever seepage of one into the other, a tainting of his non-professional life by what he did in daylight hours; it was as if the evil that men did not only lived after them, but was a contagion that he had caught and of which he could not be cured.

Even Charlie, who had at least had professional training in aspects of the world in which he found himself, could not cope, it seemed. If she could not, could anyone? Was he doomed to choose between marrying another forensic pathologist or a life alone?

Yet Helena had, at least for a while, endured him . . .

For the first time for many months, he really *thought* of Helena.

He saw her, remembered her, experienced her as if she were still with him.

She became real, just for an instant, as she had not been for so long, not since before she had died.

He had not argued with Charlie, had not even thought of doing so. He had the emotional awareness of a codfish, but even he had experience enough to appreciate that this was not a debate that could be won by intellectual acumen, that she was not putting forward a proposition, that he had just been given a description of how it was.

He began to weep.

What did he have now? Where could he go?

Just what was he?

Without prior awareness of the intention, he suddenly stood up and went to the kitchen to find some whisky; he had unexpectedly discovered that he intended to get himself thoroughly fucking drunk.

'Go home.' With these two words, Beverley stood and went to the door, opened it and stood to one side. 'Go home and go to sleep. You're on sick leave as of now.'

Lancefield stared at her; she did not get out of the chair and did not appear to be about to. 'Sir . . .'

'You've lost your mother, inspector. Even a bitch like me wouldn't have a problem with you taking compassionate leave.'

But Lancefield did not move and did not even change her facial expression. She said slowly and firmly, 'I don't want to go home.'

'You aren't in any sort of emotional state to do your job properly. I don't need someone wandering around like a zombie, bumping into the furniture.'

'I know I haven't been pulling my weight, but I promise I'll pull myself together. Don't make me go home.' She was pleading and Beverley was both surprised and rather disgusted by the realization.

'It would be for the best.'

But Lancefield was vehement. 'No, it wouldn't be. I have no one to talk to there.'

'What about your father? He's still alive, isn't he?'

'We . . . don't see eye to eye.'

Which found Beverley nonplussed. She considered. Losing Lancefield would be a temporary problem whilst someone else was drafted in, but it was not insurmountable. On the other hand, Lancefield was normally efficient and reliable – if anything, too efficient. She said, 'No more fuck-ups, Lancefield. If I let you stay around, you behave normally. It's your decision to carry on working, which means no special treatment, OK?'

Lancefield nodded. 'I appreciate that, sir.'

'You fucking better, Lancefield. I can't afford to cock this investigation up, and that means I can't afford to have anyone – anyone at all – not functioning at full capacity. If you let me down, I'll flay you alive and then throw you to the wolves; I've done it before, and I'll do it again, if I must. Understand?' Lancefield said nothing but it was clear from her expression that she understood only too well. Beverley continued to stare at her for a full thirty seconds more; then she said, still without dropping her gaze, 'Now, first I want you to find out all you can about a place called Colberrow. It's in the north of the county.'

'What do you want to know?'

'Everything, inspector. Absolutely everything.'

'What then?'

'Keep digging for a connection between the victims we've so far managed to identify.'

Which Lancefield thought was a waste of time. Nothing had come up so far and she strongly suspected it never would. 'Anything else?'

'You can go through those Internet postings again.'

An inexplicable spurt of panic ran through her at this. 'Again? But . . .'

'Yes, Lancefield. Again.'

Lancefield was about to ask why, then decided against it; she guessed that it would not be a wise move.

Lancefield found that she could not stop herself watching the Internet postings again and again. It had started as merely her obedience of a superior's orders but, as awful as the images were, it imperceptibly became a compulsion. A voice in her head kept telling her not to, kept telling her that there was perversion in her desire to see what the killer had seen, seek what the killer had sought, but she could not desist. And with each showing she trod deeper and deeper into a mire that sucked at her soul, that insinuated itself into her being and corroded it. This killer scared her but beckoned her somehow; he whispered to her, sought what she sought, wondered the same things that she wondered. She felt a dreadful affinity for him, a hypnotic entrancement by his thinking . . .

Abruptly she pulled herself from the brink.

But brink of what?

She was cold, she suddenly realized; cold, hungry and ragingly thirsty. It was past midnight and darkness had fallen in her small terraced house without her realizing it.

It was with a feeling of nauseous fear, as if she had looked into the mirror and seen a corrupted vision of herself, that she turned the computer off at the wall, eager to see that screen fade to black. She was hungry, but she knew that she could not eat that night.

FORTY-NINE

panic bloomed like a devouring plague

E isenmenger rang his secretary at eight thirty the next morning, claiming sickness; it was not altogether a lie, because he had indeed vomited twice. He felt almost overwhelming guilt at this subterfuge, yet at the same time, and considering what was happening to him, he tried to reason that he had some right to take a break; such reasoning, however, sounded to him specious and had the sound of sophistry in his ears. He was well aware that he was dumping his colleagues in it, and he did not like to do things like that. Yet, he just could not find it within himself to carry on as normal, as if his personal life had not just been blown asunder; if normally the stiff upper lip was not far from his face, today it was absent without leave; it was on someone else's face, perhaps,

someone who did not feel as if one of the legs on which his life
was based had just been blasted away by a shotgun.

Having phoned in his apologies, he made some coffee and retired
to bed on a breakfast of caffeine and paracetamol. For the next two
hours he drifted in and out of dreams that were soon forgotten yet
left an aftertaste of unpleasantness, before becoming suddenly
awake. It was quite abrupt this transition, and it found him without
a headache, although with a dry mouth and sore throat. He got up,
and tried to fight the feeling of guilt that he really should have
gone into work, that he had let himself down. More coffee down
and he debated whether to go to work, but decided against it; Charlie
would presumably be in the hospital and, although it was unlikely
they would meet, he did not want even to chance it. Besides, he
felt something at the back of his head, something about the murders
that was there to be seen, but had so far eluded him.

Accordingly, he settled down in his small study with a cafetière
of fresh coffee and began to collate all the findings on all the bodies
thus far found.

Feeling much better, Antonia was up early the next morning. Andrew
who, since his retirement, had become something of a late riser
unless he had to be otherwise, joined her in the kitchen at just after
nine thirty. 'What are you doing today?'

'I need to take the children into Hereford to get them new clothes
for school. What about you?'

'Cutting the grass. If I get the time, I'll start pruning the roses
out the front.'

'Would you? They desperately need it.'

There was a period of companionable silence as he munched
muesli and she took delicate, perfect semicircular bits of brown
toast and apricot jam, while someone read out the Radio Four book
of the week and told them all about life during the London Blitz.
They drank the breakfast tea that she liked and could only get in
Waitrose. It was too early for the paper or the post, so she read a
magazine and he a book on the history of gynaecology.

The doorbell rang. It was Ellie Taylor to pick up Darren. It took
a few moments, but when it sank in with all concerned that the
boys were missing and had been all night, panic bloomed like a
devouring plague.

The news of the missing boys had broken in Inspector Smillie's
office at eleven o'clock that morning. He had an unfortunate manner

that did not endear him to his colleagues, and he was well aware of this, but this did not mean that he was a bad or incompetent police officer. Far from it, in fact. He had constantly impressed superiors wherever he had been stationed and, the scuttlebutt predicted confidently, he was destined for great things, perhaps even for a post as Chief Constable. He went straight to the small village of Colberrow to question Ellie Taylor and Antonia and Andrew Barclay. He then organized house-to-house enquires of the entire village.

At three minutes past twelve, Eisenmenger stood up from the desk, stretched, winced and sighed. He had not moved beyond his despair at Charlie's phone call, but he had at least found a distraction. In fact, after reading and rereading his reports, making copious notes all the while, he now thought he had found an altogether very interesting distraction. He looked at his watch and decided that he and the environment in general would benefit if he took a long shower. Then he would contact Beverley and see if she agreed that he had found something useful.

He had a feeling he had.

FIFTY

they're of the social class who get murdered

'It's not all bad news.'

'Go on.'

Eisenmenger could hear weary cynicism in Beverley's voice. She had spent most of the morning collating all that she had, and had found it was precious little; she felt like someone who had just gone to get money from the bank, only to find that the account was overdrawn. 'The DNA tests confirm that the head in the slurry pit and the body from outside the mortuary match; likewise, the head with the body from the mortuary matches the body in the compost bin.'

'How is that good?'

'It's conclusive proof that I was right and you don't have to look for two more headless bodies and two more bodiless heads.'

She was patently less than impressed and showed this with a soft grunt and with no change in expression. 'At the rate that other types of dead bodies are turning up, that's little comfort, John.'

'None of the victims is known to the national DNA database, though.'

'You surprise me,' she said with irony that was so heavy it left him slightly winded. 'I've yet to find any victim or suspect who is.'

He shrugged. 'I suspect the mathematics are that you need a DNA database in order of magnitude bigger than the one we've got before you see real benefits.'

She looked less than content, saying only sourly, 'Thanks.'

'And all the toxicology has come back completely negative so far, although we're waiting on the results from the last two.'

'No drugs, no alcohol?'

'Nothing in the blood. As I said, they'd been given Rohypnol at some point, but when they died, that had passed out of their system. They were completely compos mentis when they were killed.'

Under her breath, he heard her say, *Shit*. More loudly, she then observed sourly, 'Lucky bastards.' A snort, then: 'I thought you said it wasn't all bad news. Where's the good in any of this?' He was surprised; she was not usually so morose. The Beverley Wharton he knew well was driven, cocksure, almost arrogant; this one was hung around with a necklace of defeatism. Interestingly, she did not seem quite so attractive now, he thought, and that was a shame. 'Haven't you got anything at all to help me?'

'You've got four of the victims identified. Sooner or later that ought to highlight a common theme.'

She picked up four pink cardboard folders and chucked them across the desk to him. 'This is all we've found so far on all of them. I've had Lancefield trawling again, but I doubt she'll find anything new. Go through what we've got so far, if you like. I can't see anything that links them.'

He did as he was told, not because he expected to spot something that she had missed – he knew that she was too good a detective to have missed the obvious, and he was too inexperienced a detective to find the obscured – but because he had something buzzing around the back of his mind; it was a feeling he had had before, and it occasionally meant that he had his fingertips on a thread that led to a string, that led to a cord, that led to an answer. As he read, she explained tiredly, 'Dominic Trelawney was something of a recluse, the more so following his diagnosis of malignancy. He kept himself to himself; his neighbours tended to avoid him, since he was at best uncommunicative, at worst bloody rude and abusive. Malcolm Willoughby was a no-hoper from the day his mother said, "yes"; or rather, his father said, "get your legs apart", and he was barely known at his digs. He could have been dragged from his bedsit by purple monsters with ten eyes and no one would have bothered except to take snapshots with their smartphones to put on YouTube.' She threw a pencil across the room; it bounced off the edge of the wastepaper bin and hit the wall before skedaddling behind the filing cabinet, perhaps fed up with being flung around. 'And as for the Whitakers, they were on all the social benefit they could lay their hands on; I'm expecting someone to tell me that they were receiving war disability benefit at any moment. The daughter spent more time truanting than she did attending classes, and the mother has never spent more than a month in paid employment. The area they lived in, they could have been kidnapped by a gang firing AK-47s and rocket-powered grenades in the air and no one would have thought it odd.'

He observed, 'He's choosing his victims very wisely.'

'He is.'

'A clever murderer, then . . .'

'Tell me about it.'

He took a deep breath in. 'They're all of a certain social class, though.'

She shook her head. 'They're of the social class who get murdered, John. Agatha Christie might have polished off the nobility, but in my world, it's the ones who don't have social networks who die, the ones who don't matter, except to very few, very unimportant people.'

'If I were a serial killer, I'd choose people like this,' he commented. 'It's the logical pool to fish in.'

'Which doesn't help me . . .'

'No,' he agreed.

There was silence for a short while before she said, 'I did wonder if he was enticing them with money. He could be placing small ads somewhere, but trying to find out where without any hints would be a colossal task.'

He appeared not to hear and, when she looked at him, she saw that he wasn't paying her any attention at all. She called, 'John?' He grunted softly, but not so softly that she did not hear it. 'John?' she repeated when he made no pretence at reaction.

For a while Eisenmenger still appeared to be uncomprehending, for he just carried on leafing through the reports, then he asked without his head rising, 'Did either of the Whitakers drink?'

She leaned towards him. 'John?'

He looked up. 'Did they?'

'I don't know. I could find out, though.'

'I think the mother did. I think she had an alcohol problem.'

'How do you know?' He hesitated and she picked up on this, narrowed her eyes, became a touch more animated. 'John?'

'A curiosity,' he said. 'Probably nothing more.'

'Go on . . .'

'Three of them had fatty livers.'

She knew him well enough to know that he did not like talking about hypotheses that might not pan out. 'And?'

'The fourth had cirrhosis.'

She also knew him well enough to remember how bloody infuriating he could be. 'Which means fuck all to me, John.'

It was two o'clock and he was hungry. Without any prior planning, he asked suddenly, 'How about some lunch?'

They went to a bar near the Rotunda in the Montpellier district of Cheltenham. She had a Caesar salad and he a croque-monsieur; with it, she drank Sauvignon Blanc, he lager. He found himself experiencing curious feelings as they sat at a street table under the awning; they had known each other for many years and during those years there had been an underlying mutual attraction that neither of them had openly acknowledged yet both had been fully aware of. Only the strength of his relationship with Helena had stopped him on some occasions from taking things further; he wondered as they sat there what was going on in his subconscious, given Charlie's announcement of the night before. Beverley, though, was too preoccupied with the case to be dwelling on past – perhaps present – feelings. 'So what are you talking about?' she had demanded as soon as they had ordered.

'A liver gets fatty – pathologists call it steatosis – for a variety of well-defined reasons. Diabetics tend to have it because insulin is the hormone that regulates the conversion of sugar into fat and vice versa, and a lot of sugar is stored in the liver; you can also get the same phenomenon just because you're obese and, perversely, if you're starved.' The waitress brought cutlery; she had a smile on her face but it was as meaningful and dislocating as that on a clown; her eyes were constantly looking outside at

the passing traffic and Beverley wondered if she were near the
end of her shift and waiting for a lift. Eisenmenger continued,
'But the commonest reason, at least in the developed world, is
drugs; and one drug in particular.' He raised his glass and took
a drink. 'Alcohol.'

'They all had a drink problem?'

'They all drank enough alcohol to affect their liver; I leave it to
you to decide whether that's "a problem".'

She considered this. '*If* it's a common theme, it may not be *the*
common theme. A lot of people drink too much. It could be entirely
coincidental.'

He held up his hands as if in surrender. 'I know that, Beverley.
I'm only pointing out an interesting observation.'

She was thinking things through. 'Even if it is the link we've
been looking for, what does it mean? Is the killer a pub landlord?
Perhaps he owns an off licence?'

He smiled tiredly. 'Maybe.'

She was concentrating hard now, weighing up the implications
of what she had been told, performing a cost-benefit analysis;
should she listen to him, and devote resources to what might be
a complete waste of time, one that might delay her discovering
the real linking theme? Or should she dismiss this as coincidence,
look elsewhere, and possibly miss scooping the prize? Either
way, if she got it wrong, she was going to look both stupid and
incompetent, and she would be deeper in the mire than ever.
Eisenmenger had a habit of being right when it came to finding
odd, previously overlooked clues, but he was not infallible, and
his suggestion that drink was the thread that she should follow
was vague enough and nebulous enough to mean that it would
not prove advantageous without considerable resource. The more
resource that she committed to it, the greater her risk. It was a
high-stakes gamble to listen to him, but was it a higher stakes
gamble not to?

'Jesus, John. You and your "interesting observations".'

He bowed his head in mock apology. Their food arrived; his had
mustard on and was therefore, in his opinion, spoiled; when he
asked her how she found the salad, she shrugged and made a face
to tell him that it was merely OK. They were barely halfway through
the meal – with little more said between them – when her mobile
rang. As she listened to what the caller had to say, her face became
first grave and then, if anything, vacant; noticing this, he put his

knife and fork down and waited. She said a brief, 'OK. I'll be back in ten minutes,' then ended the call.

'Another body?' he guessed, but she shook her head.

'Two young boys have disappeared.'

A bad occurrence for sure, and extremely worrying, but he could not see why she should have taken the news so badly. She had produced a twenty-pound note and put it now on the table beneath the salt and pepper. He asked, 'And?'

She was already up and walking to the door and he had to hurry after her to hear her reply. 'They live in Colberrow.'

FIFTY-ONE
it probably means nothing at all

On the way to the village of Colberrow, Lancefield told them what she knew. 'Josh Barclay and Darren Taylor.' She showed them pictures that had she had taken off the intranet; one was of a thin, handsome boy with Afro-Caribbean features and a shy smile; the other of a slightly more thickset, Caucasian lad with sandy hair and a freckled complexion. 'Their families are neighbours in the village. Josh and his sister live with their grandparents – their parents are both dead; Darren with his mother and two younger sibs – the father is not at home. They went off for the day on their bicycles yesterday morning, taking a packed lunch. Each family thought that the boys were spending the night with the other, so they weren't missed until this morning.'

'Who's the CIO?'

'Chief Inspector Smillie.'

Despite her personal antipathy towards the man, Beverley was relieved at this news, for she appreciated that whilst he was a complete dickhead on a personal level, as Chief Investigating Officer he would prove professional and competent. She said, 'Where's Fisher?'

'I told him to find out all he could about Betty Williams.' She spoke with a hint of questioning temerity in her voice, as if she feared that Beverley might not approve; in the event, her superior merely nodded.

They arrived in the village, saw that Smillie had set up a

temporary headquarters in the assembly hall of the local school.
In the lane outside it were five marked police cars and a further
three unmarked cars; she recognized Braxton's among the latter.
In the entrance hall of the school there hung the unmistakeable
shade of school dinners past – stale, overcooked cabbage and
something definable only by its acrid unpleasantness. The ceilings were low and the walls festooned with paintings, collages,
photographs and displays that varied wildly in ability; Beverley
felt a vague reminiscence stealing upon her as she walked past
them, a reminiscence that was not entirely happy. In the assembly
hall – one, she saw, that doubled as dining room and gymna-
sium – trestle tables had been set up along one wall and on this
were computer stations manned by police personnel. Along the
opposite wall were two desks facing one another; at one was
Inspector Frobisher – Smillie's usual assistant – while the other
was unoccupied. Smillie was standing up, talking earnestly to
Braxton whilst gesticulating at three large portable whiteboards
– presumably borrowed from the school – on which was pinned
a large-scale map of the area, lists of names, photographs of the
two boys and various notes; there were also numerous jottings
and notes written on in marker pen. A continuous trickle of
people, some in uniform and some not, were entering, then
reporting, then going out again.

Beverley walked over to Braxton and Smillie, both of whom
expressed surprise that she should be there. Braxton vocalized his.
'I appreciate that you are keen to help, Beverley, but I think Frank
here can handle things.' Smillie said nothing; his expression was
one of wary defensiveness as he nodded enthusiastically at Braxton's
words. Braxton continued, 'I need your full energies applied to this
mad bastard who's killing people in the name of science.'

'There's a chance the two cases may be linked, sir.'

At which news, both Smillie and Braxton visibly started. Smillie
said, 'Connected? How?'

'The name of this place, Colberrow, keeps cropping up.'

Braxton was looking at her appraisingly. He said after a moment,
'Perhaps we'd better discuss this in private and sitting down.'

The head teacher's office was Spartan and small, but adequate.
Braxton as senior officer, sat behind the desk while Smillie and
Beverley took the place of parents, perhaps worried about their child's
SAT results, perhaps there to be told of some heinous misdemeanour
which would mean exclusion for their offspring.

Beverley quickly went through her hypothesis after which Braxton looked still more thoughtful and Smillie said at once, 'It's a coincidence, nothing more.'

'You know as well as I do that it's bad policing to write off anything as "coincidence" without checking first,' she countered.

'I thought your madman was taking people who wouldn't be missed; he could hardly have done anything more likely to attract publicity than taking two young boys from their families in the middle of rural Gloucestershire.'

'I admit that goes against what we thought might be part of his MO.'

Smillie turned to Braxton. 'And we only have one pathologist's opinion that the old lady was murdered; even if she was, it doesn't fit the MO of the other killings.'

Beverley could see that Braxton was becoming convinced by Smillie's reasoning; actually, she was becoming convinced herself and it was as much to reassure herself as Smillie that she said, 'The killer *has* no MO. He doesn't operate in his own socio-economic group, he doesn't kill his own racial type or gender. He just kills to kill and to examine the process while he does it.'

Smillie jumped in triumphantly. 'But he didn't "examine the process" when he supposedly killed the old woman, did he?'

Braxton looked at Beverley questioningly. 'Good point.'

Smillie hadn't finished. 'And as for the message written in blood, it's a complete red herring. Len Barker lived in Bromsberrow Heath which is barely five miles from here. It isn't that surprising that the registration number came from a vehicle registered to an owner from Colberrow. It probably means nothing at all.'

'He wrote it whilst he was dying, for God's sake! That surely suggests he thought it significant.'

Smillie was unimpressed. 'I understand that your enquires about the vehicle came to nothing,' he pointed out.

Braxton looked at Beverley, his eyebrows raised in query. She admitted, 'The keys to the van are kept securely in the estate manager's office; they have to be booked out and booked back in again. For the time in question, the van was in the charge of Shaun Carter, an estate worker. He was tasked with picking up an antique dresser for the estate owner, Mr Wallace Parker. He had to drive to Inverness – an overnight journey. We've checked and he at least was there, although we cannot confirm that the van was.'

'But forensics say the van is clean,' said Smillie with a grim smile. Beverley admitted this, and Smillie turned to Braxton. 'This is nothing to do with the body in the quarry. Len Barker was a good copper in his time, but he'd lost it when he had stroke.'

Braxton at last decided to contribute to the conversation and, as usual, it was to decide not to make a decision. 'We must keep our options open. I admit that there does seem to be *tenuous* evidence that there may be a link' – his accentuation of the adjective was enough to tell both Beverley and Smillie that he did not really believe it – 'but I think it would be unwise to work on that assumption to the detriment of all other possibilities.' Which was an easily deciphered code for 'I am not about to be party to a decision that might ruin my record.' 'Therefore I suggest that Frank here continues with his enquires bearing in mind what you have told us, and I am sure he won't mind you keeping a watching brief, as long as you don't neglect other lines of enquiry.'

Having made this indecision, he thought about it, nodded (presumably at its wisdom) and then looked up beaming at both of them. 'I'm going back to HQ. Keep me fully informed.' It was a sign that they should go.

FIFTY-TWO

'and yesterday? What were you doing yesterday?'

That Smillie did not agree with his commanding officer's strategic decision was clear from his whole demeanour as he briefed Beverley on the operation to find the two children. He was defensive and curt, sounding as if he had been tasked with a waste of time, and one which was keeping him from matters that urgently required him and him alone. Beverley was well used to such an attitude and was open-minded enough to acknowledge that she would probably have reacted similarly herself; it didn't mean, though, that she took it meekly.

'I've got four teams of two on house-to-house in the village and surrounding area . . .'

'You think that's enough?'

'It's standard.'

She made a face, bobbed her head from side to side slightly. 'In an urban setting, of course, but around here, I don't know . . .'

He frowned but refused to engage in argument. 'We know from

the mother of Darren and Josh's guardians that they were in the habit of playing on estate land – Colberrow Estate is over a thousand acres and effectively surrounds the entire village.'

'Did they have a special place on the estate that they went? Have you asked?'

A spasm of irritation crossed Smillie's face. 'If they did, no one except the two boys knows about it.' He smiled a bitter smile. 'Yes, we have asked, OK?'

She returned the smile. 'Just trying to help.'

In a whisper, Smillie said aggressively, 'This is *my* case, Beverley. Not yours. I'll keep you informed because I've been ordered to, but don't make the mistake of thinking you're welcome here. Just keep your nose out of it.'

Her lips stretched into a shallow smile while her eyes stayed aloof and just stared at him; she might have been calculating the best temperature at which to roast him. He turned to the large map on one of the whiteboards. 'We're working on the assumption that it was to the estate that they went yesterday morning. We know that they left at just after nine on bicycles and, Darren's mother seems pretty sure, with some sort of picnic. At present, though, we know nothing of what happened to them after that.'

'How are you organizing the search of the estate?'

'We're using the village as a centre and working our way out from there; I have forty officers forming a cordon, but we're going to need more pretty soon.'

Beverley was looking at the map, not even appearing to hear. Smillie was on the point of speaking again when Frobisher called to him from his desk. 'Sir? They've found two bicycles.'

'Where?'

Frobisher repeated the question into the phone, then came to Smillie and Beverley. He pointed at the map at a point along a small, twisty road that headed north of the village. 'There.'

Smillie took a moment to examine the map in detail before saying to Frobisher, 'Right, reorganize all the teams so that the search is centred on that location, radiating out from there as before, OK?'

Frobisher was about forty and prematurely balding with a ginger moustache that Beverley found unnecessarily bushy. He nodded and was about to return to his desk when Beverley asked, 'Were the bikes in plain view?'

He shook his head. 'Hidden under undergrowth.'

'Any sign of a struggle?'

Again he shook his head. With a final glance at Smillie, Frobisher returned to his desk. Beverley said to herself, 'Maybe abducted, maybe not . . .'

Smillie snapped, 'How they came to disappear isn't our immediate concern; we can investigate that when we have them back safe and sound.' He called to Frobisher, 'Where's the estate manager? What's his name? Somersby?'

'He's on his way in now. Should be here in a couple of minutes.'

'Where the hell's he been?'

Frobisher shrugged.

Somersby came in, as promised, two minutes later, accompanied by a uniformed policewoman. He looked harassed and decidedly unhappy. Smillie took him into the head teacher's office, annoyed to find that Beverley tagged along; he gave her a warning look but said nothing. Smillie took up Braxton's seat, with Beverley standing to one side of him, leaning against the wall.

Smillie said, 'You know why we're here?'

Somersby nodded. 'It's an awful business. I hope to God that they're safe and well.'

'Where were you this morning? We couldn't find you.'

'I had arranged to meet some contractors to discuss some work that needs doing.'

'What work would that be?'

'Drainage. We've got a bad problem with flooding in the northwest corner of the estate, at a place called Fairman's Wood.'

'And yesterday? What were you doing yesterday?'

Somersby frowned, looked across at Beverley, then back to Smillie. 'Am I being accused of something?'

'We have reason to believe that the boys went missing when they were on estate land. Were you on the estate yesterday?'

'I spend most of my time on it.'

'Which part were you on yesterday?'

Somersby looked slightly nonplussed. 'I couldn't say for sure. All over the place.'

'Just driving around?' Smillie's tone contained a hint of disbelief and it stung Somersby. 'No. We're coppicing in two different areas – Silver Hill and Langley's meadow – and there are several shoots to organize. My job isn't a bed of roses.'

'And you didn't see the two boys in question?'

'I'd have said something if I had.'

Beverley asked from behind Smillie's shoulder, 'Are there any buildings on the estate? Presumably there are barns, stores and suchlike.'

'Plenty of those.'

Before Beverley could say any more, Smillie interrupted. 'We'll need you to mark those down for us. Any mineshafts on this land?' For a moment Beverley thought that she had misheard, but then remembered that the area was technically in the Forest of Dean, where open-cast mining had once occurred. Somersby, however, shook his head. 'No coal around here.'

To Smillie's intense annoyance, Beverley asked another question. 'Any abandoned buildings, places that might be dangerous to go into?'

A look crossed Somersby's face as he hesitated; it was a look that Beverley and Smillie knew well, the look of a liar. 'No. None.' The shake of the head was emphatic – perhaps too emphatic.

There followed a brief pause as if neither Beverley nor Smillie was sure what to say, or perhaps they were each waiting for the other to speak, before Smillie asked, 'You're sure?'

'Yes.'

He nodded before saying, 'Very well, Mr Somersby. If you could let Inspector Frobisher know the locations of all the buildings on the estate before you go.'

'Of course.'

He stood and was heading rapidly out of the room when Beverley called a question to him. 'What was the name of the contractors you were meeting this morning?'

He stopped but did not turn at once, delaying the movement for a fraction. His face was bland as he faced them. 'Marcham and Son. They didn't turn up, though.'

Smillie raised his eyebrows. 'Really? How annoying for a busy man like you.'

'It was.'

With that he turned again and left them.

Beverley said as soon as the door closed. 'I wonder what he's hiding.'

Smillie might have been aggravated to the point of incandescence by his colleague's interference, but his instincts, too, were aroused. 'I don't know, but I intend to find out.'

FIFTY-THREE
'have faith in the Lord'

Antonia's migraine had returned with a vengeance and she had spent much of the day in bed. It had been with the utmost effort that she had answered all the questions put to her by Inspector Frobisher, Andrew sitting by her side while she tried to produce the answers through huge, heaving sobs. In truth there was nothing much she could tell them, and this only added to a near over-whelming sense of guilt, of failure. Since the death of her son and daughter-in-law, she had come to wear with a heavier and heavier heart a mantle of deep responsibility, and she felt that she had faltered badly. She was a woman of great sense of purpose, and she had always felt it important to do her duty and to do it properly; she had become lax, not listened to her greater instincts, not been a proper parent. If she had looked after Josh and Harriet as she had looked after James, her son, then this would not have happened. And this sense of culpability only added to the burden that was her sorrow and her dread. Stories of paedophiliac monsters crammed her senses, made thinking difficult, made sleeping impossible. Her mind was not her own to command; it vacillated wildly, caromed and cavorted as if – indeed, because it was – a thing possessed.

Downstairs, Andrew sat with Marcus Pilcher in the large kitchen, mugs of tea between them. Marcus had been there for an hour but, as he quite openly professed, doing little good. Andrew had tried to assure him otherwise, but his heart had not been in it and it had been clear to both of them that he was being merely polite and not honest.

'Does Harriet know yet?' asked Marcus.

Andrew shook his head. 'But we'll have to say something soon. The papers will publish something soon, and we can't let her learn what is going on from them.'

'No, of course.'

'But I don't know what I can say. How can I tell her that Josh is missing? She's only just got over the death of her parents.'

'I'm sure they're all right,' said Marcus for the fourth or fifth time. 'They're probably on some great adventure; thought they'd camp out or something – it was very mild last night.'

'Then where are they now?' asked Andrew.

'Well, I expect they've got lost.'

Andrew said nothing, a silence that only accentuated the banality of these hypotheses and caused the priest to become unusually interested in his mug until he said suddenly, 'Look, Andrew, I know I'm not much use in these situations – men of the cloth never are – but I really am sure that everything will turn out all right. The media have us all believing that there are paedophiles and ne'er-do-wells lurking behind every tree, but the real world isn't nearly as bad as they would have us believe.'

'No? What about these dreadful killings that have been happening recently?'

Marcus frowned and shook his head. 'I am sure that this has nothing to do with that, Andrew.'

But Andrew was sunk into despair. 'How can you be? Until they turn up safe and well, we just don't know . . .'

Marcus reached across the wooden surface of the table and clasped Andrew's left wrist with his right hand. 'Yes, they will, Andrew. Yes, they will. Have faith in the Lord.'

But Andrew, who was a good and devout member of the Church of England, could not at that point find it within himself to believe that such a course of action would help either him, or his wife, or his grandchildren in any way at all.

Smillie and Beverley returned to the assembly hall to find Frobisher and Somersby standing in front of the map. As they approached them, Frobisher was saying, 'It's completely secure, then?'

Somersby was an exemplar of confidence. 'Completely. The Grange is derelict and highly dangerous. We make very sure that no one can get anywhere near it.'

'And what is the Grange?' asked Smillie.

'It's an old country house. A hundred years or so ago it used to be the squire's house, but nobody has lived there for sixty years. It's fallen into ruin.'

Smillie said at once, 'I thought you said that there were no ruined buildings on the estate.'

Somersby looked uncomfortable. 'I forgot it. It's not really part of the estate proper. It's completely inaccessible except to a few of the estate workers. There's an outside perimeter wall made of stone and an inner chain-link fence.'

'Do you make any use of it at all, then?'

'Wallace – the owner – wants to redevelop it but I'm not sure the figures are right for that. At the moment it's just used as a general storage compound; bulk supplies such as fence posts, barbed wire, stock-proof fencing, that kind of thing. Of course we keep it locked, because we don't want the stuff stolen.'

'You check that it's secure regularly?'

'It was checked only a day or two ago.'

Beverley was examining the map. 'It's not too far from the place where the bicycles were found,' she said thoughtfully. 'We ought to confirm that it's as secure as you say, I would suggest.'

Smillie's expression might have been because he was experiencing intense indigestion or a particularly severe bout of tenesmus, but it was odds on it was because he did not need to have a fellow officer of equal rank making suggestions about how the investigation should be conducted. If Beverley realized this, she hid the knowledge well and looked at her colleague in blatant innocence. Smillie, unwilling to argue in front of juniors or a member of the public, said briefly, 'Of course.'

Somersby's reaction was interesting. 'There really is no need. That area is completely secure; I guarantee that. The Grange is in an extremely dangerous state of disrepair; it's not only a question of security, but of health and safety, and we take that very seriously.'

Smillie, though, was not to be swayed; indeed, the more Somersby talked, the more convinced he became that he wanted to take a look in the area. 'You don't have children, do you, Mr Somersby? You'll find that they are a most resourceful and irritating species, Mr Somersby. I really think we have to make absolutely sure that they're not there.'

Eisenmenger watched dusk fall through eyes that were shaded with alcohol. He found that he did not care anymore, that he had run out of emotional fuel. The impact of what Charlie had said to him was only now unfolding in his head, spreading sinuous tentacles through his mind, insidiously destroying the props that held his confidence and self-respect. It was a sadly, strangely familiar experience, one he recalled with all-too-great clarity from the weeks that had followed the suicide of Maria, a girlfriend who had immolated herself before his eyes in an explosion of petrol-driven flame. He had then tormented himself with the knowledge, the certainty, that he had been responsible, and that he was solely so. Charlie might not have committed suicide but Eisenmenger was experiencing the same emotional shock, the realization that his interests, his profession, his personality were all anathema to the business of love, that he was some sort of freak, ultimately abhorrent in the eyes of those who might otherwise love him. Even Helena had been falling – had actually fallen, he supposed – out of love with him at the time of her death.

He was a Jonah, a pariah, untouchable.

'Dr Death' Clive used to call him, and Clive was no fool.

FIFTY-FOUR
freshly dug

' I told you.'

Somersby's voice carried triumphalism but this overlaid something that Beverley suspected was relief. They were standing in front of the wooden gates in the stone wall that surrounded the Grange. They were, as Somersby had promised, securely locked and the broken glass on top of the wall was clearly a considerable deterrent to any would-be trespassers. Smillie said, 'We'll just check the perimeter, Mr Somersby. Just to make sure.'

Somersby's face didn't change, but there was a noticeable increase in the tension within him, one that neither Smillie nor Beverley failed to notice. Smillie gave orders for two teams of two officers to walk in opposite directions around the wall, then said to Somersby, 'If you could open the gates, Mr Somersby . . .'

Somersby found a key amongst a large collection and did so whilst shaking his head and muttering. He inserted it into a large black padlock that hung from a chain, pulled the chain loose of the doors and pushed them open. Smillie walked into the woods beyond with Beverley following, then Somersby and two plain clothes constables. It was cool and quiet in there; almost unnaturally so. They walked along the rough gravelled driveway, looking from side to side, occasionally startled by something scurrying through the undergrowth, although very rarely did they identify what it was. The afternoon sun was yellowing and warm, ageing and becoming more slothful and decadent; there were a lot of flies and midges buzzing around them, with the odd small wasp and bee, all seemingly sleepy and bad-tempered. The air was oppressively heavy with natural and not always entirely pleasant perfumes.

After a walk of some ten minutes' silence – nervous silence in the case of the estate manager – they reached the chain-link fence and could see the decrepit roofs of the Grange above the tree line. 'See?' exclaimed Somersby hurrying to the gates, showing them that they were padlocked. At that moment, Smillie's mobile phone rang. He answered it with a curt 'Yes?' then listened. Just before he switched it off, he said, 'Get more men and some dogs over here.' Then he looked at Somersby with eyebrows raised ever so slightly. 'My men have just found some sort of tunnel under the wall. Possibly it's a badger run, they think.'

'Well, then . . .'

'But it's quite big enough for a young boy to get through.'

Somersby looked stricken and Beverley found herself become more and intrigued doubly so because then a breeze blew through the trees and it brought with it a new perfume, one that for a moment she could not place. It seemed out of place in a wood, she thought, striving to identify it. Then she did so. Acetic acid, she thought, and she knew the significance of that. She said, 'I think we need to take a look at what's on the other side of that fence.'

Smillie hadn't caught the scent of vinegar yet and didn't therefore know what she was thinking, but he looked at Somersby who, seeming almost to be battling invisible forces that were crushing and immobilizing him, turned slowly to the padlock with the correct key selected. There was a dull metallic clank as the chain fell away against the wire and he pushed the gates open. They went through and looked around; the trees and undergrowth were thicker here, the scents even stronger, but not strong enough to hide the acidic scent of vinegar; Smillie noticed it, then glanced at Beverley who nodded imperceptibly in response. They both knew what it meant. Smillie beckoned to one of the constables and whispered to him, gesturing at Somersby's back; the man nodded.

The party moved forward in silence. After a couple of minutes, one of the constables said, 'Sir?' He was pointing to their right where there was a large low outbuilding.

Smillie asked, 'What's that, Mr Somersby?'

'Nothing. Just a storage shed.'

'I think we'd better take a look.'

'It's secured. There's no way—'

'That's what you said about the outer wall,' pointed out Smillie. 'We'll take a look nonetheless.'

They veered off, following a rough path of sorts. It was clear that it had been recently used, and used heavily. 'Do you have much occasion to come in here?' Smillie asked of Somersby, who shook his head but did so jerkily and with his eyes on the ground.

They were about a hundred metres away when Somersby suddenly made a bolt for it, sprinting away to his right. He wasn't fast enough, though, and immediately there was a policeman on his tail; within ten seconds he had brought Somersby to the ground in a clumsy rugby tackle. The estate manager was being brought back to his feet when the rest of the party came up. 'Going somewhere, Mr Somersby?' Somersby, still panting, said nothing. Smillie didn't seem to mind. 'Shall we resume? Let's see what you've been doing in that storage shed, shall we? I'll wager it's something your boss doesn't know about. Something, even, illegal.'

The vinegar could only be described as a stench as they stood outside the door to the shed; it was a large wooden building, perhaps ten by ten metres, and freshly done up. Smillie asked Somersby, 'Open up, please, Mr Somersby.'

'I don't have a key.'

Smillie held out his hand. 'Give me that impressive bunch of keys you've got in your pocket. We'll just check.'

Somersby had no alternative but to hand them over. It took Smillie four minutes to work his way through over twenty keys before the lock clicked open. He glanced across at Somersby, astonishment on his face, but he said nothing. The stench of vinegar became so strong that Beverley found her eyes watering as they trooped inside, then stood in a small knot, looking around at the large vat in the corner, at the bags of chemicals on the wall opposite, at the heavy duty electric hob and at the collapsed packing cases piled high to their left.

'What the hell is all this?' asked Somersby, his voice betraying a slight trembling, and attempting but failing to Beverley's ears, to assume a basinful of incredulity.

Smillie continued to look around as he replied. 'This, Mr Somersby, is a heroin factory. And I'm willing to bet all Chief Inspector Wharton's annual salary that your fingerprints are all over it.'

'Rubbish! I know nothing about this. I let Shaun Carter have the use of this shed; he said he wanted to store some booze he'd brought back from the continent. He said he had a nice little earner . . .'

Smillie was no longer listening, a man who had heard all the lies before and felt that life was too short to indulge in futile debate with scallywags like Somersby. To the one of two constables he said, 'Take a scout around outside. Check to see if the boys could have got in here.'

'This has nothing to do with me, inspector,' said Somersby again and with the same degree of success he had had before.

Smillie's only response was to say, 'Why don't you take a seat, Mr Somersby?' Somersby wasn't given the chance to make his own decision, for his escort pulled him down into a chair and, at Smillie's order, handcuffed him.

Beverley looked around the shed at the equipment and chemicals, whilst trying to work out where this fitted into her case. It didn't seem to, though; but then neither did it fit into the disappearance of the boys. Perhaps this was just a distraction, forwarding neither case. Smillie was on his phone, giving orders presumably to Frobisher, when the policeman who had been looking around outside rushed back in. He looked both sick and excited. 'Sir, I've found something.'

Smillie was quick, Beverley had to admit. He barked to Somersby's escort to stay put, then ran outside, followed by Beverley. Around the back of the shed, about five metres away, there was a tangle of fern, bindweed and bramble. It had been trodden down and the policeman ran to it, then stopped. As Beverley came up she saw that Smillie was staring at the middle of this.

At what appeared to be a freshly dug shallow grave.

FIFTY-FIVE
killed for their trouble

T
he phone rang irritatingly, almost painfully, inside Eisenmenger's head. His mouth felt swollen and rough, his tongue tasting only acrid mucus. He reached for the receiver, found that he had fallen asleep on his arm and it was no longer his, refusing to do as he told it; it felt heavy, lethargic and clumsy, a reluctant recruit to the cause of helping him answer the phone.

'Eisenmenger here.' As he spoke he was looking at his wristwatch, surprised to see that it was only a quarter to six in the evening. His clothes were rumpled and he knew that he looked as dishevelled and disreputable as he felt.

'John, it's Beverley.'

And he knew at once what that meant. He said tiredly, 'Another body?'

'Two. The missing boys, we think.'

'Oh, shit,' he breathed. 'Where?'

'On the estate at Colberrow.' He closed his eyes; the thought of having to watch another posting, this time involving young boys, made him feel nauseous, ready to vomit, but Beverley's next words surprised him. 'It doesn't look as though it's the Internet killer, though.'

Which piqued his interest, despite his hangover. 'Then who?'

'They stumbled across a heroin factory in the woods and got killed for their trouble. We need you here to do the autopsy.'

He felt awful, was probably still drunk, and he was on the point of suggesting they find another pathologist when he stopped. Something wasn't right, he suddenly realized; it was too much of a coincidence.

'Send a car to pick me up, Beverley. I'm not sure I'm up to driving at the moment.'

For the first time since the death of her mother, Lancefield found a small spark of the kind of enthusiasm for the job, enthusiasm even for life, that she had known such a short time before. It was minute, almost beneath her ability to perceive, but it was there. She clung to it as she pondered what to do next.

Beverley had instructed her to find a link that concerned alcohol between the victims that had thus far been identified. Lancefield had got the impression that she was being given the task because it was safe and probably a waste of time; after all (and as Lancefield had asked) what kind of link could that possibly be? Beverley had shrugged and told her to start with the pub in which Malcolm Willoughby had lately been employed – were the others customers of the pub? If that didn't pan out, her only suggestion was to talk again to the next of kin and steer the conversation around to alcohol, places where they drank, parties they had been to, that kind of thing.

And Lancefield had thought – but definitely not said – *Thanks very much.*

But after half a fruitless hour spent in the delightful company of Stan, Malcolm Willoughby's last employer, followed by a whole fruitless hour with Malcolm's mother who, understandably, was completely devastated but who, perhaps not so understandably, was off her head on cannabis, something in the back of her near moribund brain flared just briefly – a glimmer, nothing more in a fleshy nook – and she stopped abruptly. She was just walking away from the ground-floor flat that Mrs Willoughby occupied in the Benhall area of Cheltenham, picking her way amongst dog faeces in varying states of decomposition, crushed lager cans and signs of pavement pizzas long past, happy to be out of the atmosphere of sad inadequacy and damp that seemed to pervade the grieving mother's house, when she stopped walking, stared for a long time into the clouding sky, then turned around and knocked for a second time on the slightly warped, sun-bleached red front door.

Like all policemen, Smillie hated having to give the bad news, and he could have passed the task on to Frobisher, except that Frobisher was a hundred metres away doing exactly the same thing to a different grieving, devastated family. Smillie thought it important that the relatives be given the bad news – he found himself laughing inside at his use of the euphemism 'bad news' by a senior detective; the 'bad news' that all dreaded, that all had probably imagined might come to them at some time or other, that all had assumed never would come. He did not take that lightly, had a kernel of humanity – one that was deeply hidden lest it break forth and ruin his carefully crafted image of cold, mirthless sod – and was still proud to appreciate that he was in the job to serve, not just to 'catch'. He knew that Beverley and Braxton and all the rest would be astonished to find that he gave

sanctity to these thoughts – Frobisher might not, for Frobisher had
been with him for six years and had been through much with him –
but this did not bother him, indeed it made him feel secure and safe;
he was a member of the crowd, one of the anonymous, indistinguishable many.

Yet that did not make it any easier as he sat in that kitchen and
watched Antonia Barclay clutch her husband so tightly it might
have been that she wanted to squeeze him out of life, even squeeze
him out of existence itself. Her keening was dreadful, made worse
because it was an old woman's voice, bearing the grief of being
both a grandmother and a mother, trembling with both anguish and
age. He could not see her face but he could see her husband's and
could see on it stoicism undermined by the tears that trickled down
amongst the fine, grey hairs of his stubble, could hear the soft
comforting noises that meant both nothing and everything, as he
comforted her. Next to him, the large, ugly priest who had been
introduced to him as Marcus reached across, a hand on each of
them, his face contorted with grief and compassion.

It was a scene he had been forced to witness too many times
before, would have to witness many times to come, and no amount
of repetition would inure him to it; indeed, repetition seemed to
sensitize him to it, and he briefly wondered if his insistence on
performing this sorry duty implied some sort of masochistic, or
perhaps voyeuristic, streak within him.

He said in a gentle voice, 'Perhaps we should ask your GP to
call, Dr Barclay.'

Andrew's eyes flicked up to him but he didn't break off his low,
nonsensical comforting. The priest said, 'It's Dr Llewellyn, from
Newent, I believe.'

Smillie looked across the kitchen table at the fifth member of
the cast, a female police officer he did not know very well. He said
under his breath, 'See to it. Get him here now.'

She hurried outside to comply.

The glimmer had become dazzling, almost incandescent in her head;
it blotted out – no, Lancefield realized, it somehow *synergized* with
her previous despondency, turning it somehow from a thing that
fed on her to one that succoured her. Malcolm Willoughby had
attended an Alcoholics Anonymous group, albeit only for a month
or so. His mother, annoyed despite the chemicals in her system that
were damping down all but the most disruptive of emotions, had

eventually recalled that it had been one in a church hall somewhere in Gloucester, she thought.

'St Mark's?'

Lancefield had asked perhaps, she felt afterwards, too eagerly. The woman – a bloated face framed in an angular fashion by lanky, greying hair, beneath which was a figure clothed in an oversized and faded navy blue cardigan and jeans that could have fitted a bull – had appeared to think long and hard, but had eventually decided that, yes, that could have been the place. Lancefield had thanked her, but knew better, even in her slightly deranged state of mind, either to betray or to feel too much elation. She had driven back to the station in a calm, almost detached manner, but she had felt like a pressure cooker with a sticking safety valve. She considered calling Beverley, but something told her not to.

FIFTY-SIX

The Grange. It's falling to bits

Even the term 'shallow grave' was doing it a kindness. Barely any digging had gone into the disposal of the two boys' bodies; they had been laid to rest in a slight depression and then hastily covered with soil, mulch, vegetation and stones from nearby. The dying evening sun shone through the partial overhead canopy, dappling the area in a way that ought to have been enchanting, but was only deeply depressing. It was a hurried, shoddy affair.

Eisenmenger had never been able to cope too well with the murder of children. He had none of his own, did not even particularly want any, yet there it was, this weak point. He found it ironic that in any other profession and for billions of people on the planet, it would not have been considered anything other than a virtue, this squeamishness, yet for a forensic pathologist it was seen as an undesirable trait, something to be kept hidden lest it bring down shame. He had even tried to give up his chosen profession following the death in his arms of Tamsin, burned to death by her insane mother, but somehow it had never happened. Somehow, he had been dragged back, attracted against his own will once more to dance with death, to look into the heart of man's last and only true friend.

Dr Death, indeed . . .

'Strangled?'

Beverley, standing behind him as he crouched before the two bodies, clearly did not harbour such flaws in her character. Keeping his voice low and steady, he said, 'I think so.'

There had been a similarly untroubled scenes of crime officer taking photographs, but who was now finished. The forensic team, attired as Eisenmenger was in the oh-so-fetching all-in-white, new-this-season protective suit, were carefully scrutinizing the ground; they had found precious little, and little that was precious. Eisenmenger stood up and, his face composed, turned to face her. 'There are definitely fingermarks around their necks. Assuming that there are no wounds on the backs of the heads or torsos, and assuming that—'

She interrupted irritably. 'I know, I know. Wait for the post-mortem.'

He shrugged; her testiness was of no importance to him. He pointed at the derelict building that rose above the trees. 'What's that place?'

'The Grange. It's falling to bits.'

'What was it? A stately home?'

'At one time. Over the years, it's been a lot of things. During the war, it was some sort of army training headquarters. Before that it was a lunatic asylum.'

Around them, the woods were being combed by uniformed officers, and there were six police cars and a black private ambulance parked along the track to the Grange. Another car drew up at that moment, with Smillie and Frobisher climbing out. Neither of them looked happy. They strode up to Eisenmenger and Beverley. 'Well? Anything?'

The forensic team had finished and Eisenmenger just ordered the bodies brought up from their sorry sepulchre; they were laid on a pale-blue sheet of plastic and then, at Eisenmenger's order, turned. He let Beverley explain his findings to Smillie while he examined the backs of the corpses.

Smillie said, 'I think we can safely say that your Internet killer isn't responsible.'

Eisenmenger stood up. 'Certainly, there are features missing that we've come to expect – the shaven heads, for example.'

'It's quite obvious that Somersby did it, purely because the boys stumbled in on his little factory.'

'He's admitted it, has he?' asked Beverley.

'Not yet. I haven't had a chance to talk to him.'

'So it's pretty circumstantial at present.'

Smillie scoffed. 'There's "circumstantial" and there's "circum-stantial", chief inspector. I'd say that the bodies of two boys not ten metres from a highly illegal drugs kitchen will weigh fairly heavily in the mind of the average juror. Anyway, I think I can persuade Mr Somersby to tell me all about it.' Beverley said nothing and Eisenmenger was trying to attract the attention of the photo-grapher to take pictures of the back of the bodies. Smillie asked, 'When will you do the post-mortem?'

Eisenmenger looked at his watch. It was nearly eight and rapidly approaching darkness; lights were being unloaded from an equipment van that had just arrived. 'I should be ready by about ten.'

'Good.' To Frobisher, Smillie said, 'Let's go and talk to Somersby in the meantime.'

Eisenmenger walked away and having directed the photographer in which pictures he was to take, he asked Beverley, 'What do you think? Was it Somersby?'

She said hesitantly. 'He certainly has a motive and, as you said, it isn't the normal MO of the Internet killer, is it?'

Eisenmenger shook his head but said, 'There are one or two things that worry me, though, Beverley.'

'Such as?'

'Why bury them so close to where they were working? Why not somewhere else on the estate, well aware from here?'

'Because he thought he was safe here, where he has the only key and no one else comes. Moving the bodies would be riskier than burying them on site.'

'Then why not on the other side of this area, why so close? And why so shallow?'

'Perhaps he was going to come back and bury them deeper when he had more time. He couldn't be found when we first tried to talk to him; perhaps we called him in the middle of digging.'

He looked neither convinced nor sceptical. After a moment, he asked, 'Is Somersby a big man? Strong?'

'Not especially. He's fairly lean and wiry, but not a muscleman. Why?'

But, frustratingly, he would say only, 'I'll tell you after the post-mortem.'

'I appreciate that it's getting late, Dr Aldrich, but it is potentially very important.'

Dr Aldrich, the incumbent of St Mark's Church, was small and, it appeared, irascible. He was balding and clearly his physiology felt that this alopecia needed compensation, for the hair follicles in his nose, his eyebrows and his ears had leapt into action, enthusiastically sprouting a chaotic tangle at each of these sites. There were also scattered hairs around the base of his neck, popping up cheekily from the depths behind his dog collar, and the sum of this was to give the impression that he was inevitably surrendering to relentless hirsutism. He was, too, a careless shaver – as evidence by small cuts on the top lip and around the chin and so, overall, he presented a picture of a man who had higher things on his mind than physical appearance.

'I have a meeting with the bishop in ten minutes.'

'*Very* important.'

He sighed. 'Very well, but be quick.'

Lancefield and Dr Aldrich were standing in the vestry of St Mark's, a feeble light bulb bravely fighting the oncoming gloom of night, and failing; Lancefield could see that the lampshade was covered in a uniform layer of soft dust. The place smelt of damp and she wondered if that was how heaven smelt, if it was the scent of God. Around her was a mess, evidence the vestry was as much a store cupboard as an office. She had not been invited to sit and was relieved not to have been. She asked, 'Does Alcoholics Anonymous meet here?'

He shook his head at once. 'No. Is that all?' He was all but ushering her out. He had a shabby, dark-grey overcoat on and around his neck was a black scarf; since the night was quite mild, it appeared to Lancefield that he felt the cold.

'Not in the hall at the back?' The church itself, a Victorian building cloaked in the grime of fifty years of heavier and heavier traffic, was near the centre of Gloucester, on a corner by the inner ring road. Behind it was a hall made of prefabricated panels and in a poor state of repair.

'Of course not. I said that they don't meet here.'

'But have they ever?'

'Yes, but that was over a year ago. Before I arrived.'

'What about records of the meetings? Where can I find those?'

'My dear young lady, how would I know? Do they even keep records? I sincerely doubt it. Now, if that is all—'

'Do you know who ran the meetings?'

Becoming increasingly impatient, he was actually herding her out of the room as he replied, 'My predecessor here.'

'Who is that? Can I speak to him? Do you know where he is now?'

She was outside in the church proper, the empty font behind her. Dr Aldrich had his back to her, locking the door. He turned around. 'His name is Marcus Pilcher. I believe that he now serves in the parish of Colberrow.'

Fisher rang Lancefield as she was heading out of Gloucester, heading north along the A417. 'I think I've identified another victim.'

'Which one?'

'The beheaded woman, the one with "Maureen" tattooed on her back.'

'And?'

'I think it's Maureen May. She lived in Barton Street, Gloucester. She was a prostitute, living on her own.'

Which made sense. Barton Street was a black hole, a zone of anonymity in which someone could die and remain undiscovered for months. 'Did she have a drink problem?' she asked.

Fisher was taken aback. 'I didn't ask. Is it important?'

'It doesn't matter. Have you let the CI know?'

'I've left her a message. Where are you?'

Without a pause, without even a question in her mind as to why she was doing it, Lancefield replied, 'I'm on my way home.'

FIFTY-SEVEN
the normal compliment of arms

Outside it was raining heavily.

'Has Somersby confessed?'

Beverley and Smillie were standing in the corner of the dissection room, whispering to each other. It was nearly twelve and Eisenmenger had his back to them as he dissected an organ pluck that was painfully small. Smillie did not enjoy autopsies and found most pathologists arrogant and patronizing. He found the whole process upsetting and was always put off his food for at least a day afterwards. He beckoned Beverley outside into the body store where a bank of fridges formed one wall.

'He's admitted to being the brains behind the heroin factory –

he could hardly do anything else, considering his fingerprints are all over it – but he denies absolutely anything to do with the death of the boys.'

'He would, wouldn't he?'

'But he specifically accuses his associate, someone called Tom Sheldon. He's a labourer on the estate. He says that they heard the boys near the shed, Sheldon went out, and then there was a scream. When Sheldon came in, he said he hadn't been able to find the boys, but Somersby thinks he's lying.'

'Have you got Sheldon?'

'Frobisher's picking him up now.'

Beverley did not know how to react. She was pleased that the murder of the boys was to be solved relatively easily and quickly, but perturbed. Colberrow was somehow connected to the Internet killer, she knew, and it seemed incredible that there should be two completely different murders in such a small, rural location. Yet Smillie guessed from the expression on her face what she was thinking. 'I doubt that Sheldon is your Internet killer. Somersby seems to think he's little better than a Neanderthal.'

She couldn't argue, and was forced to accept that she was no further forward. She had earlier picked up Fisher's message, so there was at least a new lead there, and perhaps Lancefield had made some headway on Eisenmenger's suggested alcohol link. It wasn't all bad, she reasoned.

The Rectory, whither she had been directed by a gruff man with a lazy eye who, despite the late hour, was out walking his dog, was tucked well away from the road, itself just a lane. There was no street lighting, and the only man-made structure that was visible was the spire of a church about a kilometre away. There was an intrusive sound of traffic droning intermittently in what was otherwise country quiet as she got out of the car.

She looked around. It was just starting to rain and she had to hurry to get out of it and under the small porch. She rang the doorbell, looking around again. What, she suddenly wondered, was she looking *for*? Whatever it was, she felt it was important; important enough, she hoped, to be disturbing potentially innocent people in the middle of the night.

The door opened and she was confronted by a huge figure. For a moment it was in shadow, loomed over her, seemed about to engulf her; then, with his left hand, he switched on the porch light

and she saw that the face was smiling and there was a dog collar
beneath it. She did not produce any identification. 'Marcus Pilcher?'

The smile broadened. 'Yes. And you are?'

'My name is Rebecca Lancefield. May I come in? I realize how
late it is . . .'

There was no hesitation as he stood aside to let her enter and
asked, 'Are you in some sort of trouble?'

She surprised herself by answering, 'Yes.' He didn't react to that
beyond a small nod. The house was cold and, she thought, slightly
damp. It had been built in the Thirties and was only sparsely
furnished with what looked to her like other people's cast-offs. He
showed her into the dining room where he had been working at
the rectangular wooden table. He bade her sit and resumed his seat
in front of a thick pad of paper on which was laid a black fountain pen; beside it was a pile of magazines and leaflets. She saw
that the top one was entitled *God's Hypocrisies*.

'What kind of trouble are you in?'

Again, her answer surprised her; she had the feeling that she was
not the mistress of either her thoughts or her speech. 'You are the
Internet killer.'

What reaction did she expect? She couldn't have said, but probably she would not have put much money on the one she provoked.
'Is that what they're calling me?' He laughed softly and, she thought,
kindly. 'I suppose it was inevitable.' He looked at her questioningly. 'I suppose you want to know why?'

She shook her head. In a whisper and looking at the top leaflet
with its intriguing title, she said, 'I know why.'

'They were strangled. I doubt that they were drugged first,
although the usual proviso about the tox results applies. I've
found no indications in the modus operandi that would link them
to the previous murders.' Smillie glanced across at Beverley as
Eisenmenger said this, perhaps hoping for a visible sign of capitulation but, in truth, she had already accepted that would be the
verdict. They were facing Eisenmenger across the stainless steel
dissection table on which lay the body of Darren Taylor; even
in death they could see that he had been destined to be a handsome young Afro-Caribbean man. Eisenmenger hadn't finished,
though. 'There is something odd about the precise way they were
strangled, though.'

Both Beverley and Smillie were pulled from any thoughts by his words, both of them looking intensely at him. It was Smillie who asked, 'What?'

Eisenmenger indicated the boy's throat. He performed the dissection so that instead of the primary incision running straight up from the pubis to the Adam's apple, it split at the top of the breastbone and went off obliquely on the left and right to end at the tips of the shoulders; then he had peeled the skin away using a flat blade and delicate incisions, exposing first the throat, then the lower jaw, and then the whole of the face. It was now replaced but as he said, 'There was a huge amount of compression injury, see?' He lifted the skin away and indicated what he meant. Even the two policemen could see that there had been considerable soft tissue damage done. 'The trachea has been crushed, the jugular veins severely traumatized; there would even have been considerable compression of the carotids. It's the same pattern with the other child.'

'Someone strong, then?' asked Smillie.

Eisenmenger laid the skin back down in its proper place, then reached up and pulled down a spotlight that was suspended from the ceiling; he shone it on the skin of Darren's neck. 'The pattern of bruising would suggest that it was done with a single hand.'

'Not two hands?' Smillie was surprised.

Eisenmenger shook his head. 'Just one. The right.'

Beverley murmured, 'Why? Why use just one hand?'

Smillie was clearly having a problem with this. 'Are you sure?'

Eisenmenger looked up at him. 'Yes,' he said. His tone wasn't particularly outraged or chiding, merely puzzled that anyone should ask.

Beverley was only half-joking when she suggested, 'Perhaps the killer is one-armed or one-handed.'

But Eisenmenger said at once, 'No, he's got the normal complement of arms.'

'How can you be sure?' Smillie was sceptical.

Eisenmenger indicated the body of Josh. 'Because he killed Josh in exactly the same way, only with his left hand.'

FIFTY-EIGHT
born out of death

'I was born out of death. My mother haemorrhaged and died within an hour of my birth. My father was in the SAS and had the soulless eyes of a killer; that is all I can remember of him. I had no brothers or sisters and both of my parents were only children. There was no family to divert me from the course that God had chosen for me.' He spoke calmly, as if reading from a text, and she could hear that she was listening to a man who was used to speaking to an audience. His huge hands were interlaced on the table in front of him and his face showed extreme, almost unnerving tranquillity. 'My father did understand many aspects of love and affection but not, I think, what is required in a father. I have no reason to believe that he ever abused my mother, but I doubt that he showed her what she might consider to be affection. His world was one of valour and effort and masculine pride; I think that he thought that these were enough to love a woman or a child, too; I think that he knew no other way.

'He brought me up, then, much as a deaf man might bring up a hearing child; he neglected – how could he not? – that which he knew nothing about, yet of course he laboured ceaselessly to educate me in those things with which he was familiar, those things that he considered important. He taught me about comradeship and loyalty and he was careful to make sure that I would survive in the world and, by that, I mean survive both emotionally and physically. I had just turned five when I killed my first animal. It was a rabbit that he had snared and I was given the honour of dispatching it . . .'

Pilcher trailed off into the memory and, as he did so, he looked down at his huge hands. Lancefield could almost see him throttling the rabbit herself. After a moment he continued, 'Eventually, the camping in the forest and fending for myself became a regular thing, taking up most of my holidays. He sent me to a boarding school as soon as it was practicable; it wasn't a cruel place, except in that it was a heartless place, and if there is no affection, then there is a chance for badness to breed. There was only low-level wickedness, mainly from the older boys, but, for me, there was an ever present sense of hopelessness, because there was never a respite from the coldness; other boys looked forward to the holidays, yet all I had was a transfer from one place of desolation to another.

'I think I must have looked around to find what might rebalance what, even to a child, seemed an existence terribly out of kilter, although you would not, I think, have known my feelings had you been in my company. My father had done a good job in that, at least; I was externally composed and detached, destined in his mind, I am sure, for a successful career in the armed forces. I killed the animals with efficiency and ease, not appearing to give thought to them beyond the use I could make of their carcasses, yet inside wondering what I was doing, wondering again and again if death was all there was to life. He taught me to ignore pain, that avoidance of pain is neither necessary nor particularly desirable, that minimization of pain is not compassion. They are not yin and yang but nor are they completely separate. I would go so far as to say that they are necessary for each other's existence; without one, the other cannot be. Only in true compassion is there the most exquisite pain; only in supreme pain does the average, slothful, incerebrate human come anywhere close to touching the face of the one true God.' His voice had risen and become more impassioned, but now he stopped and looked up at Lancefield. 'But I am a poor host. Would you like some refreshment?'

She said at once no and he nodded acceptance of this refusal before continuing. 'My father was a strident atheist; not for him was there a beneficent God who overlooked killing in a just war, one waged for the greater good. For him, either there was a God and he was damned forever, or there was not; it was more comfortable for him as a human being to deny than to accept. I think that he preferred to hope that there is some certainty to be had in this universe, but I, however, was beginning to think him wrong.

'He died quite unexpectedly when I had just turned fourteen. It was an accident, when we were out walking in the Black Mountains; the weather had turned foul and there was a heavy driving, drizzle that caused us to walk with heads down and water trickling underneath our clothes. He slipped and fell perhaps twenty metres; I scrabbled down to him as quickly as I could and found him still alive, although only just. He had a terrible head injury and looked to have broken both his legs. I held him, talked to him, tried to comfort him, all the while aware that I was once again in the presence of death. It took him perhaps twenty minutes to die and, as cold and wet and shocked as I was, I was staring into his face all the while and . . .'

He stopped abruptly; Lancefield had been almost hypnotized for Pilcher was speaking in a soft, lyrical lilt, one that massaged and caressed. She came to from her reverie but before she could speak, he went on whilst looking into her eyes, ' . . . and I *felt* him die.'

She had been holding her breath, and continued to hold it. She knew that she was looking at a man who had, indeed, seen a moment of dying. He smiled, aware of her interest, aware that here was perhaps a kindred spirit. He explained slowly, 'I do not know what I felt, nor did I even "feel" it as such; I certainly did not see anything, or hear anything. I just sensed a *passing*.'

Lancefield looked at him, her heart full of curiosity, and wonder, and, perhaps even envy. 'What was it like?' she asked.

He lifted his head to look her directly in the eye and she saw a glow about his face, one of joy she could see. 'It was *ecstasy*,' he breathed.

'We've got Sheldon. Made a bit of a fuss, but he came along after a bit of persuasion.' The Smillie before them was very definitely a happy Smillie. He was rubbing his hands and, at least in Beverley's opinion the smile on his face only made him look uglier. 'Frobisher's got him tucked up in the cells now. And –' he nodded in Eisenmenger's direction – 'he's a big strong lad with large hands.'

Eisenmenger, showered and dressed in civilian clothing had been sharing a cup of coffee with Beverley as Clive tidied up in the dissection room. He said softly, 'Case closed, then?'

Smillie caught his mocking tone, paused and considered. 'No, Dr Eisenmenger. Not closed, but it's only a matter of time. With Somersby's evidence and your findings, he's certainly got one foot inside a prison cell.'

Beverley suggested, 'You'd better go and interview him, then.'

Smillie shook his head, still a lambent source of smugness for them all to warm their hands on. 'I think a few hours' sleep is called for. Let Somersby and Sheldon stew.' He was about to leave the room when he appeared to think of something. 'You'd better do the same, Beverley You've still got a madman to catch.'

With that he was gone and Beverley murmured to the space he had just now occupied, 'See you next Tuesday.'

Eisenmenger laughed, then stood up. 'He's right, though. I desperately need a few zeds myself.'

He fished in his wallet and produced five ten-pound notes, leaving them under the desk blotter for Clive as a tip. They walked out of the mortuary together having called out goodbye. Outside the rain was warm but relentless. He asked her, 'Do you think he's right? Sheldon killed the boys because they stumbled across the drugs operation?'

She made a face. 'It's plausible, but there's something not quite right about it.'

'Since when has a perfect fit been needed to convict a criminal?'

'Unfortunately, that's very true. There's always doubt, one way or the other. The only question is, how much doubt should we allow?'

'You think there's too much in this case?'

But she didn't know what she felt and turned the question around. 'What about you? Are you happy to convict Sheldon?'

He laughed. 'I'm only a pathologist, Beverley. That's outside my remit.'

'But not outside your experience. You've been involved in enough investigations to have a view.'

'Maybe.' He paused to consider, gather his thoughts. They were walking in the rain back to their cars. Suddenly he said, 'Look, I'm dog tired and so are you. Give me a few hours to sleep and think it through, then I'll tell you what I think tomorrow. OK?'

'Of course.' They had reached the cars. 'We'll talk in the morning.' She smiled at him; it was a smile that he had not seen before, one that was almost shy. He wondered what it meant.

There had been perhaps ten seconds of silence, which is a long time when it is deep in the night, and there is rain outside and the room is cold. Pilcher suddenly stood up and came around the table, pulling out a chair so that he could sit directly beside Lancefield. He said, 'You know what I'm talking about, don't you. You understand.' These were assertions. She nodded, tears in her eyes, but said – could say – nothing. 'Come here, child,' he commanded, his voice soft and overfilled with compassion. He took her hands in his, enfolded them, as if making them disappear by a conjuror's illusion. 'Tell me.'

And she confessed. She told him how she and her father had sat with her mother for hours and how she had gradually subsided, and how she thought that her mother was going to slip unseen away, as if sneaking from the room. 'My father had fallen asleep and I was close to it; I felt so tired, but I couldn't allow myself to miss her passing. I just couldn't.'

She looked into the face of the priest and he nodded and there were tears in his eyes, as there were in hers. 'Of course you couldn't,' he agreed.

'She had been deteriorating for years, and I had looked on that as dying, as a passage away from us, from her body, from life, but now . . . now I don't know.'

'What happened?'

'After so many long hours of just lying there, eyes closed, mouth open and chest barely moving, her eyes suddenly opened. For some seconds, she just stared up towards the ceiling, and then I said softly, "Mum". I thought she wasn't going to respond, but quite suddenly, she turned her head to look at me. I reached for her hand, took it, and was immediately aware that it didn't feel right.'

'How so?' he asked at once.

But she couldn't put it into words. 'I don't know. It was just different.'

He frowned, considered, then sighed slightly. 'Go on.'

'My mother's eyes were at first unfocussed, but then she seemed to see me. I was going to speak, but then, for the first time for years, she smiled and with that, her eyes lost focus and I *felt* something.'

'What?' he demanded, but again she had trouble continuing and he had to prompt her. 'Was it as if something were passing through you?'

'Yes,' she said but it was a hesitant affirmation. 'I suppose it could have been.'

'You felt it too, Rebecca. You are truly blessed.' And the tears rolled down his face.

FIFTY-NINE
true life comes after this

Eisenmenger tried to sleep but there was too much going on in his head for that. He had showered and was now back at the table, pad of paper in front of him, scribbling his thoughts as they came to him. He had a familiar feeling, one that suggested to him that he was seeing a way through the maze. He was so far behind with his work at the hospital that tomorrow he would have to spend the morning in his office, eyes stuck to the microscope. Then he would meet Beverley and take her through his thoughts.

Right at the back of his mind, beneath the part that was excitedly analysing the facts of the killings of the two boys, there was a faint wisp of a different kind of excitement, but he was too pre-occupied to consider it deeply.

At Lancefield's bidding, Pilcher resumed his story. 'I sought advice from the chaplain at school; a repressed homosexual, perhaps even a repressed paedophile, although he never made advances towards me. He was a sorry looking man, perpetually morose and subject to chronic dandruff. He was of no use, of course. He thought I was either making it up or had just dreamed it, but I knew that I had not. I had been placed with foster parents and they were kindly enough, although ineffectual, and unable to view me as anything other than a casualty, something to be cosseted, forever wrapped in childhood softness. They had something of a shock, I think, when I insisted on carrying on my hunting pursuits; certainly they did not accept my gifts of pheasants, rabbits and even the odd small dear.' Pilcher grimaced. It had grown very cold in the house, but Lancefield did not care. She did not take her eyes from his face, nor her ears from his tale.

'It became something of an obsession of mine to try to recapture that moment, snaring an animal, and then looking into its eyes, coming as close as I could to it, as it died. Yet, there was never that *frisson*; I was watching an animal die, nothing more; could it be, then, that I was looking in the wrong place? Perhaps I saw nothing because there was nothing to see. In being with an animal when it died, perhaps I was wasting my time. After all, what was

I exactly looking for? What had I experienced as I held my father and as his life left him?

'Despite the pusillanimous responses of my chaplain, it became obvious to me that it was his soul that I had experienced, that it had passed through me. I tried to explain this to my teachers, but they at best patronized me, at worst scoffed; I was a child and therefore, in their eyes, incapable of any fundamental observation, worthy only of childish delusions. I had tried to recreate the experience but had failed; I had nothing but my memory.

'That I drifted into the Church was more from pragmatic and academic reasons than pastoral ones. Where better to examine this thing that man has spent thousands of years talking about yet never seeing? How better to access the finest minds on the subject? Did I believe in the existence of God? I believed in the existence of the soul; I believed that the soul differentiates us from the animals and that it is because of it that we have self-awareness. So, yes, I supposed that I did. Yet my God has never been that of so many Christians, an idealized version of a father, one who is so comforting because he is always willing to forgive, one who beams down on us from on high, a twinkle in the eye, a softly playing smile around the lips.' He snorted in disgust. 'Those fools should look around them and see the universe in which they live.'

In a voice that was hoarse, Lancefield said, 'But you must believe in kindness and charity . . . in caring.'

He frowned. 'Of course I do. But do not for one moment believe that such things come from God. They come from us, no one else. How can a God with a universe to consider, have any regard for things as lowly as we?'

'But the soul goes to heaven, doesn't it?' She sounded in her own ears to be scared of his answer.

'Of course. This existence is merely a temporary thing. True life comes after this.'

She nodded, relieved. 'Good.'

He seemed slightly troubled, as if her interruption had broken his line of thinking. Only slowly did he begin to speak again. 'Over the years I became something of an expert in writings on the soul, on what the "experts" had to say, which was precious little. Of more interest to me was the chance it gave me to be present when death arose from life. Those were the times that I craved, that made my own soul sing, yet time after time came and never once did I feel as I had felt on that one time when my father had passed away.

Gradually, my passion faded. I concluded it must have been a fluke, or maybe my school chaplain had been right and I had deluded myself. I settled into the life of priest and would be there now if circumstances had not conspired to reawaken my desires.

'I was the incumbent of St Mark's in Gloucester. It is not a particularly attractive church, nor an attractive area, or even an attractive congregation. It was at this time that I married. Did I love my wife? I have asked that of myself many times, and still do not, perhaps cannot, find the answer. I have not been taught to love as most are; I knew that there was something missing and was unable to repair the fault. All the same, Linda was happy, I am sure. She died, though, as I knew she would, for she had myeloma when I met her.'

Which brought Lancefield up with a start. 'You knew when you married her?'

He said simply, 'Yes.' There was no inflection in his voice, no surprise that she should ask, no shame at what he had done. 'She was lonely and she fell in love with me. I showed her affection and attention and love; few people had shown her those things in her life before. She was dying and I made the last few years of her life as comfortable and love-filled as I could.'

'And you got to see her die,' guessed Lancefield.

Pilcher did not react other than to explain, 'I think that if I had not succeeded, I would have given up.'

'It happened again? You experienced the passing of the soul?'

He took a while before he nodded. 'On that final morning, I held her and we talked for long hours. She was very ill by then. The cancer had caused her to become bloated and she was prone to haemorrhage. She was drowsy, and accumulating fluid in her face and limbs. Yet, at the moment of her death, I was again the conduit, it seemed, for something, and my faith was renewed. I knew that I had not imagined or confabulated the events of my father's death. There is a soul in each of us and it is a distinct entity.'

'You decided to search for it,' guessed Lancefield.

'Linda had left me a not inconsiderable legacy; it seemed only fitting that I should use it to try to define the soul. I knew that if I were to hope to persuade a sceptical world, I would have to adopt the methods of that world. I had studied the scientific method as part of my theological training, so I had a good idea where to start.'

'Where did you get the money?'

'Linda left it to me. She was a rich woman.' Lancefield was

policewoman enough to wonder just how tangled his motives had been for marrying the poor woman, but she said nothing about this. Instead she said, 'And so you killed all those people. They were from your Alcoholics Anonymous group, weren't they? No official records and therefore nothing to trace them with.'

Without any emotion – no shame, no pride, no satisfaction, as if it all meant absolutely nothing to him, he nodded and said, 'Yes.'

'But the pain you caused, the suffering of those poor people.'

He reacted suddenly. 'People, yes! But not to their souls, not the God-given part of them. They are safe, in the afterlife; they are where they belong. I have merely released them from the captivity of an incarnate, imperfect prison.' He was suddenly animated and Lancefield was slightly afraid. She found herself wondering what she had been thinking, to come here, to think to find someone whom she understood, whose motives were known to her yet completely unknowable to the likes of Beverley Wharton and the oh-so-clever Dr Eisenmenger. He was no longer talking to her, but to someone, or something else; his own personal daemon, perhaps, or his own personal God. 'I am trying to find something that mankind has sought for thousands of years, something that could prove the existence of an afterlife. Think of it, Rebecca. The knowledge that there is an eternal, immortal soul in each and every one of us. The pleasure and relief that would bring to billions. Is not a small amount of pain for a few sorry individuals worth that?'

'But what you did to Malcolm Willoughby . . .'

'Was worth it.' This was deadpan, both in his voice and his face. 'I know that he is in the afterlife and he is happy.'

She began to think that maybe it would be a mistake to argue with him, to wonder if she were entirely safe. He was still sitting in the chair facing her, and the rain was still falling outside and it was still cold and dark in that house, and suddenly everything was scaring her. She tried to soothe him, hoping to reconnect with him, for she now saw that he was no longer looking at her as, quite literally, a soul mate. 'You've had some success, too.'

He seemed to change slightly at this. 'Yes. Just a hint, but I think that there was something. You saw it?' She nodded and hoped it wasn't too enthusiastic and counterfeit. He seemed pleased. 'It shows I am on to something. It is worth continuing, I'm convinced.'

SIXTY
in suffering is there salvation

Antonia could not sleep properly, despite the pills and potions Andrew had insisted on giving her. Believing that she was thinking clearly, she eventually could lie in her bed no longer; moving slowly and cautiously so as not to wake her husband, she got up, put on the dressing gown that lay on the end of the bed, and crept from their bedroom. She went to Josh's room as if drawn and, once there, she just sat on the end of his bed and looked around, immersed in memories, tears boiling within her.

She felt crushed by failure. She had been entrusted with looking after her grandchildren and she had failed catastrophically. 'Oh, dear God,' she whispered into the darkness of that empty room, her voice trembling. 'What can I do now?'

Antonia Barclay was a fighter, though. She knew despite her failure of duty, she could not, for the sake of her husband and remaining grandchild, afford to let self-pity engulf her. She still had responsibilities. Part of her grief, she knew, was powerlessness. She was impotent to bring Josh back, impotent to assuage the anguish that Andrew was feeling, that Harriet would feel when she learned the awful truth. She was impotent, even, to help with the conviction of the two men that Chief Inspector Smillie had caught and that he assured her were the guilty men. All she could do was what woman had done for thousands of years; all she could do was weep.

She switched on the bedside light, illuminating through the Star Wars lampshade a room that was cosy and untidy and haunted. Should she tidy it? She hated the thought of turning it into a shrine and thereby becoming chained to the past, but it seemed wrong to tamper with things that were not hers. She almost laughed. It had never bothered her before, tidying up after Josh, although she had constantly scolded him for his mess. It might even help . . .

'Antonia?' It was Andrew, standing in the doorway, sleepy, concerned, almost disorientated, and easily a hundred years old. Without saying more, he went to her, embraced her hard. They said nothing, but cried so much.

Lancefield's next question was asked at the cost of her life. Her professional instincts came to the fore before she could stop them as she asked, 'Did you kill the boys?'

Again, everything changed; it was a small, subtle alteration, but the shift in perspectives it produced was profound. Quietly and not looking at her, he said, 'Yes.'

'Why?'

'They saw too much.' He sighed. 'I liked Josh and Darren, but I could not allow them to tell others that they had seen me there. Nor could I use them, for it would have been too close to home.' He was silent for a while, brooding, although she did not think that he was particularly remorseful, just upset that he had not been able to use them in his experiments. Then, chillingly, he looked at her and said, 'But all was not lost.'

'No?'

'No, because as I killed them, it happened again. I felt it, Rebecca, just as you did, just as I had twice before. Their souls passed through me as I held them down, one in each hand, and crushed their necks.'

He was elated and she knew that unless she, too, showed him elation, she was dead.

She was dead anyway.

'You did?' she asked.

In a reverie, the boys' deaths a successful experiment rather than an obscenity, he murmured, 'If only I had been able to do it in controlled conditions . . .'

What could she say to that? In the event, she didn't need to say anything, for he came out of his trance and was back close to her again; terrifyingly close to her. He asked in a whisper, 'But what about you, Rebecca?'

What about her? She was very afraid that this was a question that had no answer, at least not one in which she continued to live. She could only look deeply into those eyes and close her throat on a dry swallow. He continued before she had rediscovered the ability to speak, 'You would not wish your soul to go to waste, would you?'

She had come to this place, to this man, because she had been living, she had believed, a half-life, had been in a kind of crazy love with the idea of dying. She found now that it had been a romanticized delusion and that she had been a fool. She very much wanted to live; she did not want to die, certainly not at the hands of a man who had cooked someone to death just so that he could search out a purely metaphysical concept.

But it was too late. His gaze was constant, without blinking, as he said softly, almost lovingly, 'Your soul is strong, Rebecca; I can tell that. You will ascend to heaven and I will see it. Together we will prove that I am right, and you will be in everlasting joy with God.'

'No . . .' She was shaking her head, and her eyes felt so wide and cold that they might been about to fall to earth.

He was smiling. 'Do not be afraid, Rebecca. For in suffering is there salvation, in pain is there joy.'

Too late to do anything by way of resistance, she began to rise from her chair. He leaned forward in his chair and his right arm stretched out and his right hand – so massive, so strong – was around her throat and pushing her down and back into the chair. And no matter how much she tried to pull it away or reach out for his face and eyes, no matter how much she tried to struggle, no matter how much she squirmed and wriggled and kicked out at his shins, no matter how strenuously she gasped for breath and tried to scream . . .

No matter how much all of these, he continued to squeeze. She lost consciousness, but he stopped immediately, smiling. 'You will see heaven, Rebecca, but not just yet.'

SIXTY-ONE
the null hypothesis

'In science, the null hypothesis is the way forward.'

Beverley Wharton didn't need another soliloquy on the philosophy of scientific method, no matter how learned it might be, and even if it was from John Eisenmenger. They were in her office and she was in a fucking bad mood because Lancefield had disappeared again. This time she had had no hesitation in reporting the matter to Braxton and he had agreed that even if Lancefield was in mourning, her behaviour was unprofessional and disciplinary action was inevitable. She had been given Frobisher as a temporary replacement. 'So you said before.'

Eisenmenger was Eisenmenger and didn't notice the inflection of her reply. 'So, we ask ourselves, what if Chief Inspector Smillie is wrong and our Internet killer did murder the two boys?'

'Except that the MO is all wrong.'

'Let's put that to one side for a moment. If our madman did kill the boys, what is he to do about disposing of the bodies? If he hides the bodies, or has some way of effectively destroying them – which, of course, is unbelievably difficult – there is still a big signpost pointing to Colberrow. In fact, it's *worse* if the bodies aren't found.'

'I suppose,' she said.

'In which case, his only safe course of action is to make sure that they are found, but make it look as if they were killed for another reason and by someone else.'

'Somersby and Sheldon, and their little drugs kitchen.'

'Which would explain why the bodies were hidden so poorly and so close to the shed where Somersby and Sheldon were working.'

'They had a very good reason for killing them, we assume that it's nothing to do with the previous killings, and our man is in the clear.'

'It makes sense to me.'

She stood up and went to the door. Opening it, she yelled out, 'Fisher? Get me coffee for two.'

Eisenmenger noted the lack of pleasantries and asked mildly, 'Is that the best use of your manpower?'

Back behind her desk, she snorted. 'Where Fisher's concerned, it is.'

He laughed. She said thoughtfully, 'There's still the problem of MO. Our killer has never done anything like this before.'

'But perhaps he didn't have any choice. Perhaps he was forced to kill the boys on the spur of the moment.'

'Because they saw something?'

'That's what I think; it wasn't Somersby's little operation, though.'

Fisher knocked and came in with two mugs of coffee, two spoons, a half full bottle of semi-skimmed milk and sugar cubes in a chipped canteen dessert bowl. Eisenmenger murmured, 'Silver service, I see.'

'Nothing but the best for Gloucestershire Constabulary.'

He put some milk in his coffee, while she took hers black; the sugar cubes were ignored. Sipping it, she said, 'If all this isn't complete rot, you're suggesting that there is something the Internet killer doesn't want us to see in or around Colberrow. Other than confirming our suspicions about the significance of the place I'm not sure that gets us any further forward.'

Eisenmenger mused for a while. After a while, he admitted, 'No, I suppose not.'

'And it could all be misdirection. If our man is clever enough – and I have a horrible feeling he is – he might be deliberately pointing us towards Colberrow so that we don't look elsewhere.'

'Maybe . . .'

They sipped the coffee for a while; Eisenmenger found himself settling into a cosy sense of companionship.

Beverley stood up suddenly, went to the door and bellowed, 'Frobisher!'

He came in at once. He was a short man, not unhandsome, and clearly a fastidious dresser; Eisenmenger even saw cufflinks, an affectation he found strangely anachronistic in the modern police force. 'Sir?' Frobisher asked, standing to attention before the desk. Eisenmenger got the impression he wasn't happy to be answering to Chief Inspector Beverley Wharton.

'Sit down.'

He complied.

'Has either Somersby or Sheldon confessed?'

Frobisher said at once. 'Don't know, sir. Not my investigation anymore.'

She cut across him, sharply. 'If I want to hear bollocks, I call in Sergeant Fisher. When I ask you a question, I want some sense and I want the truth, inspector. I don't blame you for keeping in contact with DCI Smillie, so tell me what's happening.'

He had stiffened noticeably. 'No one's confessed yet. They're both vehement that they had nothing to do with it. They've both admitted the drugs charges, though.'

Eisenmenger observed, 'Which is still going to mean a very stiff sentence.'

'But easier parole,' responded Frobisher.

'But as far as I can see, that means we still have a legitimate right to investigate the boys' murder, since I deem it to be possibly connected to the Internet killings.'

'I don't see how you can say that,' protested her new inspector, clearly demonstrating a distressing lack of team spirit.

'I don't care doodley-shit what you can or can't see, Frobisher. Shut up if you can't be constructive.'

Inspector Frobisher was clearly not used to Beverley's methods of discipline; either that, Eisenmenger reckoned, or he had just soiled his Calvin Kleins. He asked him, 'Was the Grange searched?'

'We made sure it was secure, yes.' This was said in a rather haughty tone.

'And there was no sign that anyone had got in recently?'

'None at all.'

'So what the fucking hell did they see that got them killed?' asked Beverley. Frobisher began to say something and got put straight before he had got halfway through the first syllable. 'Shut up, inspector. We're thinking outside the box here.'

'To coin a cliché,' murmured Eisenmenger almost inaudibly.

Frobisher was flushed and angry at this series of put-downs and had donned a petulant expression which did little for his innate beauty, and did even less to disturb Chief Inspector Wharton, who sat in deep thought until she said suddenly, 'Frobisher, you and Fisher find out all you can about the history of the Grange. I haven't talked to the boys' parents yet, and that's the first thing we should have done.'

Frobisher frowned. 'Shouldn't you talk to DCI Smillie first?'

'I'm going to talk to them about the Internet killer, Frobisher. Nothing to do with Smillie's investigation but, if I find you've accidentally let him know what I'm doing, I'll make sure you never make Chief Inspector. Got that?'

He didn't like what he got, but he undoubtedly got it.

SIXTY-TWO
a chat with the neighbours

Ellie Taylor had nothing to tell them. She was holding herself together with admirable courage, helped by Darren's father who had flown back from his new home in Spain to be with her. It was an awkward interview, with Beverley's tact stretched to the limits as she wrestled with the opposing demands of being considerate and trying to elicit information. Eisenmenger, who had only come because Beverley had insisted, said nothing; he felt his presence to be intrusive, almost voyeuristic.

If anything, at the Barclays, things were even more difficult. It was clear that Antonia Barclay was holding herself together with nothing less than superhuman effort, whilst her husband was operating almost as an automaton. The information they gleaned, though, was of more interest. It seemed that the boys had been in the habit of playing on the estate. Had they been into the grounds of the Grange before?

Yes, Antonia said, they had. They weren't supposed to, but they had been caught on one occasion, and reprimanded for it. Mr Somersby had been angry, and now she knew why.

She broke down in tears and was comforted in a painfully mechanical way by her husband. After a short interval, Beverley began again. Had they ever mentioned anything they'd ever seen while playing in there?

No, nothing.

Nothing at all?

Antonia became flustered. No, nothing. What were they getting at by asking these questions?

Beverley explained that whilst it was almost certain that the killers were in custody, the police had to explore every possible avenue.

They understood. She asked if they could look at Josh's bedroom; she solemnly pledged that they would disturb nothing. Antonia, still wandering in the hinterland of breakdown, said with tears in her eyes that she had been about to tidy it the night before.

Andrew took them up and then stood in the doorway, not entering as if unable to, watching them as they looked around. It was Beverley who found the camera. She asked Andrew if he minded if she looked at the photographs. He said no, as long as she didn't delete them, and she was careful not to.

'Look at this,' she suddenly said to Eisenmenger. He came to stand just behind her shoulder. She was looking at the picture of Darren with the Grange in the background. To the extreme left-hand side of the picture, at the side of the Grange, there was a small white object.

'A white van,' breathed Eisenmenger.

They looked at each other. Andrew asked, 'Found something?'

Beverley said to him only, 'Probably not.' To Eisenmenger, she said, 'We'd best go.'

They hurried downstairs, making their goodbyes as politely but quickly as they could. Antonia asked if they had found anything useful and Beverley replied as neutrally as she could that it had been very useful and that they were very grateful indeed for their indulgence. Andrew asked what they had seen in the photographs and Beverley replied neutrally that it had confirmed something that might prove to be of use.

Once in the car, she phoned Frobisher at the station. 'You said that vehicles were parked at the back of the Grange.'

'Yes. Land Rovers and tractors, and suchlike.'

'Any vans? In particular a white van?'

'Yes, I think there was a white van.' She looked at Eisenmenger and nodded to indicate Frobisher's affirmative. 'How are you doing with the background on the Grange?'

'Fisher's doing it now.'

'Well, tell him to extract his finger for once in his miserable little life. I want him at the outer gate of the Grange in thirty minutes, and I want him there with the keys and with some useful information.'

She didn't appear to Eisenmenger to wait for an answer before she cut the connection. He asked, 'What now?'

She pointed farther up the road. 'Up the road is where Betty Williams lived. It's about time we had a look, don't you think? I should have done it a while ago, but things got busy.'

'Is there likely to be anything left to find?'

She laughed, then shrugged. 'You've got a long way to go before you make a policeman, John. Your clever-clever deductions are all very well, but in the real world, most of the time they mean sweet fanny-fucking-Adam. My job is to look, look again, and then look a third time. It's all about tedious, repetitive, arse-aching searching, looking and diligence.'

'Sounds like histopathology,' he replied.

Lancefield was too befuddled to appreciate fully any relief that she was still alive. Her neck hurt and she felt as if her chest were on fire. She was stiff and sore all over and . . . and she was completely naked, bound by metal bands to an upright wooden chair.

An electric chair.

Suddenly the pain in her throat and chest didn't matter much anymore. She screamed as she had never screamed before.

There was nothing, as he had suspected, and as she had known. It was almost certainly in their imaginations, but it was more than just an empty house, it was a dead house, a small piece of a necropolis. They heard a silence that told them they were in a place lost to life, they saw shadows that hid not even ghosts, they smelled the damp and decay of a place no longer to be tended. Beverley said tiredly, 'Well, we had to check.' They went outside into humid sunshine. 'Let's have a chat with the neighbours,' she suggested after a deep breath to clear her body of the taint of death.

But this course of action proved initially unproductive. No one answered the rather shabby looking house on the left and, when Eisenmenger peered through the window, he saw that it was abandoned; a single chair lying in its side with just three legs was the sole occupant. The house on the right was in considerably better condition but again there was no response when they rang the doorbell. This time, however, they could tell that the house was clearly occupied; he was able to deduce this not just because there was furniture, but because sitting on a piece of it was a young man. True, he was staring fixedly at the television with his back to the window and seemed to be absent in a cerebral sense, but in a physical sense, he was most definitely there.

'Fuckwit,' murmured Beverley. She leaned on the doorbell, seemed to be trying to drive it into the housing and, after a goodly while, this produced a result. Eisenmenger saw the figure rise slowly, still staring at the television screen, then move with even less alacrity towards the hallway. The door opened slowly to reveal a broad face of perhaps some twenty summers with features that were never going to illuminate a room. The dark grey eyes moved slowly to the identification that Beverley was holding up in front of the face; Eisenmenger could almost see the effort that went into focusing on it. She said, 'DCI Wharton, Gloucestershire Constabulary.'

The features did not move much – Beverley suspected that they could not – but there was a subtle shift, one that induced a distinct air of wariness. She was well used to that effect. He asked, 'What do you want?'

'Could I have your name, please?'

There was a moment when he appeared to be too reluctant to give this information but then he seemed to think better of it. 'Carter.'

'First name?'

'Shaun.' Then, 'What's all this about?' Beverley thought that she knew the type well; petty criminal with a million minor misdemeanours on his mind and without the intellectual ability to hide them. She gestured with her head to the left. 'Your neighbour, Mrs Williams, has just died.'

'What about it?' Was it her imagination, or was that wariness increasing, perhaps even being tinged by fear?

'When did you last see her alive?'

'Days ago.'

'How many "days ago"?'

'Dunno.'

'Did you see her on the day she died?'

'No.'

'Did you see anyone visit her on the day she died?'

'Dunno. I wasn't here.'

'Where were you?'

'At work.'

'And where is that?'

The staccato duologue faltered and he hesitated. 'On the estate.'

'What kind of work do you do on the estate, Shaun Carter?'

Whatever he did, he seemed to find difficulty describing it. 'This and that,' he offered eventually. She waited, a perfect paradigm of patience. As she knew he would, he found the silence intolerable. 'Labouring and stuff . . . Fencing, digging, some stock work.'

Was he a murderer? She thought not, at least not *her* murderer; she found it impossible to imagine that he had any of the necessary skills – and, she had to admit, the Internet killer was undoubtedly skilled – to be her perpetrator. She had no doubt that he was capable of violence sufficient to hurt, to maim and ultimately to kill but it would be a crude, unrefined act; something done out of frustration or shame, not because of a completely misplaced need to know, as her murderer seemed to be.

And yet . . .

Carter's mobile phone began to ring. For a moment he didn't react, was content just to stare, trance-like, into her eyes, then she said, 'Aren't you going to answer that?'

He looked then briefly at the screen, putting the phone back in his pocket almost immediately without saying anything. An expression of puzzlement was manifest on Beverley's face. 'Wrong number?' she asked.

'It can wait,' was all Carter said.

She knew that there was something she was missing, but she could not identify it, and Fisher would be at the gates of the Grange soon. She glanced across at Eisenmenger who was looking at nothing in particular, as if caught by the same trance that had so recently entrapped Shaun Carter. Getting no help from him, she said merely, 'OK, Mr Carter. Thanks for your help.'

He grunted and had closed the door before they had even turned away.

SIXTY-THREE
a hundred different faces

'Inspector Frobisher's not happy,' announced Fisher as soon as he got out of his car. 'Especially about you taking the keys to the Grange.'

Beverley might have been able to care less, but Eisenmenger doubted it considering her expression. As she opened the padlock and unthreaded the heavy chain free of the gates, she asked him, 'What have you found out about this place?'

Fisher took out a notebook. 'It was built in 1763 by Sir Thomas Hobbs. The family lived in it until 1856 when the grandson, Sir William Hobbs was declared bankrupt and the estate passed into the hands of a private consortium that turned it into a lunatic asylum. They, too, went bankrupt in 1911 and thereafter it's been empty, apart from a short spell during the Second World War when it was used as a rifle training school.'

While he had been speaking, they were climbing into Beverley's car and she was driving them along the gravel track. She asked, 'Did you manage to get hold of any sort of plan of the place?'

Fisher's look of fleeting panic told the story. 'I didn't know you'd want one,' he explained.

Beverley said nothing. They had come to the inner gate and she gave the keys to Fisher and told him to unlock it. This done, they drove on towards the Grange.

It had once been magnificent. A Regency style was still apparent despite the decay. Three stories high but the top two were clearly very damaged by the weather of the decades that had passed since it was last occupied. Few of the windows had glass, and the large holes in the roof and the floors below gave the impression of a bombed-out building, one that had seen the worst of the Blitz; even so, the scale of the structure impressed. That and the intricacy of the surviving stonework that spoke of thousands of man-hours and startling levels of dedication and skill.

It was about eighty metres long, and built as a gentle curve at the centre of which was the main entrance that was about three metres high and closed by two doors that had once been painted in black paint, but were now peeling so badly that they were almost down to the original oak; heavy wooden struts had been nailed across them to make sure that even the most enthusiastic of visitors was deterred. In front was a semicircular gravel drive bounded by a low stone wall dotted with impressive urns that now sprouted only grass and weeds. In the centre was a bronze statue of a man in a frock coat and top hat; it was covered in verdigris and oxidized almost to jet. Grass and tall weeds grew everywhere, while much of the stonework was inexorably being covered and eroded by ivy and bindweed. It might have been a post-apocalyptic Britain that they saw before them.

There was quiet as they got out of the car; there were still the sounds of birds, still the breeze flitting through the trees, still the sound of their footfalls on the gravel, but these were still merely noises in a silence. There was a sense of deadness about the place, as if the air of decay was more than a passive creation of neglect but was an active thing, and one that seemed to be made by badness.

They whispered; what else could they do? Eisenmenger asked in a low voice, 'What do we do now?' Beverley reflected that he sounded unsure and even afraid, and that she did not recognize this particular John Eisenmenger.

'We look around,' she said simply.

They made their way to the side of the house, seeing nothing but elegant decay, a peculiarly British scene. There were huge glasshouses there set among wide pathways; Eisenmenger could imagine that once a veritable army of gardeners had worked in them and that the weed-strewn rectangular beds around the decrepit buildings had once been perfectly laid out in arrays of bedding plants, roses, lettuces, carrots, onions and a hundred other plant types. There was a distant red brick wall that might have been made by Winston Churchill himself and that seemed to glow in the afternoon sunshine.

A very, very British scene indeed, but one that was somehow past and no longer part of reality.

When they made their way to the back of the Grange, they came rudely back to their present, for on a wide deep back patio they saw four tractors, three trailers, two Land Rovers, two white vans, two motorbikes, two quad bikes and a single orange, flatbed truck; one of the white vans had a registration number that corresponded with the one written in Len Barker's blood. Beside these were piles of fencing posts and rails, bundles of stock fencing and barbed wire, huge bags of sand and gravel, and a large number of moveable steel stock fences.

The back of the Grange was little better than the front; in front of them was a long low conservatory stretching away into what had once been cultivated gardens, but were now almost like pampas.

It was an impressive conservatory, not quite the kind of thing that might be found at the back of the average two-up, two-down terraced in Middle England. This one stretched for a hundred metres, was made of perhaps a thousand panes of glass, and had clearly once housed a formidable arboretum. Beverley considered options. 'There's no way that those videos on the web were shot in there,' she said, indicating the ruined building.

'There's bound to be a cellar,' decided Eisenmenger. 'Places like this always had extensive wine cellars and the like.'

She turned to Fisher. 'Does it?' He just looked slightly scared and very lost, which led her to turn away in disgust; Fisher didn't need to hear her imprecations to know that he was not her favourite sergeant. With not a little asperity, she told him, 'Take a look on the far side of the conservatory.'

He was eager to comply and eager to make sure that he did nothing wrong. 'What do I look for?'

It was an innocent question, but then all of Fisher's questions were innocent, and innocence was not a thing that Beverley had much truck with. 'Jesus Christ on a bicycle, Fisher. We're on the trail of a serial killer. What the fuck do you think you're supposed to look for? Liquorice bloody Allsorts?'

As an answer it didn't give him much in the way of a clue, but he knew enough by now to shut up and try to look knowledgeable. He walked off, trying to give the impression that he knew exactly what he was doing; Eisenmenger looked after him with some sympathy, then asked her, 'And what do we do?'

'First we check the vans.'

Charlie had spent many of the last waking hours trying to come to terms with her decision to end it with John Eisenmenger, and failing. She now realized that she had mistaken the man for the job. Her training had taught her just how unbelievably complex the human psyche was, how one human being could present a hundred different faces to the world, how it could hold – and, more importantly, *believe* – a hundred different opinions, many of which were completely contradictory. Why, she kept asking herself, should it matter to her what his professional self found so fascinating? She knew from her reading and her education that such a morbid (frankly disgusting, if she found enough truth within herself to admit it) interest could be totally confined in one small compartment, and that there was no danger of leakage into the rest of the mind. She knew also that she could not judge a person by such a thing, that all human beings had such small compartments, places wherein lived the extremes, the unmentioned, the underside, the worst . . .

Yet, and for the first time in her life, she could not apply her teaching to her own life. This man whom she loved had shown a side to himself that she found intolerable and, in consequence, she now found herself to be intolerable. She was ashamed of herself. He had managed a trick that she ought to find admirable, for he could live a normal life in the knowledge of such atrocity; it spoke of great equanimity, or a degree of resolution that was admirable.

The more she thought about it, the more she hated herself.

Fisher peered into the conservatory through cracked and grimy panes of glass; inside it he saw ancient rotted cane furniture, large numbers of dead, brown plants and trees, broken glass mainly from the ceiling and dust. He looked carefully at the dust but could see no sign that it had been disturbed. He moved on to the far side of the conservatory, then to the back of the house, out of sight of Beverley and Eisenmenger. To him, it all looked pretty deserted, and he was becoming more and more convinced that there was nothing to find here, but a fear of his superior's excoriating tongue kept him looking, even if it was in a somewhat desultory fashion.

There was a lot more stuff around here – more fencing supplies, huge rolls of polyethylene sheeting and large metal hoops for poly-tunnels, bags of animal feed piled on wooden pallets – and it formed a sort of maze that obscured the base of the rear wall of the Grange. He thought he'd better at least show willing, so he edged between a tower made of bags of cattle feed supplement and another of bags of animal bedding; behind these was a row of fencing poles, leaning against the wall. He was surprised to see that there was, in fact, a narrow gap to his left, behind the animal bedding. He moved along it; its end was about four metres away and, when he reached it, he was surprised to see a set of stone steps that led down to a door. The door was completely hidden from view by a high pile of fencing rails, and it was open.

SIXTY-FOUR
less than a metre from her face

They found nothing that ought not to be found in the back of the vans, though. Mud, smears of faeces that Eisenmenger was fairly sure was animal in origin, straw, irregular strips of plastic and lengths of pink plastic twine. Beverley said, 'I can't see anything, can you?' When he shook his head, she sighed. 'I'll get the forensics team to go over these.'

But before she could make the call, her phone rang; the screen came up with Fisher's name. 'Where are you?

'On the far side of the conservatory, behind the piles of sacks. I've found something interesting.'

'What?'

'There's a hidden passage between the sacks. It leads to a door that looks like a way into the cellars.'

'OK. Stay put; don't go in. We'll be there in a moment.'

Eisenmenger felt an intense feeling of inadequacy; he felt as if he should be anywhere but where he was. 'Shouldn't we call for backup?' he enquired.

He did not get the answer he wanted. 'I want to check it out first; make sure that that moron hasn't got it wrong. I don't want to make myself look an idiot.'

They made their way quickly around the conservatory. At first sight they could see no way between the supplies; Beverley called Fisher again. 'How do we get in?'

'Look between the sacks of chicken manure and sheep feed supplements.'

'Why don't you come out and show us?'

There was a pause, but Eisenmenger who had continued to nose around, said then, 'Here it is.' He stood back to let her see. She cut the connection with Fisher, then walked down the path that Eisenmenger had found. At the end, they turned right, then came to the steps. Fisher was nowhere to be seen. Beverley muttered, 'Fucking idiot.'

She made her way down the steps, surprised at how far down they led and somewhat concerned that the steps were slightly damp and slippery. Eisenmenger followed nervously. At the bottom she pushed the door a little further open. 'Fisher?' she whispered.

Two barrels of a shotgun came into view, less than a metre from her face.

SIXTY-FIVE
the snap of bone was clearly audible

Beverley quickly discovered that, if there was one thing more terrifying than having a shotgun pointed at you, it is having a shotgun pointed at you by a man who looks as terrified as Shaun Carter did. She also made several interesting discoveries about how quickly her mouth could desiccate and how bad a tremor could be. She tried to speak with the idea of uttering reassuring platitudes, but little more than a husky croak made it out of the voice box.

Eisenmenger was struck by how cold the air had become; there was a trace of damp, no more, as they stood there. There was some illumination, although it was far from adequate, coming from yellowed and cobwebbed globe lights in the ceiling. In it he could make out that they were in a vaulted corridor of unadorned brick, with rooms leading off it; each of the rooms was closed by a stout door in which was a single, small, barred opening. They were cells.

'Where's my sergeant?' Beverley demanded. Carter gestured with his chin further up the corridor.

Eisenmenger retreated into intellectualism. 'These are what? Padded cells for the lunatics?'

'Move,' was his only reward.

Eisenmenger persisted, 'I think that these were once wine cellars.' He said it in that detached, interested, academic way that he had, the one that she had come to know, the one that was somehow one hundred percent, totally and completely inappropriate for the circumstances. He did not whisper it either, so that it echoed, as if refusing to die. From ahead of them, perhaps fifty metres distant, came a deep sonorous reply. 'They were.'

Beverley did not regard herself as in any way prone to fancies, frights or fear, but there was something about that voice, that resonance, that darkness and that coldness that made her very, very afraid. The door opened; it did not creak and, indeed, it was the silence of the movement that was truly terrifying. An impressively tall figure stepped through, bowing slightly because it was so tall. It was ugly, too, a fact not masked by the broad smile it wore. Eisenmenger was intrigued but perhaps not surprised to see it wore a dog collar. 'Welcome.'

She didn't know what to say and, to judge from his expression, neither did Eisenmenger. The man said, 'Shaun, bring our guests through.'

Eisenmenger was jabbed painfully in the middle of the back by the shotgun. They went along the corridor and through the doorway, the large man standing aside for them, exuding calmness and, inexplicably, joy. They found themselves inside a room in which were three long trestle tables on which were an array of open laptops. There were chairs set out for them, with Fisher occupying one of them. They were impelled to join him. Beverley asked him, 'You all right?'

He nodded but didn't speak. Carter took up station behind them. The big man stood in front, his back to the tables. 'You're arrival here is fortuitous,' he said.

'Who are you?' demanded Beverley.

'My name is Marcus Pilcher. I am the incumbent vicar of this parish.'

'Do you know who we are?'

'Specifically?' he asked with a faint stretch of the lips. 'No. But in a more general manner, I know that you are police.'

'You are holding us against our will. That is a criminal offence.'

The expression didn't waver, perhaps because he hadn't heard; certainly his next words implied this. 'I have something to show you. Something that validates my work.'

Shaun asked, 'Shouldn't we tie them up?'

Pilcher was aghast. 'Goodness me, no, Shaun. They are my guests. They will help to spread the word.'

'The "word"?' asked Beverley. 'Is this some sort of religious trip you're on?' She sounded scathing and Eisenmenger guessed that this was a deliberate tactic.

'I am a seeker of the truth. If you think that is a "religious trip", then yes, I am.'

'You're a homicidal lunatic, Pilcher.'

This was greeted with a shake of the massive head, nothing more. Eisenmenger guessed that Pilcher was too far gone to be affected by words. He looked at Shaun Carter. 'What's your role in this, Shaun?'

He got no direct response, although Pilcher explained, 'Shaun, too, is interested in my work.'

Beverley snorted. 'Shaun is interested only in the money and the flesh, I would guess.'

If she had hoped for a response, or at least a reaction, she was left without fulfilment, for Shaun only smirked. She tried again, asking him, 'Was it your idea to put the wrong head and the wrong body together, Shaun? Your idea of a joke?'

Pilcher's face registered brief concern, but he said nothing. Shaun's face registered anger and, from the glance he threw at Pilcher, some anxiety. 'You're talking shit,' he mumbled.

Eisenmenger saw this, and saw that Beverley had seen it too, probably more than he had seen. She smiled. 'This is serious science, Shaun. It's not a joke, you know.'

'I know that.'

'And the head in the slurry pit? How is that science? Or just you being a dick?'

With a grunt and sneer, Shaun stepped forward and brought the stock of the shotgun down hard on her right shoulder. She felt something snap – her collarbone, she guessed – and with it was washed over with pain. Pilcher shook his head. 'There really is no need for this unpleasantness.'

Fisher looked aghast and began to rise, although Carter's menacing look in his direction made him think again. Eisenmenger could only look on as Beverley swayed slightly in the chair; her shoulder was hanging forward slightly and blood was seeping through the fabric of her blouse.

It took an effort in which there was a long pause, but after a deep breath she said at last, 'You haven't got the brains of a woodlouse.'

At that, Carter stepped back, but only to aim another, mirror-image blow to Beverley's left shoulder. This time, the snap of bone was clearly audible and this time the pain was enough to wash her away. She tipped forward with a low grunt, then collapsed out of the chair. Both Fisher and Eisenmenger started to go to her assistance, but the barrels of the shotgun swung round on them; Shaun Carter was grinning and shaking his head, clearly hoping one of them would do something rash. Pilcher didn't seem to have noticed anything amiss. He was at the keyboard of a large, widescreen laptop. 'Look at this,' he said. Eisenmenger could only describe the pride and satisfaction in this strange man's voice as truly chilling.

SIXTY-SIX
in his left hand a scalpel

The screen came on, the picture shockingly clear. It showed Rebecca Lancefield, naked, head shaved, electrodes applied to her scalp, her chest and her ribs. She was awake and she was terrified; there were bruises clearly visible around her throat. Pilcher had by now the other laptops up and running, five in all; they showed the telemetric read-outs that Eisenmenger was used to from the webcasts. Pilcher came to stand behind Eisenmenger. 'I did this experiment four hours ago. Watch!'

Eisenmenger knew that he ought to be immune to what he was being forced to watch, but he wasn't; far from it. He was experiencing the fear that he knew from watching well-made horror films – the awfulness of watching someone he had come to know and identify with go through a terrible experience – but this was orders of magnitude worse. He wondered what was going to happen, how she would die, and these were questions he would ask during such films, but then it would be idle, disinterested speculation; now they were asked with a degree of dread that he had never before known. He could only beg God that it would not be slow electrocution. Fisher looked just plain sick.

From behind Lancefield, a figure appeared; the face was not visible but the frame was clearly that of Pilcher. It was dressed in black and wore black leather gloves. Lancefield looked around; there was no sound, but she was talking animatedly, hysterically; she was crying now, struggling at her implacable bonds. The telemetry readings were going wild; her blood pressure was peaking wildly, her pulse was over one-fifty and rising, and her blood was becoming less acidic because of her rapid panting; the EEG readings were just chaotic.

Pilcher said ruminatively, 'The guillotine was too quick. It happens in an instant. I see that now.' He was sorrowful, but only because he had missed a trick, not because he had indiscriminately slaughtered.

As if by saying something he could delay what was happening in front of him, Eisenmenger said desperately, 'Why did you kill the old woman, Pilcher? You did, didn't you?'

He looked uncomfortable, even annoyed, at that. There was a distinct hesitation before he said apologetically, 'She was dying anyway. It was an act of mercy . . .'

Eisenmenger suddenly understood. 'You couldn't resist, could you? This is all an excuse for glorying in killing.'

'No!' His eyes moved to Shaun and Eisenmenger braced himself for pain, but Pilcher suddenly held up his hand to stay his assistant as attention once more turned to the screen.

Lancefield's remonstrations had produced no effect.

Pilcher had in his left hand a scalpel.

Fisher moaned quietly and Eisenmenger closed his eyes, imploring a God he did not entirely believe in to make it go away. Pilcher was staring at the screens intently. He glanced around at Eisenmenger, saw that his eyes were closed and said, 'Please watch. You are here to bear witness.'

Shaun tapped him on the shoulder with the shotgun and he opened his eyes. He looked into Carter's face and saw feverish excitement; he had been wondering what he got out of this, and in that look he now understood. There was a degree of savage pleasure written across his features that chilled Eisenmenger, as if he were looking into the heart of darkness; Pilcher might be mad, but Carter was just plain *bad*. On screen, Pilcher's right hand was gripping the side of Lancefield's face, pulling it up and away from the shoulder; the left with the scalpel was just penetrating the skin. He must have been tremendously strong for it was clear the Lancefield was struggling violently, yet producing almost no movement of the neck. The blade bit deeply and blood welled up immediately; that it was blood there could be no doubt; no fake blood, no matter how expensive the film ever quite got the viscosity and the shade quite right, never managed to capture the fact that blood is alive, is in many ways *life*.

Eisenmenger was thankful that at least he could not see Lancefield's face, for that he suspected would have been beyond him, would have made him faint to escape the horror. A glance at Shaun Carter gave him a glimpse of such intense excitement, it was almost pornographic to behold. The blade began to slice through the flesh and it had not gone far before the flow of blood increased exponentially, became a fountain, ebbing and flowing but never dying; the carotid, he thought, but it was a melancholy whisper, ashamed of itself. The struggles, still effectively suppressed, became spasms. The hands withdrew. Lancefield's face was a caricature of humanity, had become animalistic in its agonies, its terrors, its dying, as the blood spurted; there was no sound but he could hear her as she keened; he could also smell that ferric odour of the blood that coated her, feel it's tackiness as it began to clot.

Real-time Pilcher turned to them. 'Watch. Watch the EEG, and the eyes.'

And what else could they do?

Beverley groaned softly on the floor.

It lasted for long, long moments, a time that was stretched yet thick, in which he held his breath while his heart pounded slowly in his chest and in his head. Gradually the flow of blood subsided, the spasms became twitching, the opened mouth became slack. Pilcher stared intently, then suddenly pounced on the keyboard. Everything froze. 'There!'

There it was again. A faint spark in the eye. Just that.

Pilcher indicated the EEG read-outs. Eisenmenger was not overly familiar with the complex read-outs of electroencephalograms, but that was alright, he had Pilcher to help him. 'At the same time as we observed the ocular phenomenon, and just as the activity in the beta wave tails off, there is a small but undoubted spike in theta wave and then in delta wave.'

'What does that mean?'

'Theta activity is typically seen in young children; delta activity in babies. Interestingly, these spikes are occurring in untypical areas of the brain, which I have yet to explain. The timing of the spike, however, suggests to me some sort of regression; I think it is the unburdening of the soul, a cleansing so that it reverts to its virginal state.'

Eisenmenger wanted to argue, but he knew better than to argue with a delusion so entrenched; he wanted to scream, too – scream that this codswallop had to end – but he knew too that it would make no difference either. He tried a different tactic. 'Maybe you're right.'

Pilcher seemed pleased. 'Yes . . . Yes . . .' He was thoughtful for a moment then he said to Shaun Carter, 'We could repeat the experiment, could we not, Shaun?'

Shaun's look was one of perpetual discontent, but the prospect of further death seemed to cheer him. 'Which one?' he asked eagerly. Eisenmenger had the feeling that Shaun's idea of a good night in was one involving slaughter and plenty of it. Beverley moaned again; she began to move her arms but this caused only more moaning. 'Her?' he asked Pilcher.

Pilcher's expression suggested that he was humouring his assistant as he said with a slight smile, 'Why not?'

SIXTY-SEVEN
the Rapture

Pilcher walked across to the far side of the room where there was a door that led deeper into the cellars.

The shotgun came round to bear on Eisenmenger and Fisher. 'Pick her up.'

Eisenmenger glanced at Fisher; he was unsure what to do, was looking to the sergeant for a lead; Beverley might have had a low opinion of him, but he was all Eisenmenger had. He was surprised, then, to see a change had come over Fisher. The slightly startled, slightly unsure, totally uninspiring look that he normally presented to the world was missing, replaced by something that Eisenmenger judged to be determination. The sergeant stood slowly. He waited while Eisenmenger did likewise, never taking his eyes from Carter. The end of the gun was about no more than a metre from his chest.

Carter repeated, 'Pick her up.'

Beverley was quite still now, lying between Carter and his captives.

Fisher took a step forward. It was not a large step. He leaned down, glancing briefly at Eisenmenger to suggest that he should do likewise. He said quietly to Beverley, 'Sorry, sir.'

He grasped her around the torso, and Eisenmenger did likewise. As gently as they could, they lifted her; she seemed to be conscious, although barely. They brought her to her knees where she slumped down. Fisher said to her, 'Come on.'

And then in an instant, he straightened up to face Carter; in the same movement, he grabbed the barrels and forced them upwards. He said to Eisenmenger, 'Run!'

But Eisenmenger could not. How could he escape and leave Fisher and Beverley? His morality refused to allow him to run. All he could do was stand and watch, spectate; it suddenly occurred to him that that was all he had ever done.

Fisher and Carter were fighting to control the direction of the barrel, the former trying to force it up, the latter down. Beverley beside them was swaying slightly. Pilcher was striding across the

room, his face no longer one of benevolence. Eisenmenger realized that he had to do something, that to stay the bystander would
be to be an accomplice. He added his strength to Fisher's, but Carter
was strong. Although Fisher and Eisenmenger had forced the gun
to point towards the ceiling, he managed to twist them both so that
it swung around in an arc. Just then, Beverley rose from her knees,
then toppled forward, crashing into the three of them. She screeched
with the pain but her weight was enough to unbalance the three of
them and they, too, lost footing and crashed to the floor. The gun,
pointing at Pilcher, went off; both barrels discharged simultaneously. The noise in that confined space was for a moment beyond
endurance, a physical force that subsumed them all completely,
made them for an instant insensate, as blind as they were deaf.
Pilcher was standing two metres from them, his face one of surprise.
There was a hole where once his abdomen had been; it seemed to
Eisenmenger that there was smoke rising from the bloodied ruin
of muscle, skin and gut. Pilcher was looking down at it as the look
changed from surprise to puzzlement, then lastly to something akin
to joy. He looked directly at Eisenmenger, then whispered, 'I can
feel it! I can feel it!'

He dropped to his knees quite suddenly. A jolt of pain passed
across his face, then he sucked in a huge chestful of air, as if
savouring something. 'Oh, the Rapture!'

He slumped backwards, still upright, head bowed down, and was
dead.

For a second no one moved, then Fisher, with a titanic effort,
rose to his knees. He grabbed the gun by the barrels and swung it
in a huge arc against Carter's head.

EPILOGUE
but he only thought about it

Lancefield was cremated with full honours, her role in the apprehension of Marcus Pilcher told sparingly, her obvious psychological problems overlooked. There was a good crowd at her funeral and perhaps no one noticed that her father was not in it; Beverley, still confined to the hospital following surgery on her shattered collarbones, was also absent. Fisher was commended for his bravery, Beverley's promotion made permanent. After the funeral, Eisenmenger went to see her. She had a room in the Nuffield Hospital, a private hospital near GCHQ and they sat together, the open windows bringing in hot summer scents. He had smuggled in a bottle of champagne and with this they toasted Lancefield.

'She was a fool. She had a bright future ahead of her,' she mused.

'Her life fell apart,' he pointed out. 'That's hardly her fault.'

Beverley was scathing. 'Shit happens. How you deal with it is all that counts. Nothing else. She paid the price.'

'*De mortuis nil nisi bonum.*'

'I never did believe that crap. If you ask me, too much good is spoken of the dead They're like all the rest of us; fools, shits and madmen.'

Before he knew he had spoken, he asked, 'And in which of those categories would you put Helena?'

For a moment she said nothing, merely staring at him; she was wondering what to say, whether to be honest or kind. She admitted at last, 'Good question, John. Was she mad or just a fool to give you up?'

'Or was she mad or just a fool to take up with me in the first place?'

She sipped more champagne, wondering why her mouth was dry. 'Feeling sorry for yourself?'

'I do seem to be bad news for those around me. Clive at the mortuary calls me Dr Death. Maybe he's not far wrong.'

'Even in the midst of life . . .'

'Some more so than others.'

There was a silence, neither finding anything more that was easy to say until she put down her glass, wincing at the pain she still felt whenever she moved her arms. 'John . . .'

He looked up, breaking away from reverie, raising his eyebrows in question. She took a deep breath, wondering why she felt so fucking awkward. 'I seem to be immune to your curse.'

He thought about this. 'Yes,' he agreed. 'You do, don't you.'

She wanted to say so much more, but found that she couldn't. He poured more champagne.

As he was leaving, his mobile phone rang; it told him mutely that it was Charlie. He thought about answering for a few moments.

But he only thought about it.

THE YOUNG GERMAN NOVEL

UNIVERSITY OF NORTH CAROLINA
STUDIES IN THE GERMANIC LANGUAGES
AND LITERATURES

Initiated by RICHARD JENTE (1949–1952), *established by* F. E. COENEN (1952–1968)
Publication Committee

SIEGFRIED MEWS, EDITOR

WERNER P. FRIEDERICH   JOHN G. KUNSTMANN   GEORGE S. LANE
HERBERT W. REICHERT   CHRISTOPH E. SCHWEITZER   SIDNEY R. SMITH
RIA STAMBAUGH   PETRUS W. TAX

65. Wolfgang W. Moelleken. LIEBE UND EHE. LEHRGEDICHTE VON DEM STRICKER. 1970. Pp. xxxviii, 72. Cloth $ 6.50.

66. Alan P. Cottrell. WILHELM MÜLLER'S LYRICAL SONG-CYCLES. Interpretation and Texts. 1970. Pp. x, 172. Cloth $ 7.00.

67. Siegfried Mews, ed. STUDIES IN GERMAN LITERATURE OF THE NINETEENTH AND TWENTIETH CENTURIES. FESTSCHRIFT FOR FREDERIC E. COENEN. Foreword by Werner P. Friederich. 1970. 2nd ed. 1972. Pp xx, 251. Cloth $ 9.75.

68. John Neubauer. BIFOCAL VISION. NOVALIS' PHILOSOPHY OF NATURE AND DISEASE. 1971. Pp. x, 196. Cloth $ 7.75.

69. Victor Anthony Rudowski. LESSING'S *AESTHETICA IN NUCE.* An Analysis of the May 26, 1769, Letter to Nicolai. 1971. Pp. xii, 146. Cloth $ 6.70.

70. Donald F. Nelson. PORTRAIT OF THE ARTIST AS HERMES. A Study of Myth and Psychology in Thomas Mann's *Felix Krull.* Pp. xvi, 150. $ 6.75.

71. Murray A. and Marian L. Cowie, eds. THE WORKS OF PETER SCHOTT (1460—1490). Vol. II: Commentary. 1971. Pp. xxix, 534. Cloth $ 14.50; Paper $ 13.00.

72. Christine Oertel Sjögren. THE MARBLE STATUE AS IDEA. COLLECTED ESSAYS ON ADALBERT STIFTER'S *DER NACHSOMMER.* 1972. Pp. xiv, 121. Cloth $ 7.00.

73. Donald G. Daviau and Jorun B. Johns, eds. THE CORRESPONDENCE OF ARTHUR SCHNITZLER AND RAOUL AUERNHEIMER WITH RAOUL AUERNHEIMER'S APHORISMS. 1972. Pp. xii, 161. Cloth $ 7.50.

74. A. Margaret Arent Madelung. THE LAXDOELA SAGA: ITS STRUCTURAL PATTERNS. 1972. Pp. xiv, 250. Cloth $ 9.25.

75. Jeffrey L. Sammons. SIX ESSAYS ON THE YOUNG GERMAN NOVEL. 1972. Pp. xiv, 187. Cloth $ 7.75.

For other volumes in the "Studies" see pages 185 ff.

Send orders to: (U.S. and Canada)
The University of North Carolina Press, P.O. Box 2288
Chapel Hill, N.C. 27514
(All other countries) Feffer and Simons, Inc., 31 Union Square, New York, N.Y. 10003

NUMBER SEVENTY-FIVE

UNIVERSITY
OF NORTH CAROLINA
STUDIES IN
THE GERMANIC LANGUAGES
AND LITERATURES

Six Essays on the
Young German Novel

by

JEFFREY L. SAMMONS

CHAPEL HILL
THE UNIVERSITY OF NORTH CAROLINA PRESS
1972

Manufactured in the U.S.A.

Der Mensch des neunzehnten Jahrhunderts ist mehr als jeder andere das Product der Umstände und seines Bildungsganges. Das Allgemeine hat die Herrschaft über das Individuum, und wol nur denen, die sich vom Allgemeinen als Dichter oder Künstler emancipiren.

Karl Gutzkow, *Aus der Zeit und dem Leben*

La marche ordinaire du XIXe siècle est que, quand un être puissant et noble rencontre un homme de cœur, il le tue, l'exile, l'emprisonne ou l'humilie tellement, que l'autre a la sottise d'en mourir de douleur.

Stendhal, *Le Rouge et le noir*

PREFACE

The following essays have a dual purpose. It has been my hope to make a contribution to the study of Young Germany (Das Junge Deutschland), a topic that is now of increasing interest. But I also hope the essays will be of value to those not directly familiar with the books here discussed. None of them are widely read and several of them are quite rare and difficult of access; therefore, I have tried to keep the reader in mind who has reason to be interested in the Young German problem but is not extensively acquainted with the primary materials. This purpose obliged me to speak in some detail of the contents of the books under discussion and to quote at length from them, as well as to rehearse some matters that are well known to specialists in the period. I hope that the latter will be indulgent about this and that they will find new perspectives in these discussions.

I am obliged to several persons who have been of great assistance to me. I owe a particular debt of gratitude to Professor Jost Hermand, who has been uncommonly generous with his advice, admonitions, and encouragement, and, on one occasion, with the loan of a book rare enough that I would have thought twice before cheerfully handing it over to another book-lover. I am also deeply grateful to Professor Horst Denkler, who was kind enough to read the manuscript and offer extensive criticisms, which I have taken to heart as far as my native stubbornness would allow and which helped me to make significant improvements. To the companionship of my colleague Professor Peter Demetz I owe much in the way of inspiration and understanding.

A special acknowledgment is due here to George Vrooman, humanities bibliographer in the Yale University Library. Young German materials, because of the onslaught of repression that befell them upon their publication and the generations of neglect afterwards, are very hard to come by and few libraries are well-stocked in this area. Mr. Vrooman, out of his enthusiasm for the purpose, his enormous knowledge of the antiquarian book market, and his astonishing memory for desiderata mentioned to him in months or years past, materially assisted me by acquiring crucial items for Yale's collection and unfailingly calling my attention to them as they came into view. Such people are the unsung heroes of the scholarly enterprise, and I wish most cordially to thank him here. I am also grateful to Mrs. Joan Hodgson of the Library of the University of California at Santa Cruz for assisting me while I was there in gaining access to materials at Berkeley, which has an unusually good collection of Young German books.

A shorter version in German of the essay on Heinrich Laube will have appeared in the *Zeitschrift für deutsche Philologie*, 91 (1972), *Sonderheft* on Heine and Young Germany, 149-163, under the title "Zu Heinrich Laubes Roman *Die Krieger.*" Thanks are due to the editors for permission to republish it in its present form.

To my wife, for her support, indulgence, wisdom, and tact, I can think of no reward other than an uncertain promise not to write another book for a while.

New Haven, Connecticut
July, 1971

CONTENTS

THE YOUNG GERMAN NOVEL

I. INTRODUCTION: ON THE TREATMENT AND EVALUATION OF YOUNG GERMAN FICTION

A set of essays about the novels of Young German, is more in need of a preliminary defense than is usual in critical studies, for queries arise at every initial point of the undertaking. Is there, after all, any such thing as Young Germany? If so, what is it? Are the books the Young Germans wrote novels, and, if so, is there any justification for talking about them, given their doubtful quality and the small place they occupy in the history of literature? In what spirit and on what premises might they be usefully talked about? It is to these questions that I shall address myself by way of introduction.

It has many times been doubted that the term "Young Germany" is useful at all; Harold Jantz expressed a not uncommon view when he called it an "empty label."[1] As a group, Young Germany was largely imaginary, a fiction put into circulation by the Federal German ban on Heine, Gutzkow, Laube, Wienbarg, and Mundt of December 10, 1835. This was an overreaction of insecure governments, which had made an illegitimate connection between the emphasis that a few writers had put upon their belonging to a young generation and some completely unrelated revolutionary organizations that called themselves such things as Young Italy, or, in Switzerland, Young Germany. Since most of the putative members of the group promptly and vociferously denied either that they belonged to it or that there was any such thing at all, one may well wonder what justification there may be for retaining a term that had so dubious a birth and, in the mainstream of literary history, was often used for abusive purposes. Even if the term is retained, one seems to perpetuate an accident of politics to refer it only to the five writers named in the decree. In recent years there has been much opposition to the splintering of literary history into ever smaller movements and coteries, and much more inclination to seek a synchronic sense of epoch and relatedness. Thus there has been a tendency to look upon Young Germany as an oppositional and dialectical segment of the Biedermeier or restoration period. Similarly, one can expand the concept, if one likes, very broadly; in his edition of exemplary Young German texts, Jost Hermand has included no fewer than twenty-five writers, ranging from the Hegelian critic Robert Prutz to the local Berlin wit Adolf Glassbrenner, and including the young Friedrich Engels.[2]

There is reason in all this, and there is no need to deplore varying usages for various purposes; literary categories are instrumental, not ontological, and may be used as best suits the enterprise in hand. The term "Young Germany" has held on, despite the opposition, and it is, I believe, still usable. Helmut Koopmann, in his recent and valuable study of the subject, argues that the federal decree itself is evidence that the group has a profile of a sort; while there was an unstable and shifting mass of writers of whom one could say that they belonged to the youth movement in literature at one time or another,

> andererseits hätte eine so breite, in ihren Konturen völlig un-faßbare Bewegung gewiß nicht die offiziellen und offiziösen Reaktionen ausgelöst, die wir kennen. Das Junge Deutschland war weder eine Untergrundbewegung noch eine Subkultur. Gewiß gab es Sympathisanten, zeitweilige Mitläufer, literarische Modefans — 'Bewegungen' kennen dergleichen ja zu allen Zeiten. Aber hier, im Jungen Deutschland, konzentrierte sich alles doch immer wieder auf wenige Namen.[3]

I would suggest, furthermore, that there are good impressionistic reasons for maintaining "Young Germany" as a usable term. In the core group of writers there is a special quality of intense urgency. It is strongest in Gutzkow and weakest in Laube, but it is present in all the works I would denominate as Young German and may account as much as considerations of content for the fact that certain writers rather than others found themselves in the baleful glare of government attention. Whenever one moves away from what Koopmann calls the center, whether, say, to a novel of Ernst Willkomm or to the urbane chatter of Prince Pückler-Muskau, one senses a lowering of the stylistic temperature. Other writers on the periphery may acquire this intensity briefly; an example is Ferdinand

2

Gustav Kühne, whom I have included here. In the older men, Ludwig Börne and Heine, the urgency is under firmer rhetorical or artistic control, and when I speak of Young Germany in these studies, I shall not normally be thinking of them, although their involvement with and importance for the movement in general is self-evident. The stylistic quality, moreover, is time-bound, and is restricted for the most part to about a half-dozen years around 1835. The earliest writings of Gutzkow and Mundt, for example, have less of it than those published right around the crisis, and by 1838 it is practically nowhere to be seen. The specific Young German style is *sui generis* and is not wholly captured by attempts to catalogue the terms and slogans that were central to writers' concerns.[4] It is more a matter of pitch and gesture, simultaneously robust and bewildered, crowding insistently close to the reader in the effort to arouse in him some resonance and motion. At the same time, much intellectual pain is communicated, for common to the Young German experience is a powerful feeling of the intolerableness of the world the writers lived in.

Since the toe-to-toe relationship with the reader is the characteristic Young German posture, it sometimes seemed to matter little to them whether they expressed themselves in expository or imaginative writing. Their primary concern was to communicate and disseminate into an age characterized by stagnation and regressiveness what appeared to them to be the best modern thought; therefore the choice of vehicle often seemed to them a practical question only. It is well known, for example, that Gutzkow undertook his novel *Wally, die Zweiflerin* after having been frustrated in his effort to continue Lessing's project of publishing the fragments of the free-thinker Reimarus. The choice of fiction in this as in other cases is motivated by the insistent desire to find a way to smuggle contraband into the consciousness of the public. All the Young German novels and novellas are thesis works of one kind or another. Therefore the question arises whether it is justified to single out the longer prose fiction from the corpus of Young German writing for special attention. With very few exceptions, scholarship on Young Germany has tended from the beginning to draw from writings irrespective of their expository or fictional character, and by and large the Young German novels have not been regarded as such at all, but as fictionalized tracts that pursue the Young German mission by different means. Among the writers themselves there was an extreme and studied vagueness about genre distinctions, about the boundaries between novel and novella, between either and just stories, true or fictional, and between any of these and indefinable mixed bags of fiction, reportage, and speculation.[5]

Yet that the Young German novels are novels can hardly be doubted today. They represent, however, a substantial expansion from what had already become in the 1830's the traditional form of the *Bildungsroman* or the artistic and symbolic novel oriented on the Romantic tradition or Goethe's *Wahlverwandtschaften*. The Young German novel, writes Koopmann, "hatte mit dem überlieferten Bildungsroman allerdings kaum mehr gemeinsam als den größeren Umfang und die ihm damit auferlegten strukturellen Eigentümlichkeiten. Aber er war nicht mehr als rein poetisches Gebilde, sondern als Spiegelbild der Wirklichkeit konzipiert und folgte damit automatisch anderen Gesetzen als denen der tradierten Erzählwerke, die vom Jungen Deutschland als lebensfern und lebensfremd empfunden wurden."[6] Modern readers, who have seen the passing of the well-made nineteenth-century novel form, have become more appreciative of the expanded possibilities of narrative prose achieved by Heine and the Young Germans and are less likely to decry these works as formless. There are serious and largely unresolved formal problems in these books. But, despite the load of propaganda and cultural criticism they bear, they are novels and are accessible to treatment as experimental literary efforts.

The question remains whether they are worth treating independently as such. There is little that can be said for them as enduring works of art, and, indeed, the Young Germans, in their impatience with the *Kunstperiode* of the past, claimed not to intend them to be; Mundt's hero in *Moderne Lebenswirren* asserts that "eines Buches Geist muß in das Volk übergehen, und dann als Buch aufgehört haben zu leben. Es muß wirken und in der Wirkung seinen Geist ausathmen. Die Bücherleiche wird in den Literarhistorien feierlich begraben."[7] If this is the case, it is reasonable enough to regard the novels as simply another strategy in the Young German enterprise. C. P. Magill has argued that literary scholarship is justified in ignoring them: "the eighteen-thirties saw the appearance of works by Dickens and Tennyson, Stendhal, Hugo and de Musset, Lermontov, Pushkin, and Leopardi, Mörike and

4

Grillparzer, and students of the period might well be excused, since their reading-life is short, for giving these priority over Mundt or Laube."[8] The Young German works may be, in their own way, interesting, but that is perhaps not a quality sufficient to justify pursuing them. "Catholicity of taste," David Daiches has remarked, "is a virtue in a literary critic, but only up to a point. ... Of course, bad literature of a previous age has its *interest*; it tells us a great deal about the tastes of the time and may be illuminating sociologically or historically. But there are degrees of interest, and, more important, *interest* is not the same as *value*."[9]

Granting for the moment that the assumptions underlying Daiches' view are valid and that they are applicable to the present case, a turn to the novels is nevertheless justified in a practical sense because, in order to write intelligibly about Young Germany at all, it is necessary to find a focus. The history of criticism on the subject has made this clear. In the beginning, there was an effort by liberal scholars to unearth the buried Young German phenomenon by means of positivistic research. Without the incredibly tedious labors of these scholars, especially those of H. H. Houben, we would have today little to work with. But their books are unreadable. The Young Germans were writers of stupendous productivity and loquacity, partly because they were mistakenly inspired by a goal that they thought near at hand, and partly because the perilous situation of free-lance intellectuals in the early nineteenth century, when the age of patronage had passed and the age of protection through constitutional freedoms and copyright laws had not yet arrived, obliged them to write as though their very lives depended on it, as indeed they did. Houben's efforts to resuscitate all the Young Germans' critical and essayistic writing, the reams of government documents pertaining to them, as well as all their quarrelsomeness and infighting among themselves, were admirable in every respect, but, by the very nature of the subject and material, they produced vast compendia of excerpts and materials that overwhelm the student; and it must be said that the effort to make sense out of Young Germany by organizing innumerable quotations has remained a characteristic of scholarly writing on the subject to this day. Magill remarked, not without justice, that "since recognized literary standards cannot be applied to [the Young Germans] advantageously, the critic of their work may have to improvise a cumbersome apparatus

5

compact of history, philosophy, theology and *Geistesgeschichte*, which generates, more often than not, a smoke-screen of bewildering generalizations obscuring both the writers and their time."[10]

The difficulty of which Magill complains is imposed by the nature of the subject itself, and no one writing seriously about Young Germany will be able to avoid it altogether. Young German writing is hasty, occasional, and, on the whole, impassioned; it therefore lacks compression and is riddled with contradictions and inconsistencies, so that a large amount of material must be gathered in order to draw worthwhile conclusions. The epoch in which the writers found themselves suffered from an overwhelming multiplicity of philosophies and opinions, and they themselves thought this one reason for the general incoherence. "Die allgemeine Verwirrung der Gegenwart," wrote Gutzkow, "läßt sich darum so leicht verstehen, weil überhaupt kein Gesetz herrscht, weil Jeder das Bedürfnis fühlt, sich verständlich zu machen. Jetzt, da kein Gedanke mehr an der Spitze steht vor dem die Völker sich in den Staub würfen und anbeteten, hat eine jede Meinung das factische Recht ihrer Gültigkeit."[11] Or, more succinctly: "Das Uebel ist die Ueberfülle unserer Zeit an Ideen."[12] Since the efforts of positivist scholars tended to reproduce this uproar of ideas and opinions, it became necessary to find an approach that would organize the inchoate material: Houben himself came to concentrate more and more upon the censorship issue, E. M. Butler produced a well-known interpretation of Young Germany as a Saint-Simonian movement, Günter Bliemel analyzed the Young German view of the role and mission of the writer, Walter Dietze and, more recently, Koopmann have looked upon the movement in its relationship to the literary tradition it confronted. There have been a number of other efforts to carve out an angle of vision from the recalcitrant primary material, and a treatment of the novels may modestly take its place among them.

But turning our attention to Young German fiction has, I believe, additional potential virtues. For it remains true that almost all interpretations of the movement suffer from the fact that the Young Germans were unable to find an idiom appropriate to the purposes of their literary and cultural criticism. The abstract vagueness of their concepts has not only long been noticed by all observers, but it also pained the writers themselves, who were, nevertheless, unable to find a way of coping with it. The three

6

terms that recur thematically throughout their writing — *Leben, Zeit, Wirklichkeit* — continue from the beginning to the end to lack concretion despite the efforts to give them content and definition in the process of writing about them. The leading students of the period have performed admirable feats in giving meaning and context to these and other terms of the Young German position; yet the subject has a troublesome way of remaining amorphous. The reason for this lies not only in the weakly anchored abstract terminology, but also in the persistently metaphoric manner of Young German expression, a symptom of a crisis of language with which Heine was also afflicted. I take an example quite at random; it is from Heinrich Laube's inaugural remarks on having taken over the editorship of the *Zeitung für die elegante Welt* on 1 January 1833:

> Keine Pygmäen tändeln vor uns; Adler stürmen daher und bringen den Göttergruß der neuen Zeit. Da ist Alles ernst und bedeutend! Nicht Nachtigallengesänge, nicht den heitern Lerchenwirbel hörst Du. Die Zeit hat ihre Riesenharfe ergriffen und spielt das Lied der Lieder, die Begebenheiten. Nicht das Reich des Schönen und des Reizenden darfst Du erwarten. Die Nothwendigkeit führt den ehernen Scepter.[13]

The passage goes on in this manner at some length. Now, it cannot be denied that it has a meaning of sorts, or, at least, that it expresses an attitude toward contemporary literature and indicates a new beginning with allegiances regarded as more appropriate to the imperatives of the present. So much is clear, but no more. A critical idiom that maintains this metaphorical style permanently becomes, in the long run, uninterpretable. Such writing is characteristic of the major part of the Young German critical and essayistic literature, and reading a large amount of it is a wearing experience. Despite its passionate *engagement*, there is something deeply noncommittal about it, in the sense that one often cannot see why something said in one metaphorical and allusive way could not as easily have been said in another. Interpretation, therefore, once it attempts to advance beyond the general lineaments of the Young German position, is always threatened with foundering in a morass.

It is in the nature of the situation that the style of Young German fiction should not be markedly different from that of the critical and expository writing. Much of the content of the novels is essayistic, clothed in epistolary and dialogue form, and tends to the same characteristics as the rest of the corpus. At times the writers seem to have thought that the boundary between fiction and non-fiction could be erased altogether; they had the universalistic Romantic theory of the novel and the incompletely perceived example of Heine before them. The results, however, show that the business was rather more complicated than they realized. By admitting the dimension of the imagination into their writing, the paradox and ambivalence that were fundamental to the Young German situation and that they were endeavoring to bring under rational control are released, so that the novels and stories have a strong tendency to deviate from the lines that the writers were attempting to propagate. It is therefore frequently inappropriate to adduce evidence from the novels to support interpretations of the general Young German position. The creation of a fiction brings with it a logic different from that of critical or polemical writing. If fiction, as can be reasonably argued,[14] is not natural discourse, but the mimetic representation of natural discourse, then it follows that novels, no matter how didactic, hortatory, or assertive their intent, cannot be tracts, dialogues, or epistolary exchanges, but can only be representations of these, and that consequently they cannot be argumentative utterances, but only representations of such utterances. The consequences of this distinction are several, but the one most important for our purposes is that fiction puts the writer at one additional remove from his subjects and concerns, and frees him to describe, rather than be, the exponent of attitudes and opinions. On the one hand, the will to demonstrative argument becomes weaker, although, of course, it is never altogether absent from Young German fiction; the result is that the confusion of feelings from which the writers suffered is given freer rein, and the search for meaning through expository language yields to a representation of the dilemmas that plague the whole man. The writing becomes process rather than exposition. On the other hand, the very exigency of telling an exemplary story and positing representative *personae* requires the imaginative creation of plausibly recognizable characters and situations; in other words, it involves the writers in the pursuit of realism.

To suggest this is to enter upon a battlefield from which I would gladly be exempted as a conscientious objector. But I do not think that, in talking about the Young German novel, the question of realism can be evaded altogether. The realistic novel of contemporary society is the outstanding achievement of nineteenth-century literature. Its failure to gain a foothold in Germany above the level of industrialized trivial literature, the failure of German writers to bring forth novels that could compare fairly with the achievements of other nations, is the single reason why German literature of the nineteenth century enjoys so little reputation in the world at large, despite its large body of finely wrought novellas, excellent poetry, and relatively few but outstanding dramas. So far as the facts of literary reputation are concerned, it does not help to argue that realism is not intrinsically appropriate to the German literature of the period and therefore should not be adduced as a principle of evaluation, or that the Young Germans were endeavoring to create comprehensive and populist works that transcended well-made forms and purely artistic purposes.

There is wide agreement that realism failed to take hold in Germany because of the backwardness of its society in the early nineteenth century. Ian Watt sees the realistic novel as dependent upon "two general considerations: the society must value every individual highly enough to consider him the proper subject of its serious literature; and there must be enough variety of belief and action among ordinary people for a detailed account of them to be of interest to other ordinary people, the readers of novels."[15] Friedrich Sengle sees the conditions of realism in a similar way, adding the ability to be receptive to the world as it is "gelassene Welthaftigkeit, die durch den Verzicht auf alle Ideologie und durch die Anerkennung der verschiedensten individuellen und kollektiven Substanzen möglich wird."[16] Günter Bliemel, like the Young Germans themselves, shifts the blame to the conditions of life: "Das Leben selber konnte ihnen diesen Inhalt nicht geben, da es krank war und seine Zustände sich in einem Übergang befinden."[17] Insofar as realism is connected with a capitalist order of society becoming conscious of itself, the preconditions were not present in Germany; as late as 1849 there were 196 rural dwellers for every city dweller in industrial Saxony; and what was to become the mighty firm of Krupp employed in 1846 no more than 122 workers.[18]

That the social and political conditions of Germany were inimical to a modern literature was a widespread and familiar idea in the

1830's. Friedrich Schleiermacher, writing in the previous decade, had observed that the private character of the contemporary novel was due to a major decay of public life.[19] That literature is dependent upon life and that the contemporary conditions of life were too inchoate and feeble to generate worthwhile literature are viewpoints frequently met with in Young German writings. They dominate the argument in Ludolf Wienbarg's *Ästhetische Feldzüge*. In the ninth lecture he asserts that everything in his day is so unclear and shadowy that no valid aesthetic can be deduced,[20] and in the eighteenth lecture he asserts: "Kräftigen, reinen und schönen Stil wird kein Schriftsteller in unkräftiger, unreiner und unschöner Zeit erwerben..., denn der Schriftsteller ist im höhern Grad als ein anderer, oder vielleicht nur sichtbarer, ein Kind seiner Zeit."[21] Consideration of some of the salient features of Wienbarg's argument will help to show the inhibitions that complicated the pursuit of realism at this time.

The *Ästhetische Feldzüge*, which stands at the beginning of the Young German phenomenon as I am using the term, is a disappointing work in many of its details. Not only is much of it patched together synthetically from other writers on aesthetics, but it is also carelessly argued and self-contradictory on crucial issues. Its assertive and aggressive tone, which was responsible for its effect, reflects a posture that is apparently progressive but is seriously adulterated with Wienbarg's nationalistic prejudices and a vitalistic activism that often lacks ethical balance. But, with regard to the relationship between literature and reality, Wienbarg poses an important problem that was to haunt the Young German literary effort. He does this by working a transformation upon contemporary Classical theory. He is highly attentive to the principle of *Humanität* developed by German Classicism; this is outstandingly apparent in the third lecture, where, after having excerpted in the previous one a passage from Herder critical of the Romantic medieval revival, he argues that the test of whether such a mode should be encouraged is whether its spirit is congruent with *Humanität,* a proposition that Wienbarg, in agreement with Herder, denies. It is clear here and elsewhere that Wienbarg has learned from Classicism, but he is nevertheless concerned to draw a set of different conclusions. He has a Classical vision of the whole, free man, but, unlike Schiller in his aesthetic essays, he does not see art as the medium through which

10

such humane freedom can be developed, but rather sees the free, humane, and whole society as preliminary to the development of genuine art; indeed, he argues that the development of a sense of beauty in the characterless man of bourgeois society is damaging, as it may lead to unmanliness and indifference toward the welfare of the fatherland.[22] This difference is of fundamental importance, although in one respect it is not so radical as it may appear to be. For Schiller's aesthetics is also concerned with society — specifically, with the ways in which human freedom might be developed without paying the cost of blood, terror, and tyranny he saw in the example of the French Revolution. This social orientation is one reason why Schiller's aesthetics rarely touches on specific works of art, and Wienbarg's similar motivation appears in his objection to the practice of aesthetics in treating art works rather than the whole organism of society as Plato does.[23] That his aesthetics is related in kind to Schiller's is also shown by the fact that Wienbarg, like Schiller, sees the aesthetic element as a mediating force; in Wienbarg's version it mediates between "Erkennen und Handeln."[24] But his equation is different, for his artist transplants "die Schönheit der Tat, aus dem Leben in eine andere Welt, in die Kunstwelt."[25]

He was not always consistent about this. Viktor Schweizer quotes passages from several other writings indicating that Wienbarg sometimes did entertain the proposition that poesy can have an inspirational effect on life.[26] But for the *Ästhetische Feldzüge* the opposite order of priorities is predominant, and it is an early indication of a problem that was to grow in dimensions in the socially oriented aesthetics of the nineteenth century. The twist on Schiller indicates that Wienbarg was anxious to preserve the humanitarian and libertarian impulses of Classicism without drawing the conclusion apparently suggested by Schiller and Goethe that the existing order of life and society must be quietly accepted until the spirit of man is ennobled. In the long run, Wienbarg's argument pertains to the social responsibility and function of art, as against the tendency of Classical and Romantic traditions to build barriers between reality and imagination. In a newspaper article of 1844 he wrote: "Würden die Künstler den Gedanken an die öffentliche Bestimmung der Kunst in sich wacher und lebendiger erhalten haben, so würden sie ohne Zweifel mit Erfolg die Kunst vor dem Versinken in die Privatsphäre geschützt haben."[27]

On the other hand, Wienbarg's revision of Classical theory into activism and social responsibility poses a problem of a different kind that has some serious dimensions. For the rearrangement of priorities within the context of *Humanitätsphilosophie* introduces an element of pessimism that continually rises to the surface in the argument. Despite Goethe's and Schiller's resigned acceptance of what could not be altered, German Classical thought had an optimistic view of the potential of humane pursuits to prepare humane men for a humane order of society. Wienbarg's postulation of the primacy of life over art makes this optimism impossible to sustain. Gerhard Burkhardt is not quite on the point when he argues: "Im Grunde erliegt [Wienbarg] dabei einem Zirkelschluß, denn er ersetzt die optimistische Kunstspekulation durch eine nicht minder optimistische und utopische Lebensspekulation."[28] First of all, Wienbarg denies the possibility that the impulse for regeneration can come out of art. At one point he clothes this argument in what appears to be a defense against the attribution of immoral influence to art, a live issue in this age of oafish censorship, but the formulation leads to a more radical conclusion: "Nicht die Kunst ist es, die das Leben, das Leben ist es, das die Kunst verdirbt, und zu allen Zeiten, zu den schlechtesten unter Nero, ist diese noch immer besser und heiliger gewesen als jenes."[29] The attentive reader may detect an internal contradiction in this statement, but the operative notion is that it is life that ruins art, not vice versa. For it appears in Wienbarg's argument that a wretched state of affairs in the nation and society obviates the possibility for good art. Such a view tends to call the enterprise of aesthetics into question, and Wienbarg was keen enough to see this. He argues in the ninth lecture that a historical survey shows that aesthetics is always keyed to the respective *Weltanschauung* of the time;[30] this argument, which is clearly tending toward a theory of the dependence of intellectual structures on social determinants, is a little unclear and in several places awkwardly amalgamated with a desire to believe that there are also universal principles of judgment. To pursue this difficulty in Wienbarg would lead us farther into ideological territory than I wish to go here. The passage is followed, however, by the further argument that in Wienbarg's time everything is so unclear and shadowy that no valid aesthetic can be deduced. Quickly, he is forced on his own premises to the radical conclusion that whoever were to presume to provide an

12

aesthetic "müßte vorher ... eine neue Kunst, ein neues Leben herbei-schaffen."[31] Such a conclusion seems to undermine the sense of offering aesthetic principles at all, and illustrates very strikingly how the theory of the dependence of literature upon life and reality could inhibit the literary enterprise altogether.

At the same time, another problem emerges that stands in the way of the pursuit of realism. The Young Germans often say that life and reality are not being absorbed into literature for their own sake, but to reveal a higher truth or hidden lineaments of the future in the present. In the fifteenth lecture, Wienbarg argues: "*Wäre das Wirkliche der Wahrheit und Schönheit entgegengesetzt, so müßte es der Künstler nicht idealisieren, sondern vernichten, um an dessen Stelle die Schönheit hinzupflanzen*";[32] and, in the sixteenth lecture: "Nicht das Wirkliche als wirklich will der Künstler nachah-men, sondern dem Wirklichen eine künstlerische Bedeutung ge-ben."[33] Thus, even the concept of realism tended to be, as Theodor Mundt put it in his history of contemporary literature in 1842, "idea-lischen Ursprungs";[34] he describes the literary mission of the present as "ein bedeutungsschwangerer Messianismus der Zukunft, der sich mit hochrothen Feuerzeichen an den Horizont der Zeit gemalt hat."[35] As a practical example of what this means in terms of taste, Mundt's history gives one sentence to Balzac and twenty-eight pages to George Sand. The philosophical atmosphere of the time had much to do with this attitude that the task of art is the representation, as one Hegelian critic put it, "des Werdens des Absoluten in der Zeit, nicht des schönen Seins der einzelnen Menschen."[36]

But it must not be forgotten that Young Germany is a mass of contradictory opinions and instincts pulling and tugging against one another. Friedrich Sengle, in an important section of the recent first volume of his *magnum opus* on the period, has described how the conservative and organic instinct to which the Biedermeier attempted to hold fast is permeated in a convoluted and dialectical way with an increasingly empirical sensibility,[37] and the ambivalent Young German literary situation is an analogue of that complexity. What-ever one may wish to attribute to the Young German viewpoint, the diligent reader can find evidence to the contrary. So it is with realism. The Young Germans were not capable of forming a theoretical principle of realism that could be actively pursued, but the continuous stress upon "life" and contemporary reality itself

13

implies the potential for a kind of literary realism as a solution, and much of the Young German writing suggests at least a longing both for realism and for well-made forms. This longing expresses itself in rather comic form in the criticism the Young Germans directed against one another. Never has there been a literary movement the members of which were more at odds with one another, and this atomization was intensified by the government assault, which splintered the group even further and encouraged the principle of *sauve qui peut*. The annals of Young Germany are full of such mutual criticism, as any reader of Houben's compendia knows, and it all tends to the same point: each writer accuses the other of being too abstract, of allowing ideas and fashionable theories to clog the fiction, of artificiality and excessive introspection, and of failing to produce well-ordered forms. The comedy lies in the fact that these criticisms apply equally well to the works each was writing at the time. But the continuous reiteration of these critical principles shows that there was a perceived gap between purpose and achievement among the Young German writers.

There are also more positive expressions, and they are to be found in large numbers. One of the most curious of them is in Karl Gutzkow's novel of 1833, *Maha Guru*. Suddenly, apropos of almost nothing at all, Gutzkow drops the fictional narration and inserts a personal remark. He tells of a confrontation he had with a government minister who tried to convert him from liberal attitudes. Upon returning to the street, he is especially struck by the details of commonplace reality, which are described in a kind of montage. Two dogs investigate one another's sex; shopkeepers carry on their ordinary business. The author is aware that his shoe pinches and that he has a loose thread on his sleeve. He goes to a store and buys some paper, along with various necessaries like a watch key, two oranges, a hundred matches — "und einen Monat später schickte ich an Herrn Campe in Hamburg meine Narrenbriefe."[38] This passage is uncommonly instructive because of its simple-mindedness. Two significant links are posited: the response to reactionary political pressure is a heightened awareness of mundane reality, of the surface and appearance of things. This heightened awareness then generates a book of modern relevance. Now Gutzkow's *Briefe eines Narren an eine Närrin* has all the qualities of abstractness and diffuseness that the Young Germans criticized in one another, and it is at once

14

incongruous and instructive that Gutzkow should present the inspiration for it as an epiphany of quotidian reality. Later in *Maha Guru*, the author pauses to say: "ich schildere Ereignisse und Menschen, die dem Leben und der Wirklichkeit entnommen sind,"[39] which seems like an odd comment in this imaginary and remotely allegorical story set in Tibet, and it may mean no more than that the *issues* adumbrated in the novel are those posited by life and reality; nevertheless, the fact that the Young German logic is convoluted does not alter the nature of the original impulse.

There are many passages and comments in Gutzkow's writing that could be brought to bear on the question, but there is one more that is of particular interest:

> Es gibt zwei Arten von Schriftstellern. Solche, die vor den Ereignissen kommen, und solche, die nach ihnen. Die Einen sind Vorreden, die Andern Register. Die Vorreden prahlen und versprechen oft mehr, als die Register halten. Die Masse läuft den Vorreden nach und kommt selten über sie hinaus. Die Register, oft so nützlich, sind unpopulär.
>
> Wo man jetzt hinblickt, sieht man Vorredenliteratur.[40]

What Gutzkow says here about the relative popularity of the two kinds of writing seems a little perverse, but the rest is interesting, because it is a repudiation of Mundt's notion of "Messianismus der Zukunft." Literatur as an "index" must certainly mean something similar to Sengle's realistic canon of "gelassene Welthaftigkeit." Gutzkow's metaphors of "Vorrede" and "Register" seem to me uncommonly well taken, and if they imply a rejection of almost all Young German writing as such, they express succinctly a major theme of the realism problem.

Laube, of whose views there will be more to say in a later essay, also has a number of scattered comments that are remarkably to the point. In an apologia of his description of Vienna in the *Reisenovellen*, he mounts a defense of the primacy of the disparate apperceptions of reality over the a priori organizing idea:

> Der Leser wird es empfinden, wie man hin und her geworfen wird mit seinen Anschauungen, wenn man nicht nach einer leitenden, starren Idee das Ganze beurteilen will. Dies letztere muß aber meines Erachtens am sorgfältigsten vermieden werden, es bringt nur

eine irrtümliche Einheit in die Betrachtung, das Objekt selbst wird überritten, und man konstruiert eine Stadt aus Forderungen, Möglichkeiten und Antipathien zusammen, wie sie nicht existiert.

Das Recht der einmal wirklichen Existenz muß in allen Dingen geachtet werden, und es kommt weniger darauf an, ob diesselbe vom Darsteller als harmonisches Ganze aufgenommen und verarbeitet, als vielmehr, ob sie ehrlich, unbefangen, auch mit allen scheinbaren Widersprüchen aufgefaßt worden ist.

Die Wahrheit darf hierbei der Kunst nicht einmal untergeordnet, viel weniger geopfert werden, und man hat nur zuzusehen, daß auch die gemischten Eindrücke ein Zusammengefügtes, darstellbares Ganze bilden.[41]

There is an absolute break in these remarks with the tradition of Classical aesthetics, with even as much of it as was retained by Wienbarg. The primacy of perceived *Wirklichkeit* over philosophical *Wahrheit* is asserted with unimpeachable plainness.

It is true that Laube saw realism, for the most part, not as a formal matter, but as one of content adequate to the present. "Warum dulden wir," he asks in an essay on the contemporary novel in the *Elegante* of 23 May 1833, "daß immer noch die alten gestorbenen Interessen abgehaspelt werden; warum verlangen wir nicht vom Romanschreiber, daß die neue Welt sich abspiegele in den Erzählungen! Es gibt in Deutschland kein schnelleres und sichereres Bildungsmittel als den Roman."[42] "Die Gesellschaft," he goes on, "ist eine ganz andere geworden, der Adel ist gestürzt und verlacht, das altersgraue Herkommen ist bezweifelt und angetastet, und die Poesie der Gesellschaft, der Roman ist größtentheils noch der alte"; and he asserts, with comic exaggeration, that only fifteen new novels will be needed to bring modern ideas on their way.[43] Here Laube has fallen into the confusion that Gutzkow later attempted to clear up with his distinction between "Vorrede" and "Register": on the one hand, he asserts that modern times are upon us and it is the novel that is lagging behind; on the other, that new novels are needed to bring modern times upon us. It is a dilemma familiar from the history of Marxist literary theory. But we will have more occasion to advert to the *Elegante* essays when we come to Laube's own major effort in the novel. It will be enough to say here, in view of Mundt's avoidance of Balzac in his history of literature, that Laube on one

16

occasion expresses a view that sounds very much like one of Balzac's fundamental perceptions:

> *Selbst* ist nicht mehr der Mann, aber das Geld. Darum wird es den guten Poeten heutigen Tages so schwer, einen guten Roman oder gar eine gute Tragödie zu schreiben. Sie sind noch immer der Meinung, die Menschen seyen die Hauptsache, und aus diesem Irrthume wächst ihr Unglück. Das Geld ist die Hauptperson, die Verhältnisse des Geldes sind die Nebenpersonen, und die Menschen selbst sind nur die Kleider.[44]

Wienbarg's position, too, becomes more complicated as soon as one looks beyond the *Ästhetische Feldzüge* to some of his other writings. Though probably the least gifted in a literary sense of all the major Young Germans, he felt a yearning for creative writing. In the introduction to the *Wanderungen durch den Thierkreis*, he speaks rather gloomily of a creative flow that refuses to come: "Weiß ich's doch an mir selbst, wie unflüssig und verstockt noch so viele Ideen in mir sind, die zum Strom der jungen Welt gehören, glaube ich doch noch gar nichts gethan zu haben und harre der Stunde, wo die schöpferische Kraft, die in den Tiefen meines Lebens braust, mein ganzes Ich ergreifen und glühend in die harrende Form überströmen wird."[45] Fifteen years later, when his control over the craft of writing had much deteriorated, he exclaims "Dichter, Künstler zu sein, dazu habe ich Anlage"; he is not born to be a philosopher, scholar, statesman, or demagogue.[46] But this is either whistling in the dark or evidence of a lack of self-knowledge. In keeping with his theory of the primacy of life over art, he lays the blame on the times: "Ich habe nichts geschaffen, was einem Kunstwerke ähnlich sieht. Ich kann antworten, ihr habt nichts gethan, was eines Dichters und Künstlers würdig."[47] But such a statement by a writer on his own behalf is unbecoming and, on the whole, our judgement must be that Wienbarg was, in the first instance, a scholar, essayist, and activist intellectual rather than a poet.

He did, to be sure, have some ideas on the kind of writing that the times required; most of them refer to the novel. In November, 1835, he wrote to a publisher concerning his own novel plans as follows:

> Sie wißen, der Geschmack am historischen Roman verliert sich, und wie in England u Frankreich, der psychologische, zeitgeschichtliche

17

Sittenroman schon völlig deßen Stelle eingenommen, so wird dieser auch in Deutschland sich Bahn brechen. Gegenwärtig ist freilich noch kaum der Anfang gemacht; die verschrieene, u in der Tat zu flüchtig u in vielfacher Rücksicht unbedacht geschriebene Wally von meinem Freund Gutzkow gehört hieher. Von unsern deutschen Romanschmierern läßt sich in dieser Hinsicht nichts erwarten, denn die ersten Bedingungen des Sittenromans, originelle, feine Konturen, scharfe Analyse der Stimmungen u Charaktere, poetisches Auffaßen der Zeitelemente, wie sollten diese sich vorfinden bei Schriftstellern, die gewohnt sind, mit einer großen Schere in Chronikenstoff hineinzuschneiden u ausgestopfte Romanpuppen daraus zusammenzunähen?[48]

Wienbarg repeated this opinion in his essay *Zur neuesten Literatur*, where he predicted that analytic social novels would become the main branch of literature and displace historical novels.[49]

Although a literary work of any consequence was to elude him permanently, he did engage in a good deal of experimentation, the results of which are to be found in some of the sections of the *Wanderungen durch den Thierkreis*. Most of these items are rather unpromising. One weak effort at a novella, the section entitled "Der Stier," is more profitably examined in the context of Wienbarg's interest in the political system of Norway, and I have discussed it in that connection elsewhere.[50] "Die Jungfrau" is an unprepossessing tale of melancholy and suicide, to which is appended a longish meditation in verse on the subject of passion. Mildly amusing is a Börnesque pasquille in the section appropriately entitled "Die Waage," the name of one of Börne's periodicals. None of these will bear much attention. There are, however, three items of considerably greater interest; they are "Der Wassermann," "Der Fischer," and "Die Zwillinge."

The first of these is subtitled "Die Helgolander" [*sic*] and is a genre picture of the islanders. What is remarkable about it is the degree to which Wienbarg is able to substain a mood that is appropriate to the material and does not seem to contain any overt ulterior messages. It is an impressionistic, almost plotless story. Both the island and its inhabitants are grim and bleak; the pilots of the story are men of courage, passion, and greed, and are without mercy, like the sea. The story, such as it is, tells of an American ship that refuses the local pilot's services; as the crowd ashore watches with grim curiosity, the rejected pilot leads the ship into disaster, even though his younger brother on board begs for mercy. Here there is no idealization of the men of the north; it is an account of a hardy and mean society, the members of which are pleased with the expectation that they will be able to loot the wrecked ship. Spare in its language and unpretentious, it is the best imaginative piece in Wienbarg's writing. Here is an altogether unexpected kind of realism; it is not "poetic," nor is it apparently pervaded by any ideal *Wahrheit* that transcends the *Wirklichkeit*; on the contrary, there is a representation of the cruel and unbeautiful such as was to become the hallmark of much European realism.

Whether Wienbarg would have been able to do any more with it, however, is unlikely; he himself seems not to have grasped its special character, as his further discussion of it lapses into his more familiar attitude. He begins the essay "Der Fischer," subtitled "Faule und Frische Romane," by saying that the Helgoland sketch is the way he would write a novel if he were to write one. This essay is, for the most part, a plea for novels of contemporary setting and relevance and an argument against historical novels, an antipathy he frequently expressed. It begins with some theoretical considerations on the novel, which are unconvincing and of little moment. He then goes on to discuss Walter Scott, whom he charges with a lack of "deutsche Seele" and "Poesie."[51] He sees Scott's value in making the public interested in literature, but there is no poesy in his followers, who lack a central idea; feudal novels, argues Wienbarg, are simply an anodyne. These considerations then lead into a more interesting discussion of Schiller, Jean Paul, and Goethe, and his comment shows his wish that the virtues of the great masters of the recent past might be transformed into a style adequate to the needs of the times: "Ich wünschte, wir hätten von Schillers Hand ein Paar Abhandlungen weniger und einen Geisterseher mehr; und ich wünschte, *Paul* und *Wolfgang* wären Milchbrüder gewesen und Paul hätte etwas mehr von Göthe's Kunst und Wolfgang etwas mehr von Richters überfließender Liebe und Seelenseligkeit eingesogen. Dann besäße Deutschland einen Titan, der meisterhaft und einen Meister, der titanisch."[52] Again he urges writers to reach into their own times and their own experience, and again, as in the *Ästhetische Feldzüge*, the pessimism as to whether the conditions

19

of present-day life are up to producing art asserts itself. "Woher der Stoff zu einem zeitgeschichtlichen Roman? Ich frage aber dagegen, woher entnahm Göthe ihn für Wilhelm Meister? — Versteht mich recht. Um alles in der Welt keinen Wilhelm wieder. Der ist abgethan, der ist Göthe's und seiner Zeit. Was und wer ist *euer?*"[53] Yet, he muses, the present time hardly seems to permit poetic feelings to extend beyond adolescence.

He then attempts to tell how he would go about writing his novel *Johannes Küchlein*, of which the Helgoland vignette is a part, and the incongruence of these remarks with the special character of the fragment itself is most striking. The hero, Wienbarg says, is to be a high-minded theology student who comes to grief "in dem Norddeutschland, wie es ist."[54] The lack of external action would be made up for by psychological penetration. The confusion here is evident, and in the end he seems uncertain whether he will ever do it and, in a somewhat silly way, shifts the responsibility, as it were, onto the Muse: "Und wann wirst du deinen Vorsatz ausführen? Wenn die unsichtbare Hand, die mir die Feder leitet, Erlaubniß dazu ertheilt."[55] Of course, this permission never came. The case, however, is paradigmatic for the way in which the logic of imaginative literature can carry the writer away from his apparent theoretical views.

The remaining item of interest in the *Wanderungen* is "Die Zwillinge," which is the most singular and unconventional piece Wienbarg ever wrote. The twins in question are "Wollust und Grausamkeit," and the piece begins by talking about the destructiveness of children. This beginning sets the iconoclastic tone of the whole. Romanticism, as is well known, made much of childlikeness and of childhood as a lost paradise of innocent sensibility, and it is probably connected with this myth that there is hardly a German writer between Karl Philipp Moritz and Gottfried Keller who can portray children with much verisimilitude. But Wienbarg is not only undertaking to show that lust and cruelty are natural characteristics of children; he is attempting to suggest that they may be virtues, whereby he makes some peculiar and interesting comparisons: "Die Sentimentalität ist bekanntlich keine Kinderkrankheit. Kinder leben, wie antike Dichter, in einer objektiven Welt. Jedes kräftige, lebhafte, geistreiche Kind ist ein kleiner Pantheist, ein kleiner Wolfgang Göthe, der nach Herders zürnendem Vorwurf

20

ewig ein Kind bleibt."⁵⁶ It is amusing to see some German cultural obsessions here being turned on their ear. It is also apparent that some of the barbaric quality of Wienbarg's activism is coming to the surface. He goes on to say that children are cruel and demonic. Adults are naturally opposed to these qualities, but it is a lie that adults are more humane: "Ich habe oft darüber nachgedacht, ob es nicht besser, tausendmal besser wäre, die Menschen hätten gar kein Gewissen, als ein so stümperhaftes, invalides, bürgerliches, schwächlich sentimentales."⁵⁷ The repressive conscience generates lewdness, malice, sneaky and cowardly sins, and viciousness; far better would be heroic vice.

In this controversial mood, the essay then takes an unexpected turn — Wienbarg begins to talk about the lack of feeling in God and His ironic pleasure at the tragedy of existence. "In ächter Tyrannen-laune schuf er die Welt, um sich an dem tragischen Gaukelspiel des ringenden flüchtigen Daseins ironisch zu weiden. Er zündete die Brautfackeln an, lud die Gäste ein und ließ die Bluthochzeit be-ginnen, die niemals aufhört. Er selber lächelt vom hohen sichern Balkon der Unsterblichkeit göttlich ruhig in die weite ewige Bartolo-mäusnacht hinaus."⁵⁸ How wretched it is for people to pray and sacrifice to such a God! "Sie schmeicheln dem Tyrannen in der letzten Lebensminute, die sie auf ewig seiner Willkühr entzieht. Sie bitten ihn um Verzeihung, daß sie sterben müssen, denn sie bitten ihn um Nachsicht mit ihrer Sünde und Gebrechlichkeit."⁵⁹ Wienbarg then launches into an extraordinary passage on the absurdity of immortality. But, in the course of it, he suddenly jumps the track of his argument. He had seemingly been talking about the way in which God rules the world, but now it is apparent that this is a God made by man, and Wienbarg chooses to make himself a better one. The tone softens somewhat, and the remainder of the argument is not pertinent to the subject at hand.

This curious essay invites a number of observations. For one thing, its blasphemies and apparent praise of amorality are much more like the image of Young Germany that caused the authorities to respond so immoderately than the usual tone and subjects taken by Wienbarg or any of the others. It is therefore to be regarded as an extreme example of Young German intellectual rebelliousness and not as typical. Secondly, while Saint-Simonian materials have been woven into the essay, in its radicalism it goes beyond those impulses and evinces a spirit more daring and modern than one expects to find even in Wienbarg. Thirdly, it is here that the comparison that has several times been made between Wienbarg and Nietzsche is at its most plausible.[60] This comparison has been denounced by Walter Dietze[61] and indeed should not be pressed too hard, but the evident effort here to send a rhetorical shock wave through bourgeois moral complacency and even to undertake in a cursory way a kind of revaluation of values does remind one irresistibly of Nietzsche. But the writer one really should think of here is Georg Büchner. Hovering over all the social criticism in Büchner's works is a deep and radical mistrust of the moral order of the cosmos. I know of no other place in the Young German literature where the unique tone of Büchner seems to have so clear a counterpart as in "Die Zwillinge." That Wienbarg occasionally had a vision of a literature that would do justice to the merciless and even bleak radicalism of much of this essay appears in the Helgoland fragment, as well as in *Zur neuesten Literatur*, where he rejects Tieck's worn-out irony and humor, and says that he prefers annihilation, madness, pain, and degradation to it.[62] All these things are flickers and impulses; they are not sufficiently developed in Wienbarg to be called programmatic. But they are further evidence of a potential for new directions in literature.

It is clear that Young Germany contains a variety of imperfectly realized impulses. Among these are some tending to realism, in terms of a more immediate representation of experience and perception, and of a desentimentalization, tending to a harsher literature with deeper bite, like Büchner's. I think it somewhat misleading to speak, as sometimes is done, of Young German *Frührealismus*. Realism in Young Germany is, for the most part, an unachieved purpose, and, in talking about Young German novels, our attention will be drawn to those problems and dilemmas that blocked the realistic vision. It is true that the Young Germans, as Friedrich Sengle has pointed out, were to a large extent caught in an irrationalist and anti-empirical tradition. But Sengle goes too far in denying any realistic character to their enterprise.[63] In view of the testimony of the Young Germans themselves, and in respect of a conviction that realism was the appropriate mode at that time for a European literature of any significance, it will not be out of place to use realistic principles evaluatively, both in pointing out the weaknesses of the novels and in assessing strengths where they are to be found. I mention this, and have gone into it at some length, not because the issue of realism is a consistent topic in the following essays, but because interpreters of literature are being confronted these days with demands that they confess their predilections and evaluative principles rather than pretend to scientific objectivity The foregoing discussion will give the reader some idea of how my evaluations are likely to be made.

Another of my personal predilections, I might as well confess, is a visceral hatred of censorship in all forms, and it is this that prompts me to raise the question of the relationship of the censorship crisis to the fate of Young Germany and the course taken by German literature generally. That Young Germany was a failure in every conceivable respect, no one will deny. Hardly had the writers made a modest move toward bringing themselves together into a genuine literary group than they were flung in all directions and set at odds with one another. Not a single Young German book has maintained itself in the literary canon; their works are read almost exclusively by students of the period. None of the hopes they invested in a new and vital relationship between literature and life were realized; in fact, none of their hopes of any kind were realized, not even their most elementary ideas on politics. Wienbarg preached to deaf ears of his Norwegian constitutional model; and Walter Boehlich has remarked of Gutzkow's plea for universal suffrage in the wake of the 1848 revolution that it took no less than seventy and one-half years for this plain imperative to be realized.[64] The writers themselves were altered by the Young German experience; while Wienbarg, for a time practically an outlaw, drifted obscurely into alcoholism and eccentricity, the others, with greater or lesser reluctance, accommodated themselves to the facts of life and, excepting some of the more remarkable achievements of Gutzkow, faded into the monochrome of nineteenth-century German literary life. Their realistic impulses turned to triteness, their idealism to resignation.

Four explanations for this failure have been offered. One is that the Young German enterprise was, by its very nature, doomed, insofar as the writers attempted to put literature at the service of the issues of the day, thereby making it impossible for them to create works that would survive those issues. A second is that they lacked the literary vocation in the first place, that they were not gifted enough and their brief prominence on the literary scene is due to a more or less accidental constellation of circumstances. A third is that German society was not yet sufficiently advanced to generate and support a modern literary movement; its parochial and splintered character could only yield highly individualized authors working contemplatively on small forms in various corners of the nation. A fourth is that it was government repression that destroyed the potential of the movement. The first of these explanations has little to recommend it; it is grounded in presuppositions concerning the nature of literature that are untenable, nor is it adequate to the Young Germans' self-understanding. They often did speak of writing books only for the moment and in the service of the imperatives of the times, but some of this is bravado; every one of them would have liked to have written a good and enduring book. Günter Bliemel has said fairly that the question of aesthetic evaluation of the works is justified, "weil hinter der Sehnsucht nach idealen Gesellschaftszuständen sich die Sehnsucht nach einer großen Dichtkunst verbirgt."[65] The second explanation has more plausibility. The flame of genius that we cannot fail to detect in Georg Büchner is certainly absent from these men, although it flickers fitfully in Gutzkow from time to time. Neither Wienbarg nor Kühne had any likelihood of becoming good creative writers; they were what Houben called them all, "verdorbene Privatdozenten,"[66] as was Mundt basically, although he was a better writer than either of them. Laube, although he wrote the best novel of the lot, as we shall see, found his true métier as a theater director. But judgment of this kind is difficult and perhaps futile, so great were the obstacles of their environment, intellectual and otherwise. This is why the third explanation has gained ground in recent times: a nation so backward socially and politically could not hope to produce a socially and politically relevant literature of European standards. The question remains whether the censorship, being a concentrated symptom of that backwardness, did not itself exacerbate the situation further and do serious damage to the potential of German literature.

The origins of scholarship on Young Germany are in the late Wilhelminian period, and in retrospect it is clear that the pursuit of this topic was a phenomenon of liberal academic opposition; it is roughly contemporaneous with the first thriving period of Heine scholarship

24

and doubtless should be seen as an effort on the part of scholars to recover the oppositional and progressive literary heritage. At the end of the nineteenth century there was a series of battles in Germany about intellectual and artistic freedom; the attempts to suppress Hauptmann's *Die Weber* and Frank Wedekind's troubles with the law are only among the most outstanding examples. The censorship issue consequently loomed large for liberal scholars, whose work was climaxed by the publication in 1924 and 1928 of the two volumes of Houben's *Verbotene Literatur von der klassischen Zeit bis zur Gegenwart*, a staggering encyclopedia of repression, authoritarianism, mean-mindedness, and stupidity that ought to be required reading for all who work in the field of German literature. In more recent times there has been a rebellion against this approach to the topic; it has been felt that the focus on the censorship issue resulted in the practice of bringing more and more archival material to light without adding to our comprehension. "Damit," complains Burkhardt, "verlagerte sich das Schwergewicht der Diskussion in einem kaum vertretbaren Maße vom eigentlich Literaturgeschichtlichen ins Historisch-Politische. Der Untersuchung der Zensurfrage und des Bundestagsbeschlusses von 1835 wurde ein Raum zugemessen, der diesen bei aller Bedeutsamkeit objektiv nicht zukommt. Der Versuch, die 1835 Gebannten weißzuwaschen, ging wiederum nicht ohne Verzerrungen bei der Beurteilung der Gegner des Jungen Deutschlands ab."[67] It has been objected, first, that the concentration upon the government repression has led to a misinterpretation of Young Germany as a political movement; and, second, that the censorship was more a comedy of errors than anything else: the ban of 1835 was found by Prussia's own bureaucracy to be illegal and had to be moderated; the books continued to be published, due in large part to the infinite resourcefulness of Julius Campe in Hamburg; the actual sufferings endured by the writers were not all that great; and, excepting Wienbarg, they all came out of it in one piece, properly married and at length settled in conventional and reasonably successful lives.

The first of these objections is due to the replacement of one error by another. It is true that Young Germany was not a political movement, as some of the authorities seem at first to have thought, and the political views of the Young Germans themselves were vague, imperceptive, and not infrequently quite regressive; it is easy

25

to make fun of them, as Marxist critics often do. For reasons of conviction as well as tactics the writers frequently disclaimed any political purpose to their publications. But this is to take politics in the narrow sense of constitutional systems, rights, and party allegiances; in the larger sense of politics as the mode by which society is governed, Young Germany was a threat because these writers were endeavoring to make modern ideas more accessible to all classes of readers, in the phrase of the notorious decree of 1835 itself.[68] The key to all the censorship troubles from the Carlsbad Decrees of 1819 on is the governments' determination to inhibit the spread of new and anti-traditional ideas. Metternich, to whom we may grant some understanding of politics, said that the ban of 1835 was necessary to preserve the political structure of the state.[69] The allergy of the authorities to modern thought and even to literacy itself was made plain enough after the defeat of the revolution of 1848, when the Prussian government finally reduced the curriculum in the *Volksschule* to a little arithmetic and enough reading to understand the Bible, banned even the classic authors, put the schools under the authority of the clergy, and moved the teachers' seminaries into villages in order to protect the future teachers from the influence of the "verpestetes Zeitalter."[70]

The second objection comes, I suspect, from a tendency to measure the conditions of those times against the more efficient totalitarianism of the twentieth century. It is true that the technological inefficiency of the police and the inconsistencies and jealousies among the various petty states made the imposition of complete totalitarian control impossible. The Young Germans continued to publish, after a fashion, throughout the troubles, and in the long run they did not suffer real atrocities. But the situation has to be looked at with their eyes. Laube was terrified by his incarceration in 1834, and with good reason; and, although Gutzkow's tougher character was less impressed by his jailing in 1835, the whole sequence of events surrounding his trial and conviction aroused in him a hopelessness about his aspirations and ideals. How can one say that such things are without consequence in literary life? Contemporary observers certainly thought they were; Varnhagen, whose literary connections were vast and varied, wrote to Prince Pückler-Muskau on 26 May 1836: "Die jämmerliche Kreuzfahrt gegen die junge Litteratur ist zwar in sich selber verunglückt, zersprengt und zerfallen, die Nach-wirkung dauert aber unselig fort; und das ganze Gebiet der Litteratur ist wie versenkt und verbittert, der böse Heerrauch zieht über das weite Land."[71] Ulla Otto in her recent study of literary censorship as a sociological problem has argued that censorship can have no long-term effect: "Es ist zumindest kein einziger Fall bekannt, in dem sich ein Buch durch zensorische Maßnahmen völlig und auf die Dauer hätte unterdrücken lassen."[72] Who knows? What of books that were not written at all, writers who did not emerge? She goes on: "Erst wenn die in den Büchern formulierten Ideen ihre soziale Wirkung verloren hatten, verblaßt und vergessen waren, pflegten Bücher erfahrungsgemäß tatsächlich zu verschwinden."[73] As applicable as this may seem to the Young German case, it is simply not sensible if one sees literary history as a sequence, a tradition continually regenerating itself; books and writers that are lost at the time of their relevance, no matter what their long-term stature, must be a wound in the body of literature.

The fact that the Young German writers continued to publish is not proof that the censorship was without consequence. Consider the subsequent career of Gutzkow. In 1837, he was obliged to publish a novel, *Die Zeitgenossen*, under Bulwer-Lytton's name to fool the censor. His comic novel of 1838, *Blasedow und seine Söhne*, was banned. His book of essays entitled *Götter, Helden, Don-Quixote* (1839) was banned. His play *Richard Savage* was banned in Vienna in 1840 because it suggested that it was possible for a noble lady to have had an illegitimate son. In 1841 his publisher Campe was shut down for half a year. In 1843 he was obliged, despite much twisting and turning, to submit to a loyalty oath. In 1844 his comedy *Zopf und Schwert* was banned from the Berlin stage on Tieck's advice. In 1845 all of Gutzkow's plays were banned from the Burgtheater and he himself was forbidden to set foot on Austrian soil because of official displeasure at an essay entitled *Wiener Eindrücke*. In 1846, his greatest single playwriting success, the tragedy *Uriel Acosta*, was banned after its first performance and allowed only after he had revised it to weaken the religious allusions. A play entitled *Die Diakonissin* was banned in Dresden in 1852 and had to be withdrawn and turned into a novel. In 1855 a comedy entitled *Lenz und Söhne* was banned in Dresden because it suggested a parvenu merchant could be appointed to the upper house of the legislature. So it went. Most of these works are probably

27

of small value. Undoubtedly most of them survived the prohibitions and a few may have even benefited from the "banned in Boston" effect. But is one to believe that such experiences were without consequences in a literary career? After all, these works were all written in the hope and expectation that they *might* pass the censor, which in itself cannot be without effect upon literary creativity. Perhaps the passion of Houben on the subject of censorship was overwrought, but it is wrong to bagatellize the matter, and it is wrong to survey nineteenth-century literature without considering these conditions.

The foregoing introduction is intended to indicate the spirit in which I approach the Young German novels. I believe there are reasons for talking about Young Germany in the narrow sense, that there is a style of intense urgency characteristic of Young German writing and by which it is identifiable. The writing of fiction, no matter how much pervaded by didactic and hortatory purposes, liberates the imagination and allows us to see the Young German dilemmas in their most profound and desperate form. While concentration upon the novels lacks some of the virtues of more comprehensive studies of the period, it may obviate some of the amorphousness that is characteristic of the whole Young German corpus and that affects all the comprehensive studies in some degree, despite the great feats of organization and analysis that their authors have performed; I also hope that, by focusing on the novel texts, certain misconceptions that sometimes adhere to less detailed discussions of them can be relieved. There will be no pretense that the novels are structures that can be dealt with by aesthetic criteria of interpretation; on the other hand, I shall not treat them as expository writing in a fictional form, but rather as utterances that involve thought and emotion, argument and instinct in a way that sometimes probes more deeply and deviates from the authors' stated purposes. At the same time, judgments will be made on principles of cohesion and on the adequacy of the various strategies to reproduce reality, because these desiderata are found among the admittedly complex and sometimes inchoate theoretical assertions of the Young Germans themselves and were, I believe, the impulses most suitable to their ultimate goals and their place in literature. Immermann is included by way of contrast and comparison, as a writer coming from a different set of ideological purposes and yet finally coming close to the Young German goals and surpassing the Young German achievements in important respects. Only in the case of Mundt did it seem necessary to speak extensively about his non-literary writings; in the other essays I endeavor to concentrate on the novel texts. The familiar themes of Young German scholarship — the relationship of literature to life and its prophetic mission, the emancipation of women, religious liberalism and Saint-Simonism, and the critique of the literary past — are less central here than the effort to capture the pattern and sense of specific Young German writings.

Finally, the studies have been written out of an attitude that is closer to that of Houben and his generation than that of the more negative critics like Magill or some of the recent interpreters. There is enough silliness, self-indulgence, pretentious confusion, and plain bad writing among the Young Germans to justify anyone's impatience with the whole phenomenon. But they were engaged in an effort to turn the direction of German literature, and for a short, chaotic time they invested a great deal of energy and not a little talent in this effort. They failed, and their failure marks the departure of German literature from the European scene for decades; therefore some attention to their unrealized potential as well as to their achievements seems only fair. The Young German crisis is important and instructive for the fate of German literature and the fate of Germany.

II. KARL GUTZKOW: *WALLY, DIE ZWEIFLERIN*

The Prussian Postmaster General Friedrich von Nagler, whose occupation it was to open other people's mail, once noted down, after some experience with Karl Gutzkow's correspondence: "Dieser Mensch ist nicht gewöhnlich."[1] Students of the Young German period are bound to agree; Gutzkow clearly possessed the most powerful and resourceful mind of them all, as well as the most rugged character, which carried him through a long and stormy literary life with pugnacious persistence. He labored tirelessly at the literary calling and thought hard about it; he shook the governments of Germany with a novel written in three weeks; and he wrote a string of successful plays, including some of the better comedies in German literature, and a massive experimental novel. It is significant that he is the only Young German who has been singled out for a comprehensive study.[2] For a fleeting moment at mid-century he probably was the leading writer of Germany, only to be promptly overshadowed by the novelists Gustav Freytag and Friedrich Spielhagen and by Hebbel in the drama. He never truly broke through to the first rank of writers. The failures and disappointments of his career are of almost tragic dimensions. E. M. Butler wrote of him: "that a man should undergo all the worst fortunes of the unknown great; that he should imagine himself one of them, know their dark despairs and their spiritual isolation; that he should be their blood-brother in sorrow, yet not their fellow in joy; and akiń to them by temperament should not rank with them by achievement, this is a refinement of cruelty against which one's sense of justice rebels."[3]

Gutzkow should probably be elevated to a more honorable place in the history of literature than he has heretofore occupied. J. Dresch thought him a more powerful social novelist than Freytag, Spielhagen, or even Fontane, though less read than any of these.[4]

30

Gutzkow's enormous "Roman des Nebeneinander," *Die Ritter vom Geiste* (1850/51) is the most remarkable German experiment in the novel form between Goethe and Fontane and deserves more scholarly attention than it has received. Of his numerous plays, four seem to me at least as readable as many other works in the traditional canon. They are the tragedy *Uriel Acosta* (1846), Gutzkow's greatest stage success, and three comedies of unexpected lightness of touch: *Zopf und Schwert* (1844), a cheerful spoof of court life at the time of Frederick William I; *Das Urbild des Tartuffe* (1845), a literary comedy in the best sense, in which Gutzkow transformed his experiences with *Wally, die Zweiflerin* into a portrait of Molière's troubles with the pompous authorities of his time — the only German comedy I know of that has anything of Molière's spirit; and *Der Königsleutnant* (1849), a witty portrait of Goethe as a teenager that was written for the centennial of his birth and ran into a wall of humorlessness. A comparison of *Der Königsleutnant* with Heinrich Laube's more conventional portrayal of the young Schiller, *Die Karlsschüler* (1846), plainly shows the difference of imagination and *esprit* in the two men.

That Gutzkow never achieved the reputation he potentially deserved is due partly to the Young German crisis: not only because he was forever after type-cast in the victorious ideology as an enemy of the existing order, an unpatriotic rascal, an immoralist, or a degrader of literature to mundane purposes, but also because the brouhaha of 1835 derailed his literary development at a crucial point and obliged him to wrestle for years with a mass of recalcitrant difficulties. But some of the reason lies in Gutzkow himself and in the deficiencies that must be measured against his virtues. First of all, even the most sympathetic observer is frightened off by his incredible productivity, a curse that lies upon the whole Young German generation but upon Gutzkow most heavily of all. I cannot imagine that anyone who ever lived has read his complete works, not even the indefatigable Houben, who remarked: "Wer einen Überblick über seine Thätigkeit hat, kann ihn sich nicht anders als am Schreibtisch stehend und mit hastender Hand die Feder führend vorstellen. Er hat in einem 67jährigen Leben mehr geschrieben als Goethe."[5] This obsessive need to write as much as possible had a catastrophic effect upon his style, which seemed to worsen in the Young German period; I agree with Dobert, who observed that the

31

style of *Maha Guru*, written just before the Young German situation began to take shape, is more refined than that of the later writings, from which Dobert quotes some awful grammatical and syntactical howlers.[6] Gutzkow was aware of his problem and was troubled by it; he wrote in 1836:

> Ich besitze noch immer nicht jenen Abandon des Styls, der die Lectüre meiner Bücher zu einer Erholung machte.... Der Pegasus der Literatur von 1830 lernt jetzt erst Manège reiten.
>
> Das Fatale meiner Schreibart ist ihre Unruhe. Ich scheine oft das Widersinnigste in einander zu mischen, und fehlte doch nur darin, daß ich die Uebergänge zu schwach andeutete.[7]

And, although this semi-apology occurs in one of his relatively lucid and pleasantly written essays, he confesses: "Bei meiner Revision dieses Buches empfand ich recht lebhaft die Betrübniß, daß sich in ihm wieder so viel Verhaue, Verhacke und Gedanken-Anacoluthe finden, und daß ich mich von der Vorstellung nicht losmachen konnte, als wären Bücher, die man schreibt, nur Beschäftigungen mit uns selbst."[8]

"Verhaue, Verhacke und Gedanken-Anacoluthe" is an even more exact description of Gutzkow's style than René Wellek's "fuzzy, flabby, diffuse."[9] Both formulations suggest that behind the problem of style there is one of clarity of thought. Walter Hof has asserted in an exceptionally biting phrase that the expression in *Wally, die Zweiflerin* "krankt, wie Gutzkows Gedanken meist, an seiner miserablen Formulierung, die auf einem seltsam schleimigen Denken beruht."[10] Cruel as this remark is, it is true that his writing can often be quite weird, so that attempting to extract its plain meaning can be difficult and establishing a consistent position in his writings as a whole exceptionally challenging, for his attitudes were extremely mercurial, sometimes necessarily opportunistic, and occasionally rather unprincipled. Though he acquired a grotesque reputation as one of the most dangerous radicals of his time and often seemed to be propagating advanced positions, as early as the beginning of 1835 his statements are interspersed with remarks that show him fleeing simultaneously into the autonomous realm of art. He wrote to Gustav Schlesier: "Meine Narrenbriefe wurden doch geboren in einer aufgeregten Zeit, wo man überall hörte *Qui vit?* u seine Parole sagen mußte: aber später schickt' es sich doch, einzulenken, in die Form, in die Einheit, in die Kunst."[11] To a publisher he wrote about the same time that the writer should not keep concerning himself with the issues of his time, for such literary concern means a great deal less than real deeds; literature is not action, but "ich glaube, daß die Schriftsteller die Zeit nicht zusammenfassen u über sie räsonniren sollen, sondern sie vereinzeln u ihre Eindrücke, als unvergänglich in die Kunst über tragen."[12] This is an example of a typical confused train of thought that arises directly out of the Young German dilemmas. Yet he had the nerve to say of himself that he was, unlike the others, "kein Confusionär."[13]

The abstraction and frequent incomprehensibility of his writings made a bad impression on the reading public; as early as 1831 a reviewer remarked of the first fascicle of his periodical *Forum der Journal-Literatur*:

> Es wird dahin kommen, dass Jeder, der vor dem grösseren Publikum auftreten will, und sich der Schulsprache nicht enthalten, sondern von der "Emanation des Objects aus dem Subject" [the title of Gutzkow's first article in the periodical] und dergleichen schönen Dingen reden will, unfehlbar ausgepocht werden wird. Es muss dahin kommen. Gebildete Geschäftsmänner, und gebildete Frauen, haben aufgehört, von dem heillosen Abracadabra etwas Gutes zu erwarten. Wer sich nicht so auszudrücken weiss, dass man ihn verstehen kann, ohne ein philosophisches Wörterbuch nachzuschlagen, der muss es lernen, oder darauf verzichten, von den Gebildeten gehört zu werden.[14]

This criticism is of some interest because it indicates what the sociological audience of a literature striving to be modern and progressive should have been.

Gutzkow is in some respects the most courageous of the Young Germans; he fought hard to avoid co-optation and submission. When confronted with the loyalty oath that was required in 1842 to free the Young Germans from the special censorship that had been imposed on them in the wake of the ban of 1835, he attempted to protect his integrity by evasiveness and guile. For a long time he refused to sign it altogether. Then he talked the officials into releasing him without a specific promise on his part, but the king intervened. In May, 1843, he asserted vaguely that he had switched to the track of the existing order, but refused to go any farther.

Then he produced a carefully convoluted promise to support the existing order "wo die Heiligkeit des Bestehenden mit den Resultaten eigenen Nachdenkens zusammenfällt,"[15] a formulation that, of course, committed him to nothing. On the basis of this empty formula, the authorities, evidently weary of the whole business, lifted the restrictions on him in July, 1843. Frederick William IV attempted to countermand the order, but was unable to do so because it had already been made public. Thus Gutzkow, with his characteristic tenacity, was the only Young German to defeat the loyalty oath (Wienbarg never signed anything, but he had disappeared from the literary scene; Heine was not given the opportunity to release himself by this means).

Yet Gutzkow is also, to my knowledge, the only Young German to have actually written a *defense* of censorship. It appeared in a review of a reactionary book on the press law, which he included in his essay collection of 1838, *Götter, Helden, Don-Quixote*. Here he says that he does not demand "eine zur Unzeit geforderte Preßfreiheit."[16] He continues: "Wenn man nicht annehmen will, daß sich alle gesellschaftliche und politische Ordnung auflöse, so kann die Presse nie in dem Grade unabhängig werden, daß der Staat sie nicht controlire, richte, bestrafe."[17] Gutzkow supports this view by extensive reference to the Hegelian principle that the state is "die vollkommenste Blüthe der Humanität."[18] He is, in fact, arguing against the authoritarian position of the book under review and offers his own draft of what he considers a moderate and reasonable press law: "Preßfreiheit ist der Normalzustand der Literatur; Censur ist eine Ausnahme"[19] — a curious remark by one who at that very time was himself still an "Ausnahme," being subject to the special censorship devised for the Young Germans. While no prince may have the right to abolish censorship, it must be flexible, reticent, and speedy, and, of course, the censors should be literati themselves. They also must have "Scheu vor dem heiligen Autorrechte,"[20] as though justice depended upon the good will of bureaucrats rather than upon constitutional guarantees. This strange and shameful essay is a good example of what has caused those for whom "liberalism" is a pejorative category to present Young Germany as a chain of opportunistic betrayals of the progressive cause. One can easily imagine what Gutzkow's admired model Ludwig Börne would have made of this waffling.

34

As is well known, Gutzkow became insane towards the end of his life. A certain unstable eccentricity of mind and character is evident in him, I believe, from the beginning. There are times when our failure to understand him is not due solely to the peculiar opacity and illogic of his manner of writing; he was himself so unstable, hagridden, and pugnacious that there is reason to believe that his powerful mind was somewhat out of balance. His exceptional belligerence, which was much complained of in his time and which is evident to anyone who has read much of his criticism and correspondence, may be due in part to the social disabilities he had to overcome in order to rise from unlovely proletarian beginnings as the son of a horse trainer in the stables of the Berlin court to a respected and sometimes feared member of the bourgeois intelligentsia. Doubtless the melancholy and sometimes violent environment of his youth had something to do with the foundations of his character, as the tenacity and single-mindedness required by his upward fight had something to do with the formation of it. But we should not put too much stress on the class background. Laube, the son of a poor stonemason, from an environment wholly devoid of cultural inspiration, turned out to be a notably sane and amiable human being. Gutzkow was one of those people one sometimes encounters who are incapable of grasping the distinction between frankness and rudeness. He made a virtue out of the latter; he wrote to Varnhagen on 7 October 1835: "Man sagt, gewissermaßen sey ich von einem angeborenen Instinkt der Aufrichtigkeit so durchdrungen, daß ich Alles ausspreche, was mir vom Hirn auf die Zunge gleitet. Ich freue mich auf dieser Charakteristik; eben sie drückt mein ganzes Wesen aus und macht meinen Stolz."[21]

His fierce independence was, to be sure, a virtue; even in his courting of Wolfgang Menzel in the first fascicle of the *Forum der Journal-Literatur* he stressed to the "pope of literature" "dass ich nicht blos Menzels Anhängsel sein möchte, sondern zugleich Ich selbst."[22] But he carried his individualism to the point where he wilfully destroyed any possibility of literary community. He wrote to Alexander Jung on 7 July 1838:

Ich muß meine eigenthümliche Stellung in der Literatur, wenn sie irgendwie vorhanden ist, auf das Entschiedenste abgränzen u mir laue Freunde [the other Young Germans] lieber in Gegner verwandeln, als daß ich mich kümmerlich von ihrer matten Toleranz nähre. Dazu kömmt, dß ich die heilige Ueberzeugung habe, weder Mundt noch Kühne vermögen etwas Besonderes u Merkwürdiges zu leisten; wozu sollt' ich mich auf ein Kinderstühlchen setzen lassen? Eine Gemeinschaftlichkeit der *Sache* erkenn ich nicht an in einer Zeit, wo ich nur im schaffenden Talente Heil für die Literatur erblicke; es ist recht gut, dß es dahin gekommen ist.[23]

His denunciatory propensities inhibited the judiciousness of his critical perception, damaged his influence by making him the most generally disliked figure in the literary world, and contributed to the dissolution of Young Germany. Indeed, the very character of his first publishing venture, the negative criticism of all other contemporary periodicals, is characteristic of his strategy in life. His poison pen got so much on the nerves of Heine and Laube that in 1839 they conspired for a while to strike back with "Gutzkowyaden."[24] Yet he was easily hurt and sometimes sorely lacking in self-criticism. Mundt's impression upon first meeting him in the autumn of 1835 was of a man suffering from emotional distress: "Ich halte ihn trotz der Kälte, Ruhe und Besonnenheit, die sich in seinem Wesen ausdrückt, für sehr unglücklich."[25] Gutzkow was at this time smarting from a broken engagement, for which he took revenge in public print, but his grumpiness did not abate much over the years and continually tended to flame into ferocity. When one combines these character traits with the recurring weirdness of his argumentive tactics and the curious contrast between the violence of his opinions and their instability, one concludes that Gutzkow was rather more disturbed mentally and emotionally than the general confusion of the Young German situation can wholly account for. This may be the reason why, despite his large resources of talent and industry, he failed in his long career to produce a literary work that can be read today with unstinting admiration.

It would, of course be unfair to judge Gutzkow by *Wally, die Zweiflerin*, which is only an embarrassing episode in the context of his whole career. It concerns us here because it was and remained the primordial Young German novel in the consciousness of the public, the authorities, and posterity; it is the only Young German fictional work to have been republished in our generation. Just because it was so hastily conceived and superficially written, it exposes some of the problems of Gutzkow's thinking and imagination. Furthermore, it is entirely in keeping with his character that a book of his should have ignited the explosion that, at the end of 1835, blew the Young German movement apart.

This kind of book presents a methodological challenge to literary scholarship that is not easily solved. No one is likely to be impressed by it as an artistic achievement. There are no literary grounds for attempting to save a novel like this for the canon. Indeed, the book is in some respects so bad that it is oddly striking for that reason. Its plot is roughly as follows: Wally is a young and beautiful noble lady who covers her inner emptiness and uncertainty with fashionable pursuits and coquetry. She falls in a sort of love with Cäsar, of whom it is said that he sees everything immediately and abrades what he sees on his own individuality, and that he has transcended idealism and advanced to skepticism. She agrees, however, for a reason not clear, to marry a repellent Sardinian gentleman named Luigi. Cäsar induces her, in order to prove her undying love for him, to reenact a scene from the *Jüngerer Titurel* in which Sigune shows herself nude to Schionatulander as a mutual pledge of immortal trust and loyalty. This was the scene that purportedly outraged and shook the whole moral and political structure of Germany; one police spy reported to Vienna that even eighty-year-old men were lusting after the book.[26] Wally then accompanies her husband to Paris to live a life of empty frivolity. Here Jeronimo, a brother of Luigi, turns up; he has fallen passionately in love with Wally on the basis of Luigi's descriptions of her in his letters. Jeronimo is a weakling and quite out of his head, while Luigi is an avaricious schemer who is systematically doing his brother out of his inheritance. Reduced to penury and lunatic infatuation, Jeronimo blows out his brains in Wally's sight outside her window, an event that she finds extremely annoying, so that she flees with Cäsar, who has meanwhile materialized in Paris. She is unable to hold him, however, as he drifts away to court a young Jewess; and she begins to keep a diary in which she discusses her religious uncertainties. She appeals to Cäsar for help; he sends an aggressively free-thinking interpretation of the life of Jesus, which so shakes Wally's last foundations that she stabs herself to death.

The vulgarity and triviality of this plot are not to be denied. In the second of the three books, which narrates the events and the catastrophe in Paris, the reader has the feeling from time to time that he is faced with a hack writer of the most uninspired kind. Our judgment on the achievement is not improved by the fact that Gutzkow thought he was creating a female counterpart to Goethe's Werther. The narrative strategy at the very end of the book is a travesty of the end of *Werther*; after setting up a similar pattern of introspective writing interspersed with narrator's comments on the activities of the deceased's last day and her appearance when discovered, the novel ends with the same cool, antiseptically objective, and ironic kind of report with which Goethe describes Werther's death and burial. It seems pretentious of the author to call up such a parallel. A similar pretentiousness appears when Gutzkow attempts to reach for symbolism. The novel begins with Wally riding upon a white horse that, unbeknownst to her, is blind. But then the great nemesis that plagues Gutzkow's writing sets in: a convoluted interpretation of symbol and situation appears that lacks all the concreteness and effortless motivation of inspired symbolic writing; and when he begins to speak of traces of fear in the horsewoman not visible to the ordinary man, but perhaps to the jockey, who knows that the horse is blind, the attentive reader is only befuddled. That Wally does not know that the horse is blind, but is perhaps, nevertheless, fearful; that the jockey, who has no further role in the story, knows the horse is blind and perhaps senses the fearfulness — it all crumbles to the touch.

One reason for this poor writing is, of course, haste, the demon that continuously plagued Gutzkow. So carelessly is the book written that on one occasion he even confuses the names of the two brothers in a conversation (p. 174).[27] It is clear that no critical method that seeks for aesthetic unities or hermeneutic interpretations can be applied to *Wally*, for the level of artistic achievement forbids worthwhile results. Therefore the temptation is strong for the scholar to forget about the book as a novel at all. One may well argue that its form as a novel is merely accidental, that Gutzkow had things to say to the public that he was prevented from expressing in any other way, and that what is at issue for the interpreter is not the aesthetic failings of the book as a work of literature, but its character as a vehicle for issues and ideas. When shifting to this tack, one thinks rather sadly of Lessing, especially when one considers that it was the same religious liberalism of the Reimarus manuscripts that inspired Lessing to *Nathan der Weise* and that Gutzkow found nearly sixty years later was still too hot to be published in a straightforward way and had to be re-formed into a literary work. But *Nathan der Weise* is a great play, organized with professional and dramatic cunning and wit, and it is one of the triumphs of the creative intellect over those who would bind it in orthodoxies and repressive ideologies, whereas no such claims can be made of Gutzkow's literary effort. As Dobert not unfairly says:

> Bei Gutzkow ist nichts zu finden von Lessings ruhiger Sachlichkeit, seiner messerscharf aufgebauten Argumentation, hinter der sich nichtsdestoweniger ein großes Temperament ahnen läßt. Bei Lessing ist jeder Satz durchdacht, und wenn er auch den Leser in die Ecke treibt, so beschämt er ihn nicht. Er bringt ihn auf seine Seite, indem er ihm erlaubt, selbst die notwendigen Schlüsse zu ziehen. Mag der Leser sich ruhig einbilden, auf eigenen Wegen zu dem von Lessing gewünschten Ergebnis gelangt zu sein. Auf das Überzeugen kommt es Lessing an! Gutzkow überredet den Leser, er überrumpelt ihn. Er läßt erst gar keine Bedenken aufkommen, daß der Angesprochene verschiedener Meinung sein könnte. Bespricht Gutzkow ein Buch, einen Essay, ein Drama oder nur ein Gedicht, so scheint er selten fähig zu sein, mit unvorgefaßter Meinung an das Werk zu gehen.[28]

Nor is this all. Just as the artistic stratagems of the novel crumble when fastened upon by the literary interpreter, so does the intellectual message of the book give way when approached as an ideological tract. Everywhere one has a sense of inconsistency, of bumbling, of jejune and stilted thinking.

The question is now whether these alternatives — hermeneutic literary criticism and retrospective ideological criticism — are adequate to assess *Wally*. Perhaps one should not take too lightly the fact that it was this novel that finally set off the explosion of 1835. Houben reported in 1911 that he owned no less than forty contemporary books, not to speak of newspaper articles and the like, about the novel, which suggests that the book did challenge the public at the time.[29] Perhaps it is worthwhile to stay with this poorly conceived and poorly written novel a little longer to try to understand how it was capable of generating so immoderate a response.

If one leaves aside questions of literary quality and of ideological perception and reads it just as a human utterance, one feels first of all the impact of a weird and amorphous intensity. That such a book should ever have been written at all, by anyone, is evidence of a fierce crisis, and the earthquake it set off suggests that the crisis was not the peculiarity of one odd individual. In it, paradoxes and dilemmas, rather than being put into an ironic or humorous perspective or being resolved into dialectical syntheses, are strained desperately to the breaking point, so that the book is more than anything else a cry of pain and anxiety, for all that its intention may have been to set out solutions to problems rather than just problems themselves. It is in the nature of the affair that the question of intent should be particularly opaque and elusive. In his rebuttal of Menzel's attack, Gutzkow wrote that the purpose of the novel was a reform of Christianity and an effort to show the nearness of despair to religion,[30] picking up one element (p. 21) of the conflicting messages of the book. In a diplomatic letter to the Austrian ambassador to the Frankfurt Diet of 25 April 1836, Gutzkow naturally trivializes the active thrust of his writing and remarks: "Meine Schriften sind nicht klug berechnet,... sondern es sind Explosionen eines krankhaften Gemüths."[31] Closer acquaintance with Gutzkow, as I have argued, makes one ready enough to believe in the "krankhaftes Gemüth," but reflection on the circumstances suggests that, in this case, the sickness was related to a general condition. What seems in fact to have happened is that a more or less rationally conceived project ran away from the author under the pressures of personal distress, resentment, and haste in composition, and turned out to be something quite different and more threatening than the author himself may have intended.

Although the *Wally* affair was a political one first and last, Gutzkow was ultimately convicted, essentially, of pornography and blasphemy, and if the novel is to be regarded in terms of the events it set off, the real nature of its sexual and religious challenge requires some attention. The search for the link between these two realms will take us through some considerations on the state of society as it is portrayed in the novel. Much has been written, at the time and since, and more unthinkingly copied, about the Young German theme of "emancipation of the flesh," but as an erotic or sensually liberating novel, *Wally* has some peculiar characteristics, to say the

40

least.[32] In line with my initial concentration upon the way in which the book was perceived, I begin with a few words about the notorious nude scene. Its tastelessness lies partly in the fact that it is offered as an episode in a struggle for naiveté and frankness in human relations, while in truth it is extremely stilted and stylized. The force of a kind of perverse Romanticism is felt in it. The passion of the embrace between Cäsar and the betrothed Wally is shifted into literature, and when Wally at first rejects Cäsar's suggestion that she should appear nude before him, he haughtily disengages himself from all feeling for her on the ground that her petty morality has insulted poesy. Wally herself comes to see that the poetic stands higher than all laws of morality and tradition and thus should not be opposed. All this is really a regressive re-Romanticization, which explicitly argues the cause of human emancipation through art and the imagination (pp. 124-125). The appeal to a model in medieval literature also has its Romantic side. Yet the model is wholly inapposite to the tense and modern tone and atmosphere of the book, and its very incongruity tells us something about what is going on in this post-Romantic age. In the *Jüngerer Titurel*, the bond between the lovers is not only imperishable in the face of all obstacles and of death itself, but in the scene to which Gutzkow alludes, it transcends common morality itself, *not* because in general love is higher than morality, but because *this* love is so chaste and constant that sanctions of any kind are not needed and fall away before it. Nothing of the sort is true, of course, of the relationship between Wally and Cäsar. In *Wally*, the relationship is technically chaste, but certainly not constant, and it is hardly presented as love at all, as we shall see. The Romantic effort to recapture an ideal of purity through the aesthetic realm by an appeal to "poesy" rather than to a high but perhaps attainable human condition that the poesy represents is a forced, hothouse endeavor from the outset. In one of the curious narrative gestures with which Gutzkow suddenly distances himself from his narration,[33] he calls the whole scene "ein Frevel; aber ein Frevel der Unschuld" (p. 131). This may be a defensive sop to the prudish reader, but there is something seriously wrong with the scene, given these characters and this frantic story. It is not without its force, for it projects an image of unencumbered sensual beauty against the background of artificiality and disingenuousness that pervades the whole novel. At the same time, the beauty of the nude Wally is aesthetic, distanced, statuesque, marmorean. As Friedrich Sengle not unfairly says, the scene "scheint geradezu aus dem Kloster zu kommen."[34] And here we come to something that has not been sufficiently considered in the assessment of the novel: that its erotic aspect is so exceptionally chilly.

Although Wally falls in love with Cäsar, then marries another, and finally flees with Cäsar, who stays with her for a time, she remains a virgin throughout — as she makes explicit in her diary (p. 217). Although this may strike the modern reader as a strange way to advocate the "emancipation of the flesh," it is consistent with the tone of the book, which is strangulated and anxiously repressed throughout, and, in the account given of the unconsummated marriage with Luigi, oppressively grotesque. Wally's coquetries are from the beginning noncommittal and joyless; she takes a new admirer every month, obliges him, as she puts it, to buy his way into her favor with a ring, and at the end of the year she flings all of the rings to the poor. Interpersonal relations are being acted out in a ritualistic way without any emotional depth. The first love scene between Wally and Cäsar is quite strangely organized. At first it is indicated that a flow of genuine feeling in Wally is released by love. In the next moment it is said that Cäsar is not overcome by love at all, but by "der Gedanke an eine Humanitätsfrage" (p. 75). This is followed by a plea for freedom from convention and prudery, in fact a statement for free love, but it remains unspoken in Cäsar's thoughts. He does not actually address it to Wally in the words reported, thus intensifying the sense of tentativeness and noncommunication felt throughout the book. Then Gutzkow, in another of his distracting authorial gestures, comments that this form of love is a lie, born of the "Zerrissenheit" of the age, and, with another evasion into the realm of "poesy," compares it unfavorably to the truth of Romeo and Juliet.[35]

It is this kind of strategy that makes the book hard to understand in any logical sense. For one thing, although one can often read that Cäsar is a heightened self-portrait of Gutzkow himself, and although the author seemed to think that Cäsar represented the first citizen of a new realm of political and moral freedom,[36] his character throughout is put in a dubious and unamiable light, and his thinking, as here, is subjected to sharp criticism. One might at first think that this is just a trick to hoodwink the censorious reader while

42

smuggling the radical ideas past him. Such I believe is not the case. The problem lies in another area altogether and is characteristic of Young German writing generally: the moral, social, and psychological ideas that are continuously tested and debated are abstractions without roots in living substance. One example of this among several is the edgy debate between Cäsar and Wally on the true character of courage, which remains a logical exercise in manipulating the categories of the faculty psychology of the eighteenth century, to which the young Schiller was much addicted and the use of which suggests the influence of Schiller as an early formative reading experience of these writers. A really striking and illuminating example of this is found in a letter of Theodor Mundt to Charlotte Stieglitz of 26 October 1834. Mundt has just come across the machine called the psychometer, which determines by magnetism whether one possesses a particular personal quality out of a list of 150, a toy Mundt judges to be "eine unendlich wichtige anthropologische Entdeckung."[37] Similarly, the whole matter of love in *Wally* is divorced from any genuine eros and is constantly deflected into abstractions that are clearly desolate and unfulfilling. Gutzkow is no less a prisoner of this insubstantial intellectualism than the other Young German writers, but to a certain extent he is a more intelligent one, for the chaos of abstractions and reified categories is presented in this book as an endlessly revolving machinery that expresses the despair of these characters and the emptiness of their lives and social surroundings. Such things as the negative comment on Cäsar's theories of free love, or Cäsar's tendency to mount sophistical religious arguments, only to laugh at the result of his own proof, indicate an infinite interchangeability of arguments of this kind, which are free-floating and unable to bridge the painfully felt gap between the consciousness of the characters and real life and substance. What I am suggesting is that Gutzkow, far from having written a homiletic, radical tract disguised as a novel, in fact has written, willy-nilly perhaps, an unresolved, rather desperate account of a kind of alienation.

Thus the pursuit of the erotic aspect of *Wally* leads to the periphery of social problems, and some comments may be made in this place about the attitude toward women in the novel. The exceptional interest of Young Germany in the social situation of women has, of course, been much commented on. It would be hard to argue, however, that Young Germany is a kind of women's liberation movement, despite the great admiration for Rahel Varnhagen as the prototypical German-Jewish bluestocking and the morbid fascination with the suicide of Charlotte Stieglitz. Much of the interest in the emancipation of women, in Laube's case notoriously, is a desire that women might be emancipated from their sexual inhibitions in order to make life more pleasant for men. Although Gutzkow suggests something similar in his novel *Maha Guru,* his case is a little different, for he had been deeply scarred and embittered by the negative outcome of his engagement and brooded about the resources of courage and independence in the female character. He took many occasions to speak condescendingly of women; as early as the *Briefe eines Narren an eine Närrin* he mentions his "Abneigung gegen schreibende Damen," and he asserts bluntly: "Zum Empfangen, nicht zum Schaffen sind die Weiber geboren."[38] At the same time he claims to be the warmest defender of the female sex.[39]

One may well ask whether it was wise of him to write a novel from the perspective of a woman, always a challenging undertaking for a male writer even of exceptional gifts, and it may be that Gutzkow, having been impelled into this experiment partly by personal resentment, for that reason wrote so incoherent and unconvincing a book. Much space in it is given over to Wally's own ruminations on the limitations of women, their cruelty and insensitivity, and one may fairly wonder whether a woman would see these things in the same perspective as the jilted male intellectual. There is one moment in which the cause of emancipation is given expression: when Wally broods about the vegetative unconsciousness in which women are kept und asks herself why women should not be allowed to read *Faust* — by which is meant, why women should not be allowed to become acquainted with the dilemmas and issues of modern life. But even at the point where Gutzkow attempts to put Wally in touch with literary issues of the time, something odd happens. Wally is said to find the late Romantic Swabian poets boring and to prefer the second volume of Heine's *Der Salon* (the essay *Zur Geschichte der Religion und Philosophie in Deutschland*), the reason being that Heine's bonbons make philosophy palatable. Referring to the fact that Heine's book was originally aimed at a French audience, Wally remarks: "Welch gesunkenes Volk müssen die Franzosen sein, daß sie gerad' auf der Stufe in den Wissenschaften stehen, wo in Deutschland die Mädchen" (p. 18). The universal polemicist Gutzkow has got three at one blow: Heine, the French, and the intellectual level of women in Germany! Wally is said to be too frivolous and vain to be interested in general topics; she does not try to be a bluestocking because she is beautiful; Cäsar believes her incapable of speculation. This curious emphasis on the superficiality of the heroine is maintained through most of the book and provides a puzzle for the reader, who does not know quite how to take it, for Wally indeed engages in a great deal of speculation, although at one point she must herself laugh at the shallowness of it (p. 97), making one wonder whether Gutzkow is not himself uncertain about the depth and importance of the issues he is raising. Of Rahel Varnhagen, Wally is made to remark that only men are capable of producing anything, even thoughts (p. 242).

Of course, both Wally's subjective failings and her objective troubles are functions of her social situation. Gutzkow, however, does not manage to penetrate to a social typology, probably because of his generalized bitterness at his former fiancée. In one curious episode of the novel, Cäsar tells some fairly grim anecdotes of local love tragedies. Wally finds them unedifying because they do not speak directly to her own concerns. Perhaps these anecdotes that Cäsar recites are examples of a kind of literature no longer important and are rejected because they are not relevant to the modern reader. One of the stories, of a girl torn between two suitors, a trumpeter and a drummer, does seem to suggest some symbolic potential with regard to the uses of art, for the trumpet is a beautiful instrument that drowns out the cries of the wounded, whereas the drum, perhaps like activist prose and perhaps also in consideration of Heine's activist image of the drum major,[40] is both rhetorical and useful; but the knot is never really tied. In any case, Wally's incapacity to sympathize with the sufferings of other women in these stories is claimed by the author to be an example of the lack of feeling true of all women, so that Gutzkow misses the opportunity to develop a social typology.

Despite the muddle and confusion, it is plain that Wally is in a condition of extreme alienation — from other human beings, from her own social context, from any sort of meaningful life and activity. The special problem of women, which is not very precisely defined, is part of a more general situation. A word may be said parenthetically about the fact that Gutzkow puts his story into an

45

aristocratic milieu. It has often been observed that the bourgeois intelligentsia of this time regarded the aristocracy with a combination of class-conscious resentment and envious admiration; E. K. Bramsted has analyzed this complex throughout the history of the nineteenth-century German novel.[41] Houben had argued earlier that "dies zeigt klassisch das Emporstreben einer ganzen Generation in eine höhere Bildungs- und Lebenssphäre."[42] There is some justification in this, but the reason for the aristocratic milieu in this particular case is of a different order. It has to do with the characteristic lack of realistic skills, or, to put it another way, the will to write a modern bourgeois novel is present, but the substance and techniques that made the great European bourgeois novels possible are not available to German writers at this time. The aristocratic milieu is not due, I think, to any particular predilection on Gutzkow's part for the nobility, nor, as Sengle would have it, to the aristocracy's continued visibility and prominence in the backward German society,[43] but is chosen because aristocrats can be presented has having nothing to do, no genuine, differentiated activity that the author would have to describe in a realistic manner. There is a long history in the German novel, going back at least to Heinse, of this kind of setting being used because the creative imagination is capable only of incarnating problems, dilemmas, and ideas, not concrete settings or characters of the class to which the authors themselves belong (Goethe's *Wilhelm Meisters Lehrjahre* is a partial but important exception in this regard). Thus the aristocratic setting is really a capitulation to the unsolved problems of creating a prose fiction adequate to the modern context. Gutzkow was, or came to be, aware of this. In his polemic of 1855 against the mundane, unpoetic material of Freytag's *Soll und Haben*, he confesses that the German novel of the past had been too remote from the world of work: "Jene Goetheschen Gestalten aber und die meisten von Jacobi, Jean Paul und anderen, die bis auf den heutigen Tag die von jenen aufgestellten Persönlichkeiten variierten, scheinen allerdings nur von der Luft zu leben. Sie sind nichts, tun nichts, sie reflektieren nur und folgen den Eingebungen, die ihnen der Dichter gibt, um irgendeine seiner allgemeinen Wahrheiten zu beweisen."[44] But Gutzkow's own practice shows that this mode was very difficult to escape. Even in 1855 he continued to insist that the novel should describe man "in seiner träumerischen und idealen Neigung" and should focus on his "ewiger

46

Sonntag," "sein Lieben, sein Gefühl für Freundschaft, seine Religion, sein Geschick,"[45] not on his workaday existence.

This is part of a larger problem that we will confront again when we come to look at Laube. Once having granted it, however, we may leave class considerations aside for the time being and concentrate on the exceptional alienation of the characters within their milieu. From the very beginning there is an explicit stress on the disingenuousness, pretense, and affectation in the actions and even the opinions of the characters. Wally's chilly coquetry is one example; Cäsar's calculation, his laughter and scorn as the last residue of an outgrown idealism, his disdainful Don-Juanism are others. One reason that is given for his attitude is that there is no outlet for his activity (p. 10), a problem characteristic, of course, not of the aristocracy, with its avenues to power, but of the bourgeois intelligentsia with its frustrated, boiling energy. The continued emphasis on the insipidness of social relations is not new in literature, and it is one of the specific *Sturm-und-Drang* elements picked up by Young Germany. But here there is another example of how Gutzkow's wayward intelligence sometimes works a little more deeply. For the characteristic *Sturm-und-Drang* posture, as indeed that of Romantic social criticism, is to confront the ossification and dehumanization of society with vigorous assertiveness and intellectual *esprit de corps*. It does not happen here, however, for both Wally and Cäsar are embedded in society and share its diseases. Furthermore, the mindless round of social life is treated, not as a condition to be opposed and defeated, but rather as a form of narcosis for the feelings of helplessness, pointlessness, and lack of guidance in modern life; Wally attempts not to oppose society or escape from it, but to benumb herself in it. This is a perspective fairly peculiar to Gutzkow and it is a notably modern element in what is otherwise a sometimes regressive novel. Wally tries to evade the dilemmas that are undermining her sanity by a flight to the surface of a fashionable life: "Roth oder blau zum Kleide, das ist die Frage" (p. 107). She willingly joins the society of Paris, "eine fleißige Bundesgenossin des großen Feldzuges gegen Natur, Wahrheit, Tugend und Völkerfreiheit" (pp. 136-137), for she has, as the author remarks, no capacity for philosophy; yet it is claimed that her activity is not harmonious with her inner soul. Is there in her, then, a potential for a reunified soul, repressed only by what neo-Marxists would call "false consciousness"?

To say so would be to do Gutzkow too much credit at this point. He is neither a very self-aware proponent of ideology, nor is he a critic of ideology. Rather, like so many of his contemporaries, he broods over the apparent lack of a sustaining ideology in the modern world. At one point, he has Cäsar make a curious remark on Kleist: "die Furcht vor dem Tode, der Schmerz, nicht wie Brutus, der alte und der junge tödten, nicht wie Cato sterben zu können, die Bitte des Prinzen von Homburg, ihn leben zu lassen — das ist das Tragische unsrer Zeit und ein Gefühl, welches die Anschauungen unsrer Welt von dem Zeitalter der Schicksalsidee so schmerzlich verschieden macht" (p. 89). This observation puts the whole issue of skepticism, programmatically announced in the novel's title, in a particular light. Gutzkow's novel is not an argument for skepticism, although that the authorities thought it was, is in the last analysis the reason he went to jail; rather, it describes a condition of skepticism, a lack of deep-rooted ideal allegiance in the modern world, and it treats some of skepticism's spiritual and intellectual consequences.

Now, for Gutzkow at this moment, the consequences of modern skepticism were most severe and agonizing in the realm of religion; this is, after all, what the book was taken to be about and what, in large measure, it is about. For Gutzkow, the lapsed theologian, the religious problem was first of all a matter of personal history; beyond that, it was at least paradigmatic for the generalized feeling that society had lost its compass and anchor. In Wally herself, the resolution of the religious problem becomes literally a matter of life and death. But it only becomes central for her when the external supports of her life are removed. In her diary she says that all doubts can be withstood if the protective love of a man is available; the withdrawal of Cäsar's love requires her to construct a system of religion, which, of course, she is incapable of doing (pp. 217-218). Here, as elsewhere, the religious problem as such is adulterated with Gutzkow's views about women. As long as Wally's life is at least superficially intact, her forays into skepticism are more in the way of an amusing excitation and do not involve commitment or despair. When she finds a misprint in the Bible, she remarks, "Es ist hübsch, in der Bibel Irrthümer zu entdecken" (p. 19). The Bible lies on her table among a number of Young German books, and, at the sight of this contradiction and at the sound of the church organ, she melts into tears. "Diese Thränen flossen aus dem Weihebecken einer unsichtbaren Kirche. Die Gottheit ist nirgends näher, als wo ein Herz an ihr verzweifelt" (p. 21). Here the theme is set that is developed later in the book, for Wally does not experience any genuine religious despair until Cäsar leaves her for another. Indeed, in conversation with Cäsar, his critique of religion frightens her and she evades it (p. 84). Her rather feeble mental activity is derived from "einem religiösen Tik" (p. 91), and it is said that she had no desire to seek for a midpoint in her thinking, but only wished to find the naive, unreflected religion that would give her an occasional vantage point.

Thus the religious problem does not seem to be grave for Wally, merely a mildly troubled preoccupation. Only when she begins to lose Cäsar to the Jewess Delphine does she come to reflect upon it intensely; she envies Delphine's advantage in having been brought up free of any natural religion, with the result that she is neither bigoted nor *zerrissen* (p. 213). Thus, Delphine's love can be "ganz pflanzenartiger Natur, orientalisch, wie eingeschlossen in das Treibhaus eines Harems" (pp. 213-214). This is one of those passages that make so little sense that they must be charged to Gutzkow's inchoate prejudices and instincts. However, as Wally continues to brood on the problem, the novel becomes more and more an essay on religion, or, rather, two essays, for Wally becomes entangled in the paradoxes of atheism, while Cäsar sends her a debunking historical discourse on the origins of Christianity.[46] Wally's ruminations contain themes that one finds elsewhere in Young German writing; the poverty and frustration of life, she says, should make us angry with God, which reminds us somewhat of Wienbarg's essay, "Die Zwillinge," in the *Wanderungen durch den Thierkreis* (see above, pp. 20-22), and even more of Thomas Payne's arguments in Büchner's *Dantons Tod*, the manuscript of which Gutzkow had received from Büchner a few months before writing *Wally*. She goes on to lament the possibility of asking questions without answers, which foreshadows lines Heine was to write years later in his last collection of poems:

Also fragen wir beständig,
Bis man uns mit einer Handvoll
Erde endlich stopft die Mäuler —
Aber ist das eine Antwort?[47]

But her head spins from all her speculation about nothingness, her desperate effort to think her way through dilemmas without any hold on a world of reality; it is at this point that Cäsar parodies speculation by arguing religious proofs and then overturning them.

The details of Cäsar's argument need not concern us here; they belong to a context of theological dispute that has long ceased to be of interest. They suggest to me that Gutzkow did not have a very sensitive feel for religious matters, as in the place where Cäsar asserts that the admonition to love one's neighbor as one's self belongs neither to religion nor to philosophy, and that because Jesus failed to say, love your neighbor more than yourself, he showed himself unable to transcend his Jewishness. What is significant about Cäsar's argument is that, for its time, it is unusually aggressive and shocking in manner. To describe Jesus as a confused fellow, as not the greatest, merely the noblest man of history, or to say that his miracles suggest a charlatan, not a prophet, and that the account of them is due to the limited intelligence of the apostles is to go farther than David Friedrich Strauss in his theological mythologizing; it is a radical challenge to the sensibilities of the authorities and the public. Gutzkow was, of course, not alone among the Young Germans in mounting such provocations; two years before, in *Die Poeten*, Laube had allowed his radical Constantin to speak of the Bible with similar disrespect: "Auch les' ich jetzt fleißig in der Bibel; ich will doch mit Vernunft über den Unsinn raisonniren, nach 1800 Jahren noch immer ungestört von einem Buch sich gängeln zu lassen, das unwissende Schüler einem großen Meister nachlallten."[48] But this opinion is just an element in the kaleidoscope of attitudes and arguments in Laube's book, whereas in *Wally* it is in sharp focus. Its effect on Wally is apocalyptic: "Das tragische und der Menschheit würdige Schicksal unsers Planeten wäre, daß er sich selbst anzündete, und alle, die Leben athmen, sich auf den Scheiterhaufen der brennenden Erde würfen" (p. 309). Wally's suicide is a kind of partial fulfillment of this sacrifice, performed out of "Haß gegen den Himmel" (ibid.), an act of despair in a world in which the

50

alienation of men can no longer be compensated for by the shared consolations of faith.

Wally, die Zweiflerin exhibits the characteristic problems of the Young German novel in an extreme form. The gap between intent and result is especially noticeable here. All available evidence suggests that Gutzkow intended to write a modern novel, by which the Young Germans meant one that embodies and transmits the most promising modern ideas. A liberating skepticism in religicus matters and emancipation from the confining conventions of society are certainly among them. But the choice of fiction as a vehicle has unforeseen consequences. The characters must act out their thoughts and feelings in some sort of recognizable context, and, although a lack of realistic skills obliges the choice of a flimsy and irrelevant milieu, the logic of fiction forces the characters out of a prescribed role as exemplars of liberated man and into a representation of the painful homelessness that is Gutzkow's most fundamental feeling about his relationship to his environment. At the same time an unresolved elegiac idealism generates, not prescriptive criticism, but despair at a society lacking in focus; it is also largely responsible, I believe, for the curious process by which Gutzkow's alter ego in the story turns out to be an insincere cynic and his female Werther a shallow debutante and something of a ninny. All sorts of private matters are dredged up from Gutzkow's disquiet and intermingled in an imprecise way. This runaway fiction indicates a remarkable disparity between thought and feeling. *Wally* shows that the Young German "ideas," which have been so much written about, are not at all congruent with the human condition and environment as Gutzkow instinctively perceived it. The failure to pursue the logic of fiction whither it was leading is the fatal failing of this, as of many other Young German novels and stories. But as an outcry of pain and bewilderment at the alienation of the individual and the erosion of sustaining values in society, it is a symptomatic event of this turbulent year of 1835.

III. THEODOR MUNDT: A REVALUATION

With Theodor Mundt, wrote E. M. Butler in her best trenchant style, we are "face to face with a perfectly mediocre mind and but a moderate intelligence; a fact which moreover is not counterbalanced by any distinctive gift of temperament"; we hear in him "the voice of the normal man."[1] Reasons of several kinds can be found for holding such a view of Mundt. He shares with Goethe and Heine the misfortune of having a wife of whom the critics have not approved. In 1839, while his life was still quite troubled, he married Klara Müller, who under the pseudonym of Luise Mühlbach wrote more than 250 volumes of irredeemably trivial historical novels. "Both husband and wife," reports Butler, "sank comfortably ever lower in the scale of literature."[2] Houben memorably referred to Luise Mühlbach as "ein Papierdrache von gewaltigen Dimensionen."[3] Mundt's friend Kühne complained that she supported and encouraged her husband in his weaknesses.[4] But one would think that a man, even a writer, may be permitted to choose the wife who best meets his needs, as Goethe and Heine did, without being subjected to this kind of judgment. Mundt himself insisted that Luise Mühlbach was nothing like her books, which she turned out only to give herself something to do, complacently adding, to be sure, that his beloved fiancée was rather too plump.[5]

It is also true that he did not distinguish himself by conspicuous bravery during the Young German troubles. But in saying this, one must also recognize that he felt himself improperly named with the group, especially with Gutzkow, whom he did not admire — a sentiment Gutzkow reciprocated. At no time, as far as I can see, was Mundt ever very far exposed on the most oppositional salient of literature. He opened the first issue of his *Literarischer Zodiacus* in January, 1835, with an essay entitled "Ueber Bewegungspartien in der Literatur," in which he vigorously denounced Heine and Börne in favor of "die kernhaften und positiven Elemente dieser Zeitbewegung, für die *Production* zu retten und im *Kunstwerk* zu organisi-ren."[6] Jost Hermand has called attention to the anti-Semitic aspect of Mundt's frequent critiques of Heine.[7] For Mundt the crisis was purely a difficulty between himself and the authorities, whose pro-scription hindered him for several trying years from reaching his career goal: a university instructorship. On 29 April 1835, he stood a few steps and a few minutes away from this goal when the door was literally shut in his face. On that day Mundt was to have given his inaugural lecture at the University of Berlin, but Henrik Steffens, who was rector of the university and was peeved at the treatment Mundt had given him in one of his books, caused the lecture to be cancelled.[8] Further stymied by his inclusion in the December ban on Young Germany, Mundt was not permitted to take those last few steps until 1842. During this time he did what he could to put himself in the odor of sanctity, appealing repeatedly to the Prussian authori-ties and even, on occasion, to the king. He tried as explicitly as possible to dissociate himself from the Young German movement; he wrote, for example, to his publisher on 20 June 1836: "Sie wissen, daß die Ideengemeinschaft, die man mir mit Gutzkow und A[nde-ren?] aufgedrungen, eine Ungerechtigkeit gegen mich ist, und in meinen bei Ihnen erschienenen Schriften sich nicht wirklich nach-weisen läßt. Um so mehr werden Sie daher voraussetzen, daß ich in meinen neuen Büchern, die ich nur unter eine etwas freiere Censur stellen möchte, diese Freiheit nicht dazu benutzen werde, gegen Moral und Religion anzustoßen..., oder mit der Politik des Tages in Con-flict zu treten."[9] The road was not easy, however. Mundt vigorously denounced *Wally, die Zweiflerin* in the *Literarischer Zodiacus*, but the periodical was banned anyway for, in the eyes of the authorities, Gutzkow's atrocious book should not have been mentioned at all.[10] With single-minded persistence, however, Mundt managed to publish a variety of works under the special censorship and, in the spring of 1842, freed himself from it by the required loyalty oath.[11] This is to make a very long story short; Mundt's struggles with the censorship fill 135 pages in Houben's *Verbotene Literatur*; of the victims chronicled in the two volumes, only Fichte and his troubles with the University of Jena in the late 1790's take up more space. If Mundt did not distinguish himself as a hero in these years, it certainly must be the effect of living in such a pressure cooker to encourage mediocrity.

Perhaps, however, the impression of mediocrity is reinforced by Mundt's manner of writing. Of all the Young Germans, he has the easiest style and the most fluent pen. If toil, trouble, and effort seem too much in evidence in the writing of Wienbarg or Gutzkow, perhaps they seem too little evident in Mundt's, nor does he have the engaging artlessness of Laube. He is glib and resourceful, insouciant about organization, and tends to garrulousness. The light, seamless parlando of Mundt's prose can weaken the confidence of the reader that anything worth attending to is being said. Indeed, his productivity in the very years of his struggles with the censorship is remarkable. By 1837 he had written a large number of journalistic articles, book reviews, and characterizations; a novel, *Das Duett* (1831), several novellas, a collection of essays entitled *Kritische Wälder* (1833), a sort of novel, *Moderne Lebenswirren* (1834), the memoir *Charlotte Stieglitz, ein Denkmal* (1835); the novel *Madonna* (1835), two volumes of *Charaktere und Situationen* (1837), as well as publishing two periodicals, the *Literarischer Zodiacus* in 1835 and *Dioskuren für Wissenschaft und Kunst* in 1836-37, and making continuous efforts to replace them with publications under new names as they were banned. Hyperproductivity was the curse of all the Young Germans at this time, but Mundt's fluency is such that one imagines he would have written more, not less, under more peaceful circumstances. When one reads around among all these publications, one finds here and there achievements of real distinction. He could, from time to time, write pithy and stimulating essays on literary personalities, and a few of them, such as his remarkable analysis of the letters of Rahel Varnhagen,[12] can fairly be called brilliant. Furthermore, he was really a journalist and novelist by circumstance only. Although he continued to write indifferent novels for the rest of his life, his true métier was to be a university professor and his works of an academic nature turned out to be of some value and interest. A few observations on the two most important of them may help to make Mundt's intellectual position clearer.

The first of these is *Die Kunst der deutschen Prosa*, published in 1837.[13] The problem confronted by Mundt in this book was of no little importance for the literary situation of the time. Despite the refined prose art of the late eighteenth century, despite the achievements of Goethe and Heine, there existed at this time a wholly false categorical distinction between poetry and prose, illustrated by the differing evaluation, which is still maintained in our language usage, given to the adjectives "poetic" and "prosaic." The "poetic" is the artistic, the beautiful, perhaps also the idealistic; the "prosaic" is the pedestrian, the common, often also the materialistic. This distinction was maintained quite strictly by Hegel in his treatment of the novel as a genre.[14] It is self-evident that a generation of writers concerned to involve literature with the broad substance of life and the realities of contemporary society must overcome such prejudices if they are not to lose their self-esteem as artists. Heine, although he was acutely aware of the problem and was plagued by it, never quite got his hands on it. His own turn from poetry to prose often seemed to him a necessity imposed by the conditions of the age rather than a break-through to a new dimension of literary art. If one believes that prose is a medium qualitatively inferior to poetry, and is aware at the same time that literature reflects the conditions of society, then one is logically bound to think that an age that demands prose is one of degeneration. Heine was never able wholly to shake off this elegiac attitude, and it is a fundamental weakness in him as a writer that still awaits analysis.[15] Mundt, who was of a more sanguine temperament than Heine, makes an effort in *Die Kunst der deutschen Prosa* to undermine the foundations of the prejudice.

He does so initially by making use of the insights of Herder without accepting all the consequences of his position. Mundt is conscious of the value of Herder's views on the interrelationship between language and national life, and announces that he intends to follow Herder's principle that human reason and human language are identical and simultaneous at their source.[16] We are now in an age that requires the development of a refined prose; Mundt quotes Jakob Grimm: "Die *Poesie* vergeht, und die *Prosa* (nicht die ge-meine, sondern die geistige) wird uns angemessener."[17] Mundt is concerned to argue that this is a justified historical change, not a pattern of decay. He adverts to the interpretation placed by the then young science of linguistics upon the fact that the morphology of the Indo-European languages has become progressively simpler and less rich in its variety of forms. It was customary at that time to deplore the alleged loss of variety and regard it as a process of degeneration; Mundt appears to accept this interpretation, but he does not really believe that it has a practical evaluative consequence, for he remarks tersely and intelligently: "es [hat] mit dem grammatischen Paradies ohne Zweifel diesselbe Bewandtniß ... wie mit dem Unschuldszustande der Menschheit. Man beklagt ihn häufig, aber man vermißt ihn selten."[18]

The importance of this remark, apparently tossed off in passing, should not be missed. With it a Romantic, Rousseauistic ideology that had been imposed upon a set of observed scientific facts is thrown overboard. If it is not necessary to believe that the progressive morphological simplification of language is a process of degeneration from a primeval state of bliss, then it is not necessary to believe that the turn to prose as a mode of literary expression is such a process, either. The pejorative distinction can be removed: "Die Schranke zwischen Poesie und Prosa ist im *Gedanken* durchbrochen, sie bezeichnen nicht mehr verschiedene Ideenkreise, und wenn man auch dem Verse seinen poetischen Heiligschein und die Berechtigung für einen gewissen Inhalt nie wird abläugnen können, so büßt dagegen die Prosa durch dessen Entbehrung keine innerlichen poetischen Vortheile der Darstellung mehr ein."[19] This awkwardly stated point is important; by making verse a sub-category of the poetic and considering communicated content (understood here, of course, in the widest sense), Mundt opens the way toward an acceptance of prose as a form of literary art.

To mount such an argument at all requires an awareness of the relationship of literature and its forms to historical change. Mundt does have such an awareness, but for him the problem lies on a more fundamental level, namely, the condition of the German language. He takes a strongly populist position that undoubtedly owes a good deal to Herder and is not unlike some of the views of Wienbarg. He deplores the state of the language and believes that it is no longer capable of poetic expression directly from the soul, but he argues that this is not due to a degeneration of the national character, but to the nature of German society. Whenever Mundt uses the word "Gesellschaft," he means high society or the social intercourse of the cultured bourgeoisie. Of the human quality of this intercourse he took a dim view. He disliked the concept of "courtesy," for it suggested to him the ossified, feudal, and obsolete patterns of courtly behavior. In a review of a current handbook on etiquette, Rumohr's *Schule der Höflichkeit*, he quotes the observation that in the cities of Italy with a republican constitution the forms *civile* and *civilità* were in use and that similar forms were driving out

56

courtoisie and *courtesy* in French and English.[20] He was no doubt over-optimistic about this development, but he does show an extraordinary awareness of the relationship between language usage and social ideology, as well as an unusually conscious assumption of the role of the bourgeois in the sense of *citoyen*. German "society," in Mundt's sense, is "etwas von den Interessen der Nationalität ganz Abgesondertes, eine für sich bestehende Kalksteinformation unserer gebildeten Stände.... Die deutsche Gesellschaftlichkeit in ihrem gegenwärtigen Zustand ist die Selbstironisirung des deutschen Gemüths."[21] Class distinctions have been calcified in language usage; he argues that it was always the lower classes that revivified the German language,[22] and observes acidly:

> Man höre zu, wenn ein gebildeter und geistreicher Gelehrter, der wenig aus seinen Ideenkreisen herauszutreten geübt, in den Fall kommt, einem gewöhnlichen Bürger oder Handwerker etwas auseinanderzusetzen, was irgendwie einen ideellen Bezug und keine äußerliche Vorstellbarkeit hat; man wird finden, daß er sich bei weitem zu geistig für seinen Zuhörer ausdrückt, zu seiner eigenen Verlegenheit. Diese Trennung der intellectuellen Anschauung und der populairen Umgangssprache liegt bei keinem andern Volke in einem so ungeheuren und beispiellosen Conflict."[23]

In France, Mundt argues, the situation is different; the public character of debate results in a mode of discourse that can be understood by all classes of the population, even the illiterate.[24] In Germany the language is splintered by the barriers between the classes, and its awkwardness of expression is a reflection of the condition of society: "Die Verrenkung der Umgangssprache entspringt nur aus der Verrenkung der ächten Situation, aus der inneren Unbefriedigung der Gegenseitigkeit, in der Ich und Du sich zu einander verhalten."[25] Thus two issues are closely involved with one another: the estrangement of class from class by language, and the barriers erected between one man and another by the artificiality and stiffness of discourse. These issues are urgent because there is so much of value and importance in modern thought to be communicated. This requires a lucid style, which is not merely a matter of decorative rhetoric, for language and thought are an organism: "Kein Gedanke ist an sich schon klar, er wird es erst durch den gestalteten Satz. Bild und Begriff, Phantasie und Schönheit, welche die Werkmeister

57

bei der Entstehung der Sprache waren, sind es auch bei der Fügung des Satzes, der vorwaltend für die Anschauung herauszutreten berufen ist. Der Gedanke tritt durch den Satz in das Gebiet der Anschauung, und so wird der Stil die eigentliche Plastik des Denkens, das Schöne des Gedachten, weil dies in ihm erst an die Sonne hinaustritt."[26] Moreover, the imperatives of the time require a more active and realistic style: "Von einer Zeit aber, in der Alles auf Instrumenten, bis zum Zerspringen gestimmt, seinen Lebenston abspielt, wo unsere Sitten, unsere Speculation, unsere Existenzfragen mit lauter noch unverarbeiteten Elementen geschwängert und überfüllt sind, da verlange man nicht ländliche Schalmeienklänge und Hirtenpfeifen mit Hintergrund friedlich stiller Abendlandschaften, wie in den einfachen rein contemplativen Literaturepochen."[27]

There is a good deal more in *Die Kunst der deutschen Prosa*, but these samples shows that Mundt had worthwhile insights into the problems of language and expression in his time and was able to formulate them lucidly; René Wellek was able to call him the best of the Young German critics.[28] Much of the remainder of the book is given to a history of German prose literature, most of the principles of which have become obsolete by now. Mundt had, for example, no appreciation of seventeenth-century literature and could not be expected to have in 1837. But he traces the problem of style in the period to the deepening class distinctions in the age of absolutism: "Die schroffe Trennung der Stände ließ kein gemeinsames geistiges Band, auch nicht das der Sprache, in Deutschland mehr zu. Die Sprache wurde gewissermaßen etwas Zünftiges. Wie jeder Stand seine Vorrechte, seine Privilegien hatte, so schien er auch ein besonderes Organ des Ausdrucks für sich in Anspruch zu nehmen, das ihm vor den übrigen eigenthümlich war."[29] Besides, there are many judgments that show an instinct for literary quality and that we would share today; he is skeptical, for example, of the achievement of Klopstock;[30] and has, uncharacteristically for his time, a good word to say for Gottsched.[31] When he gets to contemporary times, Mundt has little of much interest, perhaps out of inhibitions imposed by fear of the censorship. He makes it clear, however, that he believes the liberation of language and literature is dependent upon the liberation of the intelligentsia in society:

Der Ineinsbildung von Poesie und Prosa in der productiven Literatur ist an Bedeutsamkeit gleichzusetzen das Verhältniß, welches die Prosa oder die Sprache des wirklichen Lebens zur Weltbildung und den gesellschaftlichen Bedürfnissen aufzeigt. Nur wenigen Schriftstellern verdankt die deutsche Darstellung eine höhere Entwickelung des Welttons, eine weltmännische Freiheit und Feinheit der Bewegung, die schon deshalb eine selten oder künstlich hervorgebrachte Erscheinung unter uns ist, weil nur Schriftsteller literarisch, aber keine andern Einflüsse darauf zu wirken vermögen. Die gesellschaftlichen Mittel, unsere Sprache zu bilden und geschickt zu machen, sind bei uns gering anzuschlagen.[32]

But he fears to be more specific, and at the end of the book he deals with Gutzkow, Kühne, Wienbarg, Menzel, Heine, and Börne in one short paragraph.

Mundt's *Aesthetik: Die Idee der Schönheit und des Kunstwerks im Lichte unserer Zeit* (1845), a set of lectures delivered during the summer semester at Berlin in 1843, is of less interest here, for it falls outside the chronological limits of this study. Moreover, it is a less successful book than *Die Kunst der deutschen Prosa*. It is an example of Mundt's unhappy obsession with Hegel, which he belabored throughout most of his writing career. The obsession is unhappy because Mundt did not sufficiently understand Hegel to mount a convincing critique, yet he himself remained a Hegelian in his terminology and in much of the structure of his argument. Indeed, I would hazard a guess that the difficulty of understanding Hegel is the emotional experience that impelled Mundt to take so eloquent yet ineffectual a stand against him. For he insists, over and over and in many places, that Hegel has imprisoned perception of the world into a dead abstraction and has killed the living sources and wellsprings of poetry and beauty. Mundt attempts to oppose to the Hegelian system something he calls the "principle of directness," which he defines as follows: "Das unmittelbare Leben ist nicht das endliche Leben, sondern es ist das sich *vollbringende* göttliche Leben der Wirklichkeit."[33] Where in this formulation the radical difference from Hegel lies has been difficult for most interpreters to make out, though Mundt flays Hegel with, for him, unusual rhetorical fire:

Hierin liegt der eigentliche giftige Krebsschaden der Hegel'schen Philosophie, in diesem großartig vermessenen, aber auch wieder alle Lebenskräfte fesselnden Unternehmen, ausschließlich in diesem

Vermittlungsprozeß des Gedankens die wahre Wirklichkeit aufbauen zu wollen. Dieser verwegene Griff in die Schöpfung hinein, so titanenhaft er sich auch zunächst anschaute, beruhigte sich doch bei Hegel auch wieder in dem Frieden einer dialektischen Begriffbestimmung, die wie nasser Flugsand sich von dem hohen Meer der Wirklichkeit abgesetzt hatte, und auf deren ödem Strande sich sonst ein Titane mit wirklicher Lebenskraft nicht so leicht zufriedengegeben haben würde.[34]

What is in process in this attack is not a real analysis of Hegel, but rather an involved adumbration of Mundt's main interests. They are: the maintenance of the possibility of religion and of individualism, and the dichotomy of thought and concrete reality in the realm of literature. Eberhard Galley has called Mundt the most religious of the Young German writers.[35] Although his religious concerns were distinctly liberal, he insisted on maintaining them within the context of Christianity. In a letter to Varnhagen of 12 September 1835, Mundt fulminated against Gutzkow's *Wally* as "ein brutaler Ausfall gegen das Christenthum.... Dieser Gutzkow taugt nichts für den Fortschritt, er verdirbt uns Alles und glaubt, durch Malice lasse sich die Welt bessern."[36] A Christianity combined with "das ächte Hellenenthum des Geistes,"[37] aware of the obligation toward the poor, admitting pleasure as good, and associated with a just, constitutional state, was Mundt's purpose.[38] He was strongly influenced by Saint-Simonism and, like Heine, he pleaded repeatedly for a synthesis of the spiritual and the worldly; unlike Heine, however, he sees Christ, the incarnated God, as the true image of the genuine unity of the human and the divine,[39] and he urges a new understanding of Christian myth on that basis. In the *Literarischer Zodiacus* of 1 January 1836, he wrote, with a disapproving eye toward the other Young Germans: "Es kommt darauf an, in einer solchen Menschenepoche, wo uns Gott verlassen zu haben scheint, durch doppeltes Aufbieten der menschlichen Productionskraft für Wiederherstellung vernünftiger Zustände zu beweisen, dass ein Gott ist!"[40] This standpoint marks Mundt as a moderate rather than a radical in any sense. So does his insistence on individualism and individual genius, to which he thought Hegelian philosophy inimical. Mundt defines genius as the special power to reveal and form the higher life of "directness." It is the freedom of the highly developed individual, the

60

"Meister der Wirklichkeit,"[41] who unites idea and form, can penetrate into the world, and make the unity manifest. In this way he acts for all — "höchste Potenz der menschlichen Persönlichkeit."[42] Mundt connects this essentially *Sturm-und-Drang* concept of genius to his religious views: inspiration is sensitivity to the creative force of God; genius is thus prophetic — and good and honorable.[43]

There is not a great deal in these arguments that seems exceptionally original and progressive. Nor is it clear why this definition of genius needs to be defended against Hegel, who made so much of the "world-historical individual," except that Mundt suspects in Hegel's system a determinism that threatens the ideology of individual autonomy. Mundt accuses Hegel of making of art only a sign of thought, "als ob der Dichter und Künstler eine solche schwitzende Pythia auf dem Dreifuß wäre, die nur als ein Werkzeug des Gottes empfängt, aber nicht mit freiem Bewußtsein schafft."[44] On the other hand, in view of Mundt's populist concern with the gap between intellectual and ordinary discourse, already discussed in *Die Kunst der deutschen Prosa*, his view of the dichotomy between abstract thought and concrete reality, although probably not a pertinent critique of Hegel, is not wholly lacking in sense. For Mundt, as for the Young Germans generally, "life" is an unanalyzed, positive term. He asserts that the purpose of his *Aesthetik* is "der Anschauung und Ausübung der Kunst in unserer Zeit das Lebensprinzip zurückzugeben,"[45] and he not surprisingly adverts to Schiller, whose aesthetics he calls "eine Vorschule der politischen Freiheit."[46]

This is a theme that recurs constantly in Mundt, although immediately after the debacle of 1835 it sometimes acquires a resigned tone; a character in one of his novellas is said to have "den schönen Traum von der deutschen Literatur...durchgeträumt. Wie alle jüngeren Talente von Bedeutung war er mit großen Hoffnungen von der Literatur ausgegangen, um sie in eine neue Verbindung mit dem Leben zu setzen."[47] As in *Die Kunst der deutschen Prosa*, Mundt argues in the *Aesthetik* that literature has been removed "aus der Mitte des Volkslebens, wo sie zu stehen hat, und sie ist dafür hineingezogen worden in die Angelegenheiten der heutigen Gesellschaft [meaning, as is usual with Mundt, high society], die Alles entnervende Mode hat sich ihrer zu bemächtigen gesucht und sie soll für den Salon arbeiten, für die Liebhaberei und Eitelkeit des Sammlers, für die exclusiven Vorrechte des Reichthums und der Bildung."[48] This is

61

why Mundt argues that aesthetics must be severed from its dependence on philosophy and turned to the essentials of life, which, he argues characteristically, lie "in der Entwickelung des religiösen Bewußtseins und der politischen Freiheit."[49] Art, he insists, can never be replaced by thought, as Hegel, with his successive ages of religion, art, and philosophy, appeared to mean. But, of course, Mundt's aesthetics is not a purely activist or realistic system; it retains a good deal of Hegel's historical dynamic and is strongly idealistic, as his summary of what he has demonstrated shows: "Wir haben jetzt die Idee der Schönheit auf drei verschiedenen Stufen des Völkerlebens sich entwickeln sehn, und das Schöne darin als die ideale Form der jedesmaligen Lebensunmittelbarkeit erkannt, in welcher die ganze herrschende Weltansicht auf ihren Höhepunkt herausgetreten."[50]

Yet Mundt arrives from time to time at results that point ahead to Marx and beyond. It is quite surprising to find the result of Mundt's premise that, since Christ blessed the poor, he must be seen as the redeemer of the body as well as the soul: therefore labor in the future will be joined to pleasure, anticipating Marx's striking view that in the unalienated society all people could become artists.[51] Not without interest and elegance is Mundt's argument entitled "Die Kunst in ihrem Verhältniß zur Freiheit der Völker." If art is, as Schiller postulated, an expression of human freedom, how does it happen that art has so often flourished in times of oppression and absolutism? This is not a contradiction, Mundt argues; rather, art served in such times as the haven for freedom and the divine creative urge of man.[52] Art thus defends individuality in the face of despotism, which is why — and here Mundt is surely adverting to his own times — despots as often feared artists as they encouraged them. Tyrants, he remarks not without wit, thus are in conflict with themselves; by patronizing art, they acknowledge the force in the peoples that they have suppressed. Conversely, he is obliged to admit that in restoration times art may function as an opiate, a form of "gebildeter Despotismus," thus alienating art from the reality of the people.[53] Mundt anticipates Brecht in his insistence that art must give pleasure; he denounces the devaluation of art as pleasure born of idleness. Pleasure is necessary for man and is his true Muse; the "Drang nach Vergnügen" is as important as the "Drang nach Glück."[54]

These cursory observations do not by any means exhaust the

contents of Mundt's two scholarly monographs. They have been made here, first, to give some idea of the pattern of Mundt's thinking in his mature years and, secondly, to suggest that, despite his limitations, he cannot be disposed of as a mediocre or inconsequential writer. Behind that free-flowing, sometimes careless and imprecise style was a hard-working mind, deeply worried about the contemporary condition of literature and its relationship, or lack of it, to the problems of a society in painful and sluggish transition. Another reason for treating these books in this place is that Mundt's giftedness does not show itself to its best advantage in the literary works that were directly involved in the Young German crisis. Therefore it seemed fairer, before turning to these earlier works, to give some attention to Mundt's capacities where they appear at their strongest. Indeed, Mundt's fiction of 1834 and 1835 seems so harmless that one must marvel as he did that the juggernaut of Metternich's system was rolled over him. A strange age, indeed, when such mild books could disturb the politics of all central Europe. It has to be remembered, however, that Mundt had already acquired a certain public notoriety by his involvement in the most spectacular event in the literary world at this time: the suicide of Charlotte Stieglitz on 29 December 1834.

It is an eerie tale, and although Houben has certified that Mundt scarcely altered Charlotte Stieglitz's letters to him when he published them,[55] it does not altogether make sense. One must suspect a psychopathological dimension to the relationship among Mundt and the Stieglitzes that was beyond the conscious comprehension of the participants. For our purposes, however, psychological speculation is less interesting than what the participants and the public thought was happening, for the affair tells us something about the overwrought emotional state of the literary intelligentsia at the time. Of all the eccentric personalities that emerge in the crisis of the mid-1830's, Heinrich Stieglitz is the most pathetic — a man who either could not, or was not permitted to — it is not clear which — live with the fact that he was not a major poet. Stieglitz, a Jew converted to Christianity in his childhood, wrote in 1831-33 four volumes of poems entitled *Bilder des Orients*, epic and dramatic works inspired by the oriental atmosphere of Goethe's *West-östlicher Divan*. Goethe, with his tendency, so infuriating to Heine, to praise the most mediocre literary works as long as they exhibited allegiance

63

to his own models, spoke well of Stieglitz's poems[56] and undoubtedly did him a very dubious favor. Meanwhile, Mundt had befriended Stieglitz in Berlin and became fascinated by his wife, who was frantically concerned that Stieglitz should rouse himself to poetic genius. While Stieglitz was away in Russia on family affairs in 1833, Mundt corrected the proofs of the fourth volume of the *Bilder des Orients*. Whether he believed that the critic's function is to improve literature by honest evaluation, or for more complicated reasons, he did not, like Goethe, restrict himself to praise of the inconsequential; in May, 1834, he wrote a critical review of some of Stieglitz's poems, and Charlotte was beside herself.[57] Nevertheless, Mundt joined Charlotte in the endeavor to encourage and exhort Stieglitz to higher achievement. On 4 September 1834, Mundt wrote solicitously to Stieglitz: "Dein ganzes Wesen arbeitet an einer schönern und kräftigern Erneuerung seiner selbst, und kein Wunder, wenn in dem Kampfe zwischen den alten und neuen Göttern des Menschen Herzblut schmerzlich dahinströmt"; Mundt urged on him "*Selbstbewußtheit! — Selbstvergessenheit!! — Selbstironisirung!!*"[58]

The correspondence between Mundt and the Stieglitzes in 1834 was a painful analysis of souls according to the old faculty psychology of the eighteenth century, full of idealistic pretensions and demanding a total delicacy of understanding. Charlotte became increasingly distraught; meanwhile, Stieglitz had a dream indicating that it was the marriage that fettered him and prevented the eagle's flight. She killed herself, ostensibly to free him and deepen the resources of inspiration through tragedy. Of course, no such thing happened. Stieglitz was dismayed and embarrassed; Mundt was shaken; and the public was in an uproar: a female Werther had appeared in real life! Gutzkow confessed wryly that without the death of Charlotte he would not have written *Wally*.[59] Upon hearing the news Mundt wrote to his friend Kühne of his magnificent and pure love for Charlotte, and it was not long before he was disgusted with the way Stieglitz trivialized the "Opfertod."[60] Soon Mundt was quarrelling with Kühne, whose apprehension of this love was apparently not holy and pure enough to suit him,[61] although Kühne's account of the affair is not without a kind of pedestrian common sense.[62] But this was a sacred matter for Mundt; at the beginning of *Charlotte Stieglitz, ein Denkmal*, he urges: "Wem sie [these pages] wie ein fremdes Buch in die Hände gerathen, ohne daß sie ihm für sein Fühlen und

Denken etwas bedeuten könnten, der gehe still an ihnen vorüber, wie an einem Monument heiliger Trauer, dessen Bilder und Inschriften ihm wenigstens für unverletztlich gelten."[63]

Kühne's suspicion that there was more to the affair than Mundt had revealed is plausible enough, although, as I indicated, I think it is useless to speculate on the true nature of the relationship because Mundt sublimated it beyond all recoverable psychological reality.[64] Two aspects of it, however, impress themselves on the student of Young Germany. One, noted by Houben long ago, is the apparent recapitulation of the tense, probingly sentimental interpersonal relationships of the late eighteenth century. Characteristic of this revival of *Empfindsamkeit* is a continuous, self-conscious analysis of motive and character in terms of the abstract categories of an undynamic faculty psychology, and the pursuit of a degree of true friendship, true love, total frankness, and total understanding that, as a rule, places a heavier burden on interpersonal relationships than they can bear, for the least real or imagined lapse from complete loyalty and complete empathy creates an uproar that consumes rather than enhances emotional life. This phenomenon occurs when an awareness of the richness of individual culture and moral sensitivity has outdistanced the forms of social intercourse that express human relationships. Such a situation developed in the late eighteenth century, and both the *Sturm und Drang* and the mood called *Empfindsamkeit* are symptoms of it; both find the conventions too confining to permit the communication of a new consciousness and a new sensibility. It is striking that this situation should appear to repeat itself more than a half century later. It indicates that the forms of social intercourse were still inadequate to the modern bourgeois sensibility and were creating nearly unbearable stresses. The political malaise of the intelligentsia at the time is only a part of a much larger dysfunction of society so far as the progressive bourgeoisie was concerned.

The other interesting aspect of the Stieglitz affair is the enormous, emotionally charged prestige attached to artistic creativity. It is an odd situation when a wife and a friend are engaged in pouring all their eloquence into the task of making a literary genius out of a minor poet and that the effort should cost the wife's life. In the Young German period, there was dismay over the state of literature and a conviction that its condition was bad for the "nation," that is, for the cultivated bourgeoisie. Coupled with this was an unanalyzed paradox: although most of the Young German generation was aware of the fact that the unsatisfactory state of literature was related to the unsatisfactory state of society, there was a feeling that this relationship was in some sense reciprocal: that is, if society could not be liberated to the point where it would generate a literature adequate to modern times, then the literature must be created that would aid in the regeneration of society. This may seem a large conclusion to draw from the case of Stieglitz. But that Mundt believed this is indicated by a passage in the epilogue to *Madonna* in which he argues that the "Gesinnung" of his book serves for the time being as a surrogate for unattainable political progress:

> Ich bin und war immer der Meinung, daß die gestörte Bewegung der *Politik* in unsern Tagen in die rastlos durch die Gemüther fortgehende und nicht unterdrückbare Bewegung der *Gesinnung* mit allen ihren Hoffnungen und Wünschen einstweilen übertreten und auf diesem allgemeinen Grunde des Fortschritts doch endlich ihrer größten Erfolge gewiß werden kann. Denn wenn die Politik nothgedrungen in die Gesinnung zurücktritt, wird die Gesinnung, nachdem sie ihre innere Umgestaltung aus sich vollbracht hat, allmälig wieder in die äußere Politik, und dann unwiderstehlich, hinübertreten.[65]

Since "Gesinnung" was regarded as intimately involved with literary creativity, this would explain why a moderately engaged and progressive writer like Mundt should think it so important that a flagging talent be supported and urged to develop. Gutzkow, on the whole, agreed with him. On the one hand, he ascribed Stieglitz's creative paralysis to the impossibility in such times of bridging the causes of beauty and freedom; on the other, he judged that Charlotte rightly saw what is glorious in literary art and was only mistaken in believing she saw it in her husband.[66] But no artist can develop in the kind of hothouse into which Stieglitz was put, unless, like Mozart or Beethoven, he has huge and indestructible natural gifts. There is a tendency in the Young German period to force the end result of artistic creativity, to take the goal of being a creative writer by storm. This is quite different from the distinction that developed in the international Bohemia, born at this time in France, between being an artist and actually creating artistic works. The Young Germans are not poseurs and are wholly uninterested in artistic "life

66

style"; but, having a painful consciousness that artists adequate to the progressive imperatives of the age are needed, they transform this consciousness into an urge to make themselves — or their friends — into these artists.

That Mundt should have been involved in so excessive a display of these problems is a little paradoxical, because his literary writings in the period show only intermittently a real grasp of the progressive issues. Indeed, a review of his novel of 1834, *Moderne Lebenswirren*, praising the book for Goethean coolness and for making liberalism appear absurd, resulted in an invitation from a Prussian minister to enter the state service.[67] How this could be, a year before Mundt's proscription the length and breadth of Germany, appears from an examination of the book itself. Even by Young German standards, it is an exceptionally indecisive and open-ended piece of writing. The author distances himself from the content by presenting himself as an editor of papers for which he takes no real responsibility; he describes the writer of them, the salt-mine clerk Seeliger, as a man of contradictions, but he also emphasizes the pacific quality of the book and its virtue of inconclusiveness.[68]

The satirical tone of these memoirs appears quite promptly. The clerk Seeliger presents himself immediately as a person unfit for practical life, one who wrote twenty-three tragedies as a student rather than learning a profession. His musings are addressed to Esperance, a wise, didactic girl who has become a schoolteacher in order to support her mother and who in the course of the book comes to represent a kind of anchor of reasonableness. Early in the book Seeliger graphically describes the uproar of mind that has beset him since the July Revolution: "Der Zeitgeist thut weh in mir, Esperance! ...Der Zeitgeist zuckt, dröhnt, zieht, wirbelt und hambachert [a reference to the meeting of German liberals at Hambach in May, 1832] in mir; er pfeift in mir hell wie eine Wachtel, spielt die Kriegs-trompete auf mir, singt die Marseillaise in all meinen Eingeweiden, und donnert mir in Lunge und Leber mit der Pauke des Aufruhrs herum. Vergebens lese ich in jetziger Stimmung meinen alten gelieb-ten Goethe, um mich durch ihn wieder in die gute goldene altväter-liche Ruhe eines literarischen Deutschlands hineinzuwiegen und ein-zulullen; vergebens brauche ich seine herrlichen Werke, um sie mir gewissermaßen als Aufruhr-Acte gegen meine dermalige Zeitaufre-gung zu verlesen. Es hilft Alles nicht mehr."[69] Something new must happen to him to give him a new direction because there are too many who are pointing the way: "Die Welt hat heutzutage schon mehr dienstbare Genies, als sie brauchen kann. Wimmelt es nicht überall von Genies, wo man hinsieht, so daß keins vor dem andern mehr zu Worte kommen kann, und sie sich noch alle untereinander vertilgen werden, weil Jeder der Einzige sein will, der den Zeitgeist als Siegerroß reitet?"[70] He fears "innere Bürgerkriege der Genies."[71]

Into this situation, which is an accurate if unflattering account of the contemporary young intellectual at sea, comes a mysterious travelling diplomat named Herr von Zodiacus, who interests himself in the young Seeliger and gives him some quite unhelpful advice on several occasions. It is hinted at occasionally that Zodiacus is a devil, and so he turns out to be: the "Parteiteufel," whose function it is to befuddle the young man with various partisan ideologies. (It is undoubtedly a joke on Mundt's part that he named his first periodical *Literarischer Zodiacus*.) He begins with a praise of liberalism, which the reader, though not Seeliger, recognizes as sardonic. It is a rhapsodic prophecy of the amalgamation of freedom and love, which Mundt was indeed inclined to argue, but it arouses a suspiciously facile allegiance in the young man: "Ich bin mir klar, ich bin frei, ich bin liberal geworden! Ich bin ein Mann der Zukunft geworden!"[72] He starts to incant the word "Volk" as though it were a magic formula: "Volk! Volk! Volk! möchte ich dreimal ebenso bedeutsam ausrufen, als Hamlet seine: Worte! Worte! Worte! Was ist die neue Sache der Zeit ohne Volk? Ich suche, ich will Volk!"[73] The reader cannot fail to recognize a rather heavy-handed satire here, although this strategy is a little puzzling, for it is Mundt's own preoccupations that are being satirized: in one morning Seeliger writes two liberal manifestoes for a publication called *Dampfmaschine für Völkerfreiheit*, one against tipping the hat, the other against the present state of German epistolary style. As it happens, both these antipathies of Mundt are taken up relatively seriously in *Die Kunst der deutschen Prosa*,[74] showing the degree of self-irony in this part of the book. In any case, the experiment with liberalism ends badly, in a quarrel followed by a duel. The pistols are believed to be unloaded, but they become loaded mysteriously, presumably by the "Parteiteufel," and the duel results in the death of one man and the maiming of another.

Seeliger begins to have doubts about liberalism, and Zodiacus reappears with a completely changed line: he now makes a case for servility and absolutism. He praises the past, not the future, and the foundation of life, and argues that a democratic order will not support the arts, although he again becomes obviously sardonic, bewailing the loss of pedantic scholarship and engaging in ironic praise of a number of reactionary figures, including Henrik Steffens, the man who was was to block Mundt's faculty appointment a year later. Again Seeliger is convinced: "O, auch der Servilismus ist süß! Es ist wie mit der Liebe."[75] He praises his own existence as an insignificant official and cancels the political newspapers that, as a liberal, he had subscribed to though he could ill afford them, for now he is an absolutist who stands sublimely above all politics.[76] The curious result of this development is that it arouses in Seeliger a desire to write literature. At this point Mundt loses track of the logic of his narration. The question he has raised is whether there is a connection between absolutist ideology and a flight into the realm of art. He does not pursue it in these terms, however, but rather launches into an essay on literature in which he clearly speaks with his own voice: "Ich will aus dem Ganzen heraus dichten! In einen großen Weltstoff will ich mich vertiefen, und meine eigene Seele soll mich darin überraschen.... In unmittelbares Leben will ich mich tauchen, an frischen, fremden Gestalten gesund werden, und alle greisenhaft wissenschaftliche Anflüge von dem weißen jungfräulichen Körper der Poesie abwehren."[77] He then goes on at some length to argue that art works need not have an eternal existence; they may well reflect the passing needs of the present. It is the task of the present generation, "Pfeile des Geistes in ihre Zeit hinauszuschicken, um das Volk der Deutschen aufzuregen und aufzuschütteln. Eines Buches Geist muß in das Volk übergehen, und dann als Buch aufgehört haben zu leben."[78] This is a good Young German program, though immured in a satirical context, and it leads Seeliger to consider the possibility of relating politics to literature; and since politics is a word hated by the absolutists, he begins to doubt his absolutist allegiance. He will renounce artistic greatness and write "historisch-komische Novellen"; that is the need of the present.[79] The recognition of this literary need brings him to the conclusion that he must become apolitical. Seeliger's thinking here describes a curious ellipse, from a literary urge to considerations of political relevance to a renewed apolitical literary stance. The reason for this is that the satire has become contaminated with Mundt's own views in an undisciplined way. Although the plan to write "historical-comic" novellas is devised with the same naive hyperbole that characterizes all of Seeliger's swiftly shifting enthusiasms, it presumably does not basically belong to the satirical level, for later, in *Madonna*, this genre is seriously recommended and pursued.[80]

Zodiacus now emerges for a third time, claiming that he was only joking about absolutism; he deplores Seeliger's flight into art and literature, for literature draws Germans away from the present; he recommends writing about railroads, steam cars, and the like, for a new ideology neither of the future nor the past, but of the present: "den Sieg des *Juste-Milieu-Systems!*"[81] Against this argument in favor of the *Juste-Milieu* Seeliger resists most strongly, but he comes to accept it, and the acceptance is coupled with a typical Mundtian polemic against Hegel cast in the form of a dream. In this position Seeliger ends, and the wise girl Esperance seems to encourage the allegiance to the *Juste-Milieu*. The end of the book contains a set of aphorisms and fragments, as though to show how fragmented Seeliger's state of mind is and remains.

It is hardly surprising that Mundt was offered a government position on the strength of his book; it is an irresponsible intellectual exercise, suggesting that the author was potentially employable for any purpose. It is one thing to satirize the excesses and vagaries of ideological dispute, and there may be some justice to Bliemel's view that Mundt meant only to satirize the shallowness of fashionable allegiances, not the true voice of the *Zeitgeist*,[82] whatever that may have been; but to make all such issues the consequence of a demon of partisanship is to satirize partisanship itself and thus to ally one's self with the ideologically neutral position that appeals to conservative authority. Furthermore, the book exhibits an immature intelligence, lacking the confidence of conviction. Positions that Mundt held, after a fashion, are embedded in a generally satiric context that suggests the ultimate interchangeability of all views and an author who is unserious in a very fundamental sense. Such a man, if he is also intelligent and industrious, as Mundt was, makes the perfect intellectual bureaucrat. Surely no one would have predicted for Mundt on the basis of *Moderne Lebenswirren* either a literary career of any consequence or notoriety as a radical dangerous to society. Yet, within a year or so, the Stieglitz affair and the book entitled *Madonna, Unterhaltungen mit einer Heiligen,* accomplished at least the latter.

In form, *Madonna* is substantially under the influence of Heine's *Reisebilder.* The difference in quality is painfully evident. Of Heine's complex sense of form, his skill in integrating themes and images, in weaving together sharp observation and levels of memory, there is no trace. Rarely in Heine, except occasionally in the *Reise von München nach Genua,* does his narration come so close to the flatness of plain, factual travelogue as Mundt's account of Bohemia and of Count Waldstein's Castle of Dux, where Casanova, one of the main topics of the book, spent the last years of his life. The narrator, as Rudolf Majut has perceptively observed, is not a Romantic wanderer, but a tourist in search of diversion.[83] From time to time passages occur which remind the reader directly of models in Heine; an example is the Catholic procession during which the narrator first sees the "Madonna," which recalls a similar description in Heine's *Die Stadt Lucca.* There are also thematic parallels to Heine that will concern us shortly. As is usual in such imitations, Heine's controlled looseness of composition has become indifferent disarray, and as usual, the author attempts to make of this a virtue of the book. In a letter to Charlotte Stieglitz of 26 October 1834, he described the book as "einzelne Skizzen, Humoresken und Phantasiestücke, durch welche jedoch alle nach meiner Art ein gemeinsamer rother Faden geht,"[84] just as Heine spoke in *Die Harzreise* of "die bunten Fäden, die so hübsch hineingesponnen sind, um sich im Ganzen harmonisch zu verschlingen."[85] In the book itself, however, the author raises the question whether it is a novel or novella and concludes: "Ich erkläre mit feierlicher Resignation, daß es eigentlich gar kein *Buch* ist, das ich herausgebe, sondern bloß ein Stück Leben."[86] These ironic disclaimers, inherited from the Romantic tradition, in part via Heine, and amalgamated with the new pre-eminence of "life," are among the most tiresome aspects of Young German writing, for they serve as an apology for every kind of self-indulgence. Gutzkow, incidentally, criticized Mundt in a letter to Varnhagen for the lack of artistic concretion and plasticity.[87]

It cannot be denied, however, that Mundt's critical attitude has stabilized noticeably since *Moderne Lebenswirren*; here there are themes that are unmistakeably liberal. Most prominent among them is the desire to bring movement and progress, urbanity and rationality, into the stagnation of the times. The book begins with a "Posthorn-Symphonie"[88] in which Mundt adverts directly to the stopping up of the flow of ideas by the censorship: "Ich will mir selbst etwas blasen! Jetzt fange ich an, es zu glauben, daß von einer allgemeinen Tonlosigkeit dies unser Zeitalter ergriffen sein muß, denn auch die deutschen Postillons lassen jetzt ihr schmetterndes Mundstück ungenutzt und schläfrig herunterhängen, und jeder sagt mir miß-muthig, ihm sei das Horn verstopft."[89] Do coachmen, the author asks, fear the censorship? The traveller is off on his journey not to see sights or contemplate nature, but to see and talk to the people, to find out how much they are interested in the new times and to encourage peasants and villagers especially to read and to occupy themselves with ideas for a more humane existence. Mundt's rejection of nature as an object of his interest is a rejection of the Romantic tradition: "Der Horizont dieser gegenwärtigen Zeit ist zu bewölkt, als daß man weit ausschauen könnte von den Bergen in die Thäler und die silbernen Ströme entlang, und auf die Kuppeln und Thürme der fernen schönen Städte. Das harmlose, unschuldige Gemüth ist fort, das mit Landschaften und Gegenden sich freute, und ich suche es vergeblich in mir, und finde nichts, als daß ich kein Jean-Pauli-scher Jüngling mehr bin."[90] Nature poetry, Mundt argues, is a symptom of a frustrated and unhappy society:

> Das Unglück geht am liebsten hinaus ins Grüne und unter die Einsamkeit der wehenden Bäume, das Unglück oder die spielende Kinderunschuld. Die Kinder und die Zerrissenen, beide stehen dem Naturelement am nächsten, und beide würden darin verloren gehen, wenn es nicht ein Stärkeres gäbe als das Naturelement, nämlich den historischen Trieb in die werdende Welt- und Völker-Zukunft, die Alle aufreizt, sich zu bilden, zu bewegen und zu versöhnen. Und die Deutschen waren nie unglücklicher, nie innerlich zerrissener, als zur Zeit ihrer Natursentimentalität und Landschaftsempfind-samkeit im Leben und Dichten.[91]

The writer can always call up in his imagination the decorative aspects of nature if he needs them; but imagination will not suffice to make the world of men visible to him; it must be observed.[92] This is a doubtful argument, but one not insignificant for the time, for it suggests a recipe for realism. Mundt's revaluation of the city is a significant aspect of this realistic urge. In a passage of several pages, Mundt speaks of a desire to reverse the logic of Schiller's elegy *Der Spaziergang*, which proceeds from the city into a bucolic landscape and then into a higher realm of elegiac mythological reminiscence. Mundt would like to go the other way and write an "elegy" on the city: "Ich liebe die städtebauende Muse, welche den Nomadentrieb des menschlichen Lebens einordnet in feste Gränzen der beglückenden Harmonie."[93] This allegiance to civilization is the mark of the genuine liberal and is not common in the German literary tradition.

Progressive civilization, motion, future orientation are thus notable aspects of Mundt's attitude in *Madonna*. In his postscript he refers to the novel as a "Buch der Bewegung,"[94] which could be construed, especially by the witch-hunters, as a "book of *the* movement," of a critical and even, from time to time, radical thrust. The part of the book that caused the most offense to the governmental criticism was the long eulogy on Casanova, which the traveller recites to a bigoted and ignorant old schoolteacher in Bohemia. This is, in fact, an extensive literary essay embedded in the narrative, and it shows that Mundt had a good knowledge of Casanova's memoirs, for he knows how they came to be written and published, he stresses their value as perceptive social history, and he calls attention to the wide range of Casanova's intellectual gifts and his indefatigable vitality. But Mundt makes aggressive use of Casanova's role as an apostle of worldliness; he calls him a knight of secular life and a combination of Don Juan and Faust,[95] that is, the quintessence of modern man. His Catholicism, Mundt says provocatively, was "Weltgenuß."[96] Such phrases must have appeared to conservative minds as code words for sexual licentiousness.

It is true that Mundt treats sexuality itself, particularly in the feelings of the "Madonna" figure, with a naturalness that is unusual in this age and is certainly far removed from the cramped and timid treatment in Gutzkow's *Wally*. But Mundt is not making a brief for libertinism, although some of his language was not as carefully chosen as it might have been; he is pursuing his version of the Saint-Simonian reconciliation of the flesh and the spirit. Mundt's views on these matters show numerous parallels to those argued by Heine in *Zur Geschichte der Religion und Philosophie in Deutschland*, which had appeared in January, 1835.[97] The difference, characteristic for Mundt, is a greater confidence in Christianity as a liberal religion and as a mediator between the worlds of matter and spirit. This mediatory role of Christianity is a main theme of *Madonna*. The Virgin Mary, for example, is said to be a mediator between a familiar human experience, motherhood, and the divine spirit. There is a long discussion of Raphael, whom Mundt treats, not as the Romantics did, as the epitome of the pious artist, but as the idealizer of Catholicism who painted for the invisible church, a worldly painter who expressed the worldly freedom of thought; he built a bridge from religion to the sensory world.[98] Why this should be especially true of Raphael among all religious painters is not clear, but I suspect Mundt chose this example just because of the way it had been used by the Romantics in their pursuit of an aestheticized piety. These views of reconciliation are curiously combined with a distinctly Hegelian faith in the dynamic of history: "Christus aber schreitet als der Geist der Fortentwickelung durch die Geschichte, und die Religion bildet sich im Geist und in der Wahrheit in die Welt hinein."[99] The overcoming of the dichotomy is described as something already well in process: "Alles wird weltlich in unserer Zeit und muß es werden, selbst die Religion. Denn es kann nichts Heiligeres mehr geben, als das Weltliche, nichts Geistlicheres als das Weltliche. Alles hat jetzt eine und dieselbe Geschichte."[100] Furthermore, for Mundt the gap between the flesh and the spirit is similar to the gap between the people and the cultivated intelligentsia, a concern we have already noticed in *Die Kunst der deutschen Prosa*: "Die Welt und das Fleisch müssen wieder eingesetzt werden in ihre Rechte, damit der Geist nicht mehr sechs Treppen hoch wohnt in Deutschland."[101] While he is not explicit about it, such a parallel clearly indicates that the Saint-Simonian program has revolutionary implications for society. However, he is careful to deny any sympathy with political or class revolution. Lammenais' pioneering effort to devise a kind of Christian socialism meets with strong disapproval; Mundt denounces it as Jacobinism and accuses Lammenais of arming the most dangerous class of the people.[102]

The incarnation of sanctified worldliness is the central figure of the book, Maria, the "Madonna." As a moderate Saint-Simonian, Mundt was of course interested in the question of the emancipation of women. Among the Young Germans, he takes in some respects the least patronizing view of the matter. It is true that he would not meet with the approval of the women's liberationists of today. His apotheosis of Charlotte Stieglitz and his repeated beatification of the "Madonna" as a saint are not unlike that nineteenth-century process by which women were placed on a pedestal and thus elevated out of all significance. In *Charlotte Stieglitz, ein Denkmal*, where he praises Charlotte at length as the paragon of womanhood, he lists his ideals of women: her heart is "ein offener Liebestempel"; what is admirable in women is "das Anschmiegende," "das Dienende...," die süße Magdsnatur im Weibe, die ächt christlich ihrem Herrn die Füße wäscht," and so on.[103] He makes very clear some years later that he thought it an insult to femininity to want women to have any part in the state or in civil affairs.[104] A passage in *Madonna* suggests that Mundt believed a woman could not contend with a man in an extreme situation; it occurs while Maria is resisting an attempt at forcible seduction: "In diesem Moment erfuhr ich zuerst in mir," says Maria, "daß es eine Macht des Mannes gebe, die unserer Natur weit überlegen sei. Er [the seducer] kam mir schön vor in der Gloria des Mannes, wie noch nie, und ich dachte, daß mich nichts mehr retten könne, als Bitten."[105]

The reason for this, however, is Maria's natural sexuality, which in itself is innocent for her, and which at such a critical moment comes into conflict with her abhorrence of her would-be seducer. On the whole, Mundt shows none of the attitude that one senses in Laube, for example, that emancipation of women is primarily a matter of breaking down sexual inhibitions in order to make male life less frustrating and troublesome. Mundt is more genuinely concerned with the way the inner and outer freedom of women is violated in a repressive and bigoted society. When the narrator meets Maria in Bohemia, she is virtually a prisoner in conditions that do not allow her to unfold herself: "Und gerade weibliche Naturen sind es am häufigsten, welche man an ein solches Leben ohne Sterne verbannt findet."[106] Women live in hope, but are worn out and grow old in sacrifice for others. Because Maria is regarded by her father and the neighborhood as godless, she is subjected to humiliating punishments: she is obliged to learn the names of all the saints by heart and to memorize the catalogue of all the outlandish relics collected by Emperor Charles IV. She wishes she were a Protestant — a sign in the Young German context that she wishes to become progressive and modern — and she does achieve this, to her great satisfaction, at the end of the novel.

The story of Maria herself, to which we shall turn in a moment, is evidence enough of Mundt's sympathy, within certain limits, for the cause of female emancipation. He underlines the theme, however, by attempting to give it also a legendary treatment. The legend is based on materials of the Libussa cycle, the ancient tales about the mythical foundress of Prague and her court.[107] A Prague poet, Karl Egon von Ebert (1801-82), whom Mundt, judging from the adventures of his narrator, seems to have met, had treated a part of this material in 1829: the revolt of Vlasta and the War of the Maids after the death of Libussa and the restoration of male rule. Mundt endeavored to make the legend more satirical and to bear more on the question of women's emancipation. The details, which are fairly pedestrian, need not concern us here. What happens in essence is that the women, having been denied the intellectual, cultural, and social equality they had enjoyed under Libussa's rule, become increasingly radical, and are gradually transformed into heartless Amazons and defeated after a bloody war. In the course of the legend Vlasta is made to prophesy the future of women up to the nineteenth century: she tells of the adoration of women in the medieval *Minne* cult, of the fate of Joan of Arc, of the eighteenth century, and of Saint-Simonism and its confusions. In none of these ages are women really free, although Mundt seems to hold out some hope for the nineteenth century. The legend breaks off abruptly, and it is apparent that it was inserted only as a vehicle to discuss the Saint-Simonian issue.

Maria's story is a novella of some seventy pages inserted into the larger work. It is an autobiographical account sent by the girl to the travelling narrator and it is entitled "Bekenntnisse einer weltlichen Seele," in parodistic reference, of course, to the sixth book of Goethe's *Wilhelm Meisters Lehrjahre,* "Bekenntnisse einer schönen Seele." It has some claim to be, I believe, the best of all Young German novellas; certainly it is Mundt's best piece of fictional writing. It is a well-told story — economical, convincing, and psychologically interesting — and the plot contains a startling twist of the sort perfected in the art of O. Henry. Maria is born into impoverished circumstances and is unloved by her parents. (The unconventional theme of a child with unloving and indifferent

76

parents is used by Mundt in another, otherwise undistinguished and poorly constructed novella, *Antoniens Bußfahrten.*[108]) She develops at an early age a longing for freedom and real life; she feels that if she had wings, she would fly right into the middle of life. Just what "life" is she has no very clear idea; she reads about "life" in the Bible and in her school primers, and concludes it must be something going on elsewhere. She prays for it day and night. Then matters take a turn that leads her at first to hope that she is to find life. She is taken to live with her apparently wealthy aunt in Dresden, and the quality of her existence changes dramatically. Here she is amiably treated, lives in comfortable surroundings, has every amenity, and is provided with a good education, which she greatly enjoys. Her happiness is gradually clouded, however, with the growing awareness that it is not her aunt's resources at all that are responsible for her well-being, but the subsidies of a rich count. As she grows older, it dawns on her that she is being prepared for this gentleman's concubinage, and she develops a deep aversion to him. Among Maria's tutors is a young theologian named Mellenberg, who is unprepossessing, bookish, and monosyllabic, but Maria feels attracted to him, as well as to his Protestantism. Eventually the time comes for the count to attempt to collect his investment. Maria resists him in the scene already mentioned, and flees in desperation to the garret room of Mellenberg, now a boarder in the house, in order to hide. The unspoken love between them is made manifest, and Maria spends the night with him. The next morning, in her own room, she feels revitalized, blossoming, more fulfilled than ever before in her life. But soon she receives a note from Mellenberg, in which he apologizes for the great wrong he has done her and informs her that he must take his life out of shame, which he promptly does. Maria, in shattered despair, wanders back to her Bohemian village, where Mundt's travelling narrator makes her acquaintance.

The most striking part of this novella is the fierce irony of its climax. While Maria has found the life she has so long yearned for in her night of love with Mellenberg, he is attuned to an entirely different morality and interprets as an inexpiable wrong what for Maria has been a great blessing. In retrospect Maria interprets this as a mutual failure of understanding: "Er hatte meine Liebe nicht verstanden, und ich seine Religion nicht."[109] But the author Mundt clearly evaluates the case differently. Maria, the worldly "Madonna," the saint, is a wholly positive figure; she is the principle of honest and natural life, whereas Mellenberg's repressive morality is the principle of death that meaninglessly destroys one life and wrecks another. In passing, it might be mentioned that Mundt did something similar in another novella, although with much less success. It is a double-stranded story entitled *Der Bibeldieb*.[110] One strand concerns a pastor who has been imprisoned for political activity; in his great yearning for freedom he escapes and absent-mindedly steals a Bible in order to nourish his spirit from it; this strand ends happily, for it turns out that an undelivered pardon had been issued before his escape. The other strand concerns a crisis between two young people about to be married: the girl finds the young man too frivolous and impious in his opinions; the young man declares the girl is too repressed and prudish. Through a plot complication, the young man loses his clothes while swimming and the girl comes upon him nude. She interprets this as an attempt on his part to humiliate her and drowns herself out of shame. This grisly conclusion to what is essentially a story of comic situations is entirely inappropriate and shows bad taste. It helps, however, to illuminate the more effective climax of the *Madonna* novella. Mundt could be as vague as any Young German about what the "life" was that a truly modern literature ought to represent and celebrate, but he seems to have had a clear idea that its opposite was death. The suicide of Mellenberg takes on symbolic implications; it throws into high relief all the killing repressivenenss of an orthodoxy hostile to the natural vitality of human life. The Protestant Mellenberg clearly has no notion of the liberating implications that Protestantism had for the Young Germans and also for Maria. It is also not without interest that in the one story Mundt lays the burden of repressiveness on the male, in the other on the female; thus he avoids the not uncommon tendency to blame women for resistance to what, in the unfortunate phrase of the time, was known as "emancipation of the flesh."

The story has a few other remarkable aspects as well. One I have already touched upon: the untroubled recognition of the fact that there can be such an affect in a heroine as sexuality, not a very striking matter for our own time, but a promising development in the early nineteenth century, especially because Mundt has his "Madonna" treat it with decorum but without coquettishness or fear.

Maria describes in a fairly graphic way the experience of puberty and the awareness that sexuality is developing in her. She even tells something of her feelings at inadvertently watching Mellenberg, in a room near hers, undressing for bed, although she not unreasonably breaks off this account.[111] Another interesting point is the dilemma in which she finds herself in her aunt's house. Even as a child, she is quick-witted enough to figure out what is going on. She naturally takes a dim view of the situation; the difficulty is that she takes genuine pleasure in the advantages she enjoys; she is delighted to be educated, to live in comfort, to have all the material objects and pleasurable outings she desires. It is unusual that neither Maria nor the author sees this as a moral defect. One is given rather the impression that it is good for a human being to have pleasurable and urbane surroundings, to acquire cultivated accomplishments and love handsome possessions. Mundt's strategies here remind one of Heine's dislike of Jacobin puritanism and his belief that the reformation of society should bring more joy to more men, not less. They are a not inconsiderable virtue of this novella.

Another is Mundt's characterization of the count. Although he is engaged in a scheme that is deeply disrespectful of the personal freedom of another human being, attempting literally to buy and breed Maria as though she were a pet, he is not presented as a monster, but rather as a pleasant, urbane, and vaguely well-meaning gentleman whom Maria does not really hate; she is indifferent to him personally and dislikes passionately only the dehumanizing situation into which he has put her. With a surprising realistic instinct, Mundt here avoids a melodramatic pitfall. There is one additional and effective moment in the novella. Mellenberg's suicide and Maria's helpless despair at it occur simultaneously with a religious riot in Dresden, caused by the refusal of the Catholic authorities to allow the Protestant population properly to celebrate the tricentennial of the Augsburg Confession. As Mellenberg's death is caused by allegiance to obsolete religious principles, so the whole of society is thrown into disorder by primitive and obsolete religious passion. The Augsburg Confession had, after all, been negotiated in 1530; that society should be still tormented by it must have seemed as absurd to Mundt as the religious conflicts in Northern Ireland seem to us today. With this juxtaposition, Mundt achieved a meaningful integration of a private fate and a wider social incongruity such as is rare in Young German fiction.

These virtues of Mundt's story do not make of him an outstanding writer, nor do they suggest that, under differing circumstances, he could have become one. They do indicate that the predication of mediocrity to one of the struggling young writers of this period is beside the point. Mundt's *Madonna* shows that there was enough intellectual and realistic material at hand in 1835 to make competent and worthwhile literary writing possible. If not by Mundt, then by another; but the real issue is not the failings and limitations of Mundt, but those of a ruling class of society that strangled these beginnings in their cradle.

IV. FERDINAND GUSTAV KÜHNE: *EINE QUARANTÄNE IM IRRENHAUSE*

Ferdinand Gustav Kühne was more on the periphery than in the mainstream of the Young German movement, although from time to time he applied the label to himself. He was not named in the proscription of 1835 and, as far as I know, became involved in the mill of the censorship only twice: his *Klosternovellen* were not permitted to be published in Mundt's *Dioskuren* in 1837[1] because of their anti-Catholic tone, a theme that Kühne pursued vigorously in later years in the spirit of the *Kulturkampf*; the other occasion was a series of proscriptions and fines in the early 1850's, for Kühne became a genuine "forty-eighter," if a middle-of-the-road one, whose periodical *Europa*, which he took over in 1846, published a number of the important *Vormärz* liberals, and he fell afoul of the repressive measures of the authorities after the failure of the revolution.[2] He did grieve at the censorship under which the Young Germans suffered; he wrote to an elderly lady friend in 1837: "Die Maßregeln gegen die junge Literatur haben mich nicht vernichtet, aber gelähmt. Es ist eine böse, böse Zeit. Der innere Mensch ist so gut, warm und kräftig, aber die Objectivität der Welt erdrückt ihn. Der innere Mensch möchte auferstehen wie ein weltlicher Christus, aber der Stein über dem Grabe will nicht weichen, die Engel, die ihn heben müßten, sind verscheucht, die Engel der Unschuld, Milde und Liebe — und der Stein bleibt von der Polizei versiegelt."[3] Kühne had some fleeting acquaintance with Gutzkow, but his main line of contact to Young Germany was Mundt, with whom he maintained a life-long if not untroubled friendship beginning with their school-days together in Berlin. If we have quarrelled with the predication of mediocrity to Mundt, it is difficult to do so in the case of Kühne, for, though not insensitive or unintelligent, he was a fairly ordinary soul, almost a philistine in the mundane conventionality that underlay the superficial lability of his thought and feeling. Although he wrote prose works all his life — historical novels, mainly — and some drama and occasional verse, he seems, by the standards of a Gutzkow, a Laube, or an Immermann, to have been almost wholly devoid of literary gifts. A more justly forgotten writer is hard to imagine.

In 1835, however, the year of the crisis, Kühne published a novel that gives us a tour inside the head of a chafing young liberal of the time, and for that reason it is of value for our investigation. Kühne himself regarded it as a major breakthrough after a series of un-satisfying novellas and later called it a book of "blutige Schmerzen."[4] It is entitled *Eine Quarantäne im Irrenhause* and its plot is as follows: the unnamed hero is the son of an aristocratic mother and a bourgeois father. His mother's brother, the prime minister of a small prin-cipality, dislikes him because of this odious mésalliance and is suspi-cious of him for other reasons. The hero pursues the intellectual life without making any effort to take up a useful occupation, and his brooding and thinking upset his uncle, who, a former Jacobin enthusiast, has become a fanatic absolutist and persecutor of youth-ful demagogues. Even worse, the nephew has become attached to an opera singer named Victorine Miaska, a patriotic refugee from the crushed Polish revolution. The uncle has his nephew and, shortly thereafter, Victorine, incarcerated in a madhouse to cure them of their deviant attitudes. The hero escapes with Victorine and three other characters. Victorine returns home just at the moment when her ill mother, in despair at the rude treatment she has been receiving from the authorities, shoots herself; Victorine, while wrestling with a policeman for the pistol, is shot and killed. The uncle, meanwhile, in his fanatic hatred of the rebellious younger generation, has become genuinely insane and must be confined, although in a lucid moment just before his death, he reconciles himself with his nephew. This action, which is reported in a day-to-day diary so extensive that it is impossible to imagine its author would have had time to participate in the events described, covers eighteen days.

There are a few other complications, but this, in essence, is the story, and one can easily see that so plain if melodramatic a plot cannot account for a novel of 335 pages. It does not, although the plot itself has some clear symbolic significance. The attachment of the young liberal to the patriotic Polish girl has an obvious ideological import, as does the policeman whose grip on her is likened to the grip of Russia on Poland. The Soviet-style effort to repress dissent by ignoring its content and ascribing intellectual deviation to insanity is an acid commentary on the atmosphere of the time; it is a telling coincidence that, during the crisis at the end of 1835, the Saxon government proposed that all Young Germans be put into prison or into the madhouse.[5] It cannot be determined whether the persecuting, lunatic uncle has any reference to the Prussian censorship official, Gustav Adolf von Tzschoppe, who, as was well known within the government and to some extent outside it, suffered from serious mental disturbance, but Kühne's strategy appears apposite in retrospect. However, such observations do not define the character of this novel, which, much more obviously than Gutzkow's *Wally*, is a vessel for its author's thinking processes — one sees easily in reading Kühne's letters of the time that his hero is a more extreme case of his own bewilderment and alienation.

The main purpose served by the fiction is to permit the intellectual discourse to run on and round about without logical restraint. It is not fundamentally a question of genre, but of the quantity of interest that this interminable verbiage holds for the reader: "Für den heutigen Leser," remarked Houben sixty years ago, "ist Kühnes Buch eine ziemlich schwere Lektüre, und man kann dieses Chaos von mehr oder weniger geistreichen Paradoxien, redseligen Betrachtungen, historisch-politischen Reflexionen usw. nur überwinden, wenn man eine sehr intime Kenntnis der Zeitgeschichte, ihrer Blüten und Auswüchse zur Kontrolle gegenwärtig hat."[6] Equally to the point is the critique that the novelist Heinrich König wrote to Kühne in 1854 of his novel *Die Freimaurer*, for it shows that Kühne was never able to find his way to a more objective narrative form or to overcome his discursive, intellectualized style:

Indem Sie aber eigentliche "Familienpapiere" geben, haben Sie — absichtlich oder aus Instinkt — die weiteste und bequemste Form poetischer Darstellung für ein so mächtiges Material gewählt, und müssen nun freilich auch hinnehmen, was dem Dichter, wie Sie wissen, zu begegnen pflegt, daß er sich nämlich seine Leser nur in dem Maße fesselt, als er sich selber bindet.. .An concreten Erlebnissen fehlt es zwar in Ihren Mittheilungen auch nicht, aber nur einzelne sind wahrhaft lebendig und hinreißend ausgefallen und dazwischen kommen wieder Strecken vor, über welche hin der Erzähler im Bündel seiner *Erlebnisse* zu schwer an den *Studien* des

Dichters über Literatur und Leben zu tragen hat. Die Betrachtungen sind geistreich, treffend; gute Laune und Witz fehlen nicht, aber man fühlt zu oft lebhaft, daß alles dies Eigenthum des Dichters ist, das die wechselnden Erzähler als eigenes Gepäck tragen müssen.[7]

Similar objections can easily be made to *Quarantäne*, in which both action and characterization are submerged in the philosophical brooding of the twenty-eight-year-old author.

Quarantäne is a book about madness, not primarily in a clinical, psychological sense, although there is some concern with that. (Kühne's father was a difficult, both tyrannical and morbidly dependent person who became mentally unbalanced after his wife's death.) But its chief concern is to describe a pathology of the intellect and the times. Kühne wrote to his publisher on 26 December 1834 that the "Novelle, obwohl sie in Form eines Dichtwerks erscheint, eigentlich eine Pathologie des modernen Lebens genannt werden kann."[8] The pathology is related in a complicated way to the repressiveness of the times, of which the madhouse, a kind of compassionate prison, is a symbol. In one of the rare moments of compact writing in the book, Kühne describes an inmate who loses his grip while digging potatoes: "Einer der Arbeiter schwang plötzlich seinen Spaten wie ein grimmiger Türke über den Kopf. Er stieß ein lautes, wieherndes Geschrei aus: es war wie ein Angstruf der verzweifelnden Menschheit, die nach Ruhe schnaubt. Der Aufseher, der ihm zur Seite stand, griff ihn aber hart an die Brust und schüttelte ihn tüchtig. Da besann sich der Arme wieder und grub hastig nach seinen Erdäpfeln weiter" (p. 28).[9] The question of how the madhouse and its inmates relate to the world and the general condition of mankind is one matter of interest in trying to understand Kühne's book.

The initial question, however, is that of the sanity of the diarist himself. Almost his first assertion is that he is sane, although he admits to a physical fever and delirium from which he is now recovering. But both the validity and the meaning of this assertion are quickly called into question by the subsequent course of the narrator's brooding, which zigzags in unresolved antinomies and revolves round and round with pedantic, almost lunatic persistence. The asylum's doctor, after having read part of the diary, says not without justice that it contains "bei manchen lichten Intervallationslinien viel mystische Hieroglyphe, viel dämonisch irres Getriebe, nicht ohne Methode, aber überwacht, übernommen, mein Verehrtester" (p. 185). Persistent argumentation with constantly shifting premises was apparently a characteristic of Kühne; in a touchy letter of 1828, Mundt complained of Kühne's heat in disputation and that "Du oft den Streit um wichtige Gegenstände in precäre Kleinigkeiten concentrirt und Dich mit der Sache selbst in einem sophistischen Zirkel herumgedreht [hast]."[10] The perpetual inner monologue in *Quarantäne* is not unlike this way of arguing, although here it is objectified into a distracted and representative individual, of whom it is said in the "editor's" preface that he is a self-tormentor and a negative example of the delusion of the times (pp. v, vi). The question of the meaning of sanity is raised immediately with the hero's claim that he is sane; here, as elsewhere, it is indicated that sanity is a state of harmless normality enforced by repression; at the same time, the hero claims such normality for himself, while indicating ironically that this is hardly the whole truth and suggesting an uneasy balance between his intellectual speculations and his remoteness from active life.

At the outset of the novel, there is a certain eccentric shrewdness in this nervously oscillating self-presentation. The best way to show the character of this prose is to quote a passage at considerable length. The hero is trying to figure out the reason for his sudden incarceration:

Ich hörte auf der Reise viel munkeln von Verhaftbefehlen gegen Alle, die nur jemals im Geruche der Burschenschafterei gestanden; die frankfurter Unruhen [the storming of the constabulary in April, 1833] hatten zu dieser Maßregel einen nur zu triftigen Beweggrund gegeben, oder nicht Beweggrund, Veranlassung, Befürchtungsgrund, nicht Beweggrund. Großer Gott! Bewegung! verruchtes Wort! Wie kann ich Bewegung den Verfolgern der Bewegung zumuthen. Den Grund boten die frankfurter Trivialitäten; auf den Grund wollte man der Sache kommen, selbst wenn sie bodenlos sein sollte. Aber ich für mein Theil war nie Burschenschaftler gewesen, ich konnte nicht verdächtigt werden, ich konnte vor Gericht nichts aussagen, ich bin weit unschuldiger noch als Staberl, der mit einem Flüchtling den Rock wechselt und so dessen Signalement auf seinen Rücken nimmt. Ich war zeitlebens ein viel zu timider Mensch,

ich war zu geizig mit meinen Gedanken, um einen einzigen der-
selben für zehn Revolutionsideen umzutauschen. Ich lebte in B. so
still wie eine Kirchenmaus Jahr aus Jahr ein. Stille Kirchenmäuse
zernagen freilich oft die Hostien im Tempel und zerfressen die
Sacramente des Lebens, allein man stellt Gift hin neben die heiligen Dinge und ist dann sicher gegen den Zahn der Kritik so
kleiner Wesen. Auch für den Zahn der Zeit hat man Gift genug;
man kann ruhig schlafen und Alles gut sein lassen. Politische
Zeitungen hatte ich gelesen, politische Gedanken im Kopfe gehegt,
des Völkerlebens Lust und Leid im Herzen getragen, allein nie ein
Wort hinausgesprochen aus der verschlossenen Brust; Gedanken und
Gefühle waren unausgebrütete Eier geblieben unter den schirmen-
den Flügeln einer policeilichen Stiefmutterhenne. Mein Ich hatte ich
selten hinausgedrängt auf den Markt des Ruhmes; ich hatte mehr
als eine Persönlichkeit, mehr als mein Ich suchen wollen und war
freilich so vereinsamt geblieben, daß ich doch nichts hatte und
behielt von all meinem emsigen Forschen und Grübeln, als die
mein armes, kleines, winziges Ich. Ich schien der gefahrloseste
weil unbrauchbarste Mensch im Staate, ich war von je der stillst
Bürger dieser Erdenwelt. Elegien könnte ich schreiben über die
mein stilles wissenschaftliches Vegetiren: warum mich gefänglic
einziehn? Blos auf mein ehrlich Gesicht hin und mit einem kraf
gültigen Paß versehen, hatte ich mich in das Ausland, d. h. in e
deutsches Ausland, hineingewagt. Meiner Schulden wegen konn
ich nicht gefänglich eingezogen werden, denn mich drückten kein
ein Engagement hatte ich nicht, wie reisende und ausreißen
Künstler, im Stich gelassen, denn mich band keines; wegen ve
säumter Amtspflicht konnte ich auch nicht eingezogen werden, de
ich war ja in meiner Heimat ein eben so amtloses wie harmlo
Individuum. Ich wollte eine Vergnügungsreise machen, sowie i
überhaupt zum Vergnügen lebe und zum Vergnügen sterben w
wenn's sein muß. Ich lebe in meiner Heimat, wie man so zu sag
pflegt, ganz frei und ungebunden, amtsfrei und — so lange G
will — schuldenfrei. Sollte man diese Freiheit nicht erlauber
 Ich bin in B. blos Mensch, Doctor der Philosophie, auch Magis
der brotlosen Künste. Wäge ich diese drei Würden gegen einan
ab, so fällt auf die Menschenwürde das meiste Gewicht. Ich l
nichts, rein nichts, man kann mich nicht verhaften. Philosoph
beargwöhnt man, sie haben oft falsche Begriffe von der Freih

verbreitet. Advocaten und Doctoren der Philosophie standen an der Spitze der neuesten trostlosen Bewegungen. Allein ich als Philosoph demonstrire Jedem, nach Hegel, daß Freiheit und Notwendigkeit identisch sind, und bin demnach ein gefahrloses Wesen. Ich bin sonst ein stiller friedlicher Mensch, aber wenn man mich reizt, so habe ich einige dialektische Fünffingergriffe bei der Hand, die ich dem Inquisitor um die Ohren schlage, daß ihm seinerseits die fünf Sinne vergehen. Ich kann als Philosoph nicht arretirt werden; auch lebe ich nicht von der Philosophie, vielmehr lebt und zehrt der Philosoph in mir vom Menschen in mir; als absoluter Philosoph will ich nichts Anderes sein als ein absoluter Mensch. Bin ich nun als absoluter Mensch unschuldig: wer will mich verhaften? Als Magister der brotlosen Künste sterb' ich mehr als daß ich lebe Aber gesetzt ich hätte mein Brot von den brotlosen Künsten. bedauern mögt ihr mich; wer will mich aber verhaften? Ich lebe nur zum Vergnügen, und wenn mir Einer beweist, ich würde, falls ich länger des Vergnügens wegen lebte, vergnügenshalber umkommen, so beweist das noch nicht, daß ich vergnügenshalber gefänglich eingezogen werden darf. Das ist kein Privatvergnügen mehr, das greift in die Sache der Gerechtigkeit und Staatsverwaltung, und die Zeiten sind vorüber, wo Recht und Gerechtigkeit blos zum Vergnügen der sogenannten Großen dieser Welt gehandhabt wurden. Lebten wir in einem *ancien régime,* so wüßte ich, daß es *lettres-de-cachet* gäbe und tröstete mich dann mit dem nicht unbedeutenden Range eines Wirklichen Geheimen Staatsgefangenen; allein in dem Bewußtsein, weder innerlich noch äußerlich etwas Burschenschaftliches an mir zu tragen, glaubte ich sicher meines Weges gehen zu können und bin doch bitter getäuscht.

Aber wie trug sich die Sache nur zu? — Während ich darauf sinne, merke ich erst, wie absorbirend ein Fieber auf die Gedächtnißkraft wirkt. Das klare Denken hält noch schwer (pp. 3-6).

It takes a long passage like this to see Kühne's manner most clearly, for each element or segment of it is influenced by what comes before or after; what appears to be a series of statements in discursive prose is actually a continuous floundering about in a sea of unstable attitudes and feelings. Stylistically, the prose is haunted by the pale ghost of Jean Paul: the oblique allusiveness, the continuous punning, the onrunning chain of associations, and the frantic grasp for the integrity of the peeling, splintering self all indicate that model. The change in tone and purpose, however, is just as evident. There is no liberating humor here, very little wit, no aesthetic playfulness with language; it is all dead earnest and quite desperate. Its principle quality is an elusive irony that seems to imply more than it says. The hero insists he cannot be arrested, when in fact he has been; he appears confident that he is not living in an arbitrary *ancien régime*, but he is indeed the victim, although he does not know it at this point, of something rather similar to a *lettre-de-cachet*. He is insistent that he is by no means a revolutionary, although his side glances at contemporary political repression are bitter and the queer simile of the churchmouse introduces an attitude of critical opposition and adverts to the poisonous defenses of the status quo against it. His quietude and harmlessness are forced upon him, his philosophy condemned to inactivity, yet somehow he has come into conflict with authority despite his apparently private character. With all its irony and allusiveness, the prose is, in a sense, rich, yet, at the same time, it lacks density; what presents itself as thinking and concentration is in fact the running on of a mind threatened with diffuseness and a failure of logical control — and, one must add, an intellectual narcissism that hinders the effort to find solutions to the problems because it is part of the causes of them.

The writer of this prose is bleakly self-ironic. In another place he describes the scene of his arrest: "Der Himmel hatte sich schwarz umgezogen, ein Gewitter kündigte sich in lauten Schlägen an, der Regen goß in dichten Strömen. Das gehört zur abgenutzten Romantik der Entführungsgeschichten" (p. 12). Reactionary life imitates obsolete art, yet the writer of these lines is victimized himself by the conditions under which he tries to think and cannot get out of the maze of abstraction and disembodied conceptualizing. His intellectual equipment continually carries him away from rather than toward clarity and reality. At the beginning of the second day of his diary, he tries to mobilize his "inner freedom" in order to be "ideally" not in the madhouse (p. 21), and he experiments with a version of Fichte that turns out to be parody: "Ich bin ich, das ist das Staatsgrundgesetz des psychologischen Menschen, das Ich hat Alles in sich, begreift, beherrscht Alles. *L'état c'est moi*" (p. 22). He continues twisting and turning in this vein, again punning from dilemma to dilemma, with similes always on the periphery of critical allusion,

88

until he is indeed incarcerated. The style, therefore, can be intriguing, but after many pages of this the reader becomes distressed and wearied, not only because the interminable paradoxes seem to revolve more and more pointlessly and the jejune self-absorption of the memoirist gradually causes us to lose interest in him, but also because one gets less and less the feeling that there is a controlling intelligence behind it all; the gap between narrating author and narrated character shrinks to near zero, and what appears at first to be a kind of shrewdness in representing intellectual bewilderment turns into hopeless bewilderment itself. The author, the reader comes to feel, is permitting himself too much; the lack of discipline of which Heinrich König complained leads to self-indulgence.

The theme of madness is turned over and over, dissected and reassembled, and set into dialectical puzzles. The narrator, for good reason, fears for his own sanity. He becomes curious about the doctor's methods of treatment and thinks of pretending madness, but senses immediately the danger he is in: "O Hamlet, Hamlet! Du *wurdest* was Du schienst! — Mein Gott, führe uns nicht in Versuchung!" (p. 30). Later, after a curious disquisition on the relationship of suicide to madness, he remarks strangely that he could forgive a suicide, but would avert his eyes from a madman, because "ich hasse sein Bild meinetwegen; meinetwegen, ich fürchte, gerade weil ich ihn liebe, die Ansteckung" (p. 74). The suicide is a martyr of error, he says, but madness is "ein Vergehen gegen die Weisheit unserer Tage" (p. 72). But this statement is ironic, for competing definitions of sanity are at stake also. In arguing with the doctor, he finds his vigorous efforts to prove his sanity only make the doctor more suspicious, and he concludes that men and nations should reason less and accept more; then they would be thought mature. In this view, sanity is defined by convention as accomodation to authority: "Ich sprach von meiner gesunden Vernunft wie ein Volk, das plötzlich emancipirt sein will. Grade das Drängende der Überzeugung duldet man nicht" (p. 31). Later he determines, in order to please his doctor-jailer, to be "fromm und sanft... wie ein Lamm" (p. 148). Thus there is a tendency for sanity to take on a pejorative aspect as a kind of normality that accepts repression and avoids all creative, imaginative aberration.

But the alternatives are by no means clear. One of the patients is a demented clergyman who is obsessed with water as a panacea for all the ills of the time. He is the kind of grotesque eccentric that Karl Immermann was to make a speciality of in his two major novels. He derives soul and temperament from climatic conditions — a satirical anticipation of Taine — and wants to cure the world with laxatives. Like Immermann's characters of this type, the clergyman is not only an object of satire, but also a vehicle of it: "Philosophie, Poesie, Politik," he observes, "Alles ist bis zu einem Wahnsinnsgipfel hinaufgedrängt und möchte sich von oben kopfüber hinabstürzen" (p. 93). But the hero, in one of the idealistic rhapsodies to which he is prone, denounces the clergyman for the materialism of his views. On the other hand, the doctor recommends to the hero for emulation the clergyman's successor, whose philistine moderation is rather too pedestrian:

> ein solider Seelsorger für seine Bauern, ermahnt sie zu rechtschaffenem Wandel, tauft, traut und beackert nebenbei sein Feld, hält Land, Leute und Vieh in guter Ordnung und läßt Gott einen guten Mann sein, der im Himmel sitzt und thut was er will und was kein Mensch weiß. Der vernünftige junge Pfarrer wirft die Schöpfung nicht kunterbunt durcheinander, sucht nicht in Gott die Natur, nicht in der Natur den Gott zu deuten und hält Alles hübsch auseinander, das blöde Geschlecht der Vierfüßer, den dummen Erdenkloß, Mensch genannt, und den allmächtigen Herrn der Welt. So bleibt er fromm und moralisch gut und hält sich den Wahnsinn vom Leibe (p. 105).

Such, apparently, is the goal of mental health. Kühne's hero rebels against it; when the doctor has certified him as sane, the hero sardonically speaks of himself as now "abstract verständig, tugendhaft nüchtern" (p. 190), but he quickly becomes bored in this condition, which he identifies as one devoid of passion and imagination, and he launches, as is his wont, into a long, purple rhapsody on this theme.

These variations are complicated still further, however, so that one is eventually at a loss just how to interpret and judge the question. For it occurs to our author also to make madness a function of modern civilization, which is teetering at the height of intellectual perception between being and non-being, while just below the animal part of man threatens, Mephisto lurks, and with him, madness. "Es ist ausgemacht, daß die Zahl der Irren mit den Fortschritten der Bildung bei allen Völkern steigt" (p. 58). The doctor, for his part, suggests that the whole world should establish itself as a mental institution (p. 209), and he lectures the hero on the increase in madness that has accompanied the progress of modern philosophy (pp. 177-184). On the other hand, it may be that the conventional life of society is a refuge against madness — and, simultaneously, a flight from feeling and imagination, a view not dissimilar to that found in Gutzkow's *Wally* (see above, p. 48). The doctor flirts with the female patients because "er mochte überzeugt sein, daß es zweckmäßig sei, die Reconvalescenten allmälig an den gesammten Unsinn des Gesellschaftslebens zu gewöhnen, und er hat Recht, sehr Recht, denn wer sich mit seiner ganzen Persönlichkeit in die Manieren des Visitenlebens hüllt, der hat eine gute Schutzdecke um sich gegen alle Gefährnisse der Gemüthswelt" (pp. 108-109). If a young lady has a little religion, dabbles in manners and fashions, knows a little of languages and love, reads a little Schiller and Goethe, "wie soll da ein Wahnsinn in solch einer erbärmlich zerstückelten und verflachten Seele seine Rechnung finden?" (p. 109); the madness would die of boredom. But, our hero pontificates, woe to you when the Lord asks you to give an account of the content of your life: "welches Gefühl war der Leiter, welcher Gedanke der Träger Eurer Seele im Wandel der Vergänglichkeiten?" (ibid.). There must be something in us, even if only an eccentricity or a whim, to live for; the life of society is only a homeopathic cure. If the reader thinks he understands this, two things militate against that conclusion. One is that the hero, as often happens, winds up his whole argument by denouncing it; he criticizes himself for drawing constant distinctions between madness and reason, whereas in fact everything is a mixture (pp. 110-111). The other concerns his view of the narcotic emptiness of social life; for, as it happens, the hero's childhood was spent in salon society and is pictured as bright, happy, and full of stimulation.

The possibility mentioned above that madness might be a function of contemporary philosophy and intellectual life is yet another tangent. The reason, apparently, that this philosophical brooding cannot come to rest is because it is, by choice or by necessity, out of touch with living reality. This is perceived as a specifically German problem: "Die geistige Cultur unsrer Zeit ist so mit Dampfapparaten in die Höhe getrieben, daß mehr Wahnsinn in der Welt herrscht als man denken sollte und nach dem System der speculativen Vernunft-Wirklichkeit [whatever that may be] zu denken gestattet ist.

Und eben dies Denken und Denken-Sollen ist es, an dem wir Deutschen einen Narren gegessen haben, um nicht gefressen zu sagen. Andere Nationen werfen sich auf reelle Stoffe, und ihre Narrheit wird von dem Materiellen bezwungen" (pp. 39-40). While other nations discover new worlds, travel through the air, invent railroads and steam engines, the Germans have "wässerige Moralsysteme, luftige Naturspeculationen, eisenharte Begriffsbestimmungen und qualmige Theorien" (p. 40). Thus the hero would seem to be caught in a vicious circle, for he is committed to philosophy, yet this commitment is involved with his perilous mental state. The hero's effort to cure himself and to emancipate himself from philosophy through philosophy is one of his fundamental ambivalences.

There are many others. Pertinent to our purposes are particularly those dealing with the social and political context. In the constantly shifting dialectic of these musings, it is not promising to look for a coherent social and political position, but one can keep one's eyes open for a certain instinct, for Kühne, in the course of time, did develop a clear position: one of classical bourgeois liberalism, anticlerical, pro-parliament, national, and decidedly opposed to any revolutionary movement on the part of the lower classes. Kühne was shocked by the killing, during a popular demonstration, of two right-wing members of the Frankfurt parliament in September, 1848, General von Auerswald and Prince Lichnowsky, and he welcomed the use of soldiers "gegen die ehrlosen Räuberhorden und Barrikadenhelden, die sich Demokraten nennen";[11] on the other hand, the lawless execution of the moderate democrat Robert Blum in Vienna drew from Kühne an "objective" judgment, the main point of which was that Blum's death was his own fault.[12] These results in Kühne's maturity may be usefully kept in mind in what follows.

There are passages in *Quarantäne* that reveal some traces of an apocalyptic longing for revolutionary violence, in which revolutionary war appears as the poetic war of our time: "Nach der Liebe ist der Haß die schönste Leidenschaft. Jemand hassen, der die Krone des Lebens stahl und mit frecher Hand in dein Heiligthum griff, das macht dich zum Halbgott. Religionskriege sind die blutigsten, aber auch die schönsten, und wäre der Gott, der die Gemüther entflammt, auch nur ein Dämon, ein Phantom — die Poesie der Leidenschaft redet und tönt in tausend Zungen" (p. 9); and the passage goes on to remark that freedom is the religion of our time. Another facet of this longing is an argument recurring from time to time that sin, violence, and the diabolical are necessary to keep the dialectical forces of life in motion. Life is a tragedy, it is argued, and sin is a necessity; "die Tugend ist ein Abstractum, der lebendige Mensch in Kampf und Noth ist das Concrete" (p. 236). "Ohne Teufel [e.g., Napoleon] keine Weltgeschichte!" "Das Diabolische hat Jeder in sich: sehe nur Jeder zu, daß auch sein innerer Christus miterwache!" (p. 237). With this last phrase, of course, Kühne's closet diabolism drifts back into harmlessness. The same theme is involved in the hero's passionate defense of Don Giovanni and his dismissal of the avenging Stone Guest as a philistine: "die Philosophie, die das Leben besser gemacht hätte, die die Sünde blos verketzert und in dem Bösen und seiner Verlockung nicht vielmehr den Impuls, die Erectionskraft [!] der Menschengeschichte sieht, ist eine falsche Philosophie" (p. 239).

Once in a great while these effusions spill over into the realm of the relationship between literature and politics, with which is involved an ambivalent view of Börne and Heine, who are mentioned, usually paired, several times in the book. At one point the narrator launches upon a breathless rhapsody on the need for democratic exchange of ideas: the world is in an uproar, poets fling their verses out into the open air; the diabolical Börne sits on the ruins of the state and Heine on the ruins of Christianity (pp. 131-132). But such experimentation with radical rhetoric causes an automatic shift to a more moderate stance, for the hero then inquires plaintively whether bourgeois society must be destroyed in the process, and goes on to assert that reason is democratic, not Jacobin, it is oppositional in itself — if only its workings were not so slow (p. 132). Typically, the passage ends with the complaint that the hero cannot revolutionize anything but his own head (pp. 132-133). The turn to an inner, harmonious religiosity is characteristic of Kühne throughout *Quarantäne*. An example of this, and of the way in which each little action in the novel generates a weighty gloss, is the hero's meditation on the fact that he has put a note from Victorine in his breast pocket on the left side: "Die linke Seite ist in der Welt oft genug die rechte, die Oppositionsseite oft genug die Seite der Wahrheit. Nur das Gesuchte, das Absichtliche darf nicht hervorstecken als der Stachel des *diaconus diaboli*. Die Linksmacher sind auch immer die Rechtsverdreher. Alles muß wie eine Blume sein auf Gottes freiem Felde, keine Treibhauspflanze. So die Politik, Poesie, Philosophie, das ganze volle Leben" (p. 205). Much that is characteristic of Kühne is concentrated in this passage: the timid assumption of and then withdrawal from an oppositional posture, the punning and the strained metaphors, the insistence on keeping a religious context intact, and the drift into portentous banality.

Young Kühne shared with the Young Germans and much of the liberal movement generally a weakness for monarchy. In a discussion of the false extremes of patriotism, his hero asserts that true patriotism "huldigt der Persönlichkeit des Monarchen und lebt in der Idee, die der Staat welthistorisch dermaleinst in der Wirklichkeit zu erfüllen berufen ist" (p. 33). The Hegelian jargon points to another problem that will be touched upon presently; the difficulty with such sentiments is that it was hard to locate real kings deserving of such veneration, and, indeed, some years later, in Berlin in 1843, remarking upon the general unhappiness and depression of the atmosphere, Kühne is obliged to remark of Frederick William IV: "Der König steht schon ganz isoliert. Es wäre nicht so unerhört, machten ihn die Zustände zum deutschen sechzehnten Ludwig. Er ist so characterlos und so liebenswürdig wie dieser."[13] But when it came to liberal agitation and revolutionary threats, Kühne, despite his apparent willingness to accept the violent and chaotic as part of the dialectic of life, was by and large of a negative disposition in *Quarantäne*. It is not quite certain whether this reflects an anti-democratic attitude or whether it was that liberal behavior aroused in him a Heinesque sense of the absurd. At one point, harping on the theme of madness, the hero reflects that a general insanity might take over mankind at the height of civilization. "Ein ganzes wahnsinniges Volk gäbe ein Schauspiel, das noch nicht da war im Lauf der Geschichte!" (p. 59). We who have seen this show in our century may well be struck by this passage, but unfortunately it turns out that it is liberal and egalitarian phenomena that presage this development. One symptom of the incipient madness of civilization is the convention of German liberals at Hambach in May, 1832, "ein Haufe Menschen, die einigen Irrenanstalten entlaufen sind" (ibid.). The mad society will be one in which class distinctions are erased and the Saint-Simonian doctrine will gain the upper hand: "Jeder Lump von der Gasse wäre Souverain, die Könige knieten im Kothe vor ihm und küßten den Saum seiner

Fetzen"; everyone would be a sans-culotte and run around without trousers, nature would be the highest divinity, the rehabilitation of the flesh would be the first religious and political principle; instead of gods there would be only goddesses and women would be held in common; all life would be a "Ragout von Sodom und Gomorrah" (p. 60). One would take this to be a piece of reactionary, un-Young German satire, were it not that positions and attitudes are only tasted and tested in this work and are nowhere firmly founded; a feeble, unclear irony is characteristic of the book, and on the other occasion on which Hambach is mentioned (pp. 168-169), there is a more ironic treatment of freedom as *Schein* in the German double meaning of "shine" and "illusion."

The general tendency, however, is toward a critique and suspicion of the most exposed salients of the liberal opposition. Young Germany itself the hero apostrophizes as follows: "Junges Deutschland! ... Dein Leben scheint mir hektisch, eine rapide Schwindsucht! Du bist engathmig, Du keuchst. Tanze und rase Dich nicht zunichte und zu nichts; Deine Galopade ist weiter nichts als eine Gallomanie. Nimm Dich in Acht, daß Du nicht zu früh alt, in Deiner Jugend schon alt wirst, und dann nichts mehr jung bleibt als die alte Vernunft, der ewig alte und ewig junge Phönix deutschen Denkens und deutschen Dichtens" (p. 232) — a good passage for demonstrating that neither Kühne nor his hero know what it is they mean. Real revolution is certainly suspect in this perspective. The reactionary, absolutist uncle is said to have been, in his equally radical, Jacobin youth, a "Freiheitsschwindler" (p. 319). The metaphorical association of Kühne's hero with a patriotic refugee of the Polish revolution is not without its ambivalence, through which the typically liberal theme of sympathy for the fate of Poland is modified. Victorine is committed to the madhouse because she physically resisted an arresting officer and for that reason was thought to be mad; self-defense against arbitrary authority thus appears to be a symptom of madness, and, after a long disquisition on Poland's lamentable fate, the hero indicates that the Polish desire for freedom was a form of insanity (p. 271). This suggests, as do other aspects of the text, an ironic despair at the suppression of liberty, but it is also indicated that the suffering of the Poles is due to their own deficiencies; Victorine is said to be typically Polish, strong and firm, but unsteady and excitable in mood, unable to distinguish friend from foe (pp.

95

274-275). In retrospect, one must in fairness think that in 1830/31 it was a little difficult for the Poles to discern who their friends were.

What is detectable in all this is a steady, though perhaps not wholly conscious drift into the Biedermeier attitude: a retreat from these exacerbating dilemmas into private virtues, private relationships, and privately maintained harmonies. That this process did in fact take place in Kühne is indicated by his love-letters to his fiancée, which Edgar Pierson published at embarrassing length. In one of them Kühne asserts plainly that "es ist lohnender Wenigen viel zu sein, als Vielen wenig. Daran schließt sich mein Glaube, daß das Familienleben wichtiger ist für Herz und Geist als das Gesellschaftsleben."[14] The attractive force of private virtuousness and harmony is evident in the novel itself. After having described the mad society of lost class distinction and Saint-Simonian emancipation, the hero goes on to predict that in such a society those who pursued the old-fashioned virtues, pieties, family life, and idealism would be preserved as antiquities in madhouses that would serve also as museums; the writer of these memoirs is already there. In this context, madness is not the longing for unattainable liberties, but the maintenance of conservative virtues, and it is positive, not pejorative. It is this sort of thing that puts the novel beyond any clear ideological definition. In the very few places where it raises the question of the cure for madness, however, the conservative tendency comes into the foreground. In denouncing the clergyman with his materialistic philosophy of the constipated age and the need for a purifying water cure, the hero asserts that madness can only be cured by something harmonious, like music, which in turn is an indication of "eine tiefere Musik..., eine Musik der Poesie, die unserer Zeit fehlt, eine Harmonie der Gefühle, die uns Deutsche allein zum Verständniß unserer selber bringt und zur Überzeugung, wir seien Ein Volk im Denken und Dichten" (p. 99). Man can be above the animals only, he continues, if the spirit exists "selbständig als Ursubstanz für sich von Ewigkeit zu Ewigkeit" (p. 101). In this connection, the hero accuses the pastor of being "ein grober, ein *deutscher* Saintsimonist" (ibid.). And it turns out at last, with the example of Mozart's *Don Giovanni*, that it is art, just as the Romantics thought, that contains in its eternal verities of the imagination and the spirit the cure for modern man: "Die Kunst muß heilen vom

Wahnwitz des Lebens, sie selbst ist der schönere, der göttliche Wahnsinn. In ihr müssen wir uns Alle wieder zurechtfinden, wir Alle und alle Völker der Erde. Es bleibt der Welt nichts Anderes übrig" (p. 279).

There is another alternative to the perilous state of the modern mind, however; parallel with the longing for ordered, private, aesthetically elevated circumstances is the longing to escape from this perpetual conceptualizing and to overcome madness by entering the real world. The hero becomes weary of metaphysics, which has not made him wise or brought him to the quietude of abstraction; it only urges him toward life, and teaches him that "das Leben selber sei der Inbegriff aller Wahrheit" (p. 148), a locution that strongly recalls Wienbarg. The longing for reality generates simultaneously a desire to evade it and flee from it: "Seitdem die Empirie so verschrieen ist, wird Alles früh alt in Deutschland, schrecklich früh schrecklich alt. Das macht der speculative Gedanke! Die Empirie erhält frisch und geschmeidig, die Speculation verzehrt schnell des Lebens Öl — und da thut man immer wohl daran, recht bald in eine Klause zu kriechen, wie die Schnecke sich in die Schale flüchtet und im steinernen Häuslein selbst versteint, daß Gott erbarm'!" (p. 234). It seems that the living of real life, beyond speculation, is so unthinkable in present circumstances that the retreat into the inner realm is the only possible recourse. This is a form of social criticism, but it takes on so desperate a character because the hero's demands on life are so absolute and all-encompassing: "ich kann und will nichts Vereinzeltes im Leben, ich will das Leben selbst, will die ganze Oper einstudiren [he is refusing a role in a performance of *Don Giovanni*] und in mir tragen, nicht eine einzelne Partie" (pp. 241-242). This pursuit has frustration built into it from the outset, and it is not surprising that the hero not long afterward exclaims: "Es lebe die Freiheit des innern Menschen! Das Bischen andere Freiheit schmeckt nach Wermuth!" (p. 259). As though these issues were in any sense resolved, the memoir and the novel end with the words: "Ich selbst glaube dem Leben, seinen Freuden und Schmerzen anzugehören. Ich ziehe weiter durch die Welt" (p. 334).

The distracting and wearying effort to transcend philosophy by means of philosophy is one of the fundamental ironies of the book. There is a curious combination of faith in the labors of the intellect,

97

allegiance to the "spirit," with a recognition that there is no exit in this fantastic maze of concepts and antitheses. After having concocted with his friends a really down-to-earth, practicable, and, in the short run, successful plan of escape from the madhouse, the hero, in his euphoria at this unwonted activity, is plunged into sarcasm: "Wir fühlten uns Manns genug, gegen die ganze Welt mit unserer Vernünftigkeit zu Felde zu ziehen, wir hätten Jeden zu Tode debattirt, dialektisch zermalmt, wäre uns Einer entgegengetreten als Opponent, um zu bezweifeln, wir seien nicht ganz gescheit" (p. 280). Everything in this sentence is completely short-circuited: one does not know whether "rationality" refers to practicality or to philosophical speculation, whether the plan devised rouses this sarcasm because it is efficient or because it is illusory, whether they might be accused of being not quite right in the head because they have presumed to think a way out of their incarceration or because they are pursuing the illusion of freedom, whether or why they are deluded.

One could pick this problem apart in the novel for pages without becoming any wiser about it. A few aspects of it are striking enough to deserve some commentary, however. One is a dream experienced by the hero while still in a feverish state. He is being interrogated by his uncle as to why he is only a useless *Literat*, just lurking about "um auf der Tafel des Lebens nichts als kritische Randglossen zu verzeichnen" (p. 15). The hero attempts to answer with a complex comparison of the free *Literat* with moths that lay thousands of eggs for the coming of a new age. For this simile he is flung into a torture chamber; his inquisitors remove his entrails and read his secrets in them; even though he was isolated from the world and undertook no active life, they find black sins and crimes in him, because with his knowledge and thinking he has absorbed all the crimes of history; he has eaten of the tree of knowledge and become critical of what is sacred; he has relived all the atrocious rebellions and revolutions of history in his soul: "Eine Ideenassociation verbrüdert Dich mit allen Aufrührern, allen Neuerern" (p. 20). He is an ideal Robespierre, lacking only opportunity. He is condemned as an absolute man, a radical, and executed.

This dream is one of the few passages in *Quarantäne* that exihibits a degree of imaginative power. It is simultaneously satirical and desperately anxious. The concept of intellectual guilt by association argued by the inquisitors is grotesquely extreme, but as a caricature it was certainly not irrelevant, for all the censorship and repression of the time was motivated by a fear of new knowledge and new ideas, and it is plain to the student of the period that the conservative ruling class would have liked best to keep the largest part of the population in a state of permanent ignorance and backwardness. But the claim that the hero is, or is trying to be, "der absolute Mensch" recurs as a refrain throughout the novel. Just what it means I have not been able altogether to puzzle out. At times the stress seems to be on the "Mensch," on the striving for the wholly humane or, at least, if one takes into account the adumbrations upon the necessity for the strife between good and evil, the wholly human. At other times, and more frequently, the stress is on the absoluteness, which seems to suggest the striving for total, organic comprehension by means of metaphysical speculation and thus becomes caught in the ambivalence that adheres to the philosophical enterprise throughout the book. Three *personae* in particular play a role in connection with this theme of the absolute man: Faust, Shelley, and Don Giovanni.

The Faust motif is ambivalent and elusive to the point of incoherence. The Faustian element is introduced as a threat to mental equilibrium. Faust's drive for absolute understanding, argues the hero, should lead to madness — or he will petrify, as the objective world around him vanishes into dust. "Wir müssen entweder den Faust in uns sterben lassen oder wir werden mit ihm zu Stein!" (p. 42). What this means I am not sure, but is clearly bears upon the conflict of internalized philosophical speculation with a living subject-object relationship toward the world without. The most recent work of Faust, the hero argues in a not uninteresting passage, is Hegel's system (pp. 42-43). Hegel seems to be a kind of monster haunting Kühne in this book as he haunted Kühne's friend Mundt. As in Mundt's aesthetic writings, there is a continuing resistance to Hegel in a context that would be unthinkable without Hegel's philosophy. Mundt, in fact, saw Hegel's philosophy as the fundamental issue in Kühne's book.[15] It is not many pages after the passage alluded to just now that Hegel's essence and dialectic are praised, although they must be freed from their container, which the hero, picking up the petrification image used in connection with Faust, calls "ein steinernes Beinhaus" (p. 45). Hegel's God, the narrator says, "ist die absolute Bewegung, die ewig strömende Immanenz des Geistes im Stoffe" (ibid.), a formulation not inconsistent with the rather sentimental pantheism that seems to be the basic element of the narrator's endlessly involved speculations on religion.

Elsewhere, however, Hegel is regarded less positively. Later, the hero goes on for eight pages in a highly metaphoric critique of Hegel, which in itself is an interesting document for Hegel's effect on this generation. At first, the hero seems to align himself with the philosopher by writing rhapsodies on world-historical individuals, on the depth and daring of great thinkers, and on the dialectical temporariness of any philosophy. His diction seems to stress, as Heine did, the revolutionary implications of Hegel, who marks in the narrator's life "eine Revolutionsepoche, auf die für meinen innern Menschen noch keine Restauration erfolgt ist" (p. 142). But these implications turn out not to be so positive after all. Since studying Hegel, the hero says, he has never been happy or whole-souled, and he injects, with obscure significance: "Mag die Welt hierüber lächeln; ich kann es ihr nicht wehren, ich bin ein armer Mensch im Irren-hause" (p. 143). Hegel's philosophy disturbed his faith in Christianity and erected a new but joyless god of reason. Hegel, he goes on, again reflecting a view of Heine's, has the same role in Germany as the revolution in France: "Der nackte, absolute, radicale Mensch foderte seine Rechte und zerschlug die Gestaltungen des Lebens mit grau-samer Hand. Er kannte keine Liebe, keine Hingebung, keine Freund-schaft, keine persönliche Größe, keine fromme Andacht, keine Ver-klärung in Kunst und Poesie; er beraubte Alles seiner Idealität, wie Hegel's absolute Vernunft" (p. 145). Here the absolute man, the modern, revolutionary man of reason and philosophy, is seen in a pejorative or at least in an elegiac perspective, for the hero goes on to say that though subjective idealism — apparently the antithesis to Hegelian absolute, objective reason — rages vengefully through the world at present, this may be its last battle, and with its end will come the end of poetry (p. 147). Thus a tragic inevitability is postulated for the Faustian Hegelianism with which Kühne's narrator appears to be out of harmony.

Kühne's tendency to pin every aspect of these dilemmas upon every representation of them without any integration makes the Faust *persona* less clear than the Hegelian parallel might at first suggest. In a delirium, the hero carries on a conversation with Faust, in which he urges Faust to rejuvenate himself and attempts

100

to galvanize him by a kiss; but Faust does not permit this; he urges calm and vanishes in a "metaphysische Nebelkappe" (p. 50). Just as Goethe's Faust discerns a flash of fiery red in the wake of the black poodle that stalks him on Easter Sunday, so there is a flash of red as Faust vanishes here, the red of a Jacobin cap and Mephisto's feather, images put into significant parallel. Subsequently, the hero muses that Faust has become Satan in Börne; Faust and Mephisto have become one and haunt the people — the revolutionary implications of the Faustian absolutism are connected with radical evil — although it may fairly be doubted whether poor, honest, well-meaning Börne, whose name hardly ever appears in this book without the adjective "diabolical," is an apposite incarnation of this alliance. The hero's next endeavor is to undertake a loose parody of Faust's inconclusive exegesis of the opening words of the Gospel of John. Characteristically, he overreaches himself and sets himself the task of working out the problem "What is truth?" This question he determines to answer in a modern vein, without recourse to any of the thinking of the happy, untroubled generations of the past, for the hero knows of the pain, the dynamic striving of reality, "das Unglück des alten Faust, des alten absoluten Menschen" (p. 54). His first answer is: "Wahrheit ist das Sein Gottes in mir" (ibid.), a formulation that leads him in a mystical direction, for he quotes several lines from Angelus Silesius. Then he tries: "Christus ist die Wahrheit" (p. 55), which leads him to despair, for he does not feel Christ reborn in him. At this point we hear that *Christ* is the absolute man, for his truth is in every soul and he is the prototype of self-redemption. Here the concept of absolute man, having become adulterated with Kühne's individualistic Protestantism, goes wholly out of focus. Before abandoning this enterprise, the hero concludes with the rather obscure formulation that truth is "das Sein meiner in Gott" (p. 57). A final incongruity is that Faust, after having been brought into connection with Hegel, with the absolute intellectual striving of modern man, and with the demonic force of revolution, is also identified with the absurd clergyman who desires to cure the constipated world with water and whose pedestrian successor is referred to as his Wagner (pp. 104-105).

Insofar as the absolute man suffers from the Sisyphean labor of pursuing absolute spiritual clarity, Shelley is also made a part of this context. It may seem somewhat incongruous that so fundamentally conventional a spirit as Kühne's hero should assert a spiritual intimacy with the likes of Shelley, but the English poet is used as a demonstration of the relationship of pure speculation and madness: "bei all diesem redlichen Bemühen nach Klarheit und Frieden mit sich und der Welt, [hing] der Wahnwitz nur an einem Haar über seinem Haupte.... So wenig nutzte ihm sein Denken" (p. 70). How Shelley's profound battle with the conventions of society is to be assessed in this context is not clear, but it is fair to say that Kühne does not express the same enthusiasm for the revolutionary aspect of Shelley that Friedrich Engels was to exhibit a few years later. Of Don Giovanni there has already been occasion to speak, in connection with the tragic and dialectical need for energy and sin in order to transcend and transform present reality. As the active version of the absolute man, however, Don Giovanni's tragic rebellion exhausts itself in the sphere of the private and the personal; he fails altogether to penetrate the shell of his own self and come to some kind of viable subject-object relationship with the world.

Whatever absolute humanity may be, Kühne's hero fails to attain it. Towards the end of the novel he calls himself instead "ein gattungsloser Mensch, ein Mensch an sich, ein radicaler Mensch, nichts weiter, wahrhaftig" (p. 314), which seems to be a reductive, more negative version of the absolute man. At length he must recognize that he has not mastered life and cannot draw a sum from his inner experiences and that no resolutions are remotely in sight: "Warum soll ich die Dissonanzen für mich lösen, da sie in unseren Zeitläufen harmonielos durcheinander tönen? Ich will mich nicht täuschen und einen Frieden, den ich nicht erlebte, mir nicht mit künstlichen Tractaten zusammenstellen. Es gibt provisorische Zustände in der Literatur wie in den politischen Constellationen der Welt; ebenso gibt es auch provisorische Menschen. *Sie sind das Product einer Krisis*" (pp. 317-318, my italics). These provisional men were, in a few months, to have a name forever after — the *Epigonen* of Karl Immermann's novel. Kühne was not a writer who had the gift of naming things with precision. In view of the extreme lability of feeling and opinion in this, as in other novels at the time, it is strange indeed that his friend Mundt could write in January, 1835, that "heute... uns kein ächter Dichter ohne Grösse und stählerne Kraft der Weltanschauung, mithin ohne Einheit und Schwerpunkt des Daseins mehr denkbar ist."[16] The novel is better described by the general observation of Ruth Horovitz: "In den anarchischen Romanhelden verwirklicht sich nicht das Bild einer anderen, neuen Gesellschaft, sondern der jungdeutsche Zerrissene zeigt die alte Gesellschaft nahe der höchsten Stufe ihres Zerfalls."[17] But the crisis that generated Kühne's book was a real one, and, if nothing else, it shows spectacularly how inadequate were the resources within the reach of a normal young doctor of philosophy of the time to cope with it. It shows also how dubious it can be to mine these novels for quotations in order to elucidate the thinking of the time, without considering how shifting are the sands in which it is mired.

V. HEINRICH LAUBE: *DIE KRIEGER*

Heinrich Laube was not the sort of man who should have got into trouble in any moderately sane social and political environment, and that he should have suffered the most harrowing punishment of all the Young Germans is evidence of the grotesque conditions of the time. Laube's personality positively exudes good health and good cheer; Rudolf Majut has written of him that he was "kein 'armer' wie Heine, kein 'grüner' wie Keller, sondern ein wahrhaft 'junger' Heinrich."[1] So robust and athletic that he was once offered the post of university fencing master, he is of all the Young Germans least "sicklied o'er by the pale cast of thought." Sengle's opinion that Laube was the liveliest and freshest of the Young German writers because he had the least understanding of philosophy has much to be said for it.[2] He was also the most amiable of them by far, and remained so long into his old age. While Gutzkow's autobiographical memoirs make generally unpleasant reading, with their convoluted self-justifications and his by then pathological belligerence toward all and sundry, Laube's — which are concerned largely with his long career as manager of the Vienna Burgtheater and are important source materials for the history of the theater — are charming, good-humored, and not infrequently even wise. While he was never to become a major writer, his career and œuvre, measured by Young German standards, rank second only to Gutzkow's, and a comprehensive study of his life and works would be a welcome contribution. Gutzkow thought him a critic of crucial importance: "Die Kritiken, welche H. Laube in einer von ihm redigirten Zeitung schrieb, wurden Mittelpunkt aller der jugendlichen Kräfte, die den Geist einer neuen Literatur ahnten und an seiner allmählichen sichtbaren Erscheinung selber mitarbeiten wollten."[3] The periodical in question is the *Zeitung für die elegante Welt*, which, in the period of Laube's editorship from January, 1833, until his arrest in July, 1834, contains a great deal of interesting and instructive literary criticism ("literature" understood in a broad sense, including books on history, current events, etc.), and these essays themselves would deserve a separate study. Houben remarked that their "prickelnder, schlagkräftiger Stil und die mühelose Erfassung moderner Lebensprobleme im Anschluß an literarische Fragen stempeln diese anderthalb Jahresbände unter Laubes Redaktion zu einem der wichtigsten Manifeste des 'Jungen Deutschland.' "[4] When one considers that the formal experimentation of Laube's *Reisenovellen* has drawn the critical attention of Reinhold Grimm;[5] that Houben thought several of his later works, including the novella *Die Bandomire* (1842) and the nine-volume novel of the Thirty Years' War, *Der deutsche Krieg* (1861-66), worthy of admiring notices,[6] and that, as I am about to assert, the middle part of his trilogy *Das junge Europa* is the best of the Young German novels, it seems that he may be deserving of rather more respect than he has been accorded in recent times.

It has clearly been difficult to regard Laube's role in the Young German crisis without a queasy feeling. What is distressing is not so much that, for both private and tactical reasons, he abjured any connection to the calumniated movement, but that he did so with such obtrusive insistence, that he repeated his recantations so often and falsified his own recent past. "Wie ein Held," Houben was obliged to remark, "hat sich Laube gewiß nicht benommen."[7] But the moral outrage directed against him has sometimes exceeded reasonable limits. Walter Dietze calls him the type "des böswillig-verschlagenen Mitläufers und Karrieristen..., der sich nur nach außen hin radikal und 'stürmend' gebärdet, in Wirklichkeit aber seine Kampfgenossen beinahe Tag für Tag aufs neue verrät."[8] In other places he uses terms like "politische Charakterlosigkeit," "Renegat," and "gemeiner Gesinnungslump."[9] This manner of expression is entirely out of place for several reasons. For one thing, Laube never endangered anyone by his official statements, nor did anyone ever suffer any harm because of him. Furthermore, Laube's views had been moderating noticeably before his arrest, which made the whole proceeding seem senseless to him, as indeed it was. E. M. Butler, in regard to her negative judgment on Laube's early activist writings, concluded that his liberal commitment had never been intrinsic: "If a man of twenty-six in the grip of a great enthusiasm cannot produce something worth reading, there are only two conclusions to be drawn. Either he is incapable of literary expression, or he is following after alien gods. Laube was not incapable of literary expression, as his next book [Die Poeten] and his subsequent life were to prove; it seems therefore as if, in making himself the exponent of liberal and revolutionary ideals, he had mistaken his true vocation. And this I believe to have been the case."[10] By 1848 he belonged, as he said, "Zum Centrum u. zwar mit einer Neigung nach rechts";[11] the change in his convictions in the early 1830's can be traced,[12] and one recent student sees the coincidence of the breakdown of his progressive allegiance and his arrest as purely accidental.[13] However that may be, there can be no doubt that the fright he got at the hands of the authorities strongly reinforced his desire to live at peace with existing society.

The story bears a quick retelling here for two reasons: it illuminates aspects of the nineteenth-century literary environment to which scholarship has given too little attention; and, since Laube had a bit of luck in the long run and the affair turned out less badly than it could have, there has been a tendency to make light of it, without considering how it must have looked to him at the time or the probable effect of it upon the courage of the whole literary community.[14] The reason for the exceptionally difficult time Laube had in jail was due, paradoxically, to the fact that the authorities had great trouble finding something to charge him with. Laube's critical writings in the *Elegante* and the first volume of *Das junge Europa*, *Die Poeten*, had attracted the ill-will of the Prussian censors. His praise of Heine and Börne and his view that democracy was the basic idea of Christianity had been found especially offensive. The first problem in coping with him was to get him out of Leipzig and onto Prussian territory. The authorities at first attempted to get him drafted, but, comically, the former student athlete was rejected for nearsightedness. They then pressured the Saxon government to expel him, which it was eventually obliged to do, although the Saxon authorities indicated to Laube that some way might be found to avoid this decree and suggested in a friendly way that he not go to Berlin. But, with the cheerful insouciance characteristic of him, he went straight to Berlin to confront his accusers. He called on Varnhagen, who had been following the whole business with sympathetic concern and was shocked and amazed to see Laube turn up of his own volition in the lion's den. Sure enough, he was arrested on 26 July 1834.

He freely admitted his literary sins and defended them adeptly; they really weighed too lightly to justify imprisoning him, and anyway, he argued, he could not be legally punished in Prussia for books that had passed the censorship in Leipzig, which was true. The minister in charge of these matters, Rochus von Rochow, was by August actually on the point of ordering Laube's release. But the ineffable Gustav Adolf von Tzschoppe intervened, for he could not bear the thought of setting one of these dangerous fellows free once he was in custody. Tzschoppe countermanded the order to release Laube on the grounds that he was suspected of activity in the *Burschenschaft*. According to the Carlsbad Decrees of 1819, membership in the *Burschenschaft* was punishable by six years of fortress imprisonment. Frederick William III, however, had later amnestied all members of the *Burschenschaft* whose activity fell in the years before 1830, provided that they had behaved properly since then and not done anything else punishable; if they had, the old sentence could be invoked. Tzschoppe was determined to meet this condition, to find any kind of transgression, no matter how minor, that would permit Laube's conviction under the old law. Thus literary misdemeanors that were not in themselves of sufficient moment to justify legal action against Laube were to be used to convict him for a crime for which he had been amnestied, as there was no evidence that he had any connection with the *Burschenschaft* after 1830. For eight months, while Laube was held without trial, the authorities combed his writings and personal connections for evidence against him.

Those who make light of Laube's plight neglect to consider two important aspects of it. One is that even a relatively short period of solitary confinement under the conditions to which he was subjected, without visitors or companionship, without books, writing materials, or any diversion other than an occasional interrogation, is a quite terrible experience that has been known to break stronger men than him. Laube felt himself being brought to the brink of madness and was in a condition where his thoughts, as he wrote later in his memoirs, "einander gleichsam in die Haare [fallen], man faßt seinen Kopf in beide Hände, als wollte und könnte man verhindern, daß er im Wahnsinn auseinanderspringe."[15] The other

107

aspect is that he could have no assurance of when this torment would end, indeed, if it ever would. There was no such thing as "civil rights" in restoration Germany; the citizen had no natural rights at all, only legal ones, the interpretation of which lay with the government authorities. There was plenty of precedent to cause Laube to take a doleful view of his prospects, and one curious coincidence may have contributed to his terror. In the *Elegante* of 3 May 1833, he had included an anecdote about a political prisoner in France who had been in solitary confinement for forty-three years and who, "um nur einen Augenblick das Sonnenlicht zu genießen, sich mehrmals mit solcher Täuschung todt gestellt, daß man, als er endlich wirklich gestorben, es nicht habe glauben wollen. Es liegt wirklich etwas Schauderhaftes in dieser Sehnsucht nach dem Licht bei 43jährigem dumpfem Hinbrüten in einem unterirdischen Loche ohne Beschäftigung und Gesellschaft."[16] One can imagine that this gruesome story went through Laube's head a year later when he found himself in a similar situation.

Laube's many asseverations of loyalty while in jail and while free under indictment must be judged in the light of these considerations, and the fairest observers have always done so. Houben maintained that an experience of this kind is "eine Probe auf den Charakter, über die nur derjenige triumphiren sollte, der eine gleiche durchgemacht hat";[17] Butler made a similar judgment.[18] Even Varnhagen, who had grounds to be out of countenance at Laube's apparent defection, found his way to a generous view:

> Der Heldenmuth, lieber unterzugehen als sich zu beugen, ist groß und schön, wir müssen ihn bewundern, dürfen ihn aber nicht fordern. Galilei widerruft seine eingesehene Überzeugung, ohne daß wir ihn deßhalb verachten dürfen. Auch die größten Könige bequemen sich zu schmachvollen Friedensschlüssen. Die Freundschaft, welche der König von Preußen nach dem Frieden von Tilsit gegen Napoleon heucheln mußte, ist nicht schlimmer noch besser, als die, welche von Laube gegen Tzschoppe bezeigt wird.[19]

Nor should one draw any conclusions about the general situation from the fact that Laube's seven-year sentence was reduced to one and a half years and that he was able to pass it in relative comfort under house arrest on Pückler-Muskau's estate. The first relief was due to Tzschoppe's unpredictable arbitrariness and the second to the personal influence of Frau Laube's connections. Laube told Heine in a letter of 19 August 1837, perhaps as a sardonic joke, that the reason for the commutation to house arrest was that all the fortress prisons were full.[20] There was nothing in either piece of good luck to comfort the literary generation that was watching the affair. Laube had been in a very dangerous situation and one cannot judge his behavior in it without recognizing this. In any case, moral or political disapproval of his failings should not block the view into his literary achievements, the most important of which at this time is the second volume of *Das junge Europa*, begun, probably, during his incarceration but not published until 1837.

I hold this opinion despite the fact that the novel has received relatively little attention. Houben once characterized it fleetingly as the best of Laube's youthful works.[21] One could go farther and maintain that *Die Krieger* is, in certain respects, the most successful of all Young German prose works. The reason that the value of this novel has never been appropriately stressed is connected with the kind of question previous interpretation has put to it. The concern with content and ideas has so occupied the study of Young Germany that the inner connections between the sociological situation and questions of literary form have not always come into focus.[22] Insofar as the purely artistic achievement of Young Germany was generally quite mediocre, such a method has its justification. When the trilogy *Das junge Europa* is examined from the point of view of ideas or sociological relevance, the tendency is to look upon it as a continuing process and to put the stress upon *Die Poeten* as the starting point and then upon the Biedermeier resignation at the end of the third novel, *Die Bürger*. Since both those works exhibit a rather modest degree of artistic value, it has apparently been difficult to separate *Die Krieger* from their company and examine it more carefully. Therefore, a few words about the general problem of the trilogy may be helpful.

In the third part, the hero's correspondent Hippolyt writes the following about the English novel: "Wie arm seid Ihr [the Germans] dagegen! Wo nicht ein Lehrgedanke das Faktum, die Schilderung, die Begebenheit unterstützt oder gar rechtfertigt, da meint ihr Unnützes zu treiben; das Thörichte nennt ihr Romanhaftes, darum besitzt ihr auch den reinen Roman nicht, ihr seid verdorben für reine, bloße Bilder, die nichts sein wollen und sein sollen als Bilder."[23] Whether this attribution of self-sufficient images to the realistic English novel is an adequate interpretation does not concern us here; but we cannot fail to hear in these lines an uneasiness on Laube's part with regard to Young German experimental prose. For the lack of substance and the meagerness of characterization are just the weaknesses of a novel like *Die Poeten*. The epistolary form — "diese schwatzhafte, uranfängliche Form," as Laube later judged[24] — is chosen because it is the easiest to manage for a writer embarrassed for lack of material and substance. In this case, the figures become abstract types and the plot exhausts itself in an opaque snarl of criss-crossing love relationships, the purpose of which is to illustrate Enfantin's two categories of constancy and inconstancy in the character of men and women.[25] The ideas and the involved interrelationships that are illustrated in the book are not without interest, but the novel form itself is sadly regressive. To Heine, Laube spoke of it timidly as "die *Exposition* einer modernen Novelle."[26]

Of Laube's intimations of realism something has been said in the introductory essay. A few more of his remarks can be adduced here. Realistic standpoints appear repeatedly in his criticism in the *Elegante*. He requires "blut- und lebensvolle Darstellung" and "lebendige Romane," "irdische, materiell-poetische Substanz" and "moderne Erzählungen" in contrast to the historical novel.[27] He criticizes a minor contemporary writer this way:

> Aus dem Blute der Personen können und sollen Ideen, Meinungen, meinethalben Systeme hervorgehen, wenn denn einmal eingeschachtelt werden soll, aber aus den Ideen springt im Leben kein Blut.... Das ganze Verfahren unsers Verf. ist das eines Philosophen, welcher geschickt und gewandt raisonnirt, und zu größerer Deutlichkeit hier und da mit lebendigen Figuren etwas beweist; aber es ist nicht das Verfahren des Dichters.[28]

Such remarks, of which there are many, represent consciously or unconsciously a critique of Laube's own first novel. If his memory did not betray him in his old age, Laube was concerned to avoid pale abstractions when writing *Die Poeten*. "Handlung schien mir das Suchenswerte.... Nicht bloß Raisonnements! dachte ich; das bloße Besprechen war mir in dem Tumult der Meinungen unerquicklich geworden.... Mit einem Worte: erzählen muß man lernen — das war wohl damals mein Grundgedanke."[29] But in the same passage he intimates why he did not succeed in doing this, although he does not seem to have the problem quite in focus: "Die verschiedenartigen Meinungen um mich her versinnlichten sich mir in verschiedenartigen Menschen, und alle diese Menschen bildete ich mir aus zu eigenen Persönlichkeiten, zu Charakteren, wie man's nennt, und jeden ließ ich sprechen."[30] But opinions can be concretized into characters only with an extreme degree of artistic ability. Even the fact that Laube constructed his characters out of his own circle of acquaintances did not prevent the dissolution of reality into a mental game. A lurking conflict with reality is latent in *Die Poeten*, to be sure. Karl Häberle observed accurately: "Die Maßlosigkeit des subjektiven Anspruchs, die Erfahrungsfremdheit und der überfliegende, antizipierende, hastende Eifer werden der Begegnung mit der Wirklichkeit nicht standhalten."[31] The weaknesses of *Die Poeten* did not escape the other Young Germans and, as usual, Gutzkow was at hand with an acid comment: "So geht die Handlung die Kreuz und Quere, die Neigungen tanzen Quadrillen und Kontertänze, verschlingen sich bald hier, bald dort, so daß man sich in der Tat in einen Kaninchenbau, wo Vater und Tochter sich heiraten, versetzt glaubt."[32]

Things are even worse in the third novel of the trilogy, *Die Bürger*. It seems to me plausible that Laube had lost interest in the project altogether in the meanwhile, which would not be surprising, as the original plan could not be kept intact through the tribulations of 1834 and their aftermath. In the autobiography that Laube produced in jail, the original plan was described as follows: "In dem zweiten Theile beabsichtigte ich die Leute durch allerlei Inconvenienzen zu führen und zu erläutern, daß die Bildung nach allgemeinen Principien selten zu einer ruhigen körperlichen Existenz leite und daß es wichtiger sei aus dem Einzelnen herauszubilden, das Nächste zu beachten und statt der Allgemeinheit das Individuum ins Auge zu fassen. ... Das Ganze sollte ein Entwickelungsroman nach Art des Wilhelm Meister werden."[33] Of course, Laube was here attempting to put the novel in what he thought would be the least provocative light for his persecutors, but that the direction of it should have changed under the circumstances is not surprising. Formally, the result is altogether a catastrophe. Laube returns to the epistolary form, which is then broken in two by the long narrative report of the imprisonment of the hero, Valerius. This part taken by itself is a considerable achievement. Laube drew from his own experiences in solitary confinement, and the account of a man who is brought near to mental collapse by the complete absence of any intercourse with another human being is genuine and convincing. One might even fairly be reminded of Kafka by a sentence such as this: "Das Verhör allein kann uns fördern, den traurigen Zustand ändern, wenn nicht in einen besseren verwandeln, denn im schlimmsten Falle ist Strafgefängnis eine Erholung gegen den Untersuchungs-Arrest — und doch fürchten wir Alle das Verhör, wenigstens die Ankündigung desselben, das Klopfen, den Namensruf, das hastige Ankleiden, den Gang durch die dunklen Corridore."[34] The virtues of this section in style and content are obviously due to Laube's opportunity to make use of profound personal experience. It is a little paradoxical and ironic, however, that what is here given such impressive literary expression is not something in or of the world, but the frightening loss of an objective and responding world.

Among the evidences of loss of coherence in this novel is the fact that Valerius' correspondent Hippolyt does not react to this heart-rending account with a single word of sympathy or acknowledgment; he seems to take no note whatsoever of Valerius' sufferings. So far as the trilogy as a whole is concerned, this insensitivity cannot be accounted for by Hippolyt's demonic egoism; in the first novel, for example, he helps one of the correspondents out of an embarrassment with a loan.[35] It is rather that, in *Die Bürger*, two fates are presented that are hardly connected with one another, apart from Valerius' critique of Hippolyt's radicalism and the contrast of social attitudes that is to be revealed. The content of these contrasting views is important enough in itself, but they do not yield a novel. Much in the plot and language of the book indicates increasing carelessness of composition. Hippolyt's own affairs are melodramatic and absurd, full of lurid seductions, duels, and whatnot. He is finally murdered by a jealous rival in the midst of a racial disturbance in New York, a scene that may touch our present sense of the relevant, but that in fact shows how issues of great gravity get introduced into this kind of writing in an inadequate and haphazard way. What has happened is that Laube's ideological horizon has become too foreshortened to contain Hippolyt's radical anarchism. The Young German intellectual substance is a kind of colloid in which widely disparate standpoints can be held in suspension; thus the figure of Hippolyt could maintain some plausibility among the various incarnated viewpoints of *Die*

Poeten. Now, however, that Laube's own ideological tolerance has shrunk toward the center, Hippolyt's attitudes and doings appear increasingly outlandish and the dialectical link with the perspective from the center of the novel, that of Valerius, has snapped. The return to the epistolary form also suggests, in my opinion, that Laube had exhausted his material and that only two masses remained: the account of his experiences in jail and the ideological contrast between Hippolyt and Valerius.

Apart from the autobiographical account of solitary confinement, there is little in either *Die Poeten* or *Die Bürger* to suggest that Laube had realistic gifts. Yet, in the middle novel of the trilogy, a will to realistic form and the actual achievement are more congruent than in any other longer work of fiction among the Young Germans. Laube himself recalled in his old age: "[Ich] ging entschlossen ab von der Art des ersten Buches: 'Die Poeten', welches in doktrinärer Absichtlichkeit befangen geblieben; ich meinte der vollen Roman-form, der reinen Erzählung mich ganz hingeben zu können und in ihr einen Fortschritt für mich zu finden."[36] It is interesting that here he did not attempt to draw from his own personal experience. Although the novel is about the Polish revolution of 1830/31 and deals extensively with regular and guerrilla warfare, Laube himself never saw Poland beyond the boundaries of Silesia and never took part in any fighting engagement off the fencing floor. But such direct experience was not necessary. It was the knowledge of concrete context that he and his literary contemporaries lacked. Laube was able to acquire it when he had a burning need to do so. We know from his own account that he interviewed a wounded Polish nobleman at great length and extracted from him exact details about the atmos-phere and the events of the revolution; later he studied the materials on the revolution that Jean Paul's nephew Richard Otto Spazier had collected in Leipzig.

The subject of the novel was a fortunate choice. It is true that there had been other novels in the past describing enthusiastic German youths involved in the revolutionary struggles of other nations — Hölderlin's *Hyperion* is an example — and Wolfgang Menzel scorned them bitterly as examples of the inability of the Germans to pursue modern imperatives in their own country.[37] But Laube's choice of this strategy had specific theoretical advantages, because it preserved the virtues of the historical novel without what the Young Germans perceived as its drawbacks. When realism is in a primitive stage, the historical novel is an obvious genre to develop. Since the surrounding world and society cannot yet be comprehended with precision, the concrete materials of history offer a substitute for the lack of abundance in perception of the contemporary environment. An additional virtue is the element of adventure that holds the reader's interest and enables the writer to find a resonance in a larger public — an advantage of the historical novel that even Wienbarg, though he was very opposed to the genre, was obliged to admit.[38] In Wienbarg's view, however, the orientation on the past is bad. Instead of capturing contemporary life in a critical perspective, the author of historical novels is largely supplying opiates to the people.[39] Thus it is clear what Laube gained by choosing the Polish revolution as a subject. The excitement of adventure retains this advantage of the historical novel, while the relative contemporaneity of the revolution, which was watched from Germany with much interest, gives a suitable context for the ideological crisis through which Valerius must pass. The artistic assimilation of the current-event material with Valerius' *Bildungsroman* is, to be sure, not altogether complete; especially in the second part there is a tendency for the narrated historical and political events to separate themselves from the internal fabric of the trilogy. But complete success was hardly to be expected under the circumstances; what Laube accomplished is remarkable enough.

It is in characterization that Laube's movement in the direction of a more modern realism is most evident; Rudolf Majut, speaking of the trilogy as a whole, went so far as to draw a parallel with Thomas Mann's *Zauberberg*.[40] The contrast between *Die Krieger* and *Die Poeten* is perhaps more profound than Laube himself could know, for it exemplifies a vital change in the representation of types. Peter Demetz has distinguished between the Romantic type and the realistic type as follows: "Der romantische Typus...inkarniert zeitlose Laster, Tugenden, Energien, Kräfte und Leidenschaften in mehr als menschlichen Gestalten, welche die relativen Konturen des Humanen zu sprengen drohen; der realistische Typus soziologischer Relevanz, der aus der Praxis der Naturforscher hervorgeht, repräsentiert viele einzelne Menschen der analogen Gruppe in einer Figur, der nichts Menschliches mangelt."[41] These definitions fit Laube's two novels with but a single adjustment: the characteristics

114

of the "Poeten" are not "zeitlos," but explicitly time-bound. However, the character of each functions almost exclusively as the heightened incarnation of the quality ascribed to it. In *Die Krieger* this is no longer so. Here the characters do not, in the first instance, incarnate concepts or qualities, but rather represent types that occur in a specific and concrete social and historical situation. The gain in human substance is quite remarkable and could be shown by the example of Valerius down to the manner of his language. But the transformation that Valerius undergoes has already been sufficiently analyzed by previous interpretation; furthermore, it must be said that the presentation of this unheroic, bourgeois, indecisive hero can hardly, when one thinks of Goethe's Wilhelm Meister, be regarded as an entirely original breakthrough on Laube's part. The progress is more clearly shown by considering the ancillary characters.

It is noteworthy and, for the reader coming from *Die Poeten*, somewhat surprising that the first person who emerges at the beginning of the story is an old Jew. Opening a novel by concentrating our attention on a relatively minor character — he is hunting for his son on the field of a recent battle — is an instinctively realistic device. It draws us *in medias res* and gives an opportunity for setting the scene without obtrusive authorial presence; it also places us in that perspective below the level of high policy and decision that we all share when looking upon events as they transpire. Here, however, Laube's strategy does more; it shows us that we have left the hermetically sealed pseudo-society of letter-writers passing their limitless leisure in amorous intrigue and have entered a socially more differentiated world. The prominent role of the Jew and his son can, in addition, be taken as a modest liberal challenge. That may be a speculation, but it seems to me less speculative to suggest that the Jewish characters are symptomatic for the artistic virtues of the novel.

Even in the Young German context, Laube stands out as exceptionally philo-Semitic. The Jewish anti-Semitism that flickers from time to time in Börne und Heine is notorious; it is a partly psychological problem, partly one of social criticism. In the few places where Wienbarg comes to speak of the Jews, he makes almost exclusively deprecating remarks; he had only a shrug of the shoulders for the paragraph that banned Jews from the kingdom in the Norwegian constitution he so enthusiastically admired.[42] Gutzkow's views were,

as usual, more complex. Houben has written a long essay on Gutzkow's relations with Jews, including the prominent Hamburg
emancipator, Gabriel Riesser, and on his continuing concern with
the Jewish problem over the years.[43] But Gutzkow was obliged to
admit that he had to overcome a strong prejudice within himself
when he first discovered that Heine and Börne were Jews,[44] and
his otherwise admirable tragedy *Uriel Acosta* does not suggest that
he had penetrated very deeply into Jewish culture; his rabbis are
little more than Catholic inquisitors in disguise. Laube's special
attitude toward the Jews is traceable, no doubt, partly to his good-
humored and tolerant nature, partly to personal experiences. As
a schoolboy in Glogau he received charity meals from a Jewish
family, whose warmth and humanity he clearly appreciated; for
a companion on his Italian journey with Gutzkow in 1833 he chose
a Jewish businessman with whom he maintained a close friendship
afterward. With one distressing exception,[45] his writings and memoirs
show that, as he said, he did not have any prejudice against the
Jews.[46]

This is responsible for Laube's success with the Jewish figures in
Die Krieger — less so, perhaps, with the old, embittered Manasse,
who is somewhat overdrawn and has a little too much of Shylock,
than with his son Joel. Structurally, Joel is to be understood as a
radical parallel figure to Valerius. Like Valerius, Joel stands between
two worlds between which he cannot mediate, and this is due not
to his own failings, but to the failings of the social structure. The
remark that Valerius makes about Joel's situation — "O, können sie
denn nie aufhören, diese grellen Kontraste der bürgerlichen Gesellschaft"[47] — could as easily be applied to his own difficulties. Like
Valerius, Joel tries to break with the old society by actively involving
himself in the struggle for modern ideals, but he is obliged to
recognize that he remains, despite everything, a foreign body in
revolutionary Poland. Like Valerius, he loves a girl across class
barriers, only to be flung ever deeper into his identity crisis. Like
Valerius, he ends in profound resignation. But an important aspect
of the parallel should not be overlooked. Joel undertakes his retrans-
formation into a "Schacherjude" with extreme bitterness. The abandon-
ment of his modern, bourgeois self-identification is a kind of symbolic
suicide that is meant to chastise the inhuman order of society.

116

Valerius makes a similar decision with less aggressive bitterness and a greater capacity for rationalization:

> Es giebt nur zwei Arten, glücklich zu sein: entweder man bewegt und bevölkert sich und die Welt mit Idealen, Aussichten, neuer Zukunft, man schaukelt sich auf der wogenden Bewegung des ungezügelten Strebens, — oder man betrachtet die Welt aus einem ruhigen Herzen, freut sich des Kleinsten, hilft und fördert im Kleinsten, pflanzt mit Genügsamkeit, wartet geduldig auf das Gedeihen, gestaltet das Unbedeutende zur gefälligen Form, verlangt nichts vom Tage, als was er eben bietet, und hält den Nachbar und sein Interesse höher als das Wohl oder Wehe von Nationen.[48]

For all that Laube here begins to sound like Adalbert Stifter, Valerius' resignation, when we look closely at the process that brings it about, is not in the first instance an acceptance of a Biedermeier turn inward, but is rather something that harsh reality has forced upon him. Many years ago, Benno von Wiese spoke in this connection of the involuntary Biedermeier of the Young Germans.[49] With every recognition of the Biedermeier aspect of this process, one should not overlook the fact that it contains a reproach against a society that does not permit anything better.

But Joel's pathos is much deeper than Valerius' because the hopelessness of his situation is more radical. Valerius has the possibility of conforming to his society if he can see his way to making this capitulation, while there is no place at all in society for the emancipated Polish Jew. The scenes in which Laube shows this are among the best in the novel. Neither among the revolutionary aristocrats, nor among the democrats, nor among the rebellious people is Joel permitted to have a human relationship. Courage, kindheartedness, service in the national struggle — nothing can alter his exclusion from society. (That Laube prefigures the fate of the *German* Jews with surprising precision may be mentioned here in passing.) Valerius' growing comprehension of the hopelessness of Joel's situation contributes substantially to the erosion of his revolutionary enthusiasm. He leaves the revolutionary army out of protest against the shabby treatment Joel receives because he has dared to fall in love with the daughter of an aristocratic rebel leader. When Valerius remonstrates with Count Kicki: "Ich glaube es kaum, daß Sie mit diesen aristokratischen Bedenklichkeiten eine glückliche Revolution machen,"[50] he is simply not understood. Joel's fate is thus a kind of *Bildungserlebnis* for Valerius, forcing him to the insight that "freedom," which the young German liberals propagated with insouciant imprecision, in reality can wear quite various and disquieting faces.[51]

There are some weaknesses in the characterization of Joel. The most regrettable of them is that Laube makes Joel the son of a Christian mother, whereby the symbolism of the figure becomes muddled.[52] It is likely that Laube wanted to motivate by heredity Joel's longing to escape from the narrow environment of orthodox Judaism. This fits together with a secret family relationship between Joel and his beloved, which is revealed only towards the end of the novel — an old-fashioned convention that Laube, in such a novel as this, could easily have done without. Joel's almost uninterrupted weepy self-pity, although understandable under the circumstances, seems excessive to the reader and suggests some lack of respect for the character on the author's part. More interesting is a remark that comes toward the end of the novel, after Joel has dressed himself as an orthodox "Bandjude" (a peddler of ribbons and the like): "Die Klagen des schönen jungen Mannes, welche [Valerius] so lebhaft mitfühlte, waren ihm viel würdiger erschienen, so lange der Klagende in besserer Kleidung neben ihm hergegangen war. Er schalt sich über solche Schwäche."[53] Obviously the Jew is a more pleasant phenomenon as an assimilated bourgeois. This reaction is regretted as a weakness, but is nevertheless present. A little crack in the narrative perspective opens up here, through which Valerius is seen from a critical distance. This occurs in other places in *Die Krieger* and suggests that we should be cautious with the traditional identification of Valerius with Laube himself. On the other hand, a comparison of Laube's remarks on the Jews shows that even he, to a certain degree, shared the familiar liberal hope that the Jews would abandon their separate culture and vanish into bourgeois society, a view that, twenty years later, found its ultimate formulation in the figure of Bernhard Ehrenthal in Gustav Freytag's *Soll und Haben* (1855).

Sometime a detailed comparison between *Die Krieger* and *Soll und Haben* should be undertaken; it would be quite instructive. Both novels are literary milestones in the development of the German bourgeois ideology, and not only the lines of connection, which

118

have been stressed from time to time, but also the contrasts are of interest. In the simplest terms, one could say that, while Freytag developed the technique of realistic characterization much further, the human quality of Laube's characterization has become lost due to the hardening of the ideological position that has taken place in the meantime. One sees this above all in the treatment of the Jews. The demand for complete assimilation and *embourgeoisement*, which shows up in Laube only in hints and suggestions, has become for Freytag the absolute touchstone of human value. Freytag's Jews are not conceived as anti-Semitic caricatures; they are differentiated figures and drawn with a certain sharpness of observation.[54] But they are forced with such violence into Freytag's evaluative scheme that neither a penetration into their human substance nor a balanced judgment upon their social situation is possible. What appears in Laube as an unhappy struggle for a bearable social standpoint has become philistine conviction in Freytag. The loss of the specific virtues that appear in Laube's efforts to create Jewish characters realistically is deplorable and quite ominous for the future.

A comparison of the two novels is also suggested by the fact that both treat Polish revolutionary events. Here the difference is less striking, for. Laube's opinions of the Poles are more similar to Freytag's than his opinions of the Jews. Among the German liberals the enthusiasm for the Polish revolution is not infrequently combined with a noticeable dislike of the Polish people; Heine is a familiar example. Like most prejudices, this one is the result of observation and is strongest among those who have had the most direct experience. Laube discussed the matter at length in his memoirs:

> Ich unterschätzte diese Revolution, weil ich in Glogau und Breslau in steter Berührung mit Polen gewesen und durchdrungen davon war, daß sie in ihrem streitsüchtigen Hochmute sich nicht vertragen und nichts gestalten könnten. Der Ausdruck "polnische Wirtschaft" war in Schlesien so landläufig, daß man dort absolut nicht an die Möglichkeit eines polnischen Staates glauben mochte. Persönliche Sympathien fanden die Polen außerdem nirgends unter uns. Der Begriff einer Adelsrepublik spritzte überall aus ihnen hervor und machte sie unangenehm für unsere demokratische Empfindung. Das war ganz naturgemäß, und das gerade hat ihnen bisher jedes Gelingen erschwert. Es ist nicht ihre Schuld, es ist ihr Schicksal. Der

herrschende Stamm hat sich als Adelsstamm apart gehalten, hat die große übrige Bevölkerung niedergehalten. Was nützte es, daß der polnische Adel unter sich demokratische Gleichheit standhaft durchgeführt und dem ärmsten Edelmanne immer ebensoviel Ansprüche zugestanden, als dem reichsten? Die erobernde Kaste ist Kaste geblieben, hat die Emanzipation der niederen Stände, des eigentlichen Volkes, zu lange versäumt, und hat damit versäumt, ein gleichmäßig teilnehmendes Volk heranzubilden.... Wäre unser Feudaladel nicht vom deutschen Bürgerthume überflutet worden, so wäre es uns vielleicht ähnlich ergangen; in Polen aber ist das Bürgerthum ausgeblieben, und an dieser Lücke krankt das polnische Wesen immerdar.[55]

Laube could not even stand the Polish nobleman whom he interrogated for the novel.

In *Die Poeten*, Valerius' decision to join the Polish revolution is accompanied by similar feeling, which, characteristically for that book, he resolves aesthetically:

Ich gehe morgen nach Warschau, um für das heilige Recht eines Volkes gegen die Tyrannen zu fechten. Ich liebe das polnische Volk nicht eben sehr, aber für seine Sache will ich bluten und sterben.... Es ist noch viel roh Asiatisches an ihnen, aber ihre überwältigende Poesie der Vaterlandsliebe, dieses Käthchen von Heilbronn in einem ganzen Volke, ist zauberhaft, ihr Kampf ist der reinste und edelste, der gefochten werden kann.[56]

For Laube as for Freytag this dislike of the Poles is socio-politically motivated — the Poles lack the class base for a successful revolution. For both, the Polish rebellion is in the interest of a partially enlightened but also feudal and regressive nobility, while the oppressed, uncultured peasantry is incapable of judgment and lacks any real revolutionary potential. Certainly the bourgeois class consciousness is stronger and more precise in Freytag. Although both writers tend to identify specifically German virtues with those of the bourgeoisie, the nationalism of the right-wing liberal Freytag is so closely involved with his bourgeois class consciousness that his double front against the aristocracy and an uncultivated foreign peasant class remains the main concern.

For Laube, however, the unadmired Poles remain human beings.

120

In accordance with the realistic tendency to push the heroic into the background, the great leaders in Laube's novel — Skrzynecki, Prondzynski, Krukowiecki, etc. — are more or less seen from below. Otherwise Laube seeks to differentiate among his Polish figures, and this in itself is an important example of the way the writing of fiction can enrich and complicate ideas and attitudes the author believes he holds, for, in a passage in the *Reisenovellen*, Laube denied the Poles any differentiated individuality:

> Man schildert mit *einem* Polen alle; sie haben keine absondernde Individualität, das ist auch ein Grund ihrer Größe: sie imponieren als *ein* Mann. Es ist bei allen halbzivilisierten Völkern so: ihre Bedürfnisse, Fehler, Vorzüge, sind einfach, ihre Verhältnisse nicht minder. Darum sind sie nur als Masse oder als Repräsentanten der Masse interessant; einzeln aber schnell langweilig, weil die innere Ausgebildetheit und Mannigfaltigkeit fehlt, die bei näherer Bekanntschaft immer neue Seiten entwickelt.[57]

Fortunately, Laube did not work in *Die Krieger* according to this principle. He not only contrasts the figures with one another, but also attempts to exhibit the socially determined paradoxes in the individuals in order to expose the contradictions of the revolution. A good example of this is the careful unmasking of the aristocratic foundation in the superficially democratic attitude of one of the leaders, Count Stanislaus. Another, which is also relevant to Laube's handling of the Jews, is his treatment of the character of the popular hero, Florian the blacksmith, who is presented as sympathetic and attractive. When the rebel peasants, in an access of anti-Semitic fury, attack Valerius, Joel, and Joel's beloved, who are their allies, the blacksmith is obliged to calm them down and then remarks quietly: "Vater Kosciusco, das sind Deine Polen."[58] But when Joel, during an attack of the enemy, for his part attempts to save Florian's life by calling out his name, the latter answers as he dies: "Schweig, Jude."[59] In this way, Laube tries to penetrate into the complications of an objective social situation that would have been inaccessible to the abstract dialectics of *Die Poeten*. None of this probing sensitivity remains in Freytag. His hateful treatment of the Poles makes a mockery of any realistic intention; his Poles are no longer complex human beings, but schematic cartoons.

My remarks on *Die Krieger* are only suggestions and certainly

121

could be refined methodologically and in regard to content. I am not contending that it is an outstanding novel; as a realistic work it is primitive enough. It is perhaps not much better than the novels that Burkhardt has asserted are the result of Wienbarg's novel theory: "Jene zahlreichen, wegen ihrer künstlerischen Unbedeutendheit längst vergessenen Zeitromane der dreißiger und vierziger Jahre des 19. Jahrhunderts."[60] But, in the Young German context, Laube's achievement takes on a relative significance. This raises another, somewhat disquieting problem: whether the original Young German radicality (using the word with all necessary qualifications) was advantageous to the development of a realistic prose art; whether, to put it another way, Laube did not *have* to fall away from his original attitude in order to write a book like *Die Krieger*. The Young German novels, beginning with Gutzkow's *Wally*, that were seeking direct confrontation, detonated some explosions at the intersection of literature and society, but do not stand up well to artistic or intellectual criticism. If we think of the names of the great realists, we find many who are quite the opposite of radical: Balzac, Flaubert, Thackeray, Fontane, Henry James, Thomas Mann. There are, of course, exceptions (Zola, Jack London, Dreiser, Dos Passos, Steinbeck), as well as others who are hard to discuss in such terms (Hugo, Dickens). But, aside from the fact that the concept of realism becomes a little difficult when applied to Dickens or Zola, it is perhaps not insignificant that Dos Passos and Steinbeck made sharp shifts rightward in later years. These remarks are offered here only as a possible starting point for the theme of "Jungdeutscher Frührealismus." For it would not be an exaggeration to claim that where we find realism, we do not find the specific Young German quality, and vice versa. This thesis seems to apply also to the drama of the *Vormärz*, as Horst Denkler has recently shown.[61]

Reality has, of course, the tendency to escape ideologically preconstructed categories, and no ingenious distinctions between *Wirklichkeit* and *Wahrheit* can prevent this. When the world is seen under relatively simply defined ideas or attitudes, art is very possible, but it will hardly be realism. For the realistic writer is wholly occupied with impressing an artistic order upon a chaotic abundance of experience and perception. This in itself obvious observation seems to me pertinent here, because it is just such reflections upon the complexity of experience, illustrated by the hard reality of the

122

Polish revolution, that play a large part in the tormenting revision of conviction that Valerius must go through. These considerations appear most succinctly in a passage that has been pointed out by Nolle, von Wiese, and Häberle,[62] and that also struck me upon a first reading:

> Und doch waren es nicht jene Freiheitsgedanken an sich, die er jetzt bezweifelte, es waren die Verhältnisse im Großen, die allgemeinen historischen Entwickelungen, die ihm den Geist mit Dämmerung bedeckten. Er ahnte das Tausendfältige der menschlichen Zustände, die tausendfältigen Nuancen der Weltgeschichte, die millionenfachen Wechsel in der Gestalt eines Jahrhunderts und in der Gestalt seiner Wünsche und Bedürfnisse. Er sah die Armuth des menschlichen Geistes, der reformiren will, neben dem unabsehbaren Reichthume, der unendlichen Mannigfaltigkeit dieser Welt und ihres verborgenen ewigen Gedankens.[63]

The theme is picked up again at the beginning of *Die Bürger,* in a more direct and resigned way: "Unsre übermüthigen Jugendpläne, die Welt umzugestalten, haben wir wohl zum Theil aufgegeben, wir sind erschrocken vor der Mannigfaltigkeit der Welt, vor der Unerschöpflichkeit ihrer Verhältnisse und Zustände."[64] These considerations seem to me not only to have some plausibility, but also to be closely connected with the conditions that permit realistic writing. It is also understandable that they should lead to a sort of resignation, a sense for the "Grenzen der Menschheit." Whether the resignation must necessarily be of the Biedermeier or conservative kind is another question. But the comparison with Freytag permits a critical judgment. Laube's frankness, his uncertainty in the face of a world difficult to apprehend with time-bound intellectual categories, permits, despite all his technical insufficiency, a beginning of an early form of realism. Freytag's technical ability, learned, for the most part, from the English novel, is much further developed, but his writing is so thoroughly determined by a chauvinistic and class-bound scheme that one can speak of his realism only with reservations. If the conditions under which Laube was writing had been a little different, perhaps beginnings like *Die Krieger* could have borne fruit that would have put an entirely different face on the German novel of the nineteenth century.

VI. KARL IMMERMANN

The stock of Karl Lebrecht Immermann has been rising noticeably in recent years. A number of valuable studies by several scholars have now culminated in an excellent full-length critical biography by Benno von Wiese.[1] Immermann had not been in total obscurity; although he had always been something of a stepchild of literary scholarship, many creative writers over the decades expressed their admiration for him in varying degrees; von Wiese mentions Gutzkow, Laube, Heine, Eichendorff, Droste-Hülshoff, Hebbel, Conrad Ferdinand Meyer, Wilhelm Raabe, Hugo von Hofmannsthal, Jakob Wassermann, and Hermann Hesse.[2] Wilhelm Dilthey called him one of the cleverest of German writers.[3] Not all of these accolades have been without reservations, however, and indeed it is not easy to come to a firm and adequate assessment of Immermann. Martin Greiner said rather cruelly that he "gleicht einem Gastgeber, der die reichsten Vorräte in seinem Hause eingesammelt hat. Aber auf seinem Herde brennt ein so schwaches Feuer, daß er nur ein wenig davon zubereiten und seinen Gästen vorsetzen kann, während das meiste in Muff und Moder verdirbt."[4] Robert Boxberger had said many years before, more kindly, that we admire Immermann's efforts more than his achievements.[5] There certainly is a discrepancy between his talent and ambition on the one hand and the total achievement of his twenty years of literary production on the other. He possessed limited but indisputable resources of imagination and creativity, especially in the realm of satire and, in reading him, one's attention is constantly caught by passages of subtlety and strength. But other parts of his work can be dim and commonplace, partly because, like many of his contemporaries, he tried to write so much and in so many genres, and partly because, as all his modern admirers agree, his true vocation was to be a novelist and he was slow to discover this. He was misled by his obsession with the drama,

124

which again he shared with many of his contemporaries. Unlike his friend Heine, who rather quickly got over what George Eliot called "the chicken-pox of authorship,"[6] Immermann, though he swore off the drama time and time again, could not, as Windfuhr has said, shake the "Theaterteufel" that possessed him.[7] He earned himself an honorable place in the history of the German theater by managing a "model stage" in Düsseldorf from 1832 to 1837, continuing the efforts to raise the cultural level of the theater long pursued by Lessing, Goethe, and Schiller. But his sixteen plays, even the much-noticed *Andreas Hofer* (first version, 1826; second version, 1833) and the ambitious trilogy *Alexis* (1831) are of no more than anti-quarian interest.

It is significant, as Windfuhr points out, that when Immermann planned his collected edition in 1835, he intended to include only two of his works written before 1829; chronologically, as it turned out, nearly half of his writing career.[8] Not until 1836 did the major prose works begin to appear that most interest us today. Immermann died suddenly in 1840 at the age of forty-four, and there is a feeling among his modern admirers that he was just beginning to reach a level of real greatness; his death, according to Windfuhr, "beendet ein begonnenes Lebenswerk, das die ihm zugewiesene Richtung gerade erst einzuschlagen angefangen hatte."[9] But one cannot, after all, be sure. The work that occupied him at the time of his death, a modernized version of *Tristan und Isolde*, was a cata-strophe in the making, so violently did he pursue the *embourgeoise-ment* of the material, substituting, to his friend Tieck's horror, repentence for the theme of invincible passion in the original, and garnishing the text, as was his wont, with comic and satirical whimsies. Although Immermann was clearly growing artistically and intellectu-ally when he was so regrettably taken away, there is something in the very foundation of the man that suggests his later career might have continued to be uneasy, inconsistent, and plagued with doubt and uncertainty.

Immermann has traditionally been classified as a conservative, but modern critics have seen that this is much too facile a label to define the complexity of the man. He was raised in strict idolatry of Frederick the Great, participated with patriotic fervor in the Wars of Liberation, and was a Prussian civil servant all his life; and it is true that some of his social and political opinions have little to recommend them. An anachronistic nostalgia for absolutist monarchy is among them: "Der echte Fürst," he wrote in his diary in 1832, "muß ein mythisches Gefühl seiner selbst haben, er muß sich allen andern gegenüber für ein einziges, eximirtes Wesen halten können. Hierdurch allein wird er befähigt, den Indifferenzpunkt zwischen den Persönlichkeiten und Gewalten des Staats zu machen."[10] He wrote a poem expressing scorn for the humanity of the nineteenth century that sees a brother in every rascal,[11] and of his brilliantly conceived Baron von Münchhausen, it is said that people fell for his lies as they did for the Enlightenment and the French Revolution.[12] Another constant theme is the longing for the great man, who, by the force of his personality, will cut the Gordian knot of modern dilemmas. In a letter of 7 November 1830, he comments on the July Revolution: "... die gewaltigen Ereignisse sind am Ende doch von lauter Kleinen ausgegangen — nirgends ein bedeutender Charakter, ein Held, eine wahre Apotheose der geistigen und politischen Mittelmäßigkeit — ein ungeheurer, quirlender Ameisenhaufen."[13] Although, like any writer of his time of social significance, he had trouble with the censors, he tended to support the principle of censorship.[14] He wrote a eulogy upon the death of Frederick William III in 1840 in which he incredibly calls this perjured king and terrorist of the intellectual world "Vater, Hort und Schirmherr..., redlichster Mann des Landes."[15]

Modern critics have been concerned to oppose to these opinions, which have been exploited by conservative and Fascist admirers, evidence of democratic and liberal tendencies as well. Windfuhr, in studying the manuscripts of Immermann's travel diaries, has shown how he censored his own critical observations to make them appear more legitimist, and comments that he did not have Heine's skills in masking his critique[16] — but Heine's critiques are masked only for a very obtuse reader, and Immermann, by personal ideology or public social allegiance, could not have seen any value in publishing his own. In time he did come closer to an appreciation of Young Germany; on the ban of 1835 and Wienbarg's sufferings from it he remarked: "In der That gehört jener Bannspruch, welcher die Früchte des Geistes noch ungeboren tödten wollte, zu den häßlichsten Ausgeburten eines matten Despotismus."[17] Meanwhile, his critical novels caused the Young Germans themselves to take a friendlier view of him.

In some respects Immermann suffered the familiar fate of a moderate man in a time of high political passion. The best example of this is an incident that occurred while he was still a student and that seriously affected his relationship to the intellectual community. Fraternity boys at Halle had administered a brutal beating to a nonconforming student, and Immermann, now a twenty-three-year-old war veteran, protested in two pamphlets and took his views directly to the king. Thus he acquired at the outset of his adult life the reputation of an informer and a pawn of the anti-patriotic forces; when his quondam literary mentor, Friedrich de la Motte Fouqué, heard of the incident some three years later, he broke off all relations with Immermann. Hans Mayer, while still employed in East Germany, judged that Immermann had acted from a genuine sense of justice but in political blindness.[18] I believe this assessment has little merit. The increasingly fanatical and chauvinistic student movement was only in a very limited sense a force for freedom, and Immermann's Prussian belief in ethical lawfulness cannot be said to have erred in this instance. The incident shows us, rather, how his fundamental orientation on principle tended to isolate him in his time and helps us to understand how he became the kind of writer he was. For his conservatism does not lie chiefly in his often half-baked political and social views, but in the simplicity of his ethical foundation: the plainness of his integrity, the moderation and normality of his principles in an immoderate and abnormal time. His ethical moderation was both unreflective and elegiac. It is more a product of instinct than of reason, and in this respect he differs from the Young Germans, who wrestled, however clumsily, for a critical, analytical approach to the moral and ideological presuppositions of life and society in their time. The result in Immermann is what E. K. Bramsted has perceptively called "negative neutrality";[19] so remote did Immermann's prosaic principles seem from anything happening in the world that his satire acquired a negative universality that was not impelled, as the satire and criticism of the Young Germans were, by allegiance to any progressive force, real or imagined, struggling to be born in this bewildered age. Both his major novels show this to a degree that has not always been fully appreciated.

Immermann's single great coup was to give a name to the malaise that beset the bourgeois intelligentsia. To the novel he worked on intermittently for a number of years and finally completed in the fateful year of 1835,[20] he gave the title of *Die Epigonen*, from a Greek word meaning "descendants" or "those who come after." This is a true neologism, insofar as he gave a known word a new meaning. In Greek tradition, the *Epigonoi* were the sons of the Seven against Thebes, who conquered the city before which their fathers had perished. Thus the term had by no means a pejorative connotation, since the sons accomplished that which the fathers had been unable to do. It was Immermann who gave the word the gloomy sense it was to have ever after: it identifies a mediocre generation following on one of great brilliance, condemned to imitation and amorphousness. The word became a concept of intellectual history — one often abused — and found its way, in Immermann's sense, into other languages; in English it has never achieved much currency, although the larger dictionaries carry it. Windfuhr, in his discussion of the history of the concept, makes two important distinctions. *Epigonentum* is, first of all, not the same thing as a period of productive imitation, in which classical or traditional models have authoritative status and serve as a source of creative inspiration;[21] rather, in Immermann's time, the awareness of the overwhelming greatness of past accomplishment, whether of antiquity or the Age of Goethe, is coupled with a realization that these models cannot be plausibly recreated or imitated in the present situation. Secondly, Windfuhr distinguishes *Epigonentum* from decadence, which plays with aesthetic materials, is artistically self-conscious, esoteric, and unpopular,[22] whereas *Epigonentum*, especially when it is not as conscious of its own state as Immermann was, prepares for easy consumption what once had been vital and challenging.

There can be no doubt that Immermann caught with this concept, if perhaps somewhat obliquely, an important mood and process of his time. Von Wiese quotes Ernst Troeltsch, who in retrospect found Immermann a good guide for the atmosphere of the time and described the social and historical situation this way:

> Schon verdämmert der rationalistische Geist und wandelt sich teils in demokratische Opposition, teils in kapitalistische Unternehmungslust. Stärker dauert der humanisierte Individualismus romantischer und klassizistischer Prägung. Aber hinter alledem tauchen die alten Macht- und Standesverhältnisse wieder auf, die nicht vernichtet, sondern nur geschwächt sind, und in den Vordergrund

schiebt sich der Macht- und Gewaltbau der militärisch-bürokrati-
schen Monarchien, verbündet mit einer bei jeder Gelegenheit ein-
setzenden konfessionell-christlichen Restauration des Kirchentums.[23]

But this regressive restoration is not the only oppressive aspect of the
situation; von Wiese speaks perceptively of a troubling sense of
discontinuity in human affairs: "die wachsende Unselbständigkeit
und Unwahrhaftigkeit im menschlichen Zusammenleben, weitgehend
hervorgerufen durch das Diskontinuierliche der Geschichte, durch die
politischen Wirrnisse, die wie ein Unwetter über den Menschen
hereinbrechen und sie vor den 'Stürmen der Zeit' nirgends mehr
Schutz finden lassen, selbst dort nicht, wo es früher noch möglich
war, im privaten Dasein."[24] The age is clogged with transmitted
culture and with a civilization no longer organically involved with
the conditions of life; competing truths and absolutes resound in
a cacophony of windy debate. We have already seen this view expressed by Gutzkow and Mundt. There are, in a sense, too many
answers and not enough questions, or, as Koopmann put it, there
is "ein Zuviel an Orientierungspunkten."[25]

Because Immermann's realistic skills were greater than those of the
Young Germans, his representation of culture and society helps to
fill in the background of the situation that the Young Germans confronted with greater resources of prescriptive criticism but to which
they were generally incapable of giving convincing literary form.
It is therefore useful to examine Immermann along with the Young
Germans in order to acquire a sense of epoch. His representation of
the disjunction, diffuseness, and bewilderment of his own age helps
us to see the larger context more clearly because he does not keep
these things locked in the churning liberal intellect, as the Young
Germans generally do, but projects them, satirically or realistically,
into a narrated world. While he lacked philosophical genius and
could be obtuse in certain directions, there is no other writer of his
time who concentrates so effectively, not so much on sociological
analysis of causes and effects, but on the perceived situation itself.

The way from perception to creation, however, was a difficult
one for him, even when he came at last to the genre most appropriate
to the situation, the novel. Like the Young Germans, he leaves much
to be desired in plot construction. In *Die Epigonen* the formal resources are still very inadequate. This is due in part to the long

129

genesis of the novel, which started out as a quite different kind of book and went through a stage in which it was meant to be more light-hearted and comic than it turned out to be.[26] The extremely complex plot turns on secret family relationships, withheld information, lost documents, and so on, all the paraphernalia of worn-out conventions. Another problem is the influence of Goethe's *Wilhelm Meisters Lehrjahre*, to which there are many slavish parallels. The plot is improbably constructed; von Wiese, in defense of it, has argued that accident is a structural principle in the novel, accident and contradiction being among Immermann's most basic concepts.[27] But Windfuhr seems to me more convincing when he says, "Die Zufälligkeiten und Abenteuerlichkeiten der Handlung müssen auf einmal den gesetzlichen und notwendig ablaufenden Gang eines Geschichtsprozesses symbolisieren. Hier wird dem Grundschema zu viel zugemutet. Die Form hat sich nicht im gleichen Tempo mitentwickelt."[28]

Of substantial interest is the treatment of the class situation in the novel. This is also partly an inheritance from *Wilhelm Meister*, although here the theme is of much greater importance. Hermann, the hero, becomes involved in a struggle over proprietary rights between a ducal family and his own uncle, a large-scale industrialist. The question turns, rather trivially, it has seemed to some readers, on whether the duke's ancestry is purely noble or contains a peasant woman in the family tree; the problem of the documentation of this matter is part of the machinery of Immermann's complicated plot. Hermann is torn between what he perceives as the beauty of the aristocratic culture and his duty to his uncle. These forces seem at first to be irreconcilable. The downward slide of the aristocratic family has proceeded in three stages: the grandfather of the duke was frugal and gave his attention to the working of his estates; the father was a sensitive, imaginative, prodigal philanderer; the present duke is proud and strictly concerned with the restoration of a status that has no objective relevance in modern society. Hermann's capitalist uncle has no sympathy for such a restoration. He believes that wealth and property should pass to those who know how to manage and increase it in a modern way; in this regard he anticipates the attitude in Freytag's *Soll und Haben*, in which the representative of the merchant ethos and the ethos of the novel remarks that money should roll freely into other hands and the plowshare should pass to those who know better how to guide it.[29] Hermann, who has practically no conscious class identity, gets himself frantically entangled in this affair from not being able to sort out his allegiances. Fancying himself enamoured of the duchess, he allies himself emotionally with the family's cause. For a time he tries to play the role of resident intellectual in the noble household.

As in *Wilhelm Meister*, however, the aristocratic milieu turns out to be a thin veneer of civilization beneath which there is much shallowness and pompous futility. No one is really interested in Hermann's evening lectures on "Poesie und Unterhaltungsliteratur," for they are stopped in the middle when dinner is served, and he must realize that nothing can be seen through to completion in this household. Immermann's critique of the aristocratic milieu proceeds through many dismaying details and weird events, and at one point explodes into a cruel grotesquerie of memorable proportions. The duchess, who has been reading and attempting to translate Scott, decides to put on a tournament with old weapons in honor of the duke's birthday. The imbecilic project is symbolic of the incongruity between phantasy and reality in the aristocratic class, and it turns into total farce. The bourgeois are to be excluded from the event, which so angers them that they decide to have their own, more expensive one. The old armor keeps falling apart and the nobles do not know how to use it. The village musicians employed play the *Marseillaise* because it is the only tune they can think of. While practicing the jousting, the horses refuse to run at one another and the men only succeed in hurting themselves. The horrified duchess cancels the jousting, which, on the day of the event, spoils the duke's pleasure, for that was the part he had been looking forward to. A disaffected participant smuggles in a disguised circus rider, who naturally outrides and outperforms all the unathletic, inauthentic "knights." The result of the affair is universal ill-humor and *blamage*. It is in such things that we see Immermann at his best. The grotesque lurked deeply in his satirical imagination, and when it was released, it could produce unforgettable results. A more imaginative and fierce deflation of aristocratic pretensions is not to be found elsewhere in the literature of the time, yet it all manages to present itself as comedy. Immermann's comedy, if not altogether what today we would call "black," is certainly of a sufficiently dark hue, for this aristocratic foofaraw is by no means all harmless nonsense. Men and horses

131

get hurt in the practice sessions, and, during the tournament, an old servant of the noble house, completely obsessed with the anachronistic ideology of loyal vassalage, attempts to assassinate the uncle who is struggling for possession of the property. The servant exhibits an internalization of what today would be called "false consciousness," a phenomenon upon which Heine had remarked a couple of years earlier in *Die Romantische Schule*.[30]

This uncle is the first modern capitalist in German fiction and *Die Epigonen* is the first German novel to describe a capitalist industrial milieu. This in itself is a breakthrough of importance, even if the industrial setting is more talked about than made palpable to us. Immermann went to some lengths to study industry where it was then most advanced in Germany, in the Wuppertal, at the time when Friedrich Engels was growing up there among the textile mills. It is known that Immermann modeled the uncle on a wealthy large industrialist of his time. He does not intend, however, as Freytag was to do twenty years later, to make his merchant prince into a hero of a healthy new class. It was Immermann's habit to caricature rather than characterize, by the systematic exaggeration of traits, and so it is also with the uncle. He is completely obsessed by rationalistic calculation; beauty, culture, even public honors mean little or nothing to him. The unpoetic rationalist is a familiar whipping-boy from the Romantic tradition, but Immermann is more subtle. For much that the uncle says and does makes genuine sense. He does not, for example, attempt to govern his diversified industries personally, but has put them in the hands of managers who have a considerable degree of executive and financial autonomy. He actually is able to issue his own currency, thus greatly increasing his credit resources, because of his insight that it is not money itself that makes wealth, but productivity. Thus the uncle gives an impression not only of rationality, but even of some degree of wisdom.

But Immermann is not buying it. His hero is impressed by the power of money, but also repelled by the "mathematische Berechnung menschlicher Kraft und menschlichen Fleißes."[31] This would be little more than an expression of Romantic anti-modernism if it were not for the observations on the condition of the workers, who are sickly and emaciated, a terrible contrast to the healthy farmers from whose families the workers have come. The description of the industrial landscape at the beginning of Book VII is a now familiar picture of a natural environment ruined by industry; a depressing pall of smoke hangs over it all. At table there is neither grace nor manners, nor is any wine served, since the uncle uses only what he himself produces; thus the furnishings are confused and without style, while the guests are served undrinkable ale and cider. What Lee B. Jennings called "the ludicrous demon"[32] is lurking here, although it does not become immediately apparent and bursts into view quite suddenly in a grotesque scene that is a fair parallel to the tournament of the aristocrats. It happens at the dedication of the mausoleum the uncle has built for himself and his late wife in the finest spirit of nineteenth-century gingerbread. The ceremony is punctuated by the sound of a machine draining away water that has flooded the building's foundations; the solemn pomposity of the occasion is disturbed in a manner that is peculiarly Immermann's. What then ensues hovers painfully between the melodramatic and the grotesque. The uncle's son Ferdinand is a ne'er-do-well who has conceived a jealous hatred of Hermann. A secret enemy fools Ferdinand into believing that lead acquired at the risk of one's life will make bullets that are infallibly fatal. Following this advice, he falls to his death from the machine draining the mausoleum during the ceremony. Now, as it happens, Ferdinand is not the uncle's son, but the product of an adulterous relationship between the uncle's wife and the prodigal nobleman who had mortgaged his estate to the uncle (this parentage accounts, presumably, for Ferdinand's dissolute uselessness; that is, blue blood can be inherited, but it is not ennobling). The uncle, meanwhile, in his purblind rationalistic way, had always believed in his marriage as a model of bourgeois virtue, and the theme of the preacher's sermon at the dedication is the perfect marriage as a symbol of true ethical purity. In the midst of this irony comes the news of Ferdinand's death. Hermann, who, for reasons too complicated to go into here, is mentally disturbed at this point, endeavors to ease his uncle's grief by explaining that Ferdinand was not his son, whereupon the uncle drops dead.

The artificial complexity of Immermann's plot structure makes analysis tedious, because it is hard to talk about details of the novel without going into endless explanation. In the scene just described, the machinery of plot creaks more deafeningly than the machinery of the water pump. But it is worth mentioning because it shows something about Immermann's peculiar strategies. Every world that he constructs houses the potential of grotesque catastrophe. The ethical underpinnings are never as they seem, and there is a disturbing incongruence between ideology and reality. Immermann should not be regarded as a humorist. A humorist shows us defects and flaws, and we can laugh at them in the shared knowledge that nothing, after all, is perfect. The failings in both the aristocratic world and the early capitalist milieu described in *Die Epigonen* are more than flaws; they are lethal incongruities. Just as the uncle dies when he discovers that a fundamental assumption of his self-understanding was a mirage, so the duke commits a dignified suicide when his claim to his estate and prerogatives turns out to be defective. This is the "negative neutrality" of which Bramsted spoke. Von Wiese says quite correctly that the only just way to see Immermann is to recognize the origin of his works in satire, which is used as a weapon against everyone.[33] Nikolaus Lenau asserted that no German writer was so sarcastic as Immermann.[34]

The universality of his caustic becomes evident in most of the details of what appears at first glance to be a moderate and leisurely book. There is, for example, the character of Wilhelmi, who, though extreme in his restorative, conservative opinions, seems in places to speak with Immermann's own voice.[35] While inducting Hermann into a new degree of a secret society, he delivers a lecture on alienation and *Epigonentum*; men today, he says, feel wretched without any specific cause for suffering; they are adrift because no one has a preordained place in society any more.[36] Hermann is overwhelmed by this wisdom, and indeed the section is often quoted by those seeking the key definition of what Immermann meant. But the ludicrous demon is again not far off; its approach is signalled at the point when Immermann speaks of his two earnest heroes as "Ritter der Wahrheit."[37] In their overexcitement they become drunk, and in an anarchic uproar make a shambles of the "temple." In Book VI, Wilhelmi delivers an anti-Semitic tirade of criticism of Madame Meyer, a Berlin salon Jewess who collects Christian art and pursues an absurd cult of pseudo-Romantic aestheticized Catholicism. "Es ist der Schachergeist ihrer Väter, welcher in der Sammelwut der Tochter fortspukt," he fulminates; Jewish emancipation is the "Erzeugnis sentimentaler Schriftsteller und schlaffer Staatsmänner"; "Im Volke hat sich vielmehr das alte Bewußtsein unzerstört erhalten, daß der Jude nichts tauge"; "Jude bleibt Jude, und der Christ muß sich mit ihnen vorsehn, am meisten, wenn sie sich liebevoll anstellen. Sie sind allesamt freigelassene Sklaven, kriechend, wenn sie etwas haben wollen, trotzig, wenn sie es erlangten oder wenn sie merken, daß es nicht zu erlangen steht."[38] It happens, however, that Wilhelmi is in possession of a piece missing from an altar owned by Madame Meyer, and the result is that he marries her.

I do not think that Immermann meant here to give expression to anti-Semitic opinions — he was, after all, one of Heine's most cordial admirers — nor to suggest that anti-Semitic opinions may easily be made to disappear. Rather, we are in a situation in which any strongly held and eloquently argued opinion or principle can change overnight into its opposite. People, events, and opinions are in a constant unstable flux; many of the characters and events in the novel turn out to be not what they seem, and the boundary of the absurd is easily crossed. Contradictory styles of life and thinking are put into what seems to be a dialectical opposition, but there is no synthesis. This is true, for example, in the hilarious Book V, in which Immermann takes out after his old enemies, the radical students. It begins with the account of a student Hermann had met at the beginning of the novel, who was on his way to join the Greek war of independence, but has instead become a police commissioner who specializes in hunting the "demagogues." On the road, Hermann meets what appears to be a radical nationalist student, who tells sadly of his sufferings in jail; he asks to ride a bit on Hermann's horse, promptly gallops off with it, and turns out to be a Jewish swindler wearing a blond, long-haired wig. At an inn, Hermann finds himself among an ineffable group of radical students. While the innkeeper enhances his income by turning such fellows in to the police, his daughter, named Sophie Christine, calls herself Thusnelda instead and tries to draw Hermann into the conspiracy. The students, with sixty-three talers in their revolutionary fund, are engaged in a solemn debate to decide whether all princes should be murdered. They conclude: "Die bis zur Leipziger Schlacht teutscher Sache noch nicht beigetreten waren, sollen sterben, und denen, die vor diesem Zeitpunkte ihre Pflicht erfüllt haben, geben wir Pension oder Leibzucht, vaterländischer zu reden"; they determine on 500-800 talers a year for a king.[39] Hermann, determined to convert the students, holds a gun on them and gives a rather silly speech of his own, in which he points out that if they want to imitate the past, they should remember that in older times the young were not allowed to speak and they should therefore leave the leadership of the state to the old men.[40] At this point the police come, the students evaporate, and Hermann, of course, is arrested as the "chief demagogue." The arresting officers discuss among themselves whether the Jews or the French are responsible for these revolutionary activities and conclude with familiar folk-logic that the French are all secret Jews anyway.[41]

It is important to remember that Immermann is here treating issues of the greatest contemporary significance. In the 1820's, the years in which the action of the novel takes place, the most severe political stress in Germany was that between the authorities and the nationalistic students. Fundamentally, the rebellious students after the Wars of Liberation were pressing for the transformation of Germany into some semblance of a unified, modern state. Due, in part, at least, to the violent repression to which they were subjected, the students were radicalized into nationalistic, chauvinistic, and often wildly regressive positions that Immermann was not alone in finding ridiculous; some of the plans of Karl Follen's Giessen "Schwarze" were downright fantastic.[42] The lapsed fighter for Greek independence belongs to a context already touched upon in the chapter on Laube (see above, p. 116); from October, 1821, to November, 1822, there had been four hundred foreign volunteers in Greece, half of whom were German;[43] and in 1822 Immermann himself considered going to fight in Greece.[44] But the radicality of Immermann's satire here is striking; he allows no trace of dignity either to the conspiring students or to the political authorities, and Hermann himself cuts a pretty poor figure. Again, it is far from being a genuinely funny situation; Hermann is indeed arrested, and it is only through luck and accident, as is usual in Immermann's plots, that he is extricated from this dangerous predicament. The issues and their possible consequences are not trivial, but the human material available is inadequate to cope with them. Like the tiny hero of Immermann's mock-epic *Tulifäntchen* (1829), modern men are too small for the great challenges confronting them. Consequently, issues of grave importance find no resolution, but simply whirl about in the maelstrom of a directionless society. Similar observations could be made on other parts of *Die Epigonen*, such as a debate between two schoolteachers, one a champion of classical-

humanistic education, the other of relevant, practical schooling —
a large issue at the time. As usual, the representatives of the opposing
positions are obsessed to the point of idiosyncracy, and there is
neither resolution nor synthesis.[45]

A few words need to be said about Medon, the strangest character
of all. He presents himself as a champion of Machiavellian authoritarianism, arguing for a system in which people are given constitutional forms to quiet them while the rule remains as autocratic
as before.[46] He expresses the opinion that all students should be
annihilated because their minds have been poisoned for the rest of
their lives. But a police official observes ominously that Médon
exactly resembles the chief radical conspirator being sought, and,
sure enough, he is arrested as one of the leaders of the demagogues.
It turns out that the Jesuit-educated Medon was neither a radical
nor a reactionary, but what is here called a "pessimist"; pessimism
is described as "das Streben der Faktionen, durch künstliche Hervor-
bringung eines allerschlechtesten Zustandes die Menschen in eine
Wut zu stürzen, welche sie blindlings den Planen [sic] der Bösen
zutreibt."[47] He works through bad advice to create hateful conditions
for the sake of anarchy; Hermann, too, whom he had tricked into
buying a piece of land in Baden, leading him to believe that this
would qualify him for political office, was to be a victim of his
machinations, and his wife, a patriotic enthusiast, was a tool also;
he married her only to be able to open a Berlin salon to pursue his
ends.

Von Wiese calls Medon the most interesting figure of the novel.[48]
He incarnates a valueless destructiveness that seems obliquely related
to Immermann's own satirical strategies. He is a symptom of a society
in which there are no viable guidelines, and he is driven beyond
Immermann's contemplation of the absurd to a nihilistic fury. But
there is here also a representation that the unrest in society is
conspiratorially generated and manipulated for evil and destructive
ends. Medon is the only conspirator who is regarded with any serious-
ness in the novel, and he is an ideological straw man, not correspon-
ding to anything in social or political reality, and he constitutes an
evasion on Immermann's part. The society Immermann describes is
completely adrift; one looks in vain for the stable center. Medon
embraces the obsessiveness of both radical extremes of society
simultaneously and erects the lack of meaningful conviction found

137

everywhere in Immermann's novel into a negative philosophy; he may be meant to objectify symbolically the forces that make contemporary German life so distressing and unsatisfying. But, insofar as Immermann makes Medon wilfully evil, he obscures the dynamic of social processes that otherwise is seen with considerable perspicacity. The injection of a conspiracy theory into this novel is a blunder that misdirects the reader's attention.

The end of *Die Epigonen* has caused some unhappiness and a certain amount of critical debate. By the complexities of the plot, Hermann becomes the heir of both the noble family and his uncle. He determines to dismantle the entire industrial enterprise and return the land to agriculture:

> Jene Anstalten, künstliche Bedürfnisse künstlich zu befriedigen, erscheinen mir geradezu verderblich und schlecht. Die Erde gehört dem Pfluge, dem Sonnenscheine und Regen, welcher das Samenkorn entfaltet, der fleißigen, einfach arbeitenden Hand. Mit Sturmesschnelligkeit eilt die Gegenwart einem trockenen Mechanismus zu; wir können ihren Lauf nicht hemmen, sind aber nicht zu schelten, wenn wir für uns und die Unsrigen ein grünes Plätzchen abzäunen und diese Insel so lange als möglich gegen den Sturz der vorbeirauschenden industriellen Wogen befestigen.[49]

Most critics have taken this ending to be a withdrawal by Immermann from the issues he himself raised; in the midst of the gloom of Hermann's depressed and lacerated mental state a form of Biedermeier resignation introduces itself, a retreat into an agricultural idyll inadequate to the thrust of an innovative social novel. This view has been challenged by Franz Rumler.[50] He points out that the chronological end of the story comes not in the ninth book, but in the eighth, the correspondence between the author and the doctor concerning the accuracy of the account so far. This correspondence is dated 1835, while Book IX concludes in 1829. Rumler observes that the correspondence ends with an optimistic quote from Lamartine to the effect that, although institutions are decaying, the men of the new age are fresh and gay. From this he concludes that Immermann meant his story to end on a similarly optimistic note, that the intention to agriculturize the industrial enterprise arises out of the depression of temporarily unhappy love, which disappears with Hermann's eventual marriage, and that the flight into the idyllic is only a whim. This argument, I believe, is unconvincing. In the first place, it hardly seems a proper method of interpretation to argue from the natural chronology of events against the structure of a novel. Secondly, the peroration of Book VIII is a general statement and is not applied specifically to Hermann. Nowhere is it said that the industries were not dismantled. Nor, in my view, does it matter a great deal whether they were or not. The retreat to an agricultural idyll does end the novel on a resigned and regressive note.

Theodor Mundt criticized it for its lack of confidence in the future and for not showing, as the modern novel should, "daß die Individuen heut besser sind, als die Verhältnisse,"[51] but this simply shows the difference between the Young German notion of how to write a modern, relevant book, and Immermann's realism. The dilemma he poses at the end of the novel is a real one, and it is difficult to see what alternative resolutions were available. A socialist solution at so early a date and by such a writer is, of course, unthinkable. The only imaginable alternative would be the establishment of a cooperative industrial community like those organized by Robert Owen, but it is probably too early in Germany for such ideas. Immermann looked as far ahead as he could into the embryonic capitalist age and saw no solutions; even Hermann's despairing decision is by no means presented as a prescriptive model, for he sees clearly that the development presented by the uncle's industries is ineluctable. Immermann's intellectual honesty was too great to allow him to put an optimistic interpretation on the capitalist development.[52] The final and largest dilemma of the book is, like all the others, bereft of any positive solution.

The question now presents itself whether Immermann's other important novel, *Münchhausen, eine Geschichte in Arabesken* (1839), may also be understood in terms of the concept of "negative neutrality." Critics, as a rule, have not thought so, but I doubt that they are correct. *Münchhausen,* like *Die Epigonen,* was born in satire, but in the process of writing, Immermann decided to oppose to the bottomlessly mendacious world of the great liar Münchhausen a description of a Westphalian peasant society; this section expanded until it came to equal the Münchhausen part in size and weight. The result was a double novel, somewhat reminiscent of Hoffmann's *Kater Murr.*[53] Dimiter Statkow has recently shown that the two parts of the novel are balanced and matched artistically to a degree that had not been previously perceived.[54] Statkow has made a good case that the charge of disunity raised against the novel by older critics is largely unfounded, and that structurally and aesthetically *Münchhausen* is no mean achievement. Certainly, whether one thinks of Immermann's perceptions as genuinely dialectical or just contradictory, the wittily intertwined double novel is more appropriate to his purposes than the *Bildungsroman* scheme of *Die Epigonen*.

We cannot spend much time here with the extremely complicated Münchhausen part, which has been extensively and well analyzed by Windfuhr and von Wiese. It is to a large extent literary and cultural satire, and as such requires a good deal of commentary to be wholly comprehensible. The tendency toward exploding grotesquerie evident in *Die Epigonen* has here become a principle of narration. The quantity of sheer uproar that Immermann can generate is astounding, although the hilarity can become a trifle wearying over several hundred pages. Herman Meyer remarks that "Immermann betreibt die Konfusion mit einer Art pedantischer Gründlichkeit."[55] On the satire itself Meyer observes: "Die Bezüge zwischen der Satire und ihren Objekten sind so grob-direkt und gleichzeitig so rechnerisch-korrekt, daß sich keine plötzliche Überraschung und kein befreiendes Lachen einstellen wollen."[56] On the other hand, Meyer's criticism is too negative. For one thing, to seek for "liberating laughter" in Immermann is to regard him as a humorist, which he is not. Furthermore, the Münchhausen sections are uneven; along with much that most readers could live without, there are passages that in their wit, absurdity, and grotesqueness hardly have a parallel anywhere in nineteenth-century German letters. An example is Münchhausen's proposal to form a *Luftverdichtungsaktienkompanie*, a commercial enterprise for manufacturing building materials out of solidified air. This proposal transforms the old Baron Schnuck from a monomaniac obsessed with the recovery of ancient privileges long since abrogated into a man possessed by the "Teufel der Industrie."[57] He begins to rehearse the role of a satanic corporation counsel, devising crooked defenses to hypothetical cases, and although he is troubled by the question whether a nobleman can lower himself to work for profit, these doubts dissolve in the intoxication of planning an empire of railroads, factories, and great industries. This is the genuine Immermann, skewering everyone and everything simultaneously, while keeping a sharp eye on social and class issues that were then beginning to make their appearance. His satire on excessive complexity of narrative levels in Romantic fiction,[58] and the problem of the incongruence of consciousness and reality and of an individualism that has lost its anchor in society and become catapulted into total, solipsistic eccentricity[59] are among the significant themes that are developed with remarkable resourcefulness.

For our purposes, however, it will be more helpful to give some attention to the other part of the novel, which became widely known under the title of Book II, Chapter 3, Der Oberhof. About twenty years after Münchhausen was published, the Oberhof part was separated from the Münchhausen part as an independent book, and by 1930 it had seen eighty editions, as compared to twenty for the novel as a whole.[60] This procedure had an ideological motive. Der Oberhof stands at or near the beginning of the genre of Dorfgeschichten, tales of village life that in the early part of the century were worthwhile developments in realism. Hebbel said that, with Der Oberhof, Immermann had hurled "ein wahrer neuer Weltteil in die Literatur,"[61] and Annette von Droste-Hülshoff was pleased to have Die Judenbuche compared with it.[62] But, in the course of the nineteenth century, the Dorfgeschichte became a sentimental, mendacious form veiling rather than revealing genuine social realities, and the tradition flowed into the Blut und Boden literature of noxious memory. By removing Der Oberhof from its original context of social criticism, Immermann's work was falsified and trivialized into this direction. Men of taste and sense have naturally always deplored this. Raabe complained that "das edle deutsche Volk sich den Münchhausen aus dem Münchhausen, um ihn sich mundgerecht zu machen, gestrichen hat oder hat streichen lassen," and remarked fairly, "wir haben uns ein Unterhaltungsstücklein aus einem weisen, bitterernsten Buche zurecht gemacht."[63] Hofmannsthal called the surgery criminal and refused to include Der Oberhof in his anthology of great German stories.[64]

Der Oberhof is an attempt on Immermann's part to break out of his persistent negativism. He wished to oppose to the bedlam of modern mendacity and eccentricity a society still organically intact, unalienated, self-reliant, and healthy — a genuine community welded together by allegiance to tradition and not subject to interference by others in running its own communal life. For this he chose a community of prosperous Westphalian peasants, dominated by

141

the *Hofschulze*, the richest farmer, who functions as elder, guardian of tradition, master of rites, and ruler. The virtues of the *Hofschulze* and his people are strictly conservative ones: self-sufficiency, frugality, modest demands on life, harmony with the natural cycle, and resistance to all change. Windfuhr has questioned whether this dialectical strategy was successful, arguing that Immermann has again just set out unresolved dichotomies: "In der Tat führt die säuberliche Trennung der Gesellschaft in eine heile und eine kranke Hälfte zur Verzeichnung nach beiden Seiten hin: die satirische wird zur Karikatur und die bäuerliche zum Idealrefugium."[65]

This comment, however, begs an important question about the ideality of the refuge. Certainly Immermann was convinced that he was producing a positive counterweight to the negativity of his satire; he wrote to Ferdinand Freiligrath as the novel was nearing completion in 1839: "Das positive Element tritt in den folgenden Bänden immer stärker auf";[66] to his fiancée he wrote at about the same time: "Zwischen allen Fratzen grünen die Wiesen des Oberhofes, tragen als liebliche Frucht das Verständnis des Jägers und Lisbeths."[67] In another letter to her he went so far as to say, "Im Münchhausen wird positiv ausgesprochen, was in den Epigonen mehr nur angedeutet ist" and "in der süßesten Gestalt vollendet sich meine Versöhnung mit Welt und Leben, der kalte Spott zieht wie ein gebrannter Schatten in den Tartarus und der Fluch wird von meinem Haupte genommen."[68] For us to judge whether this was truly the case, Immermann would have had to live longer. The question is, can the *Oberhof* section be seen in this light? Is the curse even apparently off Immermann's head?

The fact is that critics have long tended to sense something wrong about this assessment of the *Oberhof* section, without being altogether clear about what it is. Werner Kohlschmidt, in his instructive comparison of Immermann and Gotthelf, was the first, to my knowledge, to feel uneasy. He notes how rigidly the *Oberhof* world is tied to tradition, and comments: "Nähme man der bäuerlichen Welt die Sitte, und wenn sie rational gesehen noch so unsinnig, überlebt, ja unbürgerlich gefährlich erscheinen mag, so bräche man ihr das Rückgrat. Was aber ist dann noch Halt gegen die bedrohlich aufkommende Stadt?"[69] He also points out perceptively that it is not the peasants themselves who define the meaning of the peasant community, but the local clergyman, a character who will concern

142

us presently.[70] Von Wiese sees that there are odd, unbalanced characters in the *Oberhof* world, and that something berserk emerges in the *Hofschulze* when Oswald unwittingly upsets the order of ritual and the *Hofschulze* insists upon a duel to the death with axes.[71] Von Wiese also points out that although class propriety is maintained with fanatic insistence in the *Oberhof* world, the final marriage between the noble Oswald and the foundling Lisbeth goes directly against the rules of class and convention.[72] Windfuhr takes us a step farther by observing that Immermann gives us a picture of the peasant world through the eyes of a city man.[73] Michael Scherer has written that the *Oberhof* world is endangered, not from the outside, but from the rigidity within: "Nur scheinbar ist er [the *Hofschulze*] als Bauer gegen die schleichende Krise dieser Gesellschaft gefeit; tatsächlich gerät er hart an den Rand einer Scheinexistenz."[74] Statkow, who has defended the unity of the novel, argues that the *Oberhof* is not only ideal, but also dark and tragic and not free of conflict and criticism.[75] Finally, William McClain, while explicating the heroic stature of the *Hofschulze*, is obliged to note the "hideboundness" of his character and "the danger inherent in such a mentality."[76]

I would go a step farther than these critics and argue that the *Oberhof* section is not an ideal, but is subject to the same "negative neutrality" we have detected elsewhere in Immermann's novels, and I would regard this as significant because it is a matter of record that he did not intend it so. For he has been tripped up by his penchant for caricature. It is certainly possible to present a society living by traditional values and ritual symbols, but when these traditions and rituals are presented as surviving for their own sake alone, defended with fanatic persistence and without a clearly integrated function in the life and survival of the society, then that condition can no longer be called organic. In the *Oberhof*, the link between symbol and social reality has already been broken. The "sword of Charlemagne," which is the symbol of the *Hofschulze's* authority, is a fraud, and the *Hofschulze* forces a visiting scholar to certify it fraudulently. This is a clear case of the kind of obsessive eccentricity and mendacity that plagues the Münchhausen world; the *Hofschulze*, by knowingly maintaining a ritualistic fraud, has already departed from the naive and organic consciousness. The fanaticism with which both ritual and the authority of the *Hofschulze* are enforced is a clear sign that this society is on the verge of cracking to pieces. The hierarchical relationships are maintained to such an extreme that it cannot be said they enhance humane values. The story of the so-called "Patriotenkaspar" is a case in point; as a young man, full of egalitarian zeal, he wooed the daughter of the *Hofschulze*, an ambition to which his station did not entitle him. The son of the *Hofschulze* put out his eye, whereupon Kaspar killed him and has lived on as a vengeful pariah. It is he who creates a crisis by hiding the sword without which, the *Hofschulze* in his fetishistic rigidity believes, the governance of the community cannot be maintained. Statkow points out that Immermann, whether he intended to or not, shows here the beginning of a proletarian subclass of peasants: "Die Macht des Hofschulzen ist für Kaspar die Macht der Reichen."[77] What Immermann presents is a kind of rural Mafia, governed anachronistically by the rituals of the medieval *Vehmgericht*, rigidly stratified, egocentric, obsessed with ritual, and incapable of humane justice.

One explanation for this is found in Windfuhr's perception that Immermann viewed with the eyes of a city man. He lived in cities all his life, and, during most of his time in Düsseldorf, he made every effort to get himself transferred to Berlin; only towards the end of his life did he become reconciled to the smaller town. Windfuhr remarks that some of the most acutely observed materials in *Die Epigonen* are those in Books VI and VII dealing with Berlin society.[78] For the city man, the peasant rituals necessarily take on a quaint aspect: the ritualized, wooden moralizing; the nine vests worn by the *Hofschulze* both because tradition requires it and to show that he can afford it; the observation at the wedding scene that the bridesmaid's bouquet stinks; the general pretentiousness. In this regard the figure of the *Diakonus*, the city-born pastor who has become acclimated to the world of the *Oberhof*, is of importance. Although he participates in the wedding ritual, he has sufficient distance from it to warn Oswald not to laugh. In a curious passage in Book V, Chapter 4, it is said of the *Diakonus* that he knows about modern critical doubts in matters of religion, but he himself is untouched by them; he has made a decision in favor of conventional piety — but here, as with the *Hofschulze's* awareness of the fraudulence of the sword, one can see the fissures opening in the modern consciousness. In Book II, Chapter 10, the *Diakonus* gives a long discourse on the immortal folk, the free energies of the nation, "tiefsinnig,

144

unschuldig, treu, tapfer."[79] In the city he had suffered *Weltschmerz* and had wanted to reform Christianity, but now he has found true human relations among the peasants. Von Wiese has pointed out wryly that this discourse "hat freilich mit dem beschreibenden Realismus der Oberhofdarstellung höchstens indirekt etwas zu tun."[80] The long and the short of it is that, if Immermann intended to present the *Oberhof* as an ideological counterweight to his customary "negative neutrality," he failed; the perceptions of the modern city man intrude too easily, and the ludicrous demon is not to be exorcized by such means.

In considering the relevance of Immermann to a discussion of Young Germany, the question of realism offers itself as one possible approach. In some ways, he seems to have been more directly conscious of the issue of realism than the Young Germans were. "Realismus," as Windfuhr has pointed out, was one of Immermann's favorite words.[81] It always meant to him a turning of attention to the world without. At a very early stage he mounted a criticism of Romantic inwardness; in a draft of a review of Heine's *Tragödien, nebst einem lyrischen Intermezzo* (1823), he wrote: "Man hat dieser Zeit zum Vorwurf gemacht, daß sie, nach der Außenwelt gerichtet, sich in Oberflächlichkeit zu verlieren drohe; uns scheint jedoch, daß dieser Tadel die Dichtkunst unserer Tage wenigstens nicht treffe, daß diese vielmehr im Gegenteil sich zu einer einseitigen Innerlichkeit neige."[82] And he goes on: "der Trieb zur Selbstbetrachtung wird unwiderstehlich und gibt mehr und mehr das Material zur Dichtung her, je trüber die Augen der poetischen Psychologen für die Konstruktionen der Welt und des Lebens an sich werden."[83] Immermann himself worried a good deal whether he was in touch with this external reality. Windfuhr points out how his experience with legal affairs sharpened his sense for the logic of real events,[84] and Rumler has analyzed three realistic aspects of *Die Epigonen*: the subjective narrative perspective of the author, which yields credibility; Immermann's sense of the causal relationship between reality and literature; and "Verwissenschaftlichung," by which Rumler means Immermann's response to the scientific age in trying to be expert on what is described in the novel.[85] For example, the description of the Oberhof is prefaced by three paragraphs of a description of Westphalian peasant society quoted verbatim from a scholarly book. In the *Oberhof* section, Immermann explicitly opposes idyllic idealization of the peasant life; in Book II, Chapter 3, it is pointed out that "das ästhetische Landschaftsgefühl ist schon ein Produkt der Überfeinerung,"[86] that is, of the city man estranged from nature; it is not sensed by the peasants who actually live in nature. In another place the *Diakonus* explains to a courtier that the peasants are not "gemütlich," for they have no time and are not "Naturmenschen" in the Rousseauistic sense; they are strictly bound by tradition and caste hierarchy.[87] Even the peasant custom of premarital sex is presented, with the remark that writers of idylls had overlooked it.[88] Those who have published *Der Oberhof* separately often have overlooked it, also.

It is true, to be sure, that Immermann never made a clean break with the Romantic tradition, as his life-long orientation on Tieck as his literary model shows. But, by various means, he combatted the Romantic hypnosis from which most writers of his time suffered. The most prominent of these means is satire. An example is his parody of the Sternean tradition of the novel of confused chronology (and Pückler-Muskau's resuscitation of it) in *Münchhausen*, the first book of which begins with chapters 11-15, which are followed by a correspondence with the bookbinder discussing the faddishness that requires such confusion, whereupon Chapters 1-10 follow. Another example is the *Märchen*, "Die Wunder im Spessart," that Immermann, following Romantic practice, rather awkwardly inserted into Book V. It is, in fact, a kind of modernized anti-*Märchen*. The princess has been put under a spell by — a wicked textile mill owner! A scholar, in attempting to save her, plunges deeply into the mystical secrets of nature, but only grows mad and very old in the realm of the unreal. A knight releases her by a straightforward kiss; thus the right path is taken by the worldly knight, not by the dark seeker, who is unable to find the key to true awakening.

For a long time Immermann endeavored to maintain a link with idealism. Von Wiese comments of the period before *Die Epigonen*: "Noch scheint die Flucht aus der profanen Realität möglich zu sein, noch gibt es einen 'Immermann in der Idee', der an die eigene geistige Selbstverwirklichung glaubt. Aber die dämonische Gewalt der Natur und das Vielgestaltige und Widersprüchliche der modernen Gesellschaft sind bereits so mächtig geworden, daß die Dinge ihren eigenen Anspruch erheben und die Forderung einer wahrhaftigeren und menschwürdigeren Kunstwelt weitgehend nur ideolo-

146

gisch proklamiert wird."[89] Furthermore, von Wiese notes an important shift away from the Romantic function of irony: "Ironie ist bei Immermann stets der Satire verwandt. Sie zeigt den Abstand zwischen Ideal und Wirklichkeit, aber nicht zugunsten des Ideals, sondern zugunsten der Wirklichkeit. Denn das von der Wirklichkeit abgespaltene Ideal ist zur 'Lüge', zur fixen Idee, zum Wahn geworden."[90] This point is of exceptional importance and shows most clearly the parallels between Immermann and Heine. The orientation on objective, external reality is stronger and more purposeful in Immermann than it is in the Young Germans; it is a process similar to the one we noted as an exceptional example in Laube's *Die Krieger* and leads to similar virtues in the writing of fiction; Rumler has also argued that the interpenetration of social spheres with one another and a certain stylistic tendency to simultaneity of narration point ahead to Gutzkow's *Ritter vom Geiste*.[91] But it must be said on balance that Immermann's realism is a tendency, not an achievement. Hans Mayer, in drawing a parallel between Immermann and Balzac, argues that the opaqueness of the sociological situation itself was responsible for this: "die Zustände, die geschildert werden, um den Übergangscharakter dieser Epoche zu kennzeichnen, sind weitaus unreifer, schmächtiger, undeutlicher in ihrer Entwicklungsrichtung als bei Balzac. Das liegt nicht an mangelnder Kunst des Erzählers Immermann, sondern an mangelnder Schärfe der gesellschaftlichen Konturen im damaligen Deutschland."[92]

This view has already been discussed in the introductory essay. It appears to be supported empirically by the situation of the novel generally in Immermann's time. His own turn to external reality yields disparateness and chaos, manageable only by a rather atomistic satire. He lacks the disciplined, ordered consciousness that makes the social realism of Balzac, Stendhal, Flaubert possible. One might say that the Young Germans possessed a superfluity of ideological conviction and too little sense of the objective disparateness and complexity of the real world, whereas with Immermann it was the other way around. Von Wiese has made an effort to find solid ground in Immermann's mind; he argues that the resolution of accident and contradiction is in the hidden religious order in the hearts of men, in love and friendship, and in the reality of things, and that salvation in an uncertain time is in the individual who creates a new order in marriage and founding a family.[93] It is true that Immermann retained a religious orientation that grew stronger toward the end of his life, and true also that both of his important novels end in love and hopeful marriage. But such views are more evasive than productive for a social realist. Von Wiese himself is obliged to point out that, except for the two denouements, the marriages in Immermann's novels tend to be very shaky,[94] as is everything else.

Despite the *Chiliastische Sonette* (1832), which gives a Christian expression to hopefulness for the future,[95] and the massive effort to formulate a philosophical world-view in his quasi-*Faust, Merlin*, of the same year, Immermann was a bewildered and groping thinker, without much of the prophetic gift. Herman Meyer observed that "ein anderes ist es, die Diagnose einer Zeitkrankheit zu stellen, ein anderes, diese wirklich von sich abzuschütteln."[96] Lee B. Jennings sees the nature of Immermann's perceptions as closely connected to what I, following Bramsted, have called "negative neutrality": "Immermann... recognizes the power of decay and the prevalence of chaos and is under no illusions as to their role as an integral part of all existence. This recognition makes it extremely difficult for him to gain a foothold in his struggle to attain positive values."[97] Theodor Mundt, however, saw the problem somewhat differently, in a way that shows the contrast with the Young Germans: "Sein Roman [*Die Epigonen*] hat darin eine materielle Härte, daß er, ohne bis auf die allgemeinen Zerwürfnisse und Hemmnisse der Ideen zu gehen, die Zerfahrenheit der modernen Charaktere nur als eine individuelle Haltungslosigkeit vor Augen führt. Das heißt, die Individualität einer Epoche mißachten, ohne das Wesen der Epoche selbst, ihre ehrwürdigen Schmerzen, ihre berechtigten Hoffnungen, ihre Anwartschaft auf die Zukunft, zu ergründen."[98]

Mundt is mistaken to suggest that Immermann completely individualizes epochal issues. The relationship between individuality and society in his writing is a complex and strained one that cannot be gone into here, except to say that he certainly did attempt a kind of typological representation. It is Mundt's objection to the lack of future orientation that is important for our purposes, the utopianism out of which would arise a "Prinzip Hoffnung" in Ernst Bloch's sense, and which the Young Germans, at least initially, had to a substantially greater extent. Hans-Georg Gadamer has argued that "in der Tat lebt in dem Dichter ein Glaube an die Zukunft, die sich aus den abgelebten Gestalten der Vergangenheit und insbesondere aus der Reinigung von den Abstraktionen, in denen sich das erhitzte Zeitbewußtsein herumtreibt, zu einer lebensvollen Wirklichkeit erheben werde."[99] But other critics have read Immermann differently. Emil Grütter, though not the most subtle of Immermann's interpreters, has said that his world "kennt keine Zukunft. Die Gegenwart aber ist bestimmt durch eine Vergangenheit, die ihrerseits wieder nichts oder doch nur eine Schale ist";[100] and Windfuhr has drawn the comparison with Young Germany: "[Immermann] schließt sich nur während einer kurzen Phase mit seinen chiliastischen Ideen dem jungdeutschen Futurismus an,"[101] and in this I think Windfuhr is correct. The *Chiliastische Sonette* are no more than a vague expression of a secularized Messianic hope, and otherwise Immermann's utopias, like *Der Oberhof*, are not only regressive, but so clearly threatened by the ineluctable course of history that they offer scant hope for the future. Jennings is probably right in seeing the dark vision as the most fundamental one in Immermann: "... pessimism displays a fluctuating level of prominence in all his works, and it has the peculiar feature that it seems to consist of concentric layers. The peripheral layer manifests itself readily (as the representation of futile, incongruous life), but the more fearfully nihilistic core often remains hidden."[102] That such was probably not Immermann's intention matters little; the result shows only that his sensitivity to the torment of his age was greater than his resources for imposing a positive, forward-looking order on them.

It is likely in any case that Immermann did not share the Young German faith in the power of literature to reform or improve society. The concept of *Zeitgeist* did not mean the same thing to him, for it did not have the same pregnant, progressive, and hopeful content that it did for the Young Germans and Young Hegelians. Rumler has remarked perceptively: "Für Immermann hatte die Zeit nichts 'Offenbarendes'. Sein Zeitgeist-Begriff, inbesondere im 'Münchhausen', stand dem Zeitgeist-Begriff Gotthelfs näher, nämlich im Sinne von Zeitauswüchsen."[103] The conservative satirist measures by norms of moderation against which nearly all phenomena of an agitated time take on the quality of the absurd. On the other hand, Immermann may have had a more realistic sense of the nature of literature. He reports on a conversation with Gutzkow in which the latter argued the reform of social conditions by means of great social literary works, to which Immermann replied: "Die Literatur und Poesie erzeugt die Zustände nicht, sondern sie geht aus denselben hervor,"[104] thereby aligning himself with the distinction Gutzkow himself made elsewhere between literature as "Vorrede" and as "Register" (see above, p. 15). This more modest sense of the social determinism of literature barred Immermann from the enthusiastic reformism of the Young Germans, but enabled him to move farther along the road to realism than they were able to go.

NOTES

For each chapter, first references are given in full, thereafter by short titles. Titles of unpublished dissertations are in quotation marks, those of printed dissertations are italicized. The following short titles are used throughout:

Butler, *The Saint-Simonian Religion* = E. M. Butler, *The Saint-Simonian Religion in Germany. A Study of the Young German Movement.* Cambridge, Eng.: Cambridge University Press, 1926. Reprinted, New York: Howard Fertig, Inc., 1968.

Houben, *Gutzkow-Funde* = H. H. Houben, *Gutzkow-Funde. Beiträge zur Litteratur- und Kulturgeschichte des neunzehnten Jahrhunderts.* Berlin: Arthur L. Wolff, 1901.

Houben, *JdSuD* = H. H. Houben, *Jungdeutscher Sturm und Drang. Ergebnisse und Studien.* Leipzig: F. A. Brockhaus, 1911.

Houben, *Verbotene Literatur* = Heinrich Hubert Houben, *Verbotene Literatur von der klassischen Zeit bis zur Gegenwart. Ein kritisch-historisches Lexikon über verbotene Bücher, Zeitschriften und Theaterstücke, Schriftsteller und Verleger.* 2 vols., Berlin: E. Rowohlt, 1924; Bremen: K. Schünemann, 1928. Reprinted, Hildesheim: Georg Olms, 1965.

Houben, *Zeitschriften des Jungen Deutschlands*, I = Heinrich Hubert Houben, *Zeitschriften des Jungen Deutschlands.* Veröffentlichungen der Deutschen Bibliographischen Gesellschaft, *Bibliographisches Repertorium*, Vol. III. Berlin: B. Behr, 1906. Reprinted, Hildesheim and New York: Georg Olms, 1970.

Koopmann, *Das Junge Deutschland* = Helmut Koopmann. *Das Junge Deutschland. Analyse seines Selbstverständnisses.* Stuttgart: Metzler, 1970.

Wienbarg, *Ästhetische Feldzüge* = Ludolf Wienbarg, *Ästhetische Feldzüge*, ed. Walter Dietze. Berlin and Weimar: Aufbau-Verlag, 1964.

I. INTRODUCTION

1 Harold Jantz, "Sequence and Continuity in Nineteenth-Century German Literature," *Germanic Review*, 38 (1963), 27.
2 Jost Hermand, ed., *Das Junge Deutschland. Texte und Dokumente*, Reclams Universal-Bibliothek, Nos. 8703-07 (Stuttgart: Philipp Reclam Jun., 1966).
3 Koopmann, *Das Junge Deutschland*, p. 23. Friedrich Sengle, *Biedermeierzeit. Deutsche Literatur im Spannungsfeld zwischen Restauration und Revolution 1815-1848*, I (Stuttgart: Metzler, 1971), p. 160, has come to the same conclusion.
4 Wulf Wülfing, "Schlagworte des Jungen Deutschland," *Zeitschrift für deutsche Sprache*, 21 (1965), 42-59, 160-174; 22 (1966), 36-56, 154-178; 23 (1967), 48-82, 166-177; 24 (1968), 60-71, 161-183; 25 (1969), 96-115, 175-179; 26 (1970), 60-83, 162-175.
5 Cf. Reinhold Grimm, "Romanhaftes und Novellistisches in Laubes *Reisenovellen*," *Germanisch-romanische Monatsschrift*, N.S. 18 (1968), 299-303.
6 Koopmann, *Das Junge Deutschland*, p. 71.
7 Theodor Mundt, *Moderne Lebenswirren* (Leipzig: Gebrüder Reichenbach, 1834), p. 152.
8 C. P. Magill, "Young Germany: A Revaluation," *German Studies Presented to Leonard Ashley Willoughby*, ed. J. Boyd (Oxford: Blackwell, 1952), pp. 108-109.
9 David Daiches, *Critical Approaches to Literature* (New York: Norton, 1956), pp. 266-267.
10 Magill, "Young Germany: A Revaluation," p. 109.
11 Karl Gutzkow, *Briefe eines Narren an eine Närrin* (Hamburg: Hoffmann und Campe, 1832), p. 5.
12 Karl Gutzkow, *Zur Philosophie der Geschichte* (Hamburg: Hoffmann und Campe, 1836), p. 163. It is not without interest that John Stuart Mill expressed a very similar view of the English intellectual scene in 1831. See René Wellek, *A History of Modern Criticism 1750-1950* (New Haven and London: Yale University Press, 1955-), III, 86.
13 *Zeitung für die elegante Welt*, 1 January 1833, No. 1, p. 1. Sengle has written an extremely interesting and compelling chapter on the whole subject of "Symbol, Begriffsallegorie, Naturpersonifikation, Mythologie" (*Biedermeierzeit*, I, 292-367), and on the occasional efforts of progressive writers to combat irrational symbolism. Sengle shows a reasonable respect for the tradition of rhetoric of which this problem is a part. But he is right to say that it left writers in "einer in sich selbst kreisenden Sprache" and that

152

the Young Germans suffered from it even more than the strictly "Biedermeier" writers (ibid., I, 407). Perhaps one of the main failures of the Young Germans was not to have put this metaphorical and organistic-symbolic style out of the world once and for all.

14 Cf. Barbara Hernstein Smith, "Poetry as Fiction," *New Literary History*, 2 (1971), 259-281.

15 Ian Watt, *The Rise of the Novel. Studies in Defoe, Richardson and Fielding* (Berkeley: University of California Press, 1967), p. 60.

16 Friedrich Sengle, "Voraussetzungen und Erscheinungsformen der deutschen Restaurationsliteratur," *Deutsche Vierteljahrsschrift*, 30 (1956), 292. Cf. Sengle, "Der Romanbegriff in der ersten Hälfte des 19. Jahrhunderts," *Arbeiten zur deutschen Literatur 1750-1850* (Stuttgart: Metzler, 1965), esp. pp. 185-186. Sengle's *Biedermeierzeit* appeared too late to have the influence on my studies that it deserves. By restricting "realism" to the programmatic realism inaugurated by Julian Schmidt and Freytag and denying that "empiricist" aspects can be a typological sign of realism (I, 257-291), Sengle insists that realism should not be spoken of before 1850 and denies it especially to Young Germany. Rather than debate this difficult matter here, I should like merely to make two points. First, the evidence accumulated in this essay ought to suggest some moderation of Sengle's strictness. Second, because of his toleration of the harmonizing, sentimentalizing, and socially accommodated character of post-mid-century realism, Sengle does not share my regret at the loss of the critical faculty in the writer's consciousness involved in this process and the resulting trivialization of much German realism. See my essay on Laube below (Chapter V, pp. 104-126).

17 Günter Bliemel, "Die Auffassung des Jungen Deutschlands von Wesen und Aufgabe des Dichters und der Dichtung" (diss. Berlin, 1955), p. 92. A similar argument concerning the lack of realism in Germany was popularized by Erich Auerbach in the chapter "Miller the Musician" in *Mimesis* (Garden City: Doubleday, 1953), pp. 398-399.

18 Walther Roer, *Soziale Bewegung und politische Lyrik im Vormärz* (diss. Münster, 1933), pp. 13, 29-30. Even in the 1840's, when literature was becoming completely politicized, there was not a very strong sense of the poor as a class: "Es schien, als ob es nur ein Zufall sei, daß es Mangel und Besitzlosigkeit gab. Ein wenig mehr Mitleid, ein wenig mehr den Beutel geöffnet, und die ganze Armut wäre aufgehoben; aber die Reichen seien hartherzig und wollten von ihren Vorrechten nicht lassen. Die Vorstellung, die man sich von den Armen machte, verrät, daß man nur an verarmte Bürgerliche dachte" (ibid., p. 178). Certain poems of Herwegh and Freiligrath are important exceptions to this generalization.

19 Quoted by Hartmut Steinecke, ed., *Theorie und Technik des Romans im 19. Jahrhundert* (Tübingen: Niemeyer, 1970), p. 3.

20 Wienbarg, *Ästhetische Feldzüge*, p. 86.

21 Ibid., p. 146.

22 Ibid., p. 16.

23 Ibid., p. 11.

24 Ibid., p. 59.

25 Ibid., p. 94.

[26] Viktor Schweizer, *Ludolf Wienbarg. Beiträge zu einer Jungdeutschen Ästhetik* (diss. Leipzig, 1897), pp. 86-87.

[27] Quoted ibid., p. 130.

[28] Gerhard Burkhardt, "Ludolf Wienbarg als Ästhetiker und Kritiker. Seine Entwicklung und seine geistesgeschichtliche Stellung" (diss. Hamburg, 1956), p. 111.

[29] Wienbarg, *Ästhetische Feldzüge*, p. 112.

[30] Ibid., p. 83.

[31] Ibid., p. 88.

[32] Ibid., p. 130. Wienbarg's emphasis.

[33] Ibid., p. 131.

[34] Theodor Mundt, *Geschichte der Literatur der Gegenwart. Friedrich von Schlegel's Geschichte der alten und neuen Literatur, bis auf die neueste Zeit fortgeführt* (Berlin: M. Simion, 1842), p. 41. Mundt's phrase is derived from Schlegel.

[35] Ibid., p. 306.

[36] Else von Eck, *Die Literaturkritik in den Hallischen und Deutschen Jahrbüchern (1838-1842)*, Germanische Studien, No. 42 (Berlin: E. Ebering, 1926), p. 34.

[37] Sengle, *Biedermeierzeit*, I, 34-47.

[38] Karl Gutzkow, *Maha Guru. Geschichte eines Gottes* (Stuttgart and Tübingen: J. G. Cotta, 1833), II, 72-74.

[39] Ibid., II, 131.

[40] Karl Gutzkow, *Aus der Zeit und dem Leben* (Leipzig: Brockhaus, 1844), p. 115.

[41] Heinrich Laube, *Gesammelte Werke in fünfzig Bänden*, ed. Heinrich Hubert Houben with Albert Hänel (Leipzig: M. Hesse, 1908-09), VI, 35-36.

[42] *Zeitung für die elegante Welt*, 23 May 1833, No. 100, p. 398.

[43] Ibid.

[44] Ibid., 8 August 1833, No. 153, p. 609.

[45] Ludolf Wienbarg, *Wanderungen durch den Thierkreis* (Hamburg: Hoffmann und Campe, 1835), p. viii.

[46] Ludolf Wienbarg, *Quadriga* (Hamburg: Hoffmann und Campe, 1840), p. vii

[47] Ibid.

[48] Houben, *JdSuD*, pp. 194-195.

[49] Ludolf Wienbarg, *Zur neuesten Literatur* (Mannheim: Löwenthal, 1835), p. 31.

[50] Jeffrey L. Sammons, "Ludolf Wienbarg and Norway," *Scandinavian Studies*, 42 (1970), pp. 19-21.

[51] Wienbarg, *Wanderungen durch den Thierkreis*, p. 248.

[52] Ibid., p. 254.

[53] Ibid, p. 256.

[54] Ibid., p. 258.

[55] Ibid., p. 260.

[56] Ibid., p. 77.

[57] Ibid., p. 80.

[58] Ibid., p. 93.

[59] Ibid., p. 94.

[60] E.g., J. Dresch, "Schiller et la jeune Allemagne," *Revue germanique*, 1 (1905), 579; Schweizer, *Ludolf Wienbarg*, p. 55; Houben, *JdSuD*, p. 188; Butler, *The Saint-Simonian Religion*, pp. 409, 412-419; Burkhardt, "Ludolf Wienbarg," pp. 42-43; Rudolf Kayser, "Ludolf Wienbarg und der Kampf um den Historismus," *German Quarterly*, 29 (1956), 71-74.

[61] Wienbarg, *Ästhetische Feldzüge*, "Anhang," pp. 311-312.

[62] Wienbarg, *Zur neuesten Literatur*, pp. 8-9.

[63] Sengle, *Biedermeierzeit*, I, 165-167.

[64] Karl Gutzkow, *Deutschland am Vorabend seines Falles oder seiner Größe*, ed. Walter Boehlich, sammlung insel 36 (Frankfurt: Insel Verlag, 1969), p. 140.

[65] Bliemel, "Die Auffassung des Jungen Deutschlands," p. 149.

[66] Houben, *JdSuD*, p. 488.

[67] Burkhardt, "Ludolf Wienbarg," p. 2.

[68] Houben, *JdSuD*, p. 63.

[69] Karl Glossy, *Literarische Geheimberichte aus dem Vormärz*. Separatabdruck aus dem *Jahrbuch der Grillparzer-Gesellschaft*, Vols. 21-23 (Vienna: C. Konegen, 1912), I, xcv.

[70] See Friedrich C. Sell, *Die Tragödie des deutschen Liberalismus* (Stuttgart: Deutsche Verlags-Anstalt, 1953), p. 174.

[71] Houben, *JdSuD*, p. 85.

[72] Ulla Otto, *Die literarische Zensur als Problem der Soziologie der Politik* (Stuttgart: Ferdinand Enke Verlag, 1968), p. 128.

[73] Ibid.

1 Koopmann, *Das Junge Deutschland*, p. 37.
2 Eitel Wolf Dobert, *Karl Gutzkow und seine Zeit* (Bern and Munich: Francke Verlag, 1968). Dietze's account of Wienbarg in Wienbarg, *Ästhetische Feldzüge*, could also be mentioned, as it tells nearly all that is known about him.
3 Butler, *The Saint-Simonian Religion*, p. 258.
4 J. Dresch, *Le Roman social en Allemagne (1850-1900). Gutzkow — Freytag — Spielhagen — Fontane* (Paris: Félix Alcan, 1913), p. 3.
5 Houben, *Gutzkow-Funde*, p. vi.
6 Dobert, *Karl Gutzkow*, pp. 61, 107-108.
7 Karl Gutzkow, *Zur Philosophie der Geschichte* (Hamburg: Hoffmann und Campe, 1836), pp. iii-iv.
8 Ibid., p. v.
9 René Wellek, *A History of Modern Criticism 1750-1950* (New Haven and London: Yale University Press, 1955-), III, 203.
10 Walter Hof, *Pessimistisch-nihilistische Strömungen in der deutschen Literatur vom Sturm und Drang bis zum Jungen Deutschland* (Tübingen: Niemeyer, 1970), p. 183.
11 Houben, *JdSuD*, p. 27.
12 Ibid., p. 29.
13 Houben, *Gutzkow-Funde*, p. 58.
14 Houben, *Zeitschriften des Jungen Deutschlands*, I, col. 58.
15 Houben, *Verbotene Literatur*, II, 299-300.
16 Karl Gutzkow, *Götter, Helden, Don-Quixote. Abstimmungen zur Beurtheilung der literarischen Epoche* (Hamburg: Hoffmann und Campe, 1838), p. 331.
17 Ibid.
18 Ibid., pp. 352-353.
19 Ibid., p. 378.
20 Ibid., p. 389.
21 Houben, *Gutzkow-Funde*, p. 56.
22 Houben, *Zeitschriften des Jungen Deutschlands*, I, col. 47.
23 Houben, *JdSuD*, p. 659.
24 Ernst Elster, "H. Heine und H. Laube. Mit sechsundvierzig bisher ungedruckten Briefen Laubes an Heine," *Deutsche Rundschau*, 135 (1908), 93-95. Whatever Heine and Laube may have written, nothing seems to have appeared in print.
25 To Varnhagen, 14 October 1835, Houben, *Gutzkow-Funde*, p. 60.

26 Karl Glossy, *Literarische Geheimberichte aus dem Vormärz*, Separatabdruck aus dem *Jahrbuch der Grillparzer-Gesellschaft*, Vols. 21-23 (Vienna: C. Konegen, 1912), I, 47. Houben (*Verbotene Literatur*, I, 264) sensationalized this information slightly by saying merely that the elderly gentlemen had been reported to be "lüstern."

27 All the page numbers in parentheses in this essay are references to the photographic reprint of the original edition of *Wally, die Zweiflerin*, ed. Jost Schillemeit (Göttingen: Vandenhoeck & Ruprecht, 1965).

28 Dobert, *Karl Gutzkow*, p. 109. In view of Dobert's harsh opinion here, it is interesting that elsewhere he finds Gutzkow's *Uriel Acosta* better structured and more realistic than *Nathan der Weise* (p. 133).

29 Houben, *JdSuD*, p. 164.

30 Karl Gutzkow, *Vertheidigung gegen Menzel und Berichtigung einiger Urtheile im Publikum* (Mannheim: Löwenthal, 1835), p. 36. What Gutzkow meant when he said in a letter of 28 October 1835 to Varnhagen that the religious side of the book was "nur Ballast und Lockspeise für die Massen" completely eludes me. See Houben, *Gutzkow-Funde*, p. 71.

31 Houben, *JdSuD*, p. 531.

32 For objections to regarding *Wally* as a Saint-Simonian novel, cf. Koopmann, *Das Junge Deutschland*, p. 35.

33 Another example is a comment on brother Jeronimo that the character is "eine widerliche Störung dieses Berichts" (p. 165), a form of narrative irony that suggests real, rather than pretended lack of control.

34 Friedrich Sengle, *Biedermeierzeit. Deutsche Literatur im Spannnungsfeld zwischen Restauration und Revolution 1815-1848*, I (Stuttgart: Metzler, 1971), p. 176.

35 Rudolf Majut, in his discussion of *Wally* in his article on the nineteenth-century novel in *Deutsche Philologie im Aufriß*, ed. Wolfgang Stammler, 2nd ed. (Berlin: Erich Schmidt, 1960), II, cols. 1429-30, is wrong to state that Wally marries Luigi because she has taken offense at Cäsar's "Bastardierung des Liebesgefühls" in this scene. Wally is moved by Cäsar's "ächt philanthropische Vorstellung" and embraces him, not out of love, but because he has made her feel part of the great chain of being and "daß diese heißen Küsse, welche Cäsar auf ihre Lippen drückte, allen Millionen gälte [sic] unterm Sternenzelt" (p. 77). The parodic allusion to Schiller adds another irony, while the primitive grammatical error in the sentence is further evidence of haste.

36 Cf. Günter Bliemel, "Die Auffassung des Jungen Deutschlands von Wesen und Aufgabe des Dichters und der Dichtung" (diss. Berlin, 1955), p. 125.

37 Houben, *JdSuD*, p. 439.

38 Karl Gutzkow, *Briefe eines Narren an eine Närrin*, (Hamburg: Hoffmann und Campe, 1832), pp. 169-170.

39 Ibid., p. 173. Cf. Gutzkow, *Zur Philosophie der Geschichte*, pp. 148-151; Dobert, *Karl Gutzkow*, pp. 71-73; and Hof, *Pessimistisch-nihilistische Strömungen*, pp. 198-199.

40 See my treatment of this theme in Heine's *Buch Le Grand* and in the poem *Doktrin* in my study, *Heinrich Heine: The Elusive Poet* (New Haven and London: Yale University Press, 1969), pp. 139-143, 212.

[41] Ernest K. Bramsted, *Aristocracy and the Middle-Classes in Germany. Social Types in German Literature 1830-1900*, revised ed. (Chicago and London: University of Chicago Press, 1964).

[42] Houben, *JdSuD*, p. 352. Cf. Ruth Horovitz, *Vom Roman des Jungen Deutschlands zum Roman der Gartenlaube. Ein Beitrag zur Geschichte des deutschen Liberalismus* (diss. Basel, 1937), pp. 45-46.

[43] Friedrich Sengle, "Voraussetzungen und Erscheinungsformen der deutschen Restaurationsliteratur," *Deutsche Vierteljahrsschrift*, 30 (1956), 271. Cf. Sengle's discussion of the continuing prominence and prestige of the nobility in *Biedermeierzeit*, I, 17-20. Because he is looking at the society with a wide-angle lens, Sengle tends, in my view, to bagatellize the anti-aristocratic thrust of oppositional fiction.

[44] Quored in Hartmut Steinecke, ed., *Theorie und Technik des Romans im 19. Jahrhundert* (Tübingen: Niemeyer, 1970), p. 46.

[45] Ibid. On Gutzkow's later idealistic critique of realism, see Sengle, *Biedermeierzeit*, I, 290-291. Sengle does not note how sharply these polemics contrast with some of Gutzkow's own earlier insights.

[46] Gutzkow thought he remembered, forty years later, that *Wally* had been influenced by the first volume of David Friedrich Strauss' *Das Leben Jesu*, which also appeared in 1835, and many interpreters and literary historians have repeated this. From the chronology of the publications, as described by Franz Schneider, "Gutzkows *Wally* und D. F. Strauss' *Das Leben Jesu*, eine Richtigstellung," *Germanic Review*, 1 (1926), 115-119, it appears that this cannot be correct. But Schneider is wrong to argue that there was no relationship between the two books; Strauss was attempting to find a middle way through the dilemmas that are adumbrated in the third part of *Wally*.

[47] "Zum Lazarus," 1. Heinrich Heine, *Sämtliche Werke*, ed. Ernst Elster (Leipzig and Vienna: Bibliographisches Institut, [1887-90]), II, 92.

[48] Heinrich Laube, *Die Poeten* (Mannheim: Heinrich Hoff, 1836), I, 108.

III. THEODOR MUNDT: A REVALUATION

1 Butler, *The Saint-Simonian Religion*, p. 320.
2 Ibid., p. 388.
3 Houben, *JdSuD*, p. 463.
4 Edgar Pierson, ed., *Gustav Kühne, sein Lebensbild und Briefwechsel mit Zeitgenossen* (Dresden and Leipzig: E. Pierson's Verlag, [1889]), pp. 205-206.
5 Ibid., pp. 121-122.
6 Houben, *Zeitschriften des Jungen Deutschlands*, I, cols. 167-168.
7 Jost Hermand, "Heines frühe Kritiker," *Der Dichter und seine Zeit. Politik im Spiegel der Literatur. Drittes Amherster Kolloquium zur modernen deutschen Literatur 1969*, ed. Wolfgang Paulsen (Heidelberg: Lothar Stiehm, 1970), pp. 129-130.
8 Cf. Houben, *Verbotene Literatur*, II, 389-391.
9 Houben, *JdSuD*, p. 483.
10 Ibid., p. 472. Mundt went so far as to print an anti-Semitic attack on Gutzkow's publisher Löwenthal in the October, 1835, issue of the *Literarischer Zodiacus*. See Houben, *Zeitschriften des Jungen Deutschlands*, I, col. 274.
11 Houben, *Verbotene Literatur*, II, 492-493.
12 "Rahel und ihre Zeit," *Charaktere und Situationen* (Wismar and Leipzig: H. Schmidt u. v. Cossel, 1837), I, 213-271.
13 A second edition appeared in 1843. The first edition — *Die Kunst der deutschen Prosa. Ästhetisch, literaturgeschichtlich, gesellschaftlich* (Berlin: Veit & Comp., 1837) — has been reprinted by Vandenhoeck & Ruprecht (Göttingen, 1969), with a brief commentary by Hans Düvel. This edition is used here.
14 See Georg Wilhelm Friedrich Hegel, *Sämtliche Werke, Jubiläumsausgabe in zwanzig Bänden*, ed. Hermann Glockner (Stuttgart: Friedrich Frommann, 1964-), XIII, 215-217; XIV, 395-396.
15 Cf. my tentative attempt to raise the question in *Heinrich Heine, the Elusive Poet* (New Haven and London: Yale University Press, 1969), pp. 178-179.
16 Theodor Mundt, *Die Kunst der deutschen Prosa*, p. 7.
17 Ibid., p. 20.
18 Ibid., pp. 19-20.
19 Ibid., p. 47.
20 "Deutsche Höflichkeit," *Charaktere und Situationen*, I, 329-337.
21 Mundt, *Die Kunst der deutschen Prosa*, p. 74.
22 Ibid., p. 76.

23 Ibid., pp. 94-95.

24 Mundt's view of the French language is similar to one found in a letter of Wilhelm von Humboldt to Goethe of 18 August 1799, which Goethe published in the *Propyläen* the following year under the title "Ueber die gegenwärtige französische tragische Bühne." See Humboldt, *Gesammelte Schriften,* ed. Albert Leitzmann, II (Berlin: B. Behr, 1904), 391-392.

25 Mundt, *Die Kunst der deutschen Prosa*, p. 101.

26 Ibid., pp. 119-120. Friedrich Sengle, *Biedermeierzeit. Deutsche Literatur im Spannungsfeld zwischen Restauration und Revolution 1815-1848*, I (Stuttgart: Metzler, 1971), 549-552, has a generally less admiring view of Mundt's book, pointing out the ambiguities in his critique of "Ciceronian" syntax of the *Goethezeit*.

27 Mundt, *Die Kunst der deutschen Prosa*, pp. 143-144.

28 René Wellek, *A History of Modern Criticism 1750-1950* (New Haven and London: Yale University Press, 1955-), III, 203.

29 Mundt, *Die Kunst der deutschen Prosa*, p. 272.

30 Ibid., p. 326.

31 Ibid., pp. 318-319.

32 Ibid., p. 373.

33 Theodor Mundt, *Aesthetik. Die Idee der Schönheit und des Kunstwerks im Lichte unserer Zeit*. Photographic reprint of the first edition, ed. Hans Düvel (Göttingen: Vandenhoeck & Ruprecht, 1966), p. 64.

34 Ibid., p. 58.

35 Eberhard Galley, *Der religiöse Liberalismus in der deutschen Literatur von 1830 bis 1850* (diss. Rostock, 1934), p. 55.

36 Houben, *Verbotene Literatur*, II, 408.

37 Mundt, *Aesthetik*, p. 4.

38 Ibid., pp. 4-8.

39 Ibid., p. 177.

40 Houben, *Zeitschriften des Jungen Deutschlands*, I, col. 304.

41 Mundt, *Aesthetik*, p. 83.

42 Ibid., p. 84.

43 Ibid., pp. 86-87.

44 Ibid., p. 60.

45 Ibid., p. iv.

46 Ibid., pp. iv-v.

47 "Antoniens Bußfahrten," *Charaktere und Situationen*, I, 7.

48 Mundt, *Aesthetik*, p. 2.

49 Ibid., p. 10.

50 Ibid., p. 258.

51 Ibid., pp. 4-5. Cf. Karl Marx and Friedrich Engels, *Über Kunst und Literatur*, ed. Manfred Kliem (Berlin: Dietz Verlag, 1968), II, 351.

52 Mundt, *Aesthetik*, p. 23.

53 Ibid., pp. 24-25.

54 Ibid., p. 30.

55 Houben, *JdSuD*, p. 397.

56 Ibid., p. 399.

57 Ibid., pp. 423-424.

160

58 Ibid., p. 433.
59 Karl Gutzkow, *Werke*, ed. Peter Müller (Leipzig and Vienna: Bibliographisches Institut, [1911]), III, 103.
60 Pierson, *Gustav Kühne*, pp. 22-23.
61 Ibid., pp. 24-28.
62 F. Gustav Kühne, *Weibliche und männliche Charaktere* (Leipzig: Wilh. Engelmann, 1838), I, 115-154.
63 [Theodor Mundt], *Charlotte Stieglitz, ein Denkmal* (Berlin: Veit & Comp., [1835]), p. iii.
64 There are hints in *Charlotte Stieglitz, ein Denkmal* that the sexual relationship of the Stieglitzes was not good; Mundt remarks at one point that Stieglitz' poetry made up "bei fast gänzlicher Entsagung aller andern Beziehungen der Ehe, den eigentlichen Mittelpunkt ihres Umgangs" (p. 41). Charlotte herself perceived Stieglitz' incredible series of ailments as psychosomatic (p. 201).
65 Theodor Mundt, *Madonna. Unterhaltungen mit einer Heiligen* (Leipzig: Gebrüder Reichenbach, 1835), p. 435. On the undiminished prestige of literature at this time, cf. Sengle, *Biedermeierzeit*, I, 104-106. Despite all the talk about the end of the *Kunstperiode*, "meistens tritt die zum Tempel hinausgeworfene Göttin unversehens wieder ein, in einem nationalen, demokratischen, oder religiösen Gewand" (ibid., p. 106).
66 Gutzkow, *Werke*, ed. Müller, III, 106-107, 112.
67 Houben, *JdSuD*, pp. 441-444. It is true, to be sure, that in Saxony the book was thought to be demagogic, and because of it Mundt had great difficulty getting his projects for periodicals off the ground (to Charlotte Stieglitz, May, 1834, Houben, *Verbotene Literatur*, II, 373. In Houben, *Zeitschriften des Jungen Deutschlands*, I, col. 123, the letter is misdated 1835).
68 Theodor Mundt, *Moderne Lebenswirren. Briefe und Zeitabenteuer eines Salzschreibers* (Leipzig: Gebrüder Reichenbach, 1834), pp. [1], [2].
69 Ibid., pp. 11-12.
70 Ibid., p. 17.
71 Ibid.
72 Ibid., p. 43.
73 Ibid., p. 46.
74 Mundt, *Die Kunst der deutschen Prosa*, p. 92.
75 Mundt, *Moderne Lebenswirren*, p. 126.
76 Ibid.
77 Ibid., p. 146.
78 Ibid., p. 152.
79 Ibid., p. 160.
80 Mundt, *Madonna*, p. 300.
81 Mundt, *Moderne Lebenswirren*, p. 188.
82 Günter Bliemel, "Die Auffassung des Jungen Deutschlands von Wesen und Aufgabe des Dichters und der Dichtung" (diss. Berlin, 1955), p. 96.
83 Rudolf Majut, "Der deutsche Roman vom Biedermeier bis zur Gegenwart," *Deutsche Philologie im Aufriß*, ed. Wolfgang Stammler, 2nd ed. (Berlin: Erich Schmidt, 1960), II, col. 1425.
84 Houben, *JdSuD*, pp. 438-439.

[85] Heinrich Heine, *Sämtliche Werke*, ed. Ernst Elster (Leipzig and Vienna: Bibliographisches Institut, [1887-90]), III, 74.

[86] Mundt, *Madonna*, p. 433.

[87] Houben, *JdSuD*, p. 447.

[88] Such a chapter title suggests the influence of Jean Paul, but Mundt, as appears in several passages of the book, believed Jean Paul to be obsolete and did not consciously follow him in any degree.

[89] Mundt, *Madonna*, p. 1.

[90] Ibid., p. 14.

[91] Ibid., pp. 24-25.

[92] Ibid., p. 26.

[93] Ibid., p. 281.

[94] Ibid., p. 434.

[95] Ibid., p. 79.

[96] Ibid., p. 74.

[97] *Madonna* had probably been essentially completed by that time; the first part of the MS had been submitted to the censors in November, 1834 (Houben, *Verbotene Literatur*, II, 385). But the French version of Heine's book had begun to appear in March, 1834, and his views were well known.

[98] Mundt, *Madonna*, p. 130.

[99] Ibid., p. 141.

[100] Ibid., pp. 141-142.

[101] Ibid., p. 274.

[102] Ibid., p. 365.

[103] Mundt, *Charlotte Stieglitz, ein Denkmal*, pp. 54-56.

[104] Theodor Mundt, *Geschichte der Literatur der Gegenwart. Friedrich von Schlegel's Geschichte der alten und neuen Literatur, bis auf die neueste Zeit fortgeführt* (Berlin: M. Simion, 1842), p. 388.

[105] Mundt, *Madonna*, pp. 227-228.

[106] Ibid., p. 96.

[107] For a summary of the Libussa tradition, cf. Elisabeth Frenzel, *Stoffe der Weltliteratur*, 2nd ed., (Stuttgart: A. Kröner, 1963), pp. 379-381.

[108] Mundt, *Charaktere und Situationen*, I, 3-127.

[109] Mundt, *Madonna*, p. 259.

[110] Mundt, *Charaktere und Situationen*, I, 128-210.

[111] Mundt, *Madonna*, pp. 219-220.

IV. FERDINAND GUSTAV KÜHNE: *EINE QUARANTÄNE IM IRRENHAUSE*

1 Houben, *Verbotene Literatur*, II, 450-454.
2 Cf. Edgar Pierson, ed., *Gustav Kühne, sein Lebensbild und Briefwechsel mit Zeitgenossen* (Dresden and Leipzig: E. Pierson's Verlag, [1889]), pp. 175-176.
3 Ibid., p. 69.
4 Ibid., p. 20.
5 Houben, *JdSuD*, p. 65.
6 Ibid., p. 640.
7 Pierson, *Gustav Kühne*, pp. 234-235.
8 Houben, *JdSuD*, p. 638.
9 All page numbers in parentheses in this chapter are references to F. G. Kühne, *Eine Quarantäne im Irrenhause. Novelle aus den Papieren eines Mondsteiners* (Leipzig: F. A. Brockhaus, 1835). I am grateful to Professor Jost Hermand for the loan of his copy of this rare book.
10 Pierson, *Gustav Kühne*, p. 12.
11 Ibid., pp. 219-220.
12 Ibid., p. 224.
13 Ibid., p. 203.
14 Ibid., p. 159.
15 Theodor Mundt, *Charaktere und Situationen* (Wismar and Leipzig: H. Schmidt u. v. Cossel, 1837), I, 306-308.
16 *Literarischer Zodiacus*, January, 1835, p. 4, quoted Günter Bliemel, "Die Auffassung des Jungen Deutschlands von Wesen und Aufgabe des Dichters und der Dichtung" (diss. Berlin, 1955), p. 74.
17 Ruth Horovitz, *Vom Roman des Jungen Deutschland zum Roman der Gartenlaube* (diss. Basel, 1937), p. 22.

V. HEINRICH LAUBE: *DIE KRIEGER*

1 Rudolf Majut, "Der deutsche Roman vom Biedermeier bis zur Gegenwart," *Deutsche Philologie im Aufriß*, ed. Wolfgang Stammler, 2nd ed. (Berlin: Erich Schmidt, 1960), II, col. 1420.

2 Friedrich Sengle, *Biedermeierzeit. Deutsche Literatur im Spannungsfeld zwischen Restauration und Revolution 1815-1848*, I (Stuttgart: Metzler, 1971), 171.

3 Karl Gutzkow, *Vergangenheit und Gegenwart 1830-1838, Werke*, ed. Peter Müller (Leipzig and Vienna: Bibliographisches Institut, [1911]), III, 167.

4 Heinrich Laube, *Ausgewählte Werke in zehn Bänden*, ed. Heinrich Hubert Houben (Leipzig: Max Hesse, n.d.), I, 94.

5 Reinhold Grimm, "Romanhaftes und Novellistisches in Laubes *Reisenovellen*," *Germanisch-romanische Monatsschrift*, N.S. 18 (1968), 299-303.

6 Laube, *Ausgewählte Werke*, I, 193, 260.

7 Houben, *JdSuD*, p. 362.

8 Walter Dietze, *Junges Deutschland und deutsche Klassik. Zur Ästhetik und Literaturtheorie des Vormärz*, 3rd ed. (Berlin: Rütten & Loening, 1962), p. 89.

9 Ibid., pp. 89, 90.

10 Butler, *The Saint-Simonian Religion*, p. 200.

11 Ernst Elster, "H. Heine und H. Laube. Mit sechsundvierzig bisher ungedruckten Briefen Laubes an Heine," *Deutsche Rundschau*, 136 (1908), 448.

12 See especially the chapter, "Der Wandel in Laubes Anschauungen," in Karl Nolle, *Heinrich Laube als sozialer und politischer Schriftsteller* (diss. Münster, 1914), pp. 37-41.

13 Wilh. Johannes Becker, *Zeitgeist und Krisenbewußtsein in Heinrich Laubes Novellen* (diss. Frankfurt, 1960), p. 37.

14 The following sketch is a digest of the accounts given by Houben in Laube, *Ausgewählte Werke*, I, and *Verbotene Literatur*, I.

15 Heinrich Laube, *Gesammelte Werke in fünfzig Bänden*, ed. Heinrich Hubert Houben with Albert Hänel (Leipzig: M. Hesse, 1908-09), XL, 269-270.

16 *Zeitung für die elegante Welt*, 3 May 1833, No. 86, p. 344.

17 Houben, *JdSuD*, p. 386.

18 Butler, *The Saint-Simonian Religion*, p. 189.

19 Houben, *JdSuD*, p. 386.

20 Elster, "H. Heine und H. Laube," *Deutsche Rundschau*, 134 (1908), 80.

21 Houben, *Verbotene Literatur*, I, 481.

22 An example of what can be accomplished in this regard is Becker's study

164

of Laube's novellas (see above, n. 13), which elucidates the connections between form and sociological conviction more precisely than I can here; I owe his study worthwhile insights that are also applicable to Laube's novel.

23 Heinrich Laube, *Die Bürger* (Mannheim: Heinrich Hoff, 1837), p. 226.

24 Laube, *Gesammelte Werke*, XL, 184.

25 See Butler, *The Saint-Simonian Religion*, pp. 207-208.

26 Elster, "H. Heine und H. Laube," *Deutsche Rundschau*, 133 (1907), 231. My italics.

27 *Zeitung für die elegante Welt*, 23 May 1833, No. 100, pp. 398, 399.

28 Ibid., 25 July 1833, No. 143, p. 572.

29 Laube, *Gesammelte Werke*, XL, 183.

30 Ibid., pp. 182-183.

31 Karl Häberle, *Individualität und Zeit in H. Laubes Jungem Europa und K. Gutzkows Ritter vom Geist* (Erlangen: Palm & Enke, 1938), p. 41.

32 Gutzkow, *Vergangenheit und Gegenwart, Werke*, ed. Müller, III, 169.

33 Laube, *Gesammelte Werke*, XLI, 453.

34 Laube, *Die Bürger*, pp. 153-154.

35 Heinrich Laube, *Die Poeten* (Mannheim: Heinrich Hoff, 1836), [I], 113. Although this (second) edition is not explicitly in two books or volumes, there are two paginations.

36 Laube, *Gesammelte Werke*, XL, 286.

37 Quoted Eitel Wolf Dobert, *Karl Gutzkow und seine Zeit* (Bern and Munich: Francke Verlag, 1968), p. 50.

38 Ludolf Wienbarg, *Wanderungen durch den Thierkreis* (Hamburg: Hoffmann und Campe, 1835), p. 248.

39 Ibid., pp. 251-252.

40 Majut, "Der deutsche Roman," col. 1409.

41 Peter Demetz, "Zur Definition des Realismus," *Literatur und Kritik*, 2 (1967), 340.

42 Ludolf Wienbarg, *Quadriga* (Hamburg: Hoffmann und Campe, 1840), p. 136. Cf. Jeffrey L. Sammons, "Ludolf Wienbarg and Norway," *Scandinavian Studies*, 42 (1970), 21-22.

43 Houben, *Gutzkow-Funde*, pp. 144-280.

44 Karl Gutzkow, *Götter, Helden, Don-Quixote. Abstimmungen zur Beurtheilung der literarischen Epoche* (Hamburg: Hoffmann und Campe, 1838), p. 258 n.

45 Laube did once allow himself to slip into a rude tone about Jewish influence in literature, and it is characteristic of the situation of the time that the outburst was touched off by a problem of literary competition, a quarrel in 1847 concerning the subject of his drama *Struensee*, the performance of which was interfered with by the influential Giacomo Meyerbeer, whose brother Michael Beer had written a play on the same subject years before (Laube, *Gesammelte Werke,* XXIV, 130-132). The tone of these remarks is deplorable and shows how a conflict of economic interest could arouse the bacillus of anti-Semitism even in a man so thoroughly inoculated against it.

46 Examples of the nuances in Laube's judgment concerning the Jews are in Nolle, *Heinrich Laube als sozialer und politischer Schriftsteller*, pp. 46-48.

47 Heinrich Laube, *Die Krieger* (Mannheim: Heinrich Hoff, 1837), I, 157.

48 Ibid., II, 25.

49 Benno von Wiese, "Zeitkrisis und Biedermeier in Laubes 'Das junge Europa' und in Immermanns 'Epigonen,'" *Dichtung und Volkstum*, 36 (1935), 163, n. 1.

50 Laube, *Die Krieger*, I, 242.

51 To my knowledge, Wienbarg is the only one of the Young Germans to have grasped the difference between freedom as a liberal, individualistic concern and independence as a national goal (*Quadriga*, p. 140).

52 It is possible that Laube is here thinking of Heine, because he shared with Wienbarg and Johann Peter Lyser the opinion that Heine's mother was a Christian. This false information led Wienbarg in the twenty-third lecture of the *Ästhetische Feldzüge* to an assessment of Heine very much lacking in objective value. An inconclusive discussion of the possible source of this notion is in Friedrich Hirth, *Heinrich Heines Briefe* (Mainz: F. Kupferberg, 1950-51), IV, 225-226. An interesting example of how preconceptions and prejudices can interfere with direct perception is Wienbarg's description of Heine in the *Wanderungen durch den Thierkreis* (p. 150) as *black-haired*, when all other evidence is unanimous that he was blond.

53 Laube, *Die Krieger*, II, 285-286.

54 Cf. the observations in my article, "The Evaluation of Freytag's 'Soll und Haben,'" *German Life & Letters*, N.S., 22 (1968/69), 318-319.

55 Laube, *Gesammelte Werke*, XL, 135-136.

56 Laube, *Die Poeten*, [II], 186-187.

57 Laube, *Gesammelte Werke*, VI, 133.

58 Laube, *Die Krieger*, I, 127.

59 Ibid., II, 272.

60 Gerhard Burkhardt, "Ludolf Wienbarg als Ästhetiker und Kritiker. Seine Entwicklung und seine geistesgeschichtliche Stellung" (diss. Hamburg, 1956), p. 158.

61 Horst Denkler, "Aufbruch der Aristophaniden. Die aristophanische Komödie als Modell für das politische Lustspiel im deutschen Vormärz," *Der Dichter und seine Zeit — Politik im Spiegel der Literatur. Drittes Amherster Kolloquium zur modernen deutschen Literatur 1969*, ed. Wolfgang Paulsen (Heidelberg: Lothar Stiehm), pp. 134-157.

62 Nolle, *Heinrich Laube als sozialer und politischer Schriftsteller*, pp. 45-46; von Wiese, "Zeitkrisis und Biedermeier," pp. 171-172; Häberle, *Individualität und Zeit*, pp. 51-52.

63 Laube, *Die Krieger*, I, 73-74.

64 Laube, *Die Bürger*, p. 4.

[1] Benno von Wiese, *Karl Immermann. Sein Werk und sein Leben* (Bad Homburg, Berlin, and Zurich: Gehlen, 1969).

[2] *Ibid.*, p. 287.

[3] *Ibid.*

[4] Martin Greiner, *Zwischen Biedermeier und Bourgeoisie. Ein Kapitel deutscher Literaturgeschichte* (Göttingen: Vandenhoeck & Ruprecht, 1953), p. 81.

[5] Immermann, *Werke*, ed. Robert Boxberger (Leipzig: Dümmler, [1883]), I, vi.

[6] George Eliot, "German Wit: Heinrich Heine," *Essays and Leaves from a Notebook*, ed. Charles Lee Lewes (New York: Harper & Brothers, 1884), p. 80.

[7] Manfred Windfuhr, *Immermanns erzählerisches Werk. Zur Situation des Romans in der Restaurationszeit* (Giessen: Schmitz, 1957), p. 32.

[8] *Ibid.*, pp. 91-92.

[9] *Ibid.*, p. 17.

[10] MS quoted by Elisabeth Guzinski, *Karl Immermann als Zeitkritiker. Ein Beitrag zur Geschichte der deutschen Selbstkritik*, Neue Deutsche Forschungen, No. 142 (Berlin: Junker und Dünnhaupt, 1937), p. 19.

[11] *Werke*, ed. Boxberger, XI, 308, 310.

[12] Immermann, *Werke*, ed. Harry Maync (Leipzig and Vienna: Bibliographisches Institut, [1906]), I, 16.

[13] Immermann to his brother, 7 November 1830, MS letter quoted by Peter Hasubek, ed. Immermann, *Tulifäntchen*, Reclams Universal-Bibliothek, Nos. 8551-52 (Stuttgart: Philipp Reclam Jun., 1968), p. 145.

[14] Cf. *Werke*, ed. Boxberger, X, 29.

[15] *Ibid.*, I, lxxxviii.

[16] Windfuhr, *Immermanns erzählerisches Werk*, pp. 123-124.

[17] Gustav zu Putlitz, *Karl Immermann. Sein Leben und seine Werke, aus Tagebüchern und Briefen an seine Familie zusammengestellt* (Berlin: Wilhelm Hertz, 1870), II, 234.

[18] Hans Mayer, "Karl Immermanns 'Epigonen,'" *Studien zur deutschen Literaturgeschichte*, 2nd ed. (Berlin: Rütten & Loening, 1955), p. 130.

[19] Ernest K. Bramsted, *Aristocracy and the Middle-Classes in Germany. Social Types in German Literature 1830-1900*, revised ed. (Chicago and London: University of Chicago Press, 1964), p. 62.

[20] In fact, by coincidence, Immermann completed the novel on 12 December,

just two days after the Federal ban on the Young Germans. Cf. von Wiese, *Karl Immermann*, p. 172.

21 Manfred Windfuhr, "Der Epigone. Begriff, Phänomen und Bewußtsein," *Archiv für Begriffsgeschichte*, 4 (1959), 190.

22 Ibid., pp. 193-194.

23 Von Wiese, *Karl Immermann*, p. 174.

24 Ibid., p. 261.

25 Koopmann, *Das Junge Deutschland*, p. 96.

26 Cf. Windfuhr, *Immermanns erzählerisches Werk*, p. 139.

27 Von Wiese, *Karl Immermann*, pp. 187-188.

28 Windfuhr, *Immermanns erzählerisches Werk*, p. 140.

29 Gustav Freytag, *Soll und Haben, Gesammelte Werke*, IV (Leipzig: S. Hirzel, 1887), 561.

30 Heinrich Heine, *Sämtliche Werke*, ed. Ernst Elster (Leipzig and Vienna: Bibliographisches Institut, [1887-90]), V, 236.

31 Immermann, *Werke*, ed. Maync, IV, 22.

32 Lee B. Jennings, *The Ludicrous Demon: Aspects of the Grotesque in German Post-Romantic Prose* (Berkeley and Los Angeles: University of California Press, 1963).

33 Von Wiese, *Karl Immermann*, pp. 12, 14.

34 Ibid., p. 84.

35 Immermann complained in a letter to his brother about readers who insisted on making this assumption, despite the fact that Wilhelmi had been presented as "krank und hypochondrisch" (Putlitz, *Karl Immermann*, II, 148).

36 Immermann, *Werke*, ed. Maync, III, 135-137.

37 Ibid., p. 141.

38 Ibid., pp. 419, 421.

39 Ibid., p. 364.

40 Ibid., p. 366.

41 Ibid., p. 369.

42 See Hans-Georg Werner, *Geschichte des politischen Gedichts in Deutschland von 1815 bis 1840* (Berlin: Akademie-Verlag, 1969), pp. 55-58.

43 Ibid., p. 116; cf. the discussion of the whole subject on pp. 112-146.

44 Putlitz, *Karl Immermann*, I, 106.

45 Cf. the excellent analysis of this part of the novel by Franz Rumler, *Realistische Elemente in Immermanns "Epigonen"* (diss. Munich, 1964), pp. 106-121.

46 Immermann, *Werke*, ed. Maync, III, 406.

47 Ibid., IV, 138.

48 Von Wiese, *Karl Immermann*, p. 197.

49 Immermann, *Werke*, ed. Maync, IV, 265-266.

50 Rumler, *Realistische Elemente*, pp. 134-136.

51 Theodor Mundt, *Charaktere und Situationen* (Wismar and Leipzig: H. Schmidt u. v. Cossel, 1837), I, 276, 292.

52 Although Immermann was writing at a very early stage in the development of German capitalism, there were already signs during his time that an ideology was forming to neutralize optimistically or misdirect attention away from the depredations of capitalism that he was able to perceive. By

accident I have come across a book that is interesting in this regard, a German translation of Charles Babbage's textbook of capitalist industry in England of 1832, *On the Economy of Machinery and Manufactures*, translated by Dr. G. Friedenberg, *Ueber Maschinen- und Fabrikwesen* (Berlin: Verlag der Stuhrschen Buchhandlung, 1833). Of interest here is a preface supplied by one K. F. Köden, director of the Berlin Trade School. In it he raises the question whether specialized, monotonous, repetitive factory work, in contrast to obsolete craftsmanship, which made the worker responsible for a whole product, will not be harmful to the human spirit. Clearly he senses in the air the problem of what was to be called alienation. He disposes of it with ease, however, by arguing that monotonous work, rather than deadening the spirit, will free the mind to think of other things; in a characteristic, almost comic juxtaposition, he remarks that the brooding of the weavers (whose desperate conditions were to drive them, eleven years later, into the first full-scale workers' uprising in Germany) has developed in them mechanical, mystical, Pietist, and poetic talents (pp. xii-xiii). Factory work will lead men to turn inward into their souls. This being the case, however, steps must be taken to prevent workers, with so much free mental time, from developing dangerous religious and political enthusiasms, which can be accomplished by teaching them to interest themselves in the real things of their immediate world — an interesting application of Goethean principles to the class problem.

53 On the genesis of the novel, see Windfuhr, *Immermanns erzählerisches Werk*, pp. 180-181.

54 Dimiter Statkow, "Über die dialektische Struktur des Immermann-Romans 'Münchhausen.' Zum Problem des Übergangs von der Romantik zum Realismus," *Weimarer Beiträge*, 11 (1965), 200-204.

55 Herman Meyer, *Das Zitat in der Erzählkunst. Zur Geschichte und Poetik des europäischen Romans*, 2nd ed. (Stuttgart: Metzler, 1967), p. 140.

56 Ibid., p. 141.

57 Immermann, *Werke*, ed. Maync, I, 327.

58 Cf. Windfuhr, *Immermanns erzählerisches Werk*, p. 191.

59 Cf. Von Wiese, *Karl Immermann*, p. 186, and Windfuhr, *Immermanns erzählerisches Werk*, p. 84.

60 Cf. Windfuhr, *Immermanns erzählerisches Werk*, p. 183.

61 Friedrich Hebbel, *Sämtliche Werke. Historisch-kritische Ausgabe*, ed. Richard Maria Werner, XII (Berlin: B. Behr, 1903), 62.

62 Droste to Levin Schücking, 11 September 1842, *Die Briefe der Annette von Droste-Hülshoff*, ed. Karl Schulte-Kemminghausen (Düsseldorf: Eugen Diederichs, 1968), II, 77-78.

63 Quoted by Windfuhr, *Immermanns erzählerisches Werk*, p. 183.

64 Von Wiese, *Karl Immermann*, p. 11.

65 Windfuhr, *Immermanns erzählerisches Werk*, p. 202.

66 Quoted ibid., p. 181.

67 Ibid., p. 192.

68 Ibid., p. 196.

69 Werner Kohlschmidt, "Die Welt des Bauern im Spiegel von Immermanns

'Münchhausen' und Gotthelfs 'Uli,' " *Dichtung und Volkstum*, 39 (1938), 226.

70 Ibid., p. 236.

71 Von Wiese, *Karl Immermann*, pp. 228-229.

72 Ibid., pp. 241-242.

73 Windfuhr, *Immermanns erzählerisches Werk*, p. 202.

74 Michael Scherer, "Immermanns *Münchhausen*-Roman," *German Quarterly*, 36 (1963), 240.

75 Statkow, "Über die dialektische Struktur," pp. 198-199.

76 William McClain, "Karl Lebrecht Immermann's Portrait of a Folk-Hero in *Münchhausen*," *Studies in German Literature of the Nineteenth and Twentieth Centuries. Festschrift for Frederic E. Coenen*, ed. Siegfried Mews (Chapel Hill: University of North Carolina Press, 1970), pp. 55-63.

77 Statkow, "Über die dialektische Struktur," p. 208.

78 Windfuhr, *Immermanns erzählerisches Werk*, pp. 148-149.

79 Immermann, *Werke*, ed. Maync, I, 238.

80 Von Wiese, *Karl Immermann*, p. 240.

81 Windfuhr, *Immermanns erzählerisches Werk*, pp. 169-170; cf. Rumler, *Realistische Elemente*, pp. 9-11.

82 Windfuhr, *Immermanns erzählerisches Werk*, p. 247.

83 Ibid.

84 Ibid., pp. 98-99.

85 Rumler, *Realistische Elemente*, passim.

86 Immermann, *Werke*, ed. Maync, I, 183.

87 Ibid., II, 66-67.

88 Ibid., I, 269.

89 Von Wiese, *Karl Immermann*, p. 166.

90 Ibid., p. 244.

91 Rumler, *Realistische Elemente*, pp. 84-88.

92 Mayer, "Karl Immermanns 'Epigonen,' " p. 139.

93 Von Wiese, *Karl Immermann*, pp. 191-192.

94 Ibid., p. 192.

95 See Hans-Georg Gadamer, "Karl Immermanns 'Chiliastische Sonette,' " *Kleine Schriften II. Interpretationen* (Tübingen: Mohr, 1967), pp. 136-147.

96 Meyer, *Das Zitat in der Erzählkunst*, p. 136.

97 Jennings, *The Ludicrous Demon*, p. 51.

98 Mundt, *Charaktere und Situationen*, I, 278.

99 Gadamer, "Zu Immermanns Epigonen-Roman," *Kleine Schriften II*, p. 160.

100 Emil Grütter, *Immermanns "Epigonen". Ein Beitrag zur Geschichte des deutschen Romans* (diss. Zurich, 1951), p. 36.

101 Windfuhr, *Immermanns erzählerisches Werk*, p. 175.

102 Jennings, *The Ludicrous Demon*, p. 76.

103 Rumler, *Realistische Elemente*, p. 17.

104 Putlitz, *Karl Immermann*, II, 233.

BIBLIOGRAPHY

AUERBACH, ERICH. *Mimesis. The Representation of Reality in Western Literature.* Translated from the German by Willard Trask. Garden City: Doubleday, 1953.

BABBAGE, CHARLES. *Ueber Maschinen- und Fabrikwesen,* tr. Dr. G. Friedenberg. Berlin: Verlag der Stuhrschen Buchhandlung, 1833.

BECKER, WILH. JOHANNES. *Zeitgeist und Krisenbewußtsein in Heinrich Laubes Novellen.* Diss. Frankfurt, 1960.

BIEBER, HUGO. *Der Kampf um die Tradition. Die deutsche Dichtung im europäischen Geistesleben 1830-1880.* Epochen der deutschen Literatur, Vol. V. Stuttgart: Metzler, 1928.

BLIEMEL, GÜNTER. "Die Auffassung des Jungen Deutschlands von Wesen und Aufgabe der Dichtung." Diss. Berlin, 1955.

BOCK, HELMUT. *Ludwig Börne. Vom Gettojuden zum Nationalschriftsteller.* Berlin: Rütten & Loening, 1962.

BÖRNE, LUDWIG. *Sämtliche Schriften,* ed. Inge und Peter Rippmann. 5 vols. Düsseldorf: Melzer, 1964-68.

BRAMSTED, ERNEST K. *Aristocracy and the Middle-Classes in Germany. Social Types in German Literature 1830-1900.* Revised ed. Chicago and London: University of Chicago Press, 1964.

BRANDES, GEORG. *Main Currents in Nineteenth Century Literature.* Vol. VI: *Young Germany,* tr. Mary Morison. London and Paris: W. Heinemann, 1906.

BRANN, HENRY WALTER. "The Young German Movement Creates a Political Literature." *German Quarterly,* 24 (1951), 189-194.

BURKHARDT, GERHARD. "Ludolf Wienbarg als Ästhetiker und Kritiker. Seine Entwicklung und seine geistesgeschichtliche Stellung." Diss. Hamburg, 1956.

BUTLER, E. M. *The Saint-Simonian Religion in Germany. A Study of the Young German Movement.* Cambridge, Eng.: Cambridge University Press, 1926. Reprinted, New York: Howard Fertig, Inc., 1968.

COLDITZ, CARL. "Über den Denunzianten." *Modern Language Quarterly,* 6 (1945), 131-147.

171

DAICHES, DAVID. *Critical Approaches to Literature.* New York: Norton, 1956.

DEMETZ, PETER. "Zur Definition des Realismus." *Literatur und Kritik,* 2 (1967), 330-345.

DENKLER, HORST. "Aufbruch der Aristophaniden. Die aristophanische Komödie als Modell für das politische Lustspiel im deutschen Vormärz." *Der Dichter und seine Zeit — Politik im Spiegel der Literatur. Drittes Amherster Kolloquium zur modernen deutschen Literatur 1969,* ed. Wolfgang Paulsen. Heidelberg: Lothar Stiehm, 1970, pp. 134-157.

——. "Revolutionäre Dramaturgie und revolutionäres Drama in Vormärz und Märzrevolution." *Gestaltungsgeschichte und Gesellschaftsgeschichte. Literatur-, kunst- und musikwissenschaftliche Studien,* ed. Helmut Kreuzer und Käte Hamburger. Stuttgart: Metzler, 1969, pp. 306-337.

DIETZE, WALTER. *Junges Deutschland und deutsche Klassik. Zur Ästhetik und Literaturtheorie des Vormärz.* 3rd ed. Berlin: Rütten & Loening, 1962.

DOBERT, EITEL WOLF. *Karl Gutzkow und seine Zeit.* Bern and Munich: Francke Verlag, 1968.

DRESCH, J. *Le Roman social en Allemagne (1850-1900). Gutzkow — Freytag — Spielhagen — Fontane.* Paris: Félix Alcan, 1913.

——. "Schiller et la jeune Allemagne." *Revue germanique,* 1 (1905), 569-587.

DROSTE-HÜLSHOFF, ANNETTE VON. *Briefe,* ed. Karl Schulte-Kemminghausen. Düsseldorf: Eugen Diederichs, 1968.

ECK, ELSE VON. *Die Literaturkritik in den Hallischen und Deutschen Jahrbüchern (1838-1842).* Germanische Studien, No. 42. Berlin: E. Ebering, 1926.

ELIOT, GEORGE. "German Wit: Heinrich Heine." *Essays and Leaves from a Notebook,* ed. Charles Lee Lewes. New York: Harper & Brothers, 1884, pp. 79-144.

ELSTER, ERNST. "H. Heine und H. Laube. Mit sechsundvierzig bisher ungedruckten Briefen Laubes an Heine." *Deutsche Rundschau,* 133 (1907), 210-232, 394-412; 134 (1908), 77-90; 135 (1908), 91-116, 232-259; 136 (1908), 233-251, 441-455.

FRENZEL, ELISABETH. *Stoffe der Weltliteratur.* 2nd ed. Stuttgart: A. Kröner, 1963.

FREYTAG, GUSTAV. *Soll und Haben. Gesammelte Werke,* Vols. IV-V. Leipzig: S. Hirzel, 1887.

GADAMER, HANS-GEORG. *Kleine Schriften II. Interpretationen.* Tübingen: Mohr, 1967.

GALLEY, EBERHARD. "Heine im literarischen Streit mit Gutzkow. Mit unbekannten Manuskripten aus Heines Nachlaß." *Heine-Jahrbuch 1966*, pp. 1-40.

—. *Der religiöse Liberalismus in der deutschen Literatur von 1830 bis 1850.* Diss. Rostock, 1934.

GEIGER, LUDWIG. *Das junge Deutschland und die preußische Censur.* Berlin: S. Schottlaender, 1900.

GLANDER, PHILIP. "K. A. Varnhagen von Ense: Man of Letters. 1833-1858." Diss., University of Wisconsin, 1961.

GLOSSY, KARL. *Literarische Geheimberichte aus dem Vormärz.* Separatdruck aus dem *Jahrbuch der Grillparzer-Gesellschaft*, Vols. 21-23. Vienna: C. Konegen, 1912.

GREINER, MARTIN. *Zwischen Biedermeier und Bourgeoisie. Ein Kapitel deutscher Literaturgeschichte.* Göttingen: Vandenhoeck & Ruprecht, 1953.

GRIMM, REINHOLD. "Romanhaftes und Novellistisches in Laubes *Reisenovellen.*" *Germanisch-romanische Monatsschrift*, N.S. 18 (1968), 299-303.

GRÜTTER, EMIL. *Immermanns "Epigonen". Ein Beitrag zur Geschichte des deutschen Romans.* Diss. Zurich, 1951.

GULDE, HILDEGARD. *Studien zum jungdeutschen Frauenroman.* Diss. Tübingen, 1931.

GUTZKOW, KARL. *Aus der Zeit und dem Leben.* Leipzig: F. A. Brockhaus, 1844.

—. *Briefe eines Narren an eine Närrin.* Hamburg: Hoffmann und Campe, 1832.

—. *Deutschland am Vorabend seines Falles oder seiner Größe*, ed. Walter Boehlich. sammlung insel, 36. Frankfurt: Insel Verlag, 1969.

—. *Götter, Helden, Don-Quixote. Abstimmungen zur Beurtheilung der literarischen Epoche.* Hamburg: Hoffmann und Campe, 1838.

—. *Maha Guru. Geschichte eines Gottes.* Stuttgart and Tübingen: J. G. Cotta, 1833.

—. *Oeffentliche Charaktere.* Hamburg: Hoffmann und Campe, 1835.

—. *Vertheidigung gegen Menzel und Berichtigung einiger Urtheile im Publikum.* Mannheim: Löwenthal, 1835.

—. *Wally, die Zweiflerin.* Mannheim: Löwenthal, 1835. Reprint, ed. Jost Schillemeit. Göttingen: Vandenhoeck & Ruprecht, 1965.

—. *Werke*, ed. Peter Müller. Leipzig and Vienna: Bibliographisches Institut, [1911].

—. *Zur Philosophie der Geschichte.* Hamburg: Hoffmann und Campe, 1836.

GUZINSKY, ELISABETH. *Karl Immermann als Zeitkritiker. Ein Beitrag zur Geschichte der deutschen Selbstkritik.* Neue deutsche Forschungen, No. 142. Berlin: Junker und Dünnhaupt, 1937.

173

HÄBERLE, KARL. *Individualität und Zeit in H. Laubes Jungem Europa und K. Gutzkows Ritter vom Geist.* Erlangen: Palm & Enke, 1938.

HANSON, WILLIAM P. "F. G. Kühne. A Forgotten Young German." *German Life & Letters,* N.S. 17 (1963/64), 335-338.

HARSING, ERICH. *Wolfgang Menzel und das Junge Deutschland.* Diss. Münster, 1909.

HEBBEL, FRIEDRICH. *Sämtliche Werke. Historisch-kritische Ausgabe,* ed. Richard Maria Werner. Berlin: B. Behr, 1903.

HECKER, KONRAD. *Mensch und Masse. Situation und Handeln der Epigonen. Gezeigt an Immermann und den Jungdeutschen.* Das politische Volk. Schriften zur sozialen Bewegung, Vol. II. Berlin: Junker und Dünnhaupt, 1933.

HEGEL, GEORG WILHELM FRIEDRICH. *Sämtliche Werke. Jubiläumsausgabe in zwanzig Bänden,* ed. Hermann Glockner. Stuttgart: Friedrich Frommann, 1964—.

HEINE, HEINRICH. *Sämtliche Werke,* ed. Ernst Elster. 7 vols. Leipzig and Vienna: Bibliographisches Institut, [1887-90].

HERMAND, JOST. "Allgemeine Epochenprobleme." *Zur Literatur der Restaurationsepoche 1815-1848,* ed. Jost Hermand and Manfred Windfuhr. Stuttgart: Metzler, 1970, pp. 3-61.

—. "Heines frühe Kritiker." *Der Dichter und seine Zeit — Politik im Spiegel der Literatur. Drittes Amherster Kolloquium zur modernen deutschen Literatur 1969,* ed. Wolfgang Paulsen. Heidelberg: Lothar Stiehm, 1970, pp. 113-133.

—, ed. *Das Junge Deutschland. Texte und Dokumente.* Reclams Universal-Bibliothek, Nos. 8703-07. Stuttgart: Philipp Reclam Jun., 1966.

HIRTH, FRIEDRICH, ed. *Heinrich Heines Briefe.* 6 vols. Mainz: F. Kupferberg, 1950-51.

HOF, WALTER. *Pessimistisch-nihilistische Strömungen in der deutschen Literatur vom Sturm und Drang bis zum Jungen Deutschland.* Tübingen: Niemeyer, 1970.

HOROVITZ, RUTH. *Vom Roman des Jungen Deutschland zum Roman der Gartenlaube.* Diss. Basel, 1937.

HOUBEN, H. H. *Gutzkow-Funde. Beiträge zur Litteratur- und Kulturgeschichte des neunzehnten Jahrhunderts.* Berlin: Arthur L. Wolff, 1901.

—. *Jungdeutscher Sturm und Drang. Ergebnisse und Studien.* Leipzig: F. A. Brockhaus, 1911.

—. *Verbotene Literatur von der klassischen Zeit bis zur Gegenwart. Ein kritisch-historisches Lexikon über verbotene Bücher, Zeitschriften und Theaterstücke, Schriftsteller und Verleger.* 2 vols. Berlin: E. Rowohlt, 1924; Bremen: K. Schünemann, 1928. Reprinted, Hildesheim: Georg Olms, 1965.

—. *Zeitschriften des Jungen Deutschlands.* Veröffentlichungen der Deutschen Bibliographischen Gesellschaft, *Bibliographisches Repertorium*, Vols. III-IV. Berlin: B. Behr, 1906 and 1909. Reprinted, Hildesheim and New York: Georg Olms, 1970.

HUMBOLDT, WILHELM VON. *Gesammelte Schriften,* ed. Albert Leitzmann. Vol. II. Berlin: B. Behr, 1908.

IGGERS, GEORGE G. "Heine and the Saint-Simonians: A Re-examination." *Comparative Literature*, 10 (1958), 289-308.

IMMERMANN, KARL. *Münchhausen. Eine Geschichte in Arabesken,* ed. Gustav Konrad. Frechen: Bartmann, 1968.

—. *Tulifäntchen,* ed. Peter Hasubek. Reclams Universal-Bibliothek, Nos. 8551-52. Stuttgart: Philipp Reclam Jun., 1968.

—. *Werke,* ed. Robert Boxberger. Leipzig: Dümmler, [1883].

—. *Werke,* ed. Harry Maync. Leipzig and Vienna: Bibliographisches Institut, [1906].

JANTZ, HAROLD. "Sequence and Continuity in Nineteenth-Century German Literature." *Germanic Review*, 38 (1963), 27-36.

JENNINGS, LEE B. *The Ludicrous Demon: Aspects of the Grotesque in German Post-Romantic Prose.* Berkeley and Los Angeles: University of California Press, 1963.

KAYSER, RUDOLF. "Ludolf Wienbarg und der Kampf um den Historismus." *German Quarterly*, 29 (1956), 71-74.

KISCHKA, KARL HARALD. "Typologie der Lyrik des Vormärz." Diss. Mainz, 1965.

KOHLSCHMIDT, WERNER. "Die Welt des Bauern im Spiegel von Immermanns 'Münchhausen' und Gotthelfs 'Uli'." *Dichtung und Volkstum*, 39 (1938), 223-237.

KOOPMANN, HELMUT. *Das Junge Deutschland. Analyse seines Selbstverständnisses.* Stuttgart: Metzler, 1970.

KÜHNE, FERDINAND GUSTAV. *Eine Quarantäne im Irrenhause. Novelle aus den Papieren eines Mondsteiners.* Leipzig: Brockhaus, 1835.

—. *Weibliche und männliche Charaktere.* Leipzig: Wilh. Engelmann, 1838.

KURZ, PAUL KONRAD. *Künstler, Tribun, Apostel. Heinrich Heines Auffassung vom Beruf des Dichters.* Munich: Fink, 1967.

KUTHE, OLGA. *Heinrich Laubes Roman "Die Krieger" im Zusammenhang mit der Polenbegeisterung um 1830.* Diss. Marburg, 1925.

LAUBE, HEINRICH. *Ausgewählte Werke in zehn Bänden,* ed. Heinrich Hubert Houben. Leipzig: Max Hesse, n.d.

—. *Die Bürger.* Mannheim: Heinrich Hoff, 1837.

—. *Gesammelte Werke in fünfzig Bänden*, ed. Heinrich Hubert Houben with Albert Hänel. Leipzig, Max Hesse, 1908-09.

—. *Die Krieger*. Mannheim: Heinrich Hoff, 1837.

—. *Die Poeten*. Mannheim: Heinrich Hoff, 1836.

—. ed. *Zeitung für die elegante Welt*. January, 1833 to July, 1834.

LEGGE, J. G. *Rhyme and Revolution in Germany. A Study in German History, Life, Literature and Character 1813-1850*. London: Constable, 1918.

MCCLAIN, WILLIAM. "Karl Lebrecht Immermann's Portrait of a Folk-Hero in *Münchhausen*." *Studies in German Literature of the Nineteenth and Twentieth Centuries. Festschrift for Frederic E. Coenen*, ed. Siegfried Mews. University of North Carolina Studies in the Germanic Languages and Literatures, Vol. 67. Chapel Hill: University of North Carolina Press, 1970, pp. 55-63.

MAGILL, C. P. "Young Germany: A Revaluation." *German Studies Presented to Leonard Ashley Willoughby*, ed. J. Boyd. Oxford: Blackwell, 1952, pp. 108-119.

MAJUT, RUDOLF. "Der deutsche Roman vom Biedermeier bis zur Gegenwart." *Deutsche Philologie im Aufriß*, ed. Wolfgang Stammler. 2nd ed. Berlin: Erich Schmidt, 1960. II, cols. 1357-1535.

MARCUSE, LUDWIG. *Revolutionär und Patriot. Das Leben Ludwig Börnes*. Leipzig: P. List, 1929.

MARX, KARL, and FRIEDRICH ENGELS. *Über Kunst und Literatur*, ed. Manfred Kliem. 2 vols. Berlin: Dietz Verlag, 1968.

MÀYER, HANS. *Studien zur deutschen Literaturgeschichte*, 2nd ed. Berlin: Rütten & Loening, 1955.

MAYRHOFER, OTTO. *Gustav Freytag und das Junge Deutschland*. Beiträge zur deutschen Literaturwissenschaft, No. 1. Marburg: Elwert, 1907.

MENZEL, WOLFGANG. *Geist der Geschichte*. Stuttgart: Liesching, 1835.

MEYER, HERMAN. *Das Zitat in der Erzählkunst. Zur Geschichte und Poetik des europäischen Romans*. 2nd ed. Stuttgart: Metzler, 1967.

MUNDT, THEODOR. *Aesthetik. Die Idee der Schönheit und des Kunstwerks im Lichte unserer Zeit*. Berlin: M. Simion, 1845. Reprint, ed. Hans Düvel, Göttingen: Vandenhoeck & Ruprecht, 1966.

—. *Charaktere und Situationen*. Wismar and Leipzig: H. Schmidt u. v. Cossel, 1837.

—. *Charlotte Stieglitz, ein Denkmal*. Berlin: Veit & Comp., [1835].

—. *Geschichte der Literatur der Gegenwart. Friedrich von Schlegel's Geschichte der alten und neuen Literatur, bis auf die neueste Zeit fortgeführt*. Berlin: M. Simion, 1842.

—. *Die Kunst der deutschen Prosa. Aesthetisch, literargeschichtlich, ge-*

sellschaftlich. Berlin: Veit & Comp., 1837. Reprint, ed. Hans Düvel, Göttingen: Vandenhoeck & Ruprecht, 1969.

—. *Madelon oder die Romantiker in Paris. Eine Novelle.* Leipzig: Georg Wolbrecht, 1832.

—. *Madonna. Unterhaltungen mit einer Heiligen.* Leipzig: Gebrüder Reichenbach, 1835.

—. *Moderne Lebenswirren. Briefe und Zeitabenteuer eines Salzschreibers.* Leipzig: Gebrüder Reichenbach, 1834.

NOLLE, KARL. *Heinrich Laube als sozialer und politischer Schriftsteller.* Diss. Münster, 1914.

OTT, BARTHÉLEMY. *La Querelle de Heine et de Börne. Contribution à l'étude des idées politiques et sociales en Allemagne de 1830 à 1840.* Diss. Lille, 1936.

OTTO, ULLA. *Die literarische Zensur als Problem der Soziologie der Politik.* Stuttgart: Ferdinand Enke Verlag, 1968.

PIERSON, EDGAR, ed. *Gustav Kühne, sein Lebensbild und Briefwechsel mit Zeitgenossen.* Dresden and Leipzig: E. Pierson's Verlag, [1889].

PORTERFIELD, ALLEN WILSON. *Karl Lebrecht Immermann. A Study in German Romanticism.* New York: Columbia University Press, 1911. Reprinted, New York: AMS Press, 1966.

PROELSS, JOHANNES. *Das junge Deutschland. Ein Buch deutscher Geistesgeschichte.* Stuttgart: Cotta, 1892.

PRZYGODDA, PAUL. *Heinrich Laubes literarische Frühzeit.* Diss. Berlin, 1910.

PUTLITZ, GUSTAV ZU, ed. *Karl Immermann. Sein Leben und seine Werke, aus Tagebüchern und Briefen an seine Familie zusammengestellt.* Berlin: Wilhelm Hertz, 1870.

RAS, GERARD. *Börne und Heine als politische Schriftsteller.* The Hague: Wolters, 1926.

ROER, WALTHER. *Soziale Bewegung und politische Lyrik im Vormärz.* Diss. Münster, 1933.

RUMLER, FRANZ. *Realistische Elemente in Immermanns "Epigonen."* Diss. Munich, 1964.

SAMMONS, JEFFREY L. "The Evaluation of Freytag's 'Soll und Haben.'" *German Life & Letters,* N.S. 22 (1968/69), 315-324.

—. *Heinrich Heine: The Elusive Poet.* New Haven and London: Yale University Press, 1969.

—. "Ludolf Wienbarg and Norway." *Scandinavian Studies,* 42 (1970), 14-30.

SCHERER, MICHAEL. "Immermanns *Münchhausen*-Roman." *German Quarterly,* 36 (1963), 236-244.

SCHERER, WINGOLF. "Heinrich Heine und der Saint-Simonismus." Diss. Bonn, 1950.

SCHNEIDER, FRANZ. "Gutzkows *Wally* und D. F. Strauss' *Das Leben Jesu, eine Richtigstellung.*" *Germanic Review,* 1 (1926), 115-119.

SCHÖNFELD, MARGARETE. *Gutzkows Frauengestalten. Ein Kapitel aus der literarhistorischen Anthropologie des 19. Jahrhunderts.* Germanische Studien, No. 133. Berlin: E. Ebering, 1933. Reprinted Nendeln/Liechtenstein: Kraus Reprint, 1967.

SCHWEIZER, VIKTOR. *Ludolf Wienbarg. Beiträge zu einer Jungdeutschen Ästhetik.* Diss. Leipzig, 1897.

SELL, FRIEDRICH C. *Die Tragödie des deutschen Liberalismus.* Stuttgart: Deutsche Verlags-Anstalt, 1953.

SENGLE, FRIEDRICH. *Arbeiten zur deutschen Literatur 1750-1850.* Stuttgart: Metzler, 1965.

—. *Biedermeierzeit. Deutsche Literatur im Spannungsfeld zwischen Restauration und Revolution 1815-1848.* Vol. I. Stuttgart: Metzler, 1971.

—. "Voraussetzungen und Erscheinungsformen der deutschen Restaurationsliteratur." *Deutsche Vierteljahrsschrift,* 30 (1956), 268-294.

SMITH, BARBARA HERNSTEIN. "Poetry as Fiction." *New Literary History,* 2 (1971), 259-281.

STATKOW, DIMITER. "Über die dialektische Struktur des Immermann-Romans 'Münchhausen.' Zum Problem des Übergangs von der Romantik zum Realismus." *Weimarer Beiträge,* 11 (1965), 195-211.

STEINECKE, HARTMUT, ed. *Theorie und Technik des Romans im 19. Jahrhundert.* Tübingen: Niemeyer, 1970.

STORCH, WERNER. "Die ästhetischen Theorien des jungdeutschen Sturms und Drangs." Diss. Bonn, 1926.
[Upon my inquiry, I was informed that this dissertation was lost during World War II. Dietze, however, refers to it several times, so that this information may not be correct. An abstract of the dissertation is in *Jahrbuch der philosophischen Fakultät der Rheinischen Friedrich Wilhelms-Universität zu Bonn,* 3 (1924/25), 141-147.]

WATT, IAN. *The Rise of the Novel. Studies in Defoe, Richardson and Fielding.* Berkeley: University of California Press, 1967.

WELLEK, RENÉ. *A History of Modern Criticism 1750-1950.* New Haven and London: Yale University Press, 1955-.

WERNER, HANS-GEORG. *Geschichte des politischen Gedichts in Deutschland von 1815 bis 1840.* Berlin: Akademie-Verlag, 1969.

WIENBARG, LUDOLF. *Ästhetische Feldzüge,* ed. Walter Dietze. Berlin and Weimar: Aufbau-Verlag, 1964.

—. *Der dänische Fehdehandschuh, aufgenommen von Ludolf Wienbarg.* Hamburg: Hoffmann und Campe, 1846.

178

—. *Das dänische Königsgesetz oder das in Dänemark geltende Grundgesetz.* Hamburg: Hoffmann und Campe, 1847.

—. *Geschichtliche Vorträge über altdeutsche Sprache und Literatur.* Hamburg: Hoffmann und Campe, 1838.

—. *Holland in den Jahren 1831 und 1832.* Hamburg: Hoffmann und Campe, 1833.

—. *Menzel und die junge Literatur. Programme zur deutschen Revue.* Mannheim: Löwenthal, 1835.

—. *Quadriga.* Hamburg: Hoffmann und Campe, 1840.

—. *Soll die plattdeutsche Sprache gepflegt oder ausgerottet werden? Gegen Ersteres und für Letzteres.* Hamburg: Hoffmann und Campe, 1834.

—. *Wanderungen durch den Thierkreis.* Hamburg: Hoffmann und Campe, 1835.

—. *Zur neuesten Literatur.* Mannheim: Löwenthal, 1835.

WIESE, BENNO VON. *Karl Immermann. Sein Werk und sein Leben.* Bad Homburg, Berlin, and Zürich: Gehlen, 1969.

—. "Zeitkrisis und Biedermeier in Laubes 'Das junge Europa' und in Immermanns 'Epigonen.'" *Dichtung und Volkstum,* 36 (1935), 163-197.

WINDFUHR, MANFRED. "Der Epigone. Begriff, Phänomen und Bewußtsein." *Archiv für Begriffsgeschichte,* 4 (1959), 182-209.

—. *Immermanns erzählerisches Werk. Zur Situation des Romans in der Restaurationszeit.* Giessen: Schmitz, 1957.

WÜLFING, WULF. "Schlagworte des Jungen Deutschland." *Zeitschrift für deutsche Sprache,* 21 (1965), 42-59, 160-174; 22 (1966), 36-56, 154-178; 23 (1967), 48-82, 166-177; 24 (1968), 60-71, 161-183; 25 (1969), 96-115, 175-179; 26 (1970), 60-83, 162-175.

182

UNIVERSITY OF NORTH CAROLINA
STUDIES IN THE GERMANIC LANGUAGES
AND LITERATURES

Initiated by RICHARD JENTE (1949–1952), *established by* F. E. COENEN (1952–1968)
Publication Committee

SIEGFRIED MEWS, EDITOR

WERNER P. FRIEDERICH   JOHN G. KUNSTMANN   GEORGE S. LANE
HERBERT W. REICHERT   CHRISTOPH E. SCHWEITZER   SIDNEY R. SMITH
RIA STAMBAUGH   PETRUS W. TAX

For other volumes in the "Studies" see page ii and following pages.

Send orders to: (U.S. and Canada)
The University of North Carolina Press, P.O. Box 2288
Chapel Hill, N.C. 27514
(All other countries) Feffer and Simons, Inc., 31 Union Square, New York, N.Y. 10003

UNIVERSITY OF NORTH CAROLINA STUDIES IN THE GERMANIC LANGUAGES AND LITERATURES

initiated by RICHARD JENTE (1949–1952), *established by* F. E. COENEN (1952–1968)

Publication Committee

SIEGFRIED MEWS, EDITOR

WERNER P. FRIEDERICH   JOHN G. KUNSTMANN   GEORGE S. LANE
HERBERT W. REICHERT   CHRISTOPH E. SCHWEITZER   SIDNEY R. SMITH
RIA STAMBAUGH   PETRUS W. TAX

For other volumes in the "Studies" see preceding and following pages and p. ii

Order reprinted books from: AMS PRESS, Inc.,
56 East 13th Street, New York, N.Y. 10003

UNIVERSITY OF NORTH CAROLINA
STUDIES IN THE GERMANIC LANGUAGES
AND LITERATURES

Initiated by RICHARD JENTE (1949–1952), established by F. E. COENEN (1952–1968)

Publication Committee

SIEGFRIED MEWS, EDITOR

WERNER P. FRIEDERICH	JOHN G. KUNSTMANN	GEORGE S. LANE
HERBERT W. REICHERT	CHRISTOPH E. SCHWEITZER	SIDNEY R. SMITH
RIA STAMBAUGH		PETRUS W. TAX

For other volumes in the "Studies" see preceding pages and p. ii

Order reprinted books from: AMS PRESS, Inc.,
56 East 13th Street, New York, N.Y. 10003